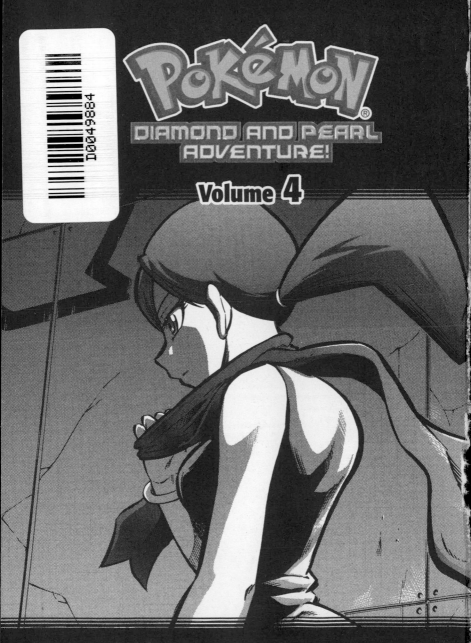

Pokémon

DIAMOND AND PEARL ADVENTURE!

Volume 4

Story & Art by
Shigekatsu Ihara

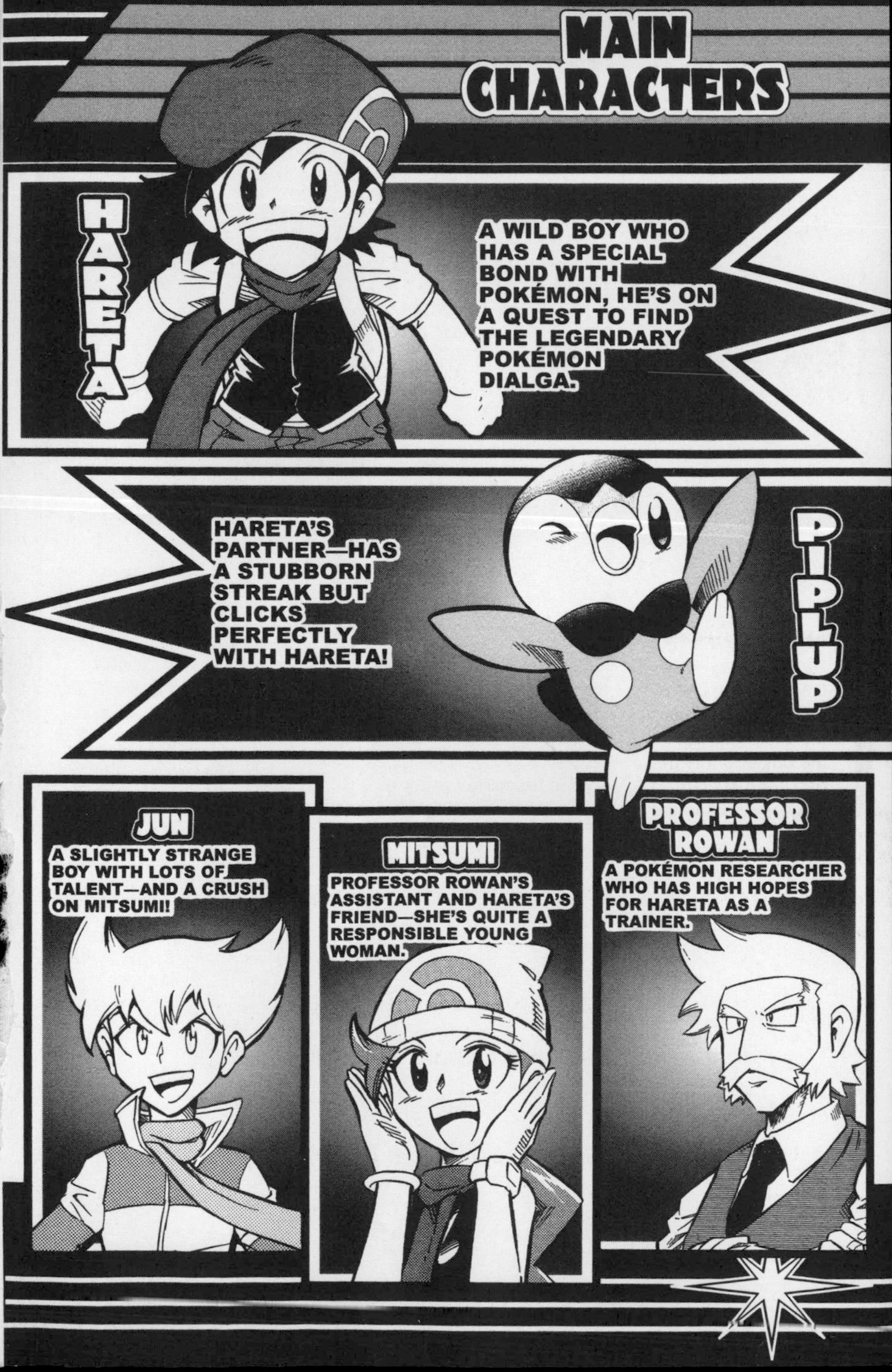
MAIN CHARACTERS
HARETA
A WILD BOY WHO HAS A SPECIAL BOND WITH POKÉMON, HE'S ON A QUEST TO FIND THE LEGENDARY POKÉMON DIALGA.
PIPLUP
HARETA'S PARTNER—HAS A STUBBORN STREAK BUT CLICKS PERFECTLY WITH HARETA!
PROFESSOR ROWAN
A POKÉMON RESEARCHER WHO HAS HIGH HOPES FOR HARETA AS A TRAINER.
MITSUMI
PROFESSOR ROWAN'S ASSISTANT AND HARETA'S FRIEND—SHE'S QUITE A RESPONSIBLE YOUNG WOMAN.
JUN
A SLIGHTLY STRANGE BOY WITH LOTS OF TALENT—AND A CRUSH ON MITSUMI!

BYRON
GYM LEADER OF CANALAVE CITY. WORKS HIS TRAINERS VERY HARD.
CANDICE
GYM LEADER OF SNOWPOINT CITY. SHE'S ALWAYS CALM, COOL, AND COLLECTED—PROBABLY BECAUSE SHE'S SUCH A SKILLED TRAINER.
TEAM GALACTIC
AN EVIL ORGANIZATION THAT SEEKS TO EXPLOIT POKÉMON.
CYRUS
LEADER OF TEAM GALACTIC. WANTS DIALGA'S POWERS.
JUPITER

THE STORY SO FAR

Hareta, a boy with a special bond to the hearts of Pokémon, and Mitsumi continue their quest to find Dialga, the Pokémon ruler of time. Hareta discovers that he must first find three special Pokémon who act as keys to unlock the location of Dialga. But the evil organization Team Galactic is already working to capture these Pokémon. As the battle for the three key Pokémon continues to escalate, Mitsumi, who until recently had been at Hareta's side, finds herself engaged in a fierce battle of her own...

TABLE OF CONTENTS

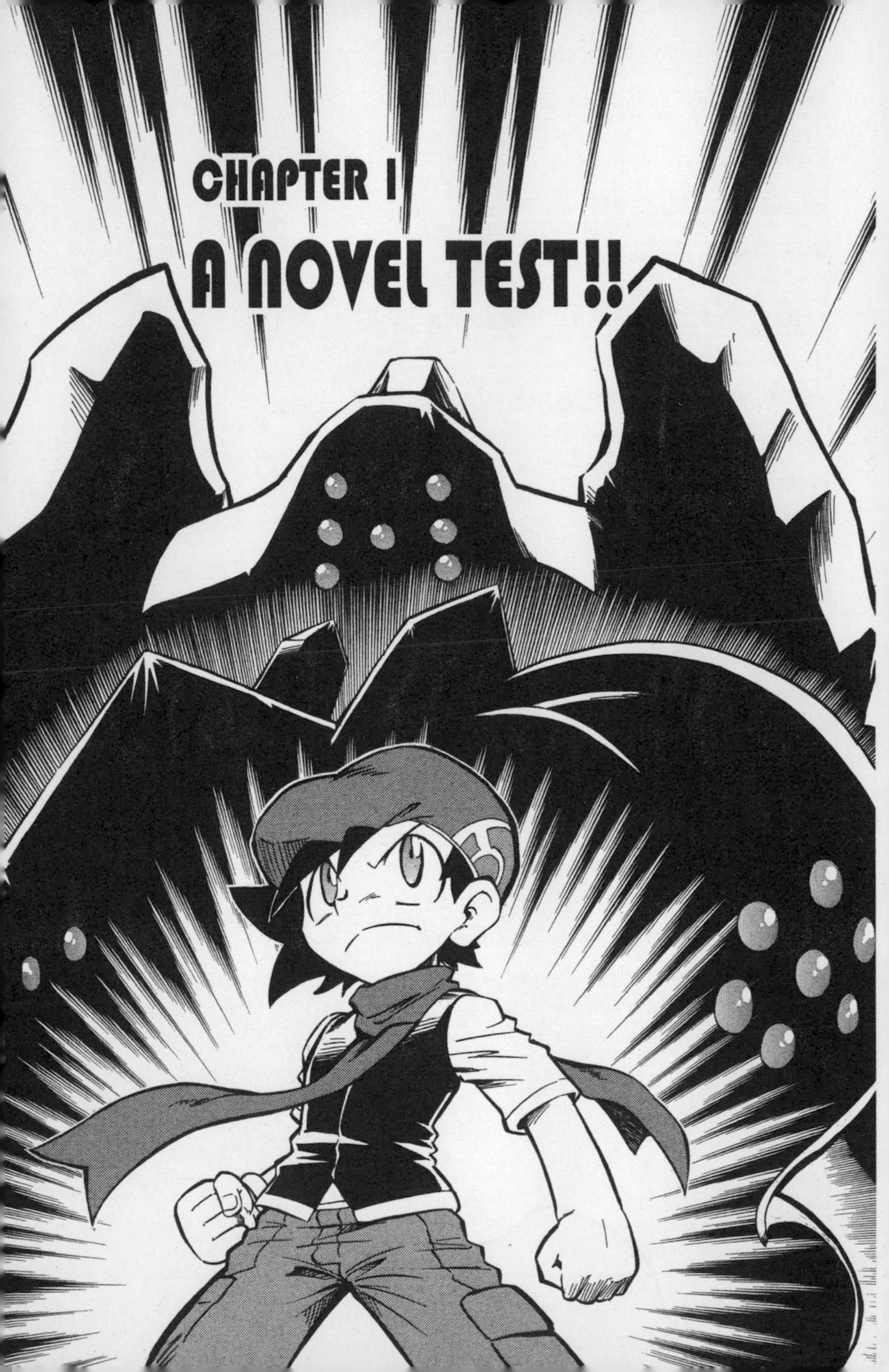
CHAPTER 1
A NOVEL TEST!!

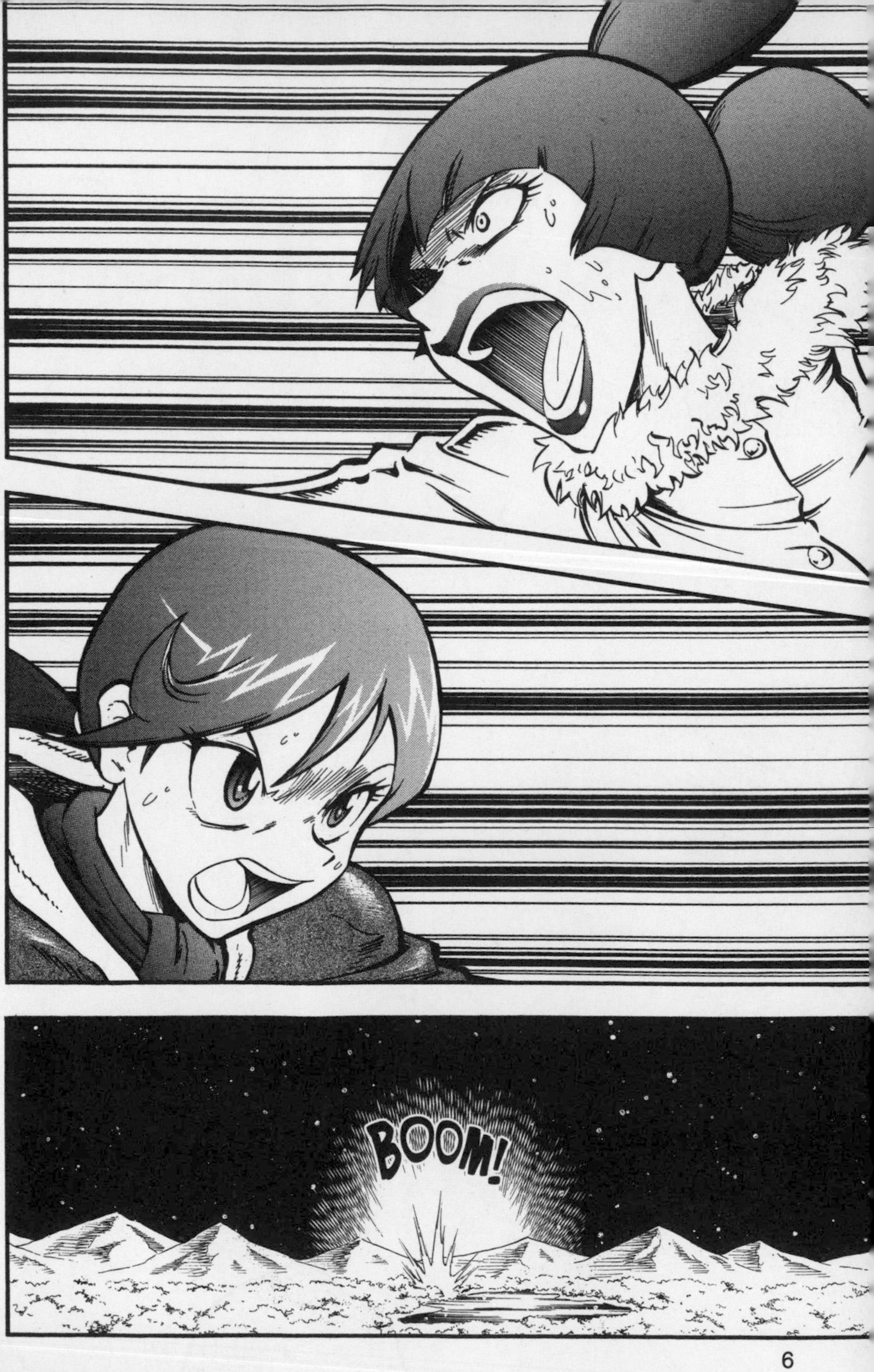
BOOM!

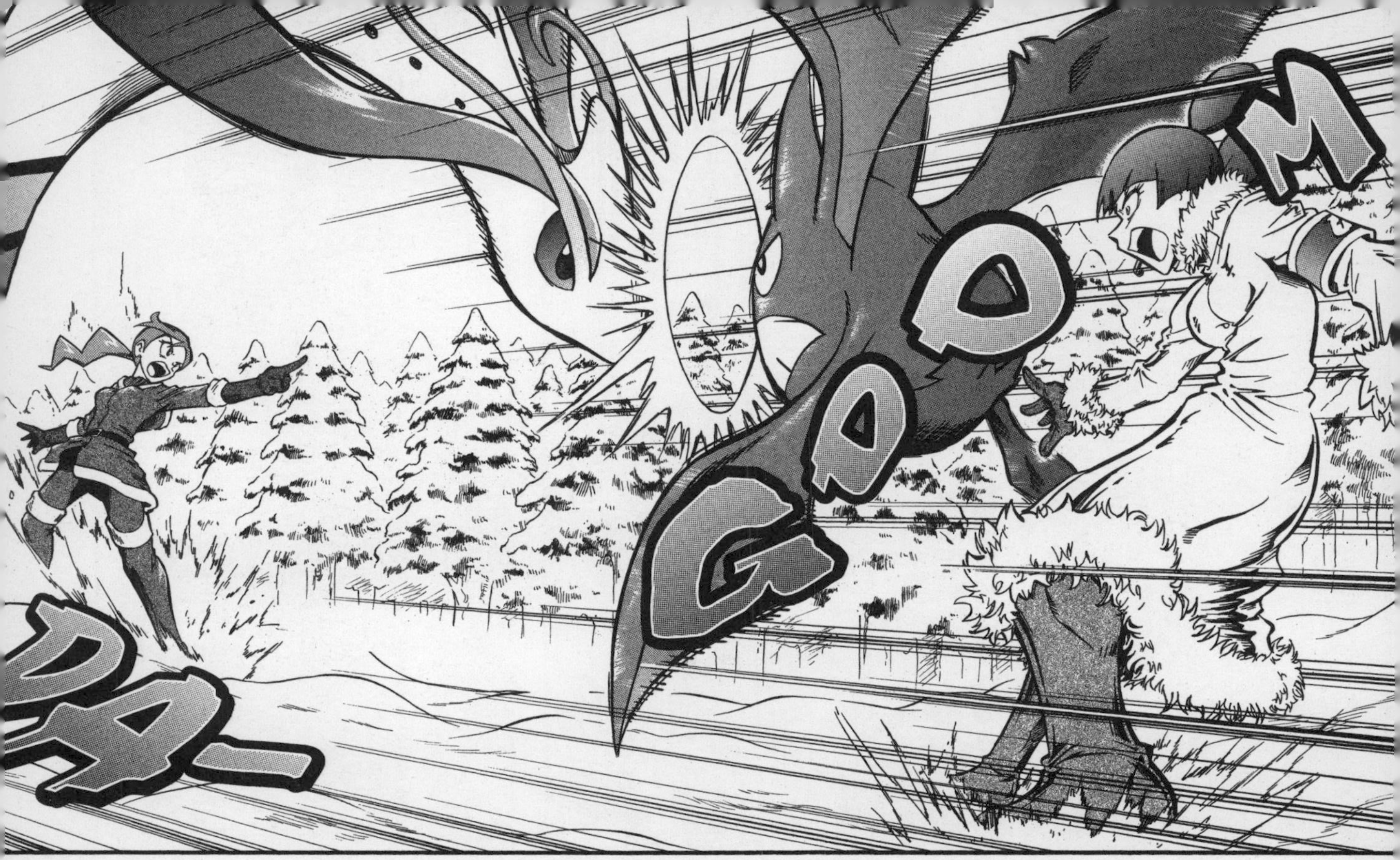

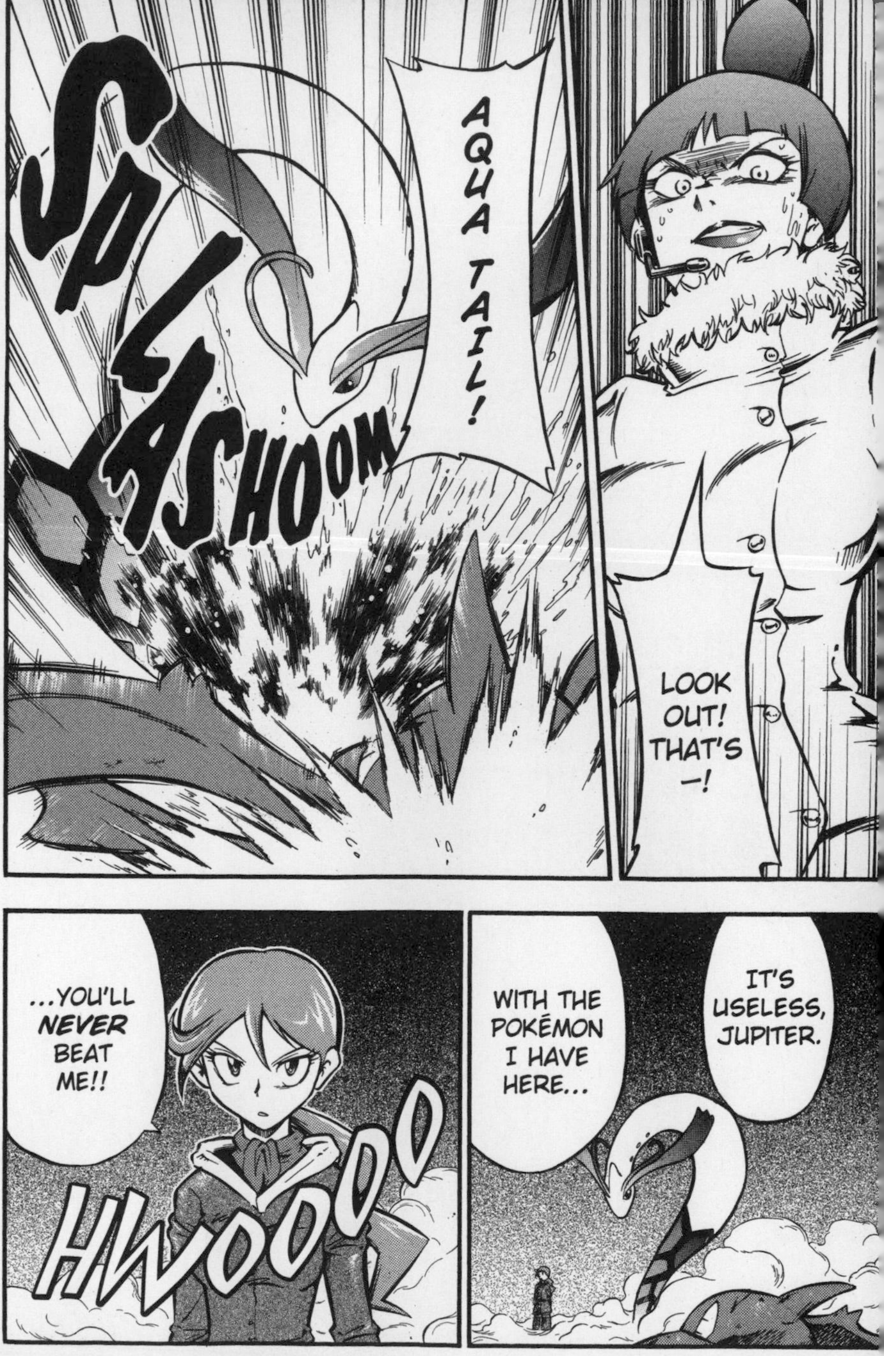
LOOK OUT! THAT'S —!
AQUA TAIL!
SPLASHOOM
IT'S USELESS, JUPITER.
WITH THE POKÉMON I HAVE HERE...
...YOU'LL **NEVER** BEAT ME!!
HWOOOO

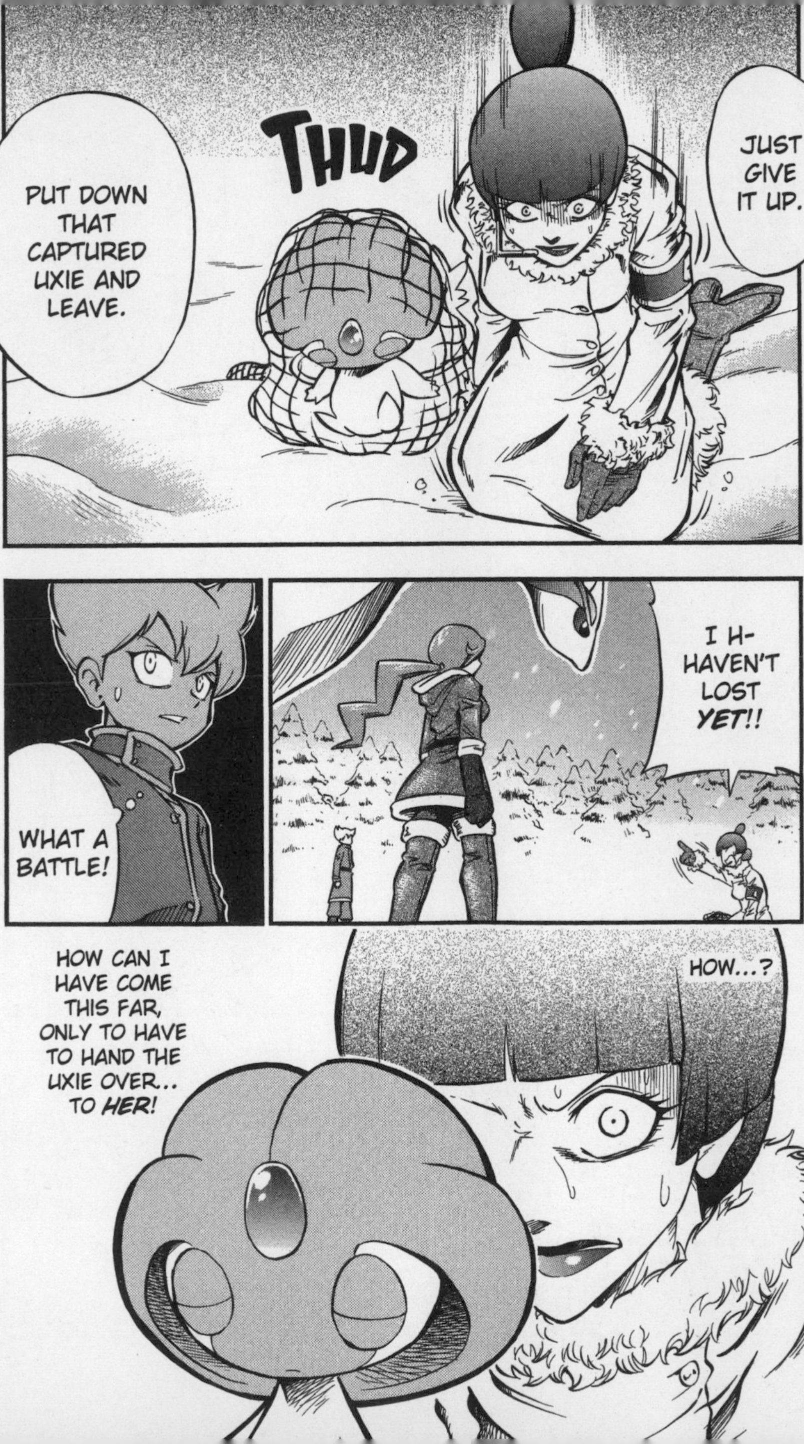
JUST GIVE IT UP.
THUD
PUT DOWN THAT CAPTURED UXIE AND LEAVE.
I H-HAVEN'T LOST *YET*!!
WHAT A BATTLE!
HOW...?
HOW CAN I HAVE COME THIS FAR, ONLY TO HAVE TO HAND THE UXIE OVER... TO *HER*!

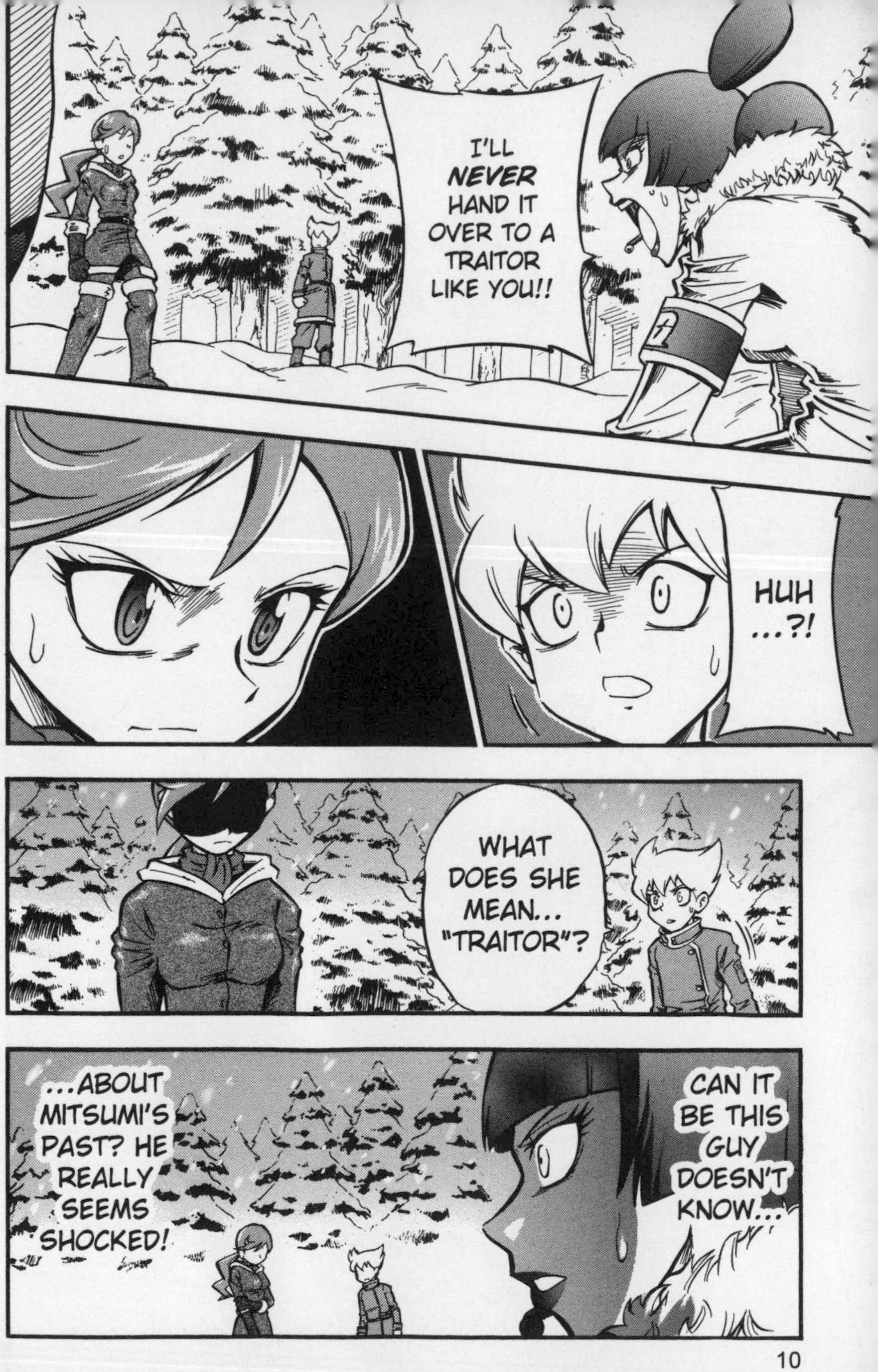
I'LL **NEVER** HAND IT OVER TO A TRAITOR LIKE YOU!!
HUH ...?!
WHAT DOES SHE MEAN... "TRAITOR"?
CAN IT BE THIS GUY DOESN'T KNOW...
...ABOUT MITSUMI'S PAST? HE REALLY SEEMS SHOCKED!

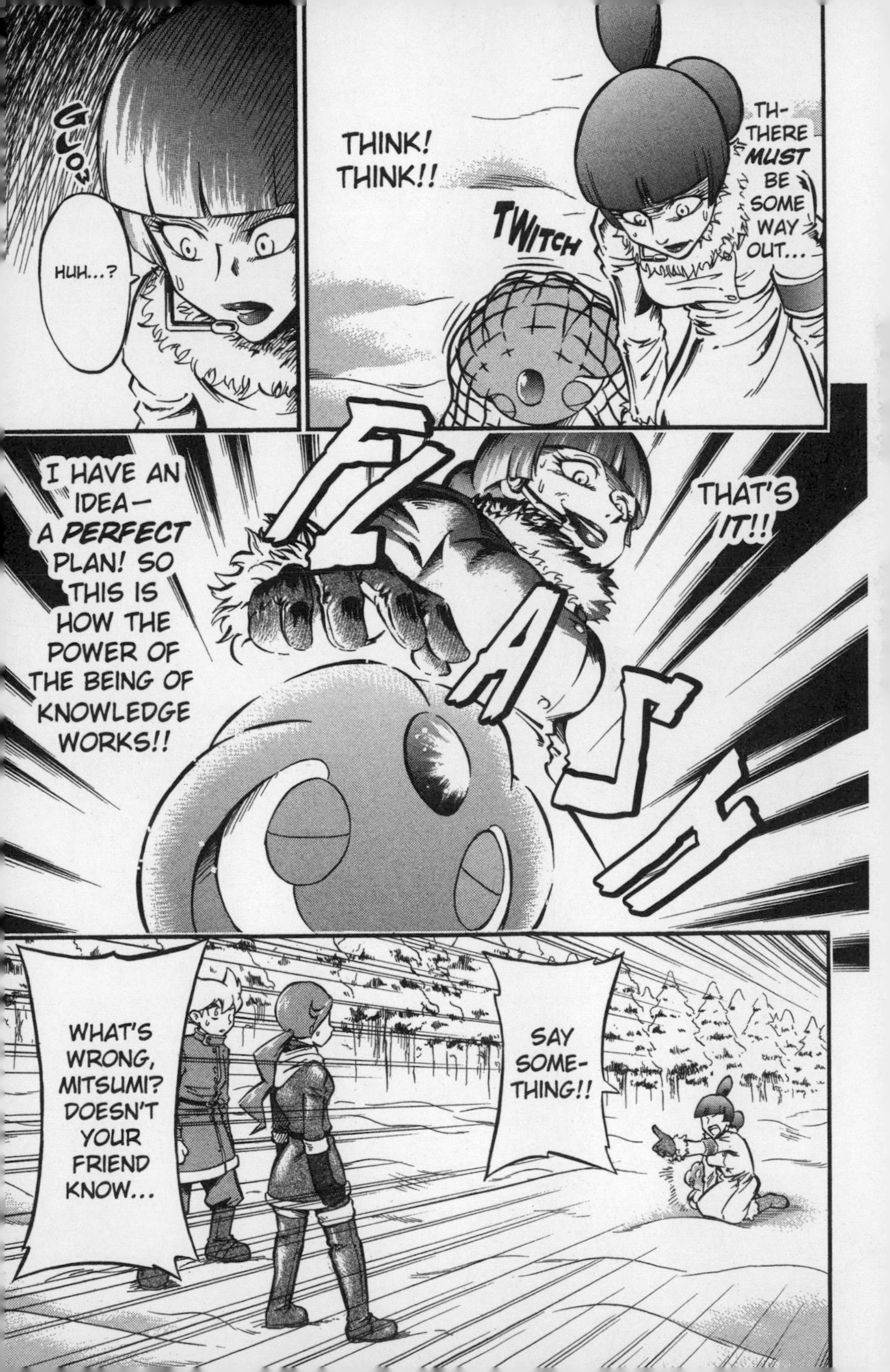
TH-THERE MUST BE SOME WAY OUT...
THINK! THINK!!
TWITCH
GLOW
HUH...?
THAT'S IT!!
I HAVE AN IDEA— A PERFECT PLAN! SO THIS IS HOW THE POWER OF THE BEING OF KNOWLEDGE WORKS!!
SAY SOME-THING!!
WHAT'S WRONG, MITSUMI? DOESN'T YOUR FRIEND KNOW...

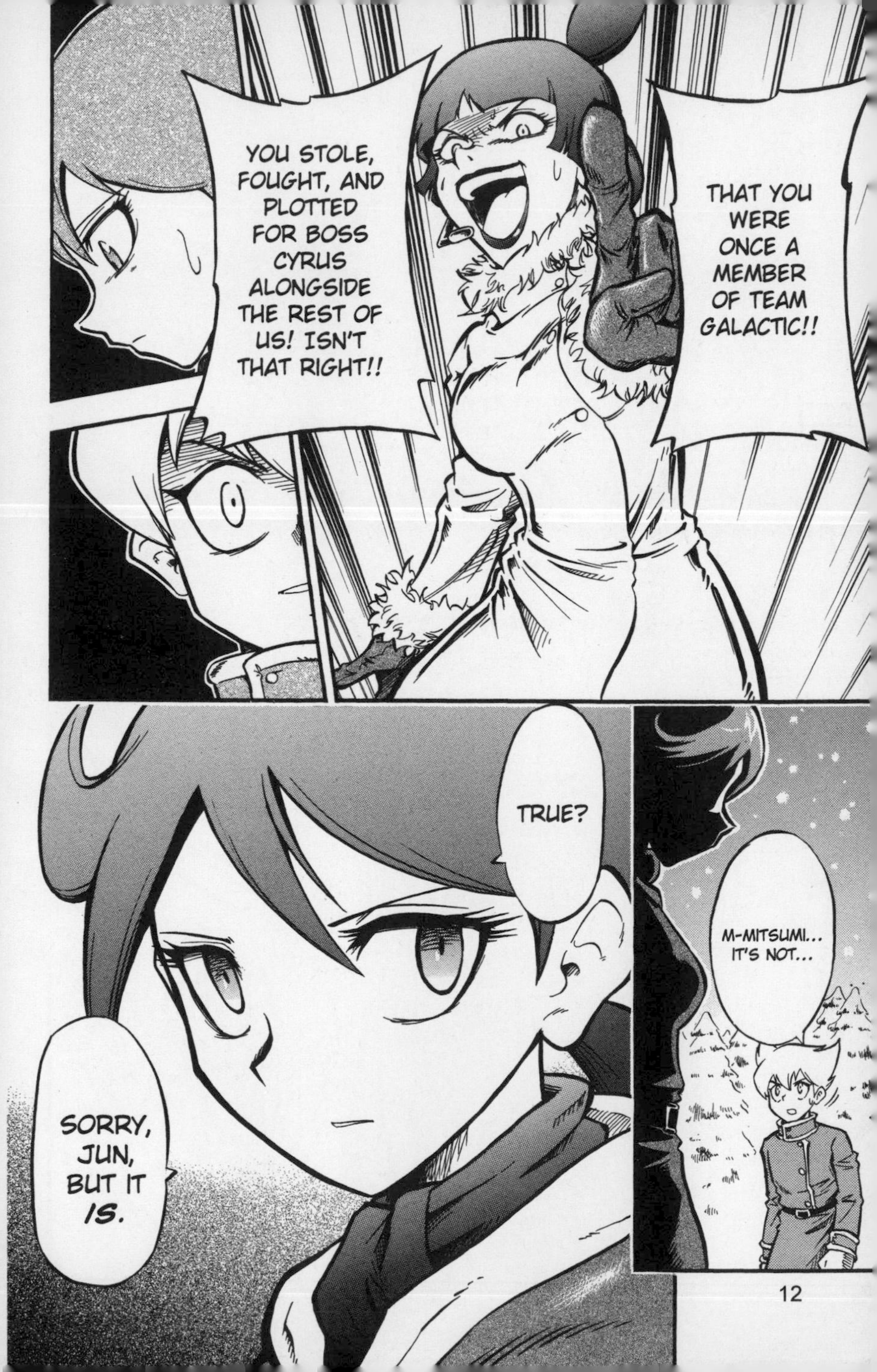
THAT YOU WERE ONCE A MEMBER OF TEAM GALACTIC!!
YOU STOLE, FOUGHT, AND PLOTTED FOR BOSS CYRUS ALONGSIDE THE REST OF US! ISN'T THAT RIGHT!!
M-MITSUMI... IT'S NOT...
TRUE?
SORRY, JUN, BUT IT *IS*.

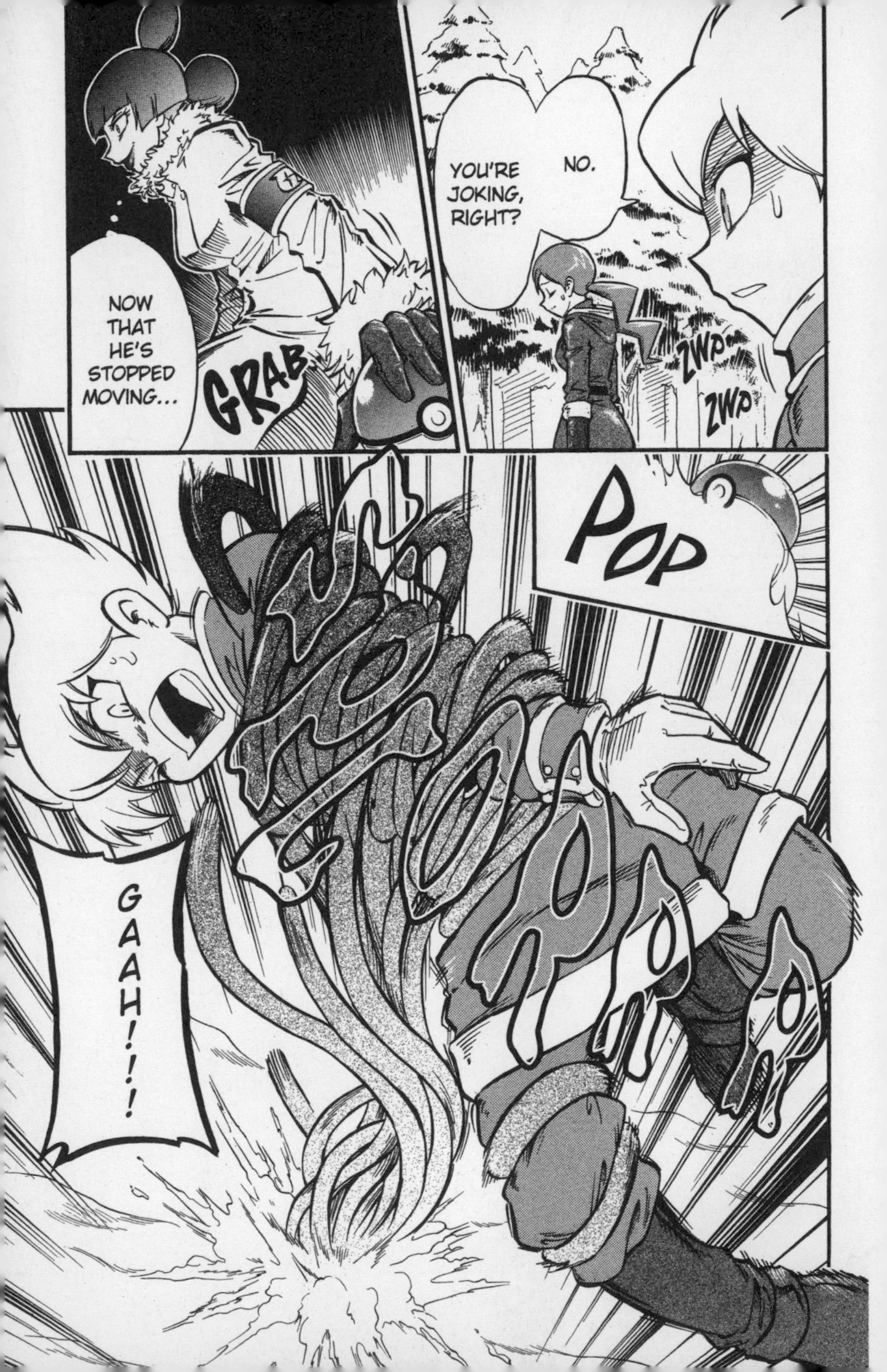
YOU'RE JOKING, RIGHT?
NO.
ZWP
ZWP
NOW THAT HE'S STOPPED MOVING...
GRAB
POP
GAAH!!!

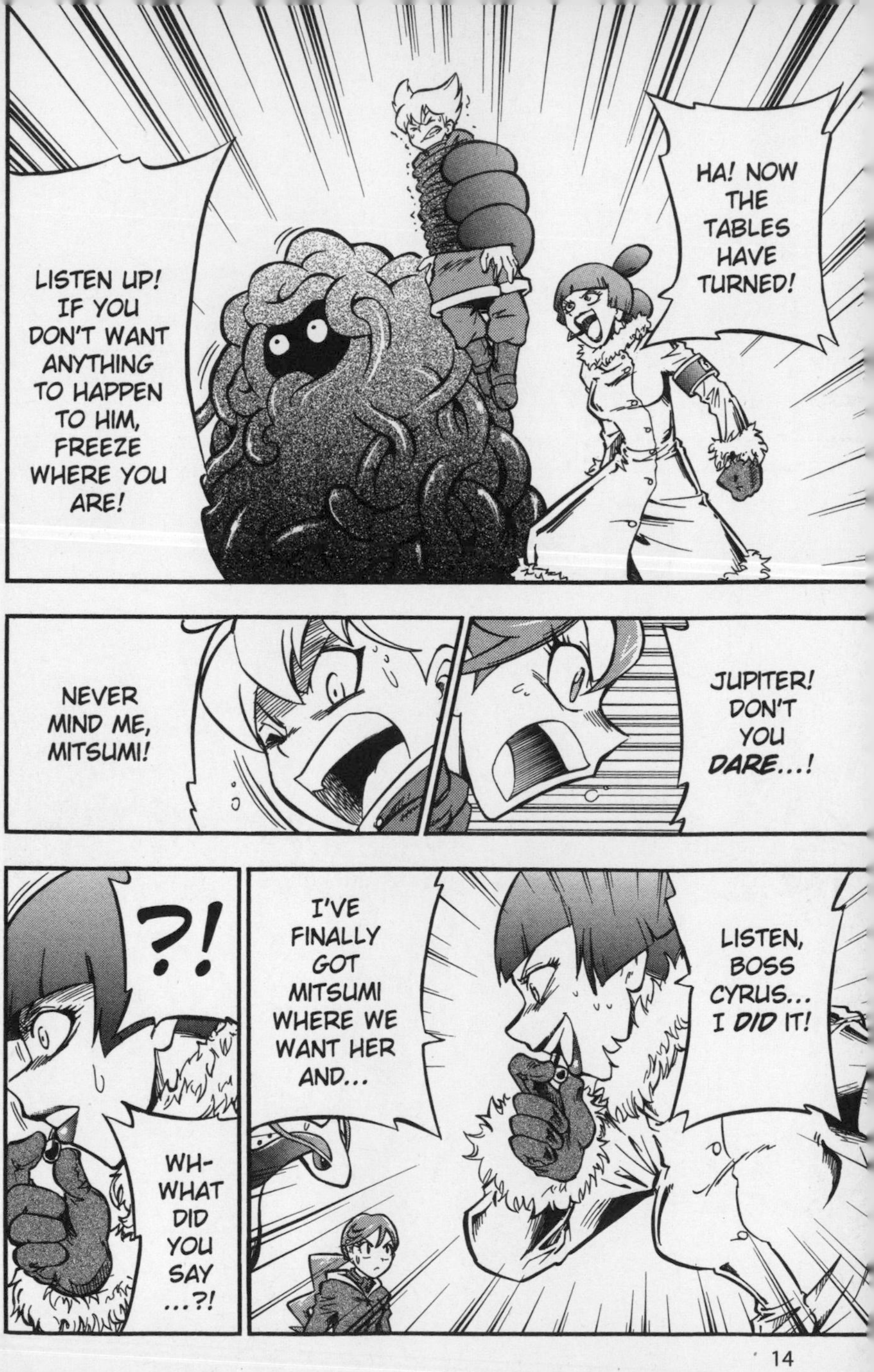
HA! NOW THE TABLES HAVE TURNED!
LISTEN UP! IF YOU DON'T WANT ANYTHING TO HAPPEN TO HIM, FREEZE WHERE YOU ARE!
JUPITER! DON'T YOU *DARE*...!
NEVER MIND ME, MITSUMI!
LISTEN, BOSS CYRUS... I *DID* IT!
I'VE FINALLY GOT MITSUMI WHERE WE WANT HER AND...
?!
WH-WHAT DID YOU SAY ...?!

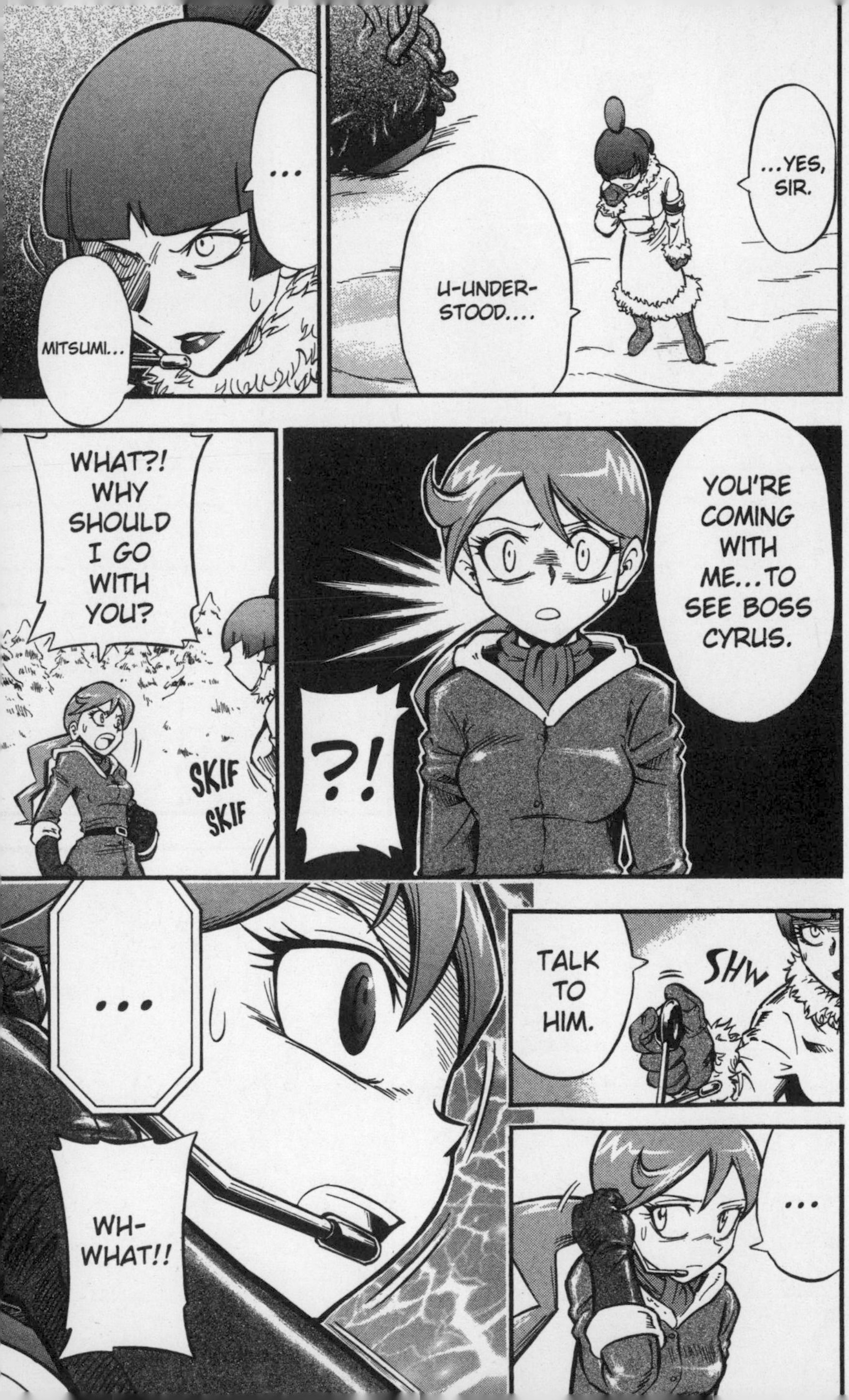
...YES, SIR.
U-UNDER-STOOD....
...
MITSUMI...
YOU'RE COMING WITH ME...TO SEE BOSS CYRUS.
?!
WHAT?! WHY SHOULD I GO WITH YOU?
SKIF SKIF
TALK TO HIM.
SHW
...
...
WH-WHAT!!

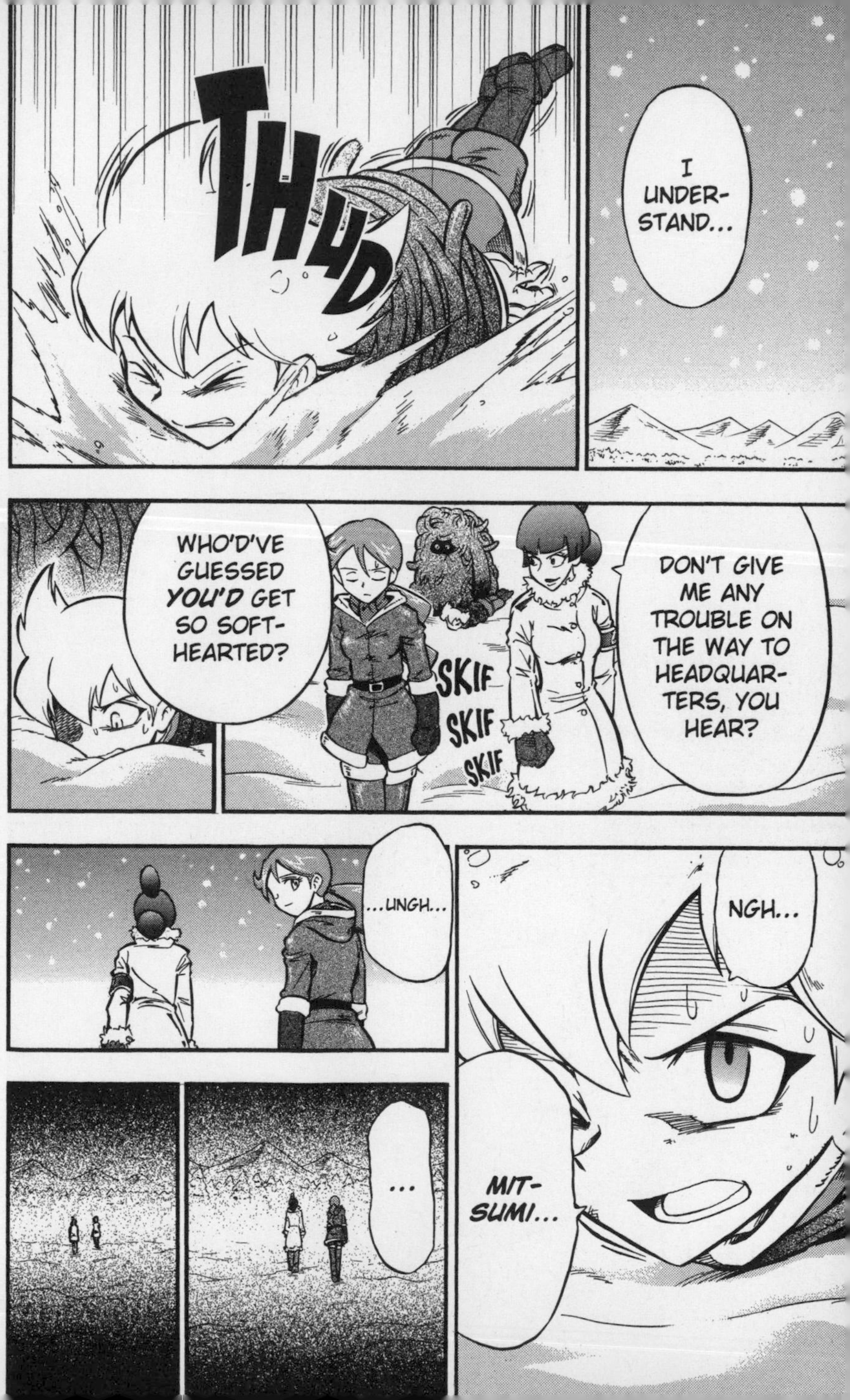
I UNDER-STAND...
THUD
DON'T GIVE ME ANY TROUBLE ON THE WAY TO HEADQUAR-TERS, YOU HEAR?
SKIF
SKIF
SKIF
WHO'D'VE GUESSED *YOU'D* GET SO SOFT-HEARTED?
NGH...
MIT-SUMI...
...UNGH...
...

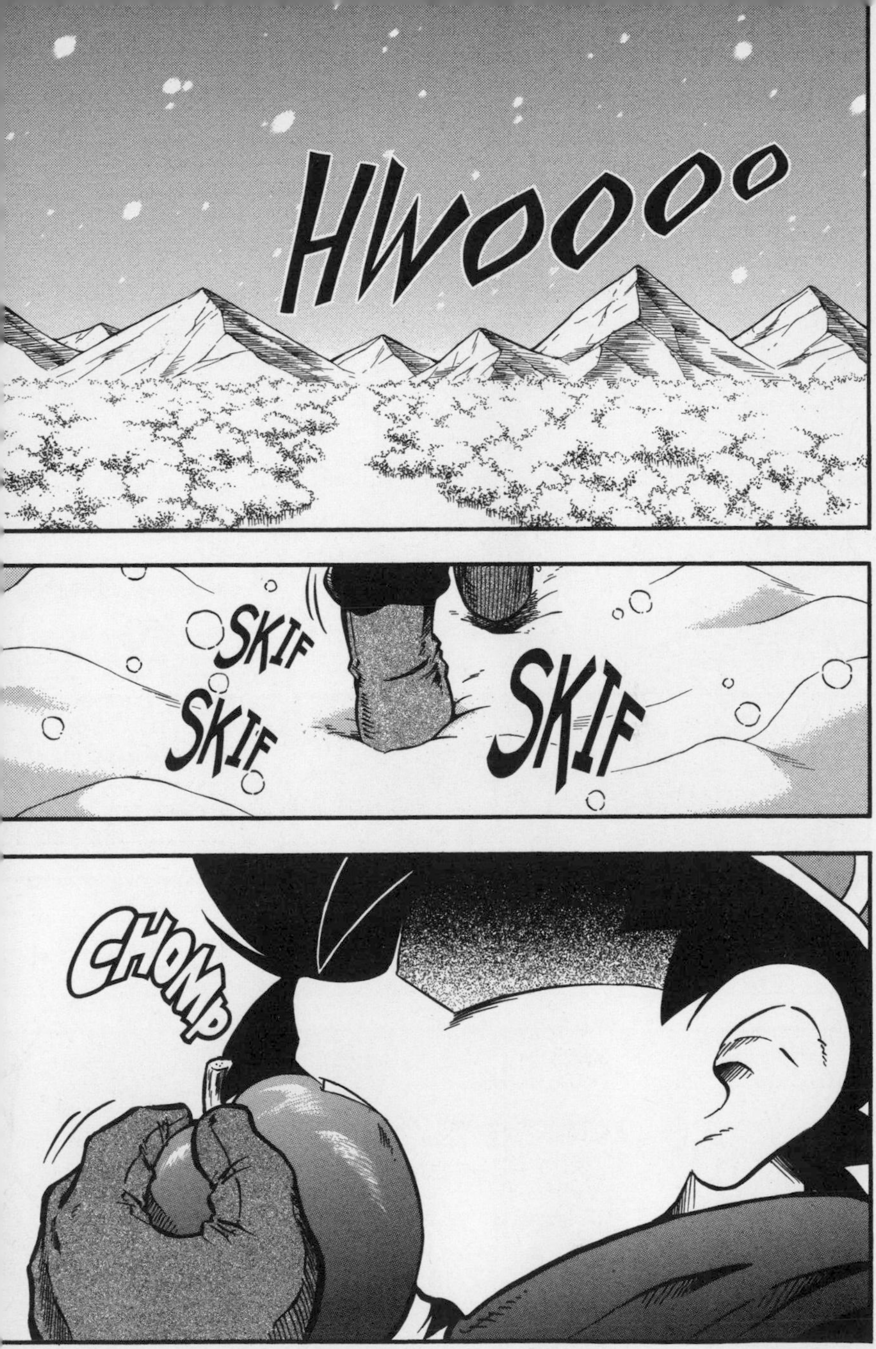
HWOOOO
SKIF
SKIF
SKIF
CHOMP

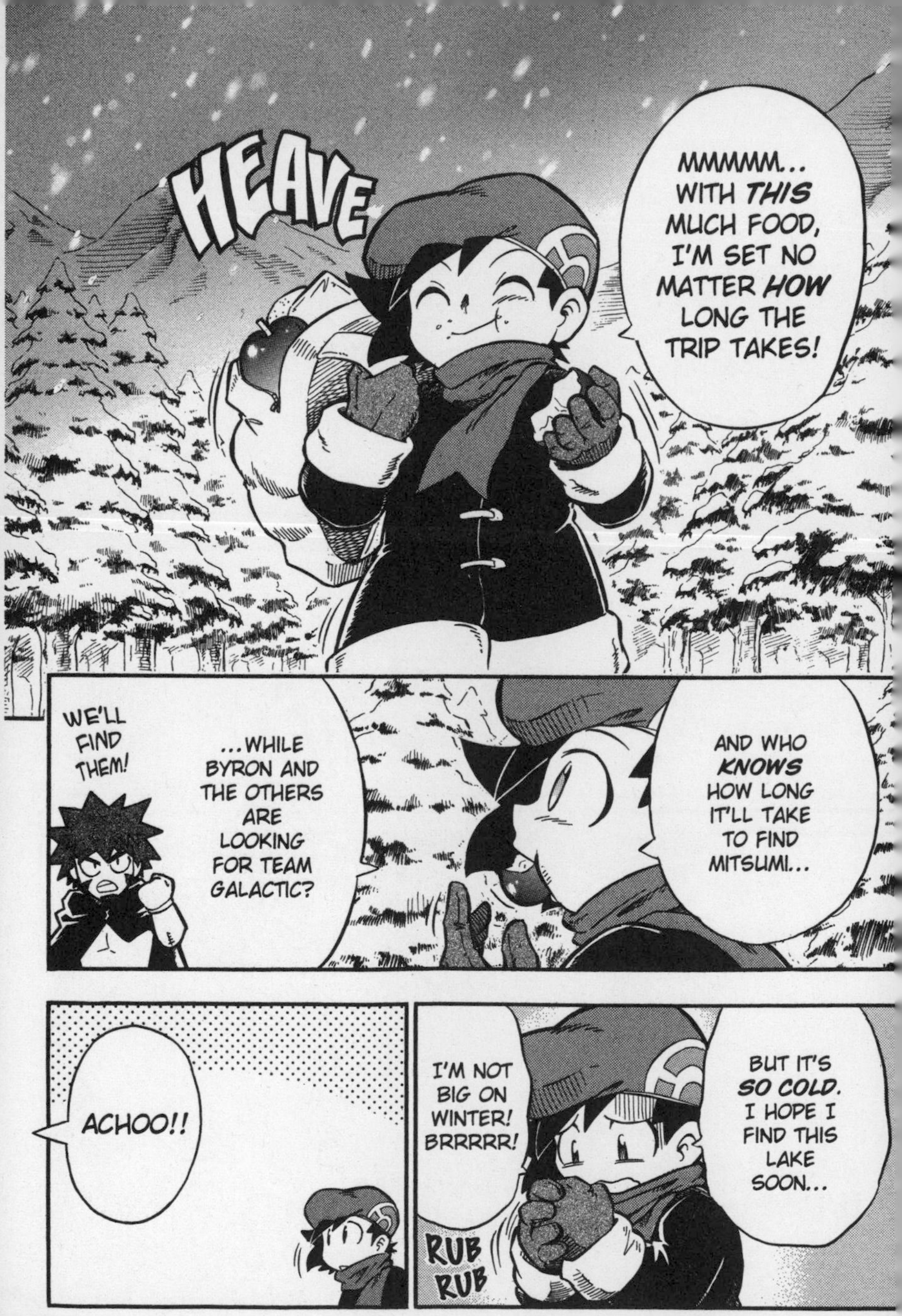
HEAVE
MMMMM... WITH THIS MUCH FOOD, I'M SET NO MATTER HOW LONG THE TRIP TAKES!
AND WHO KNOWS HOW LONG IT'LL TAKE TO FIND MITSUMI...
...WHILE BYRON AND THE OTHERS ARE LOOKING FOR TEAM GALACTIC?
WE'LL FIND THEM!
BUT IT'S SO COLD. I HOPE I FIND THIS LAKE SOON...
I'M NOT BIG ON WINTER! BRRRRR!
RUB RUB
ACHOO!!

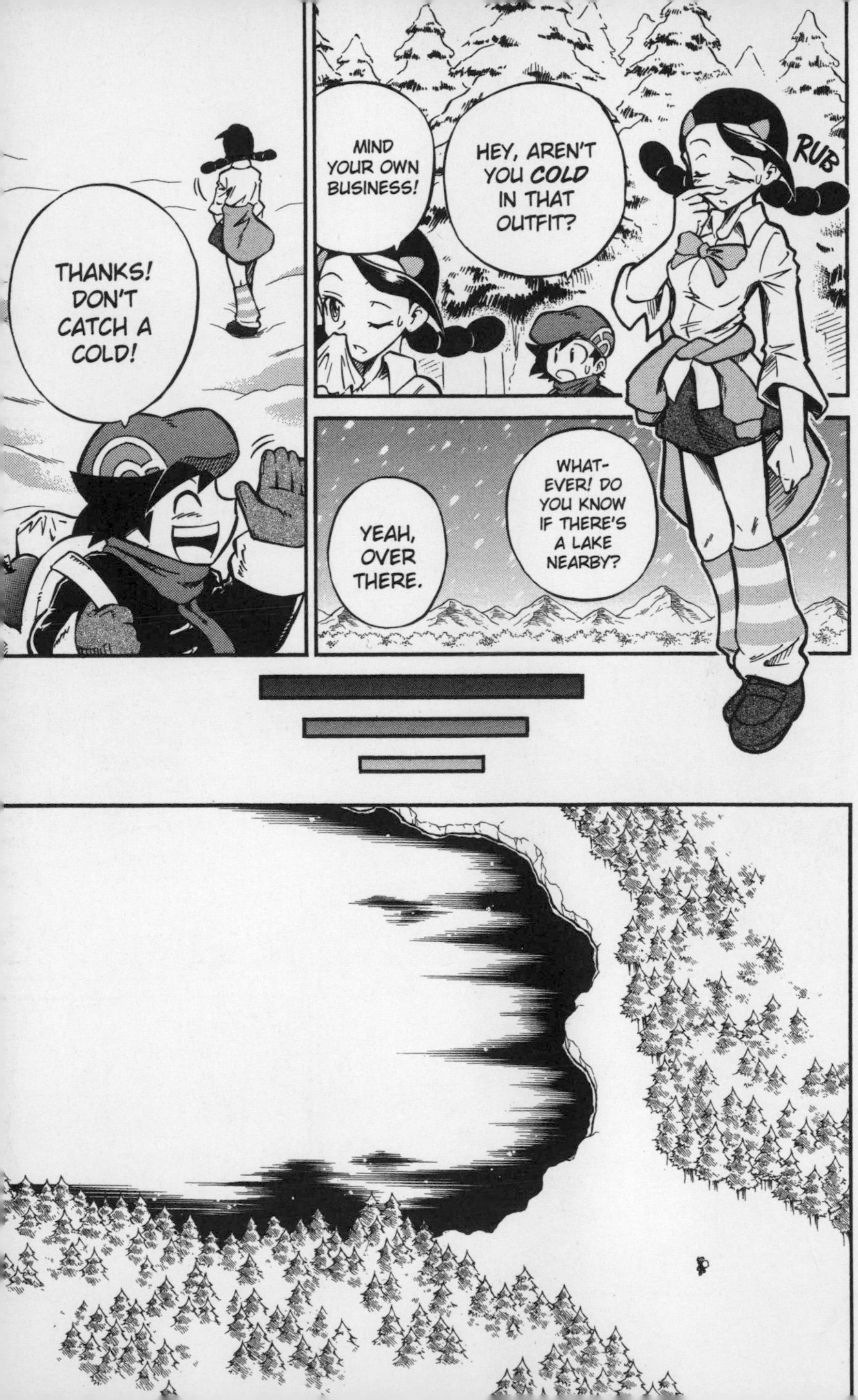
HEY, AREN'T YOU COLD IN THAT OUTFIT?
MIND YOUR OWN BUSINESS!
RUB
WHAT-EVER! DO YOU KNOW IF THERE'S A LAKE NEARBY?
YEAH, OVER THERE.
THANKS! DON'T CATCH A COLD!

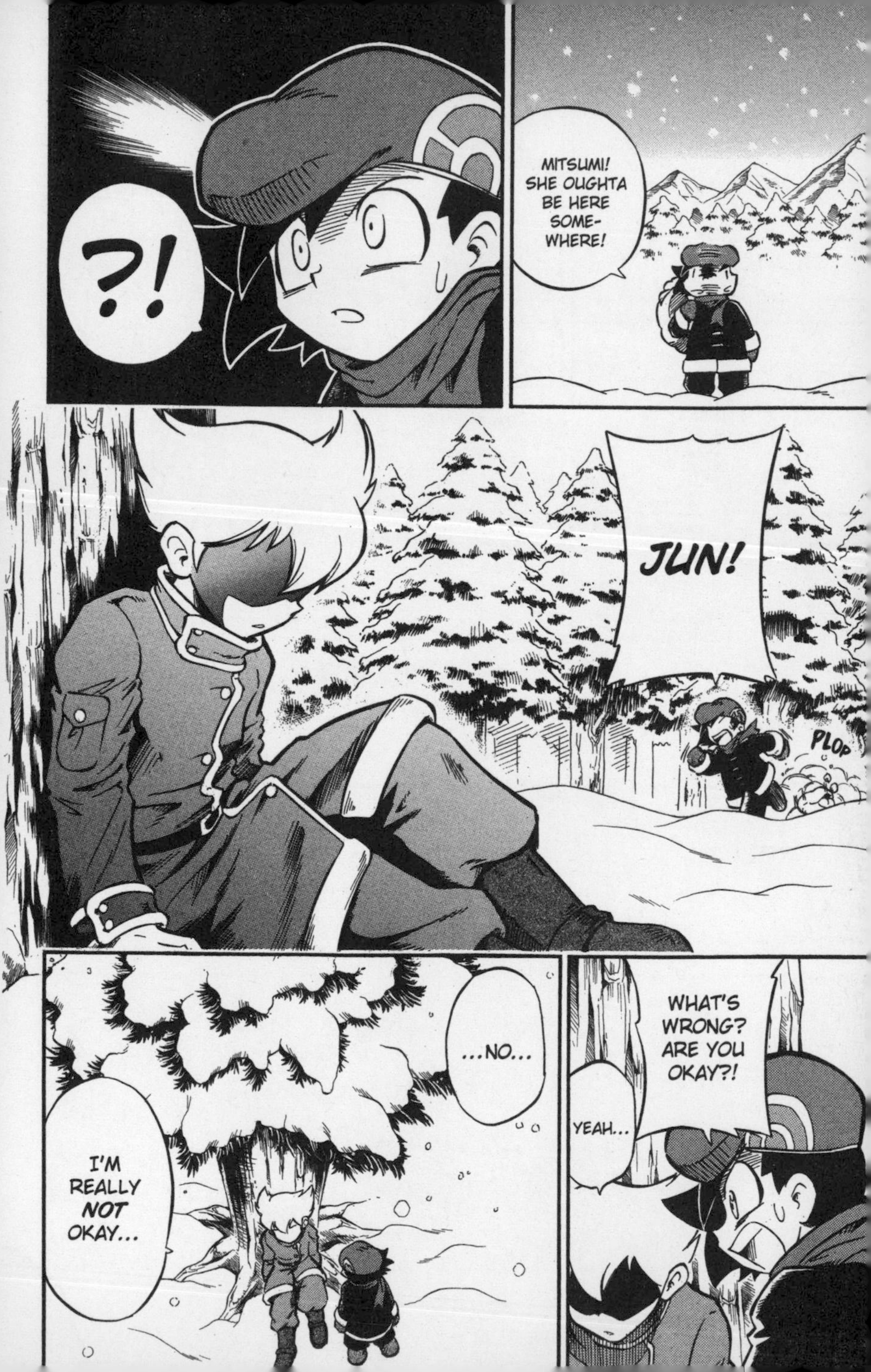
MITSUMI! SHE OUGHTA BE HERE SOME-WHERE!
?!
JUN!
PLOP
WHAT'S WRONG? ARE YOU OKAY?!
YEAH...
...NO...
I'M REALLY NOT OKAY...

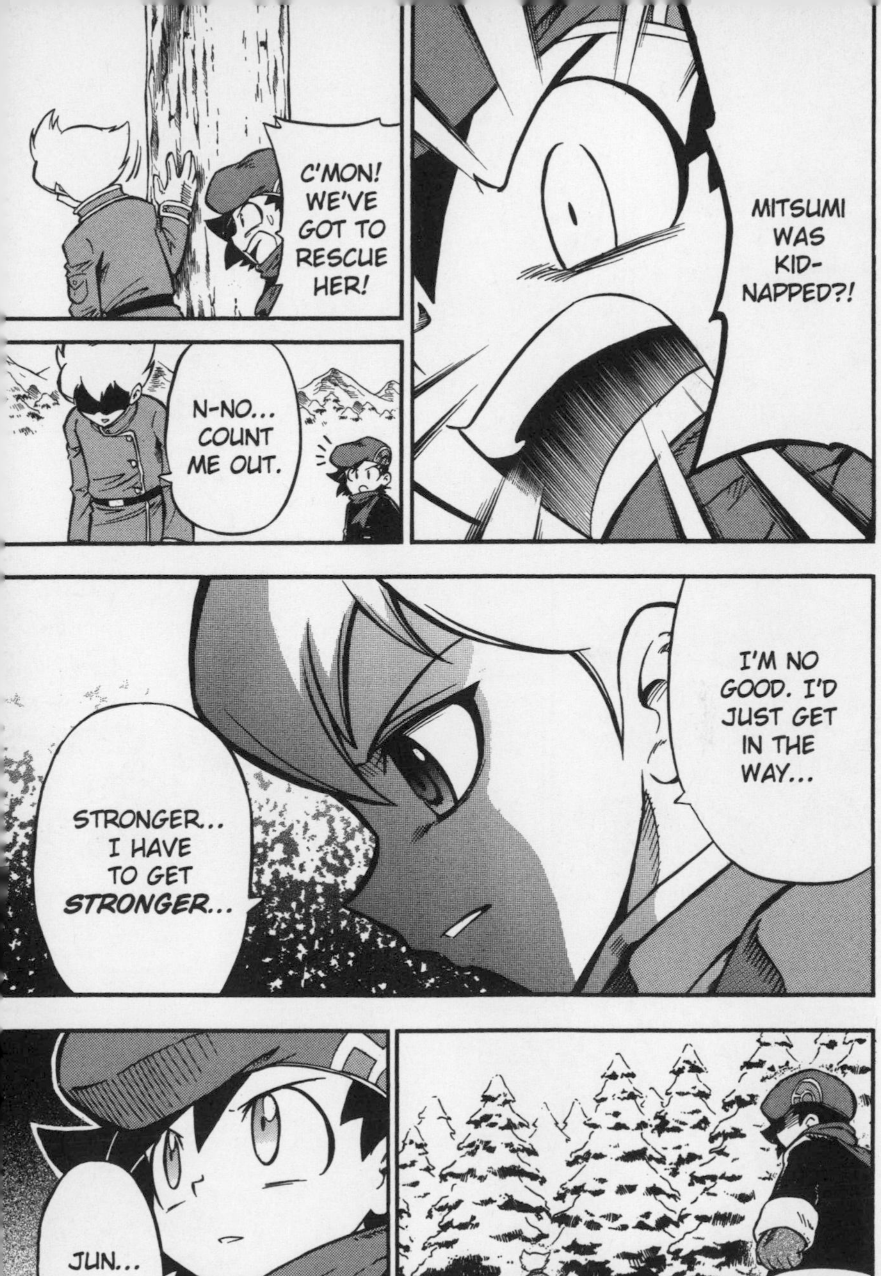
MITSUMI WAS KID-NAPPED?!
C'MON! WE'VE GOT TO RESCUE HER!
N-NO... COUNT ME OUT.
I'M NO GOOD. I'D JUST GET IN THE WAY...
STRONGER... I HAVE TO GET **STRONGER**...
JUN...

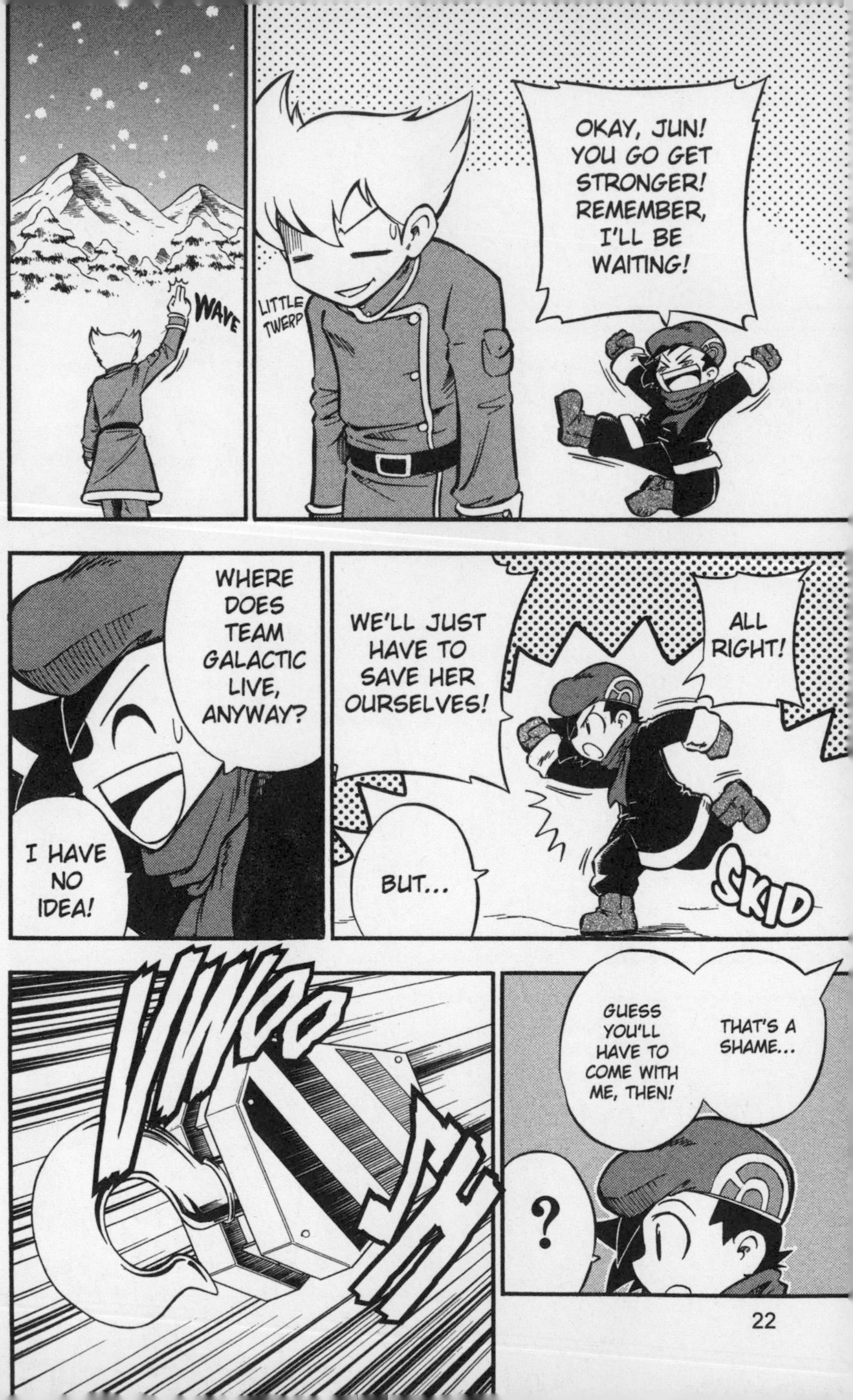
OKAY, JUN! YOU GO GET STRONGER! REMEMBER, I'LL BE WAITING!
LITTLE TWERP
WAVE
ALL RIGHT!
WE'LL JUST HAVE TO SAVE HER OURSELVES!
SKID
BUT...
WHERE DOES TEAM GALACTIC LIVE, ANYWAY?
I HAVE NO IDEA!
THAT'S A SHAME...
GUESS YOU'LL HAVE TO COME WITH ME, THEN!
?
WOOSH

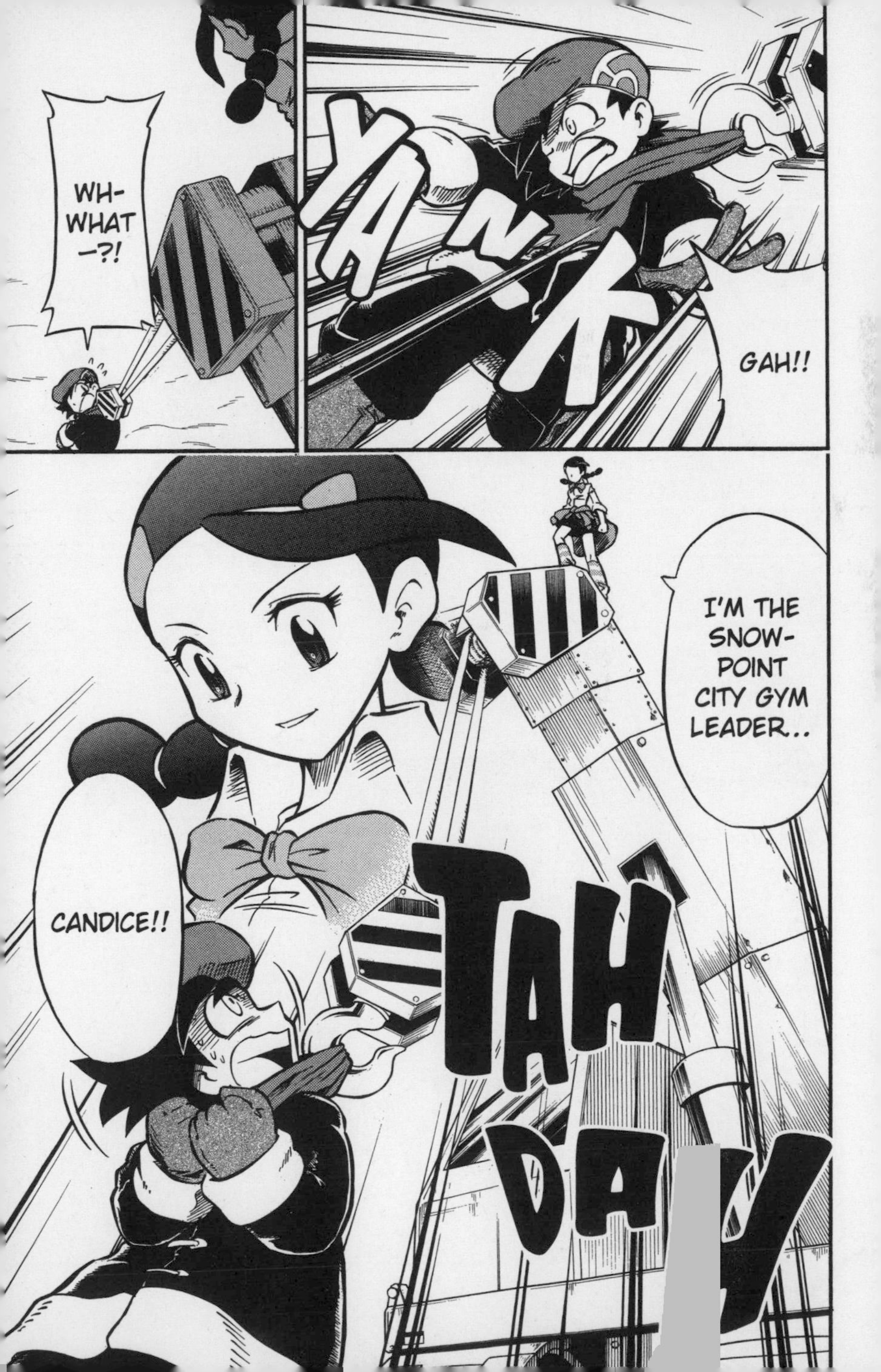
YANK
GAH!!
WH-WHAT—?!
I'M THE SNOW-POINT CITY GYM LEADER...
TAH
DA
CANDICE!!

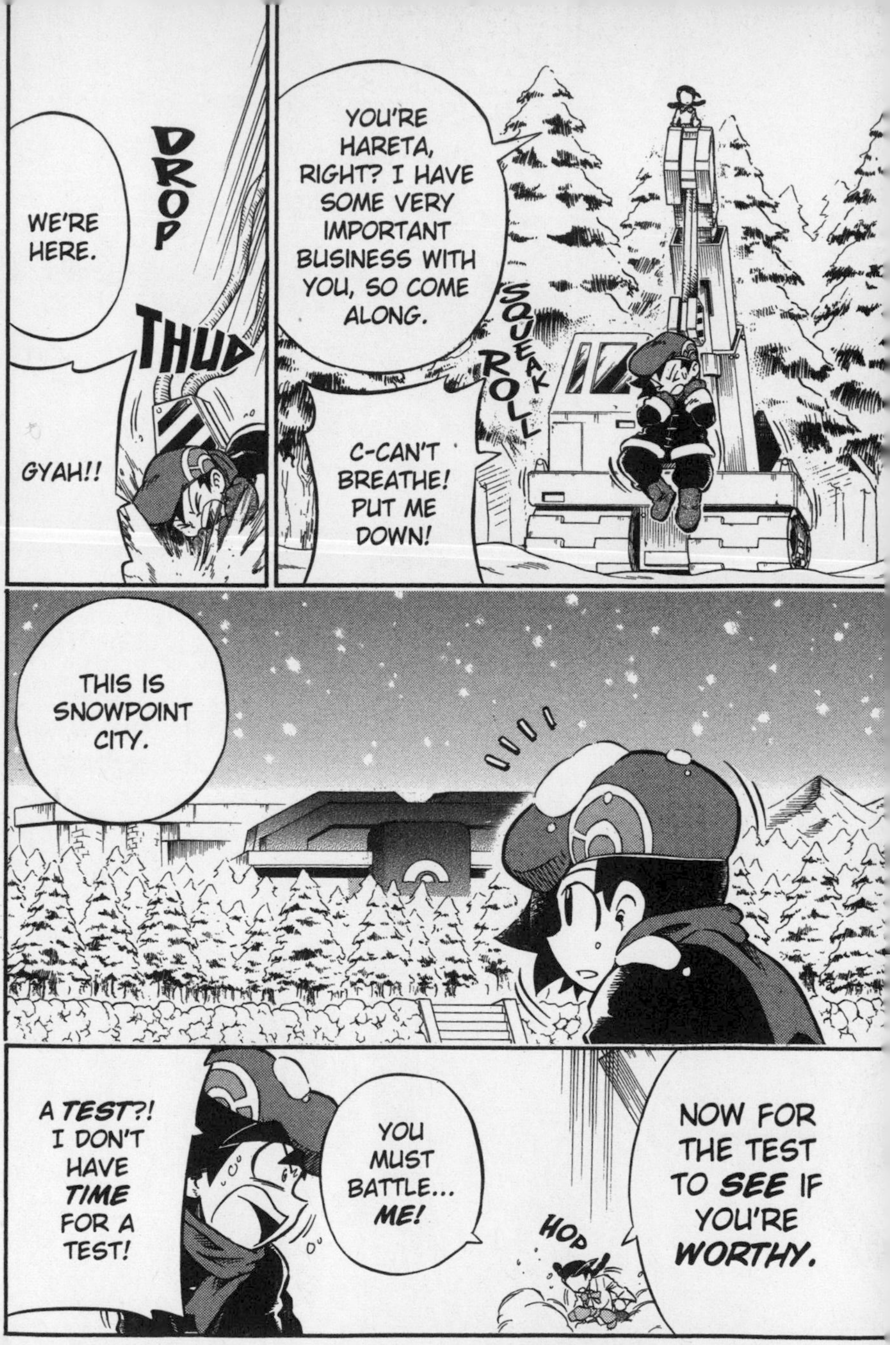
YOU'RE HARETA, RIGHT? I HAVE SOME VERY IMPORTANT BUSINESS WITH YOU, SO COME ALONG.
SQUEAK
ROLL
C-CAN'T BREATHE! PUT ME DOWN!
DROP
WE'RE HERE.
THUD
GYAH!!
THIS IS SNOWPOINT CITY.
NOW FOR THE TEST TO SEE IF YOU'RE WORTHY.
HOP
YOU MUST BATTLE... ME!
A TEST?! I DON'T HAVE TIME FOR A TEST!

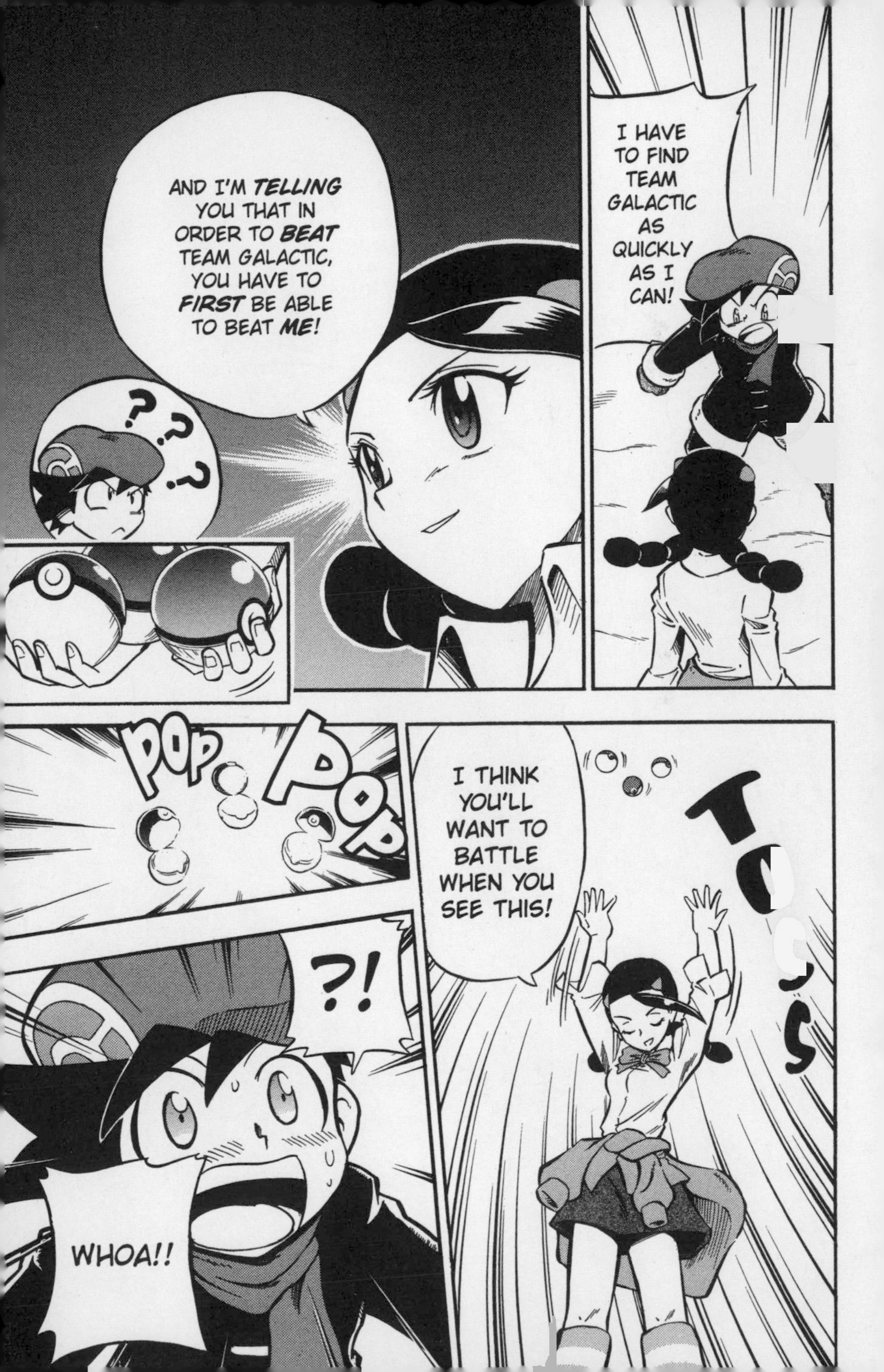
I HAVE TO FIND TEAM GALACTIC AS QUICKLY AS I CAN!
AND I'M *TELLING* YOU THAT IN ORDER TO *BEAT* TEAM GALACTIC, YOU HAVE TO *FIRST* BE ABLE TO BEAT *ME*!
???
I THINK YOU'LL WANT TO BATTLE WHEN YOU SEE THIS!
TOSS
POP POP
?!
WHOA!!

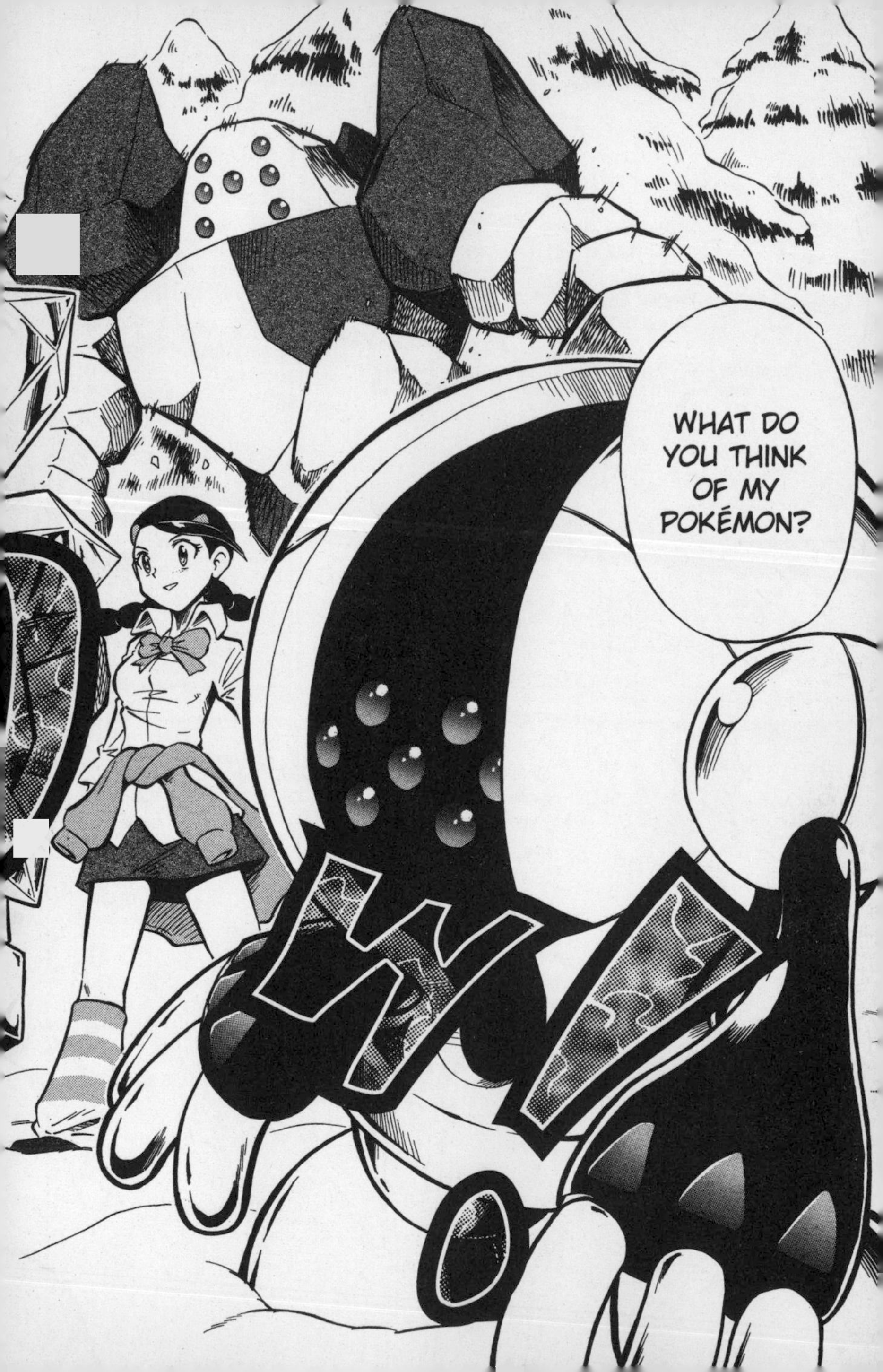
WHAT DO YOU THINK OF MY POKÉMON?

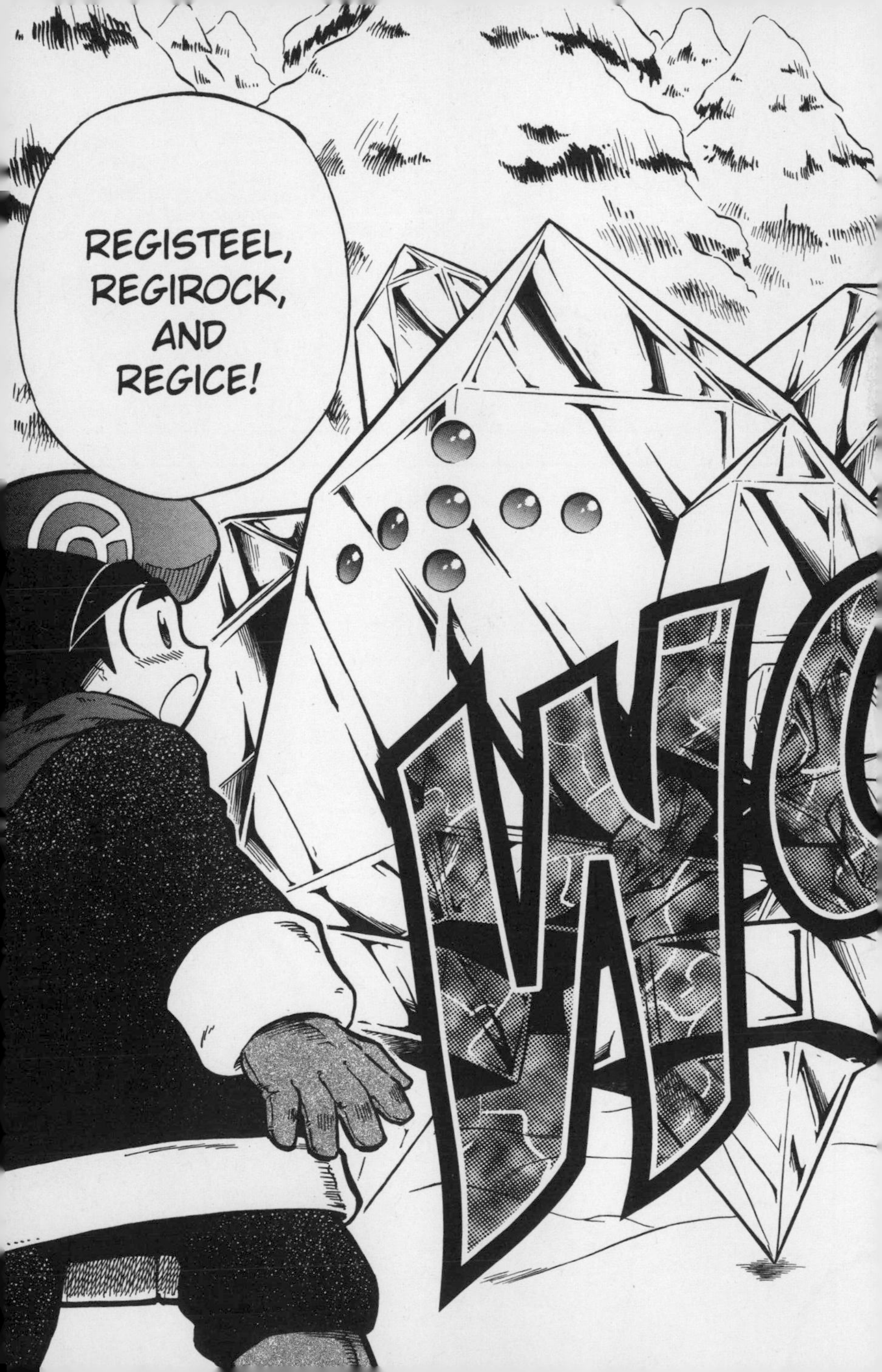
REGISTEEL, REGIROCK, AND REGICE!

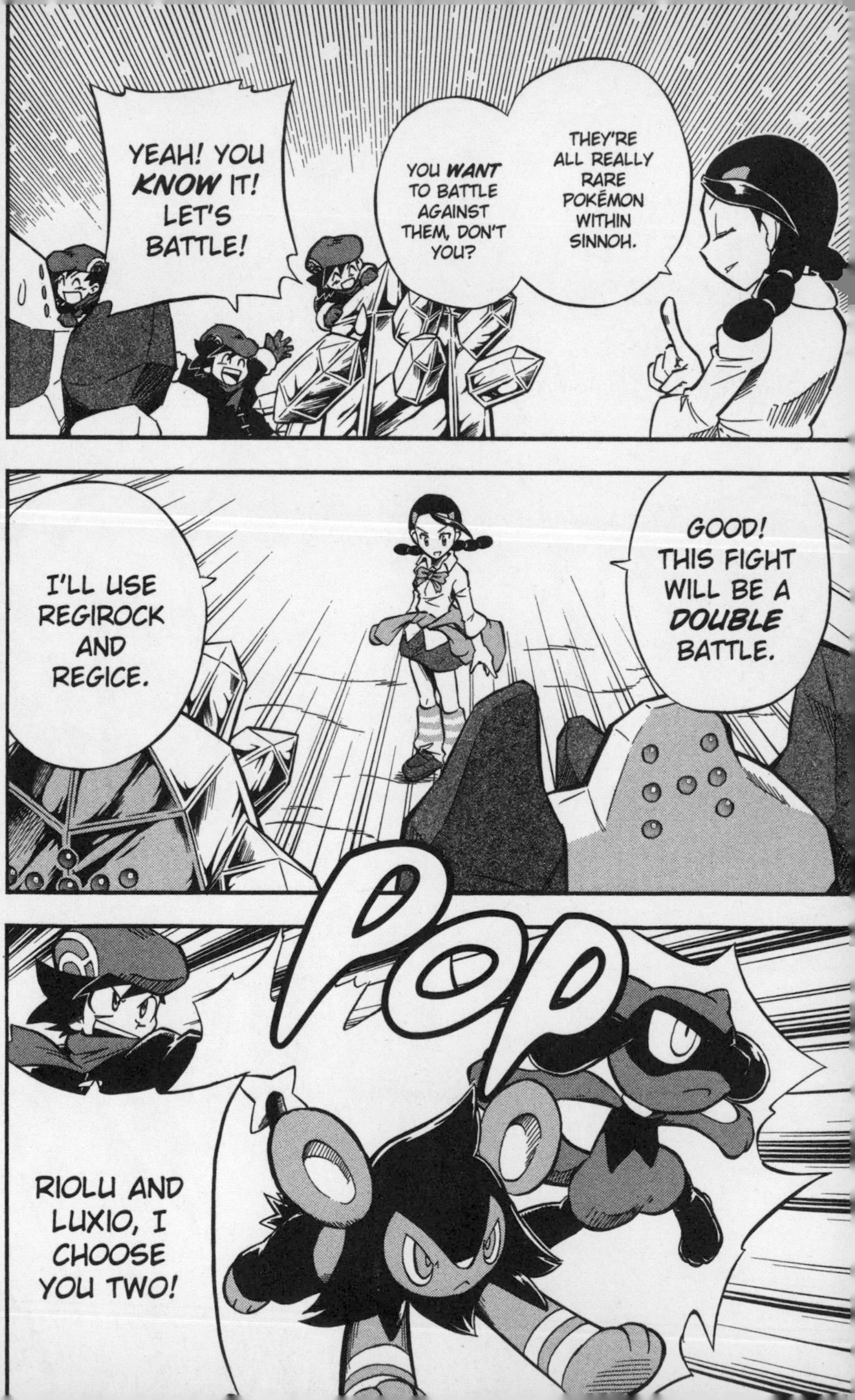
THEY'RE ALL REALLY RARE POKÉMON WITHIN SINNOH.
YOU WANT TO BATTLE AGAINST THEM, DON'T YOU?
YEAH! YOU KNOW IT! LET'S BATTLE!
GOOD! THIS FIGHT WILL BE A DOUBLE BATTLE.
I'LL USE REGIROCK AND REGICE.
POP
RIOLU AND LUXIO, I CHOOSE YOU TWO!

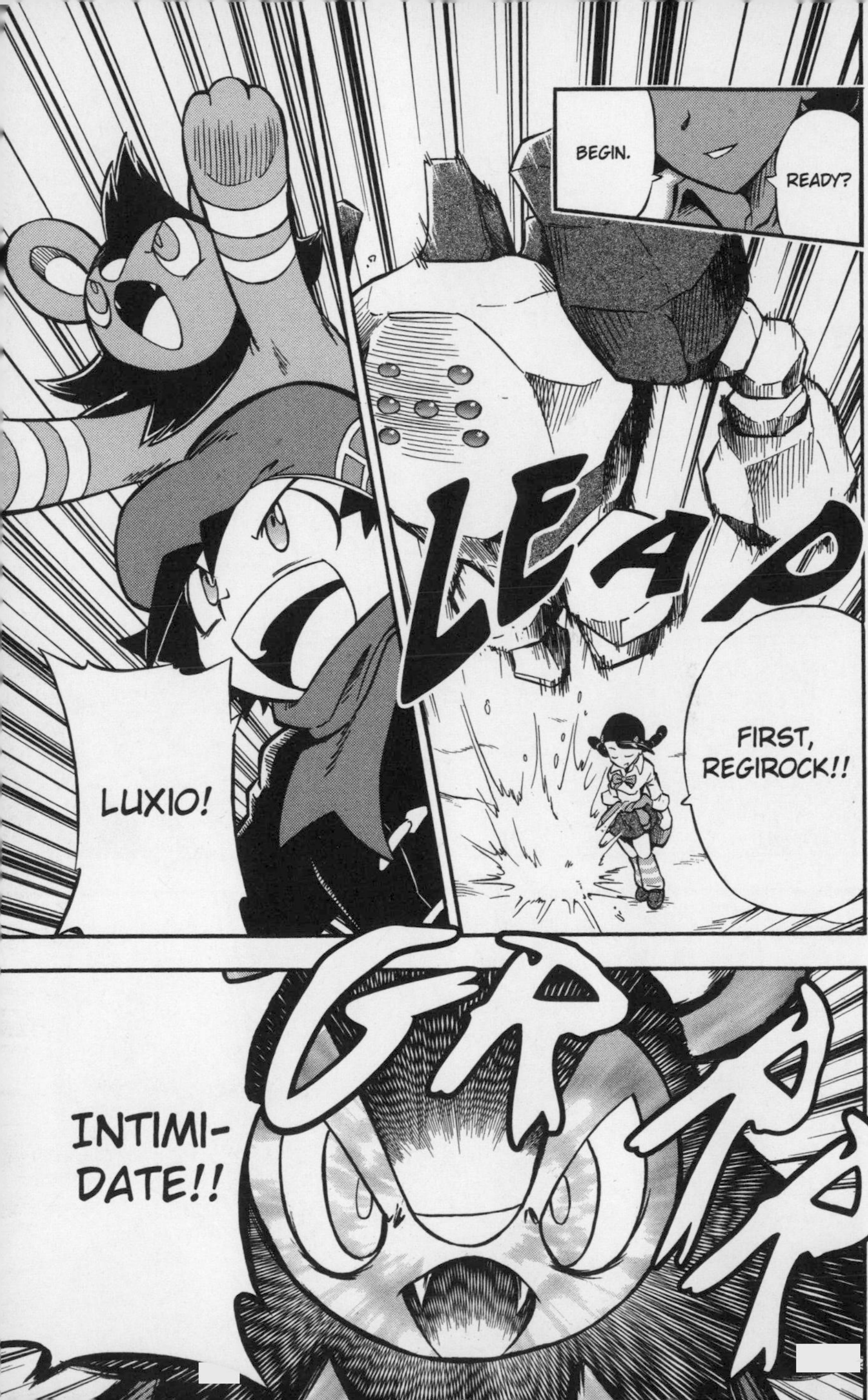
READY?
BEGIN.
LEAP
FIRST, REGIROCK!!
LUXIO!
INTIMI-
DATE!!

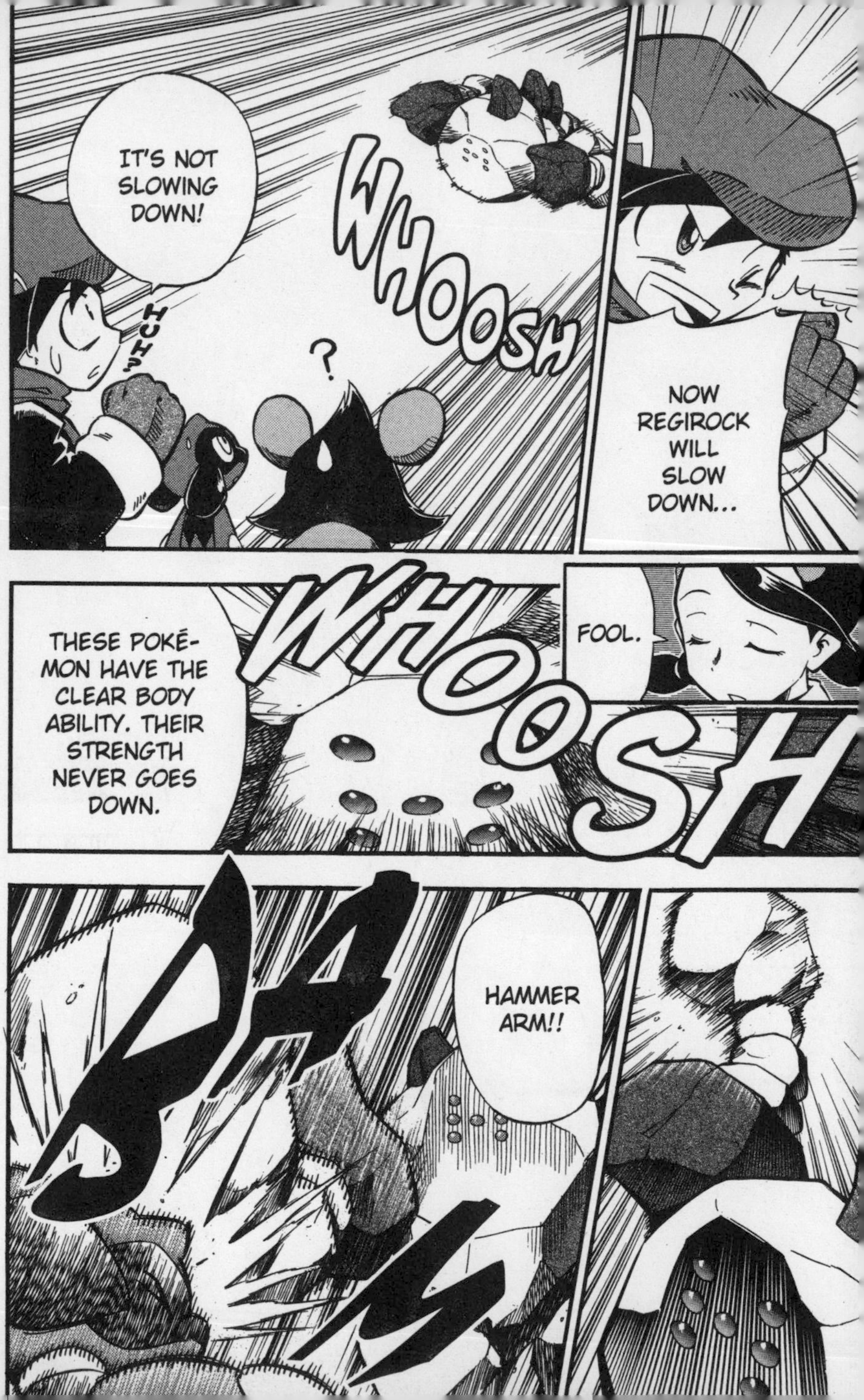
NOW REGIROCK WILL SLOW DOWN...
WHOOSH
IT'S NOT SLOWING DOWN!
?
HUH?
FOOL.
WHOOSH
THESE POKÉMON HAVE THE CLEAR BODY ABILITY. THEIR STRENGTH NEVER GOES DOWN.
HAMMER ARM!!

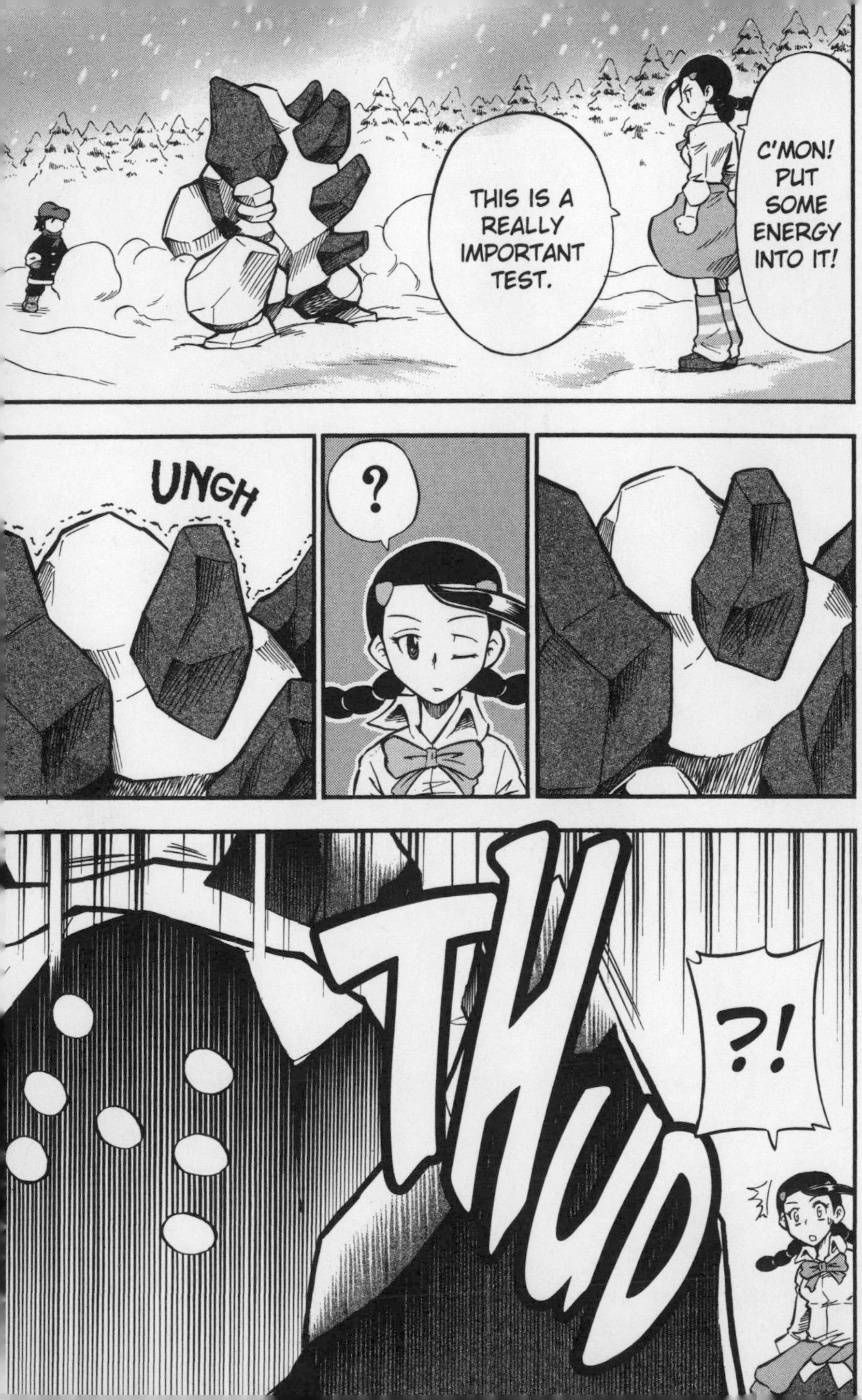
C'MON! PUT SOME ENERGY INTO IT!
THIS IS A REALLY IMPORTANT TEST.
?
UNGH
THUD
?!

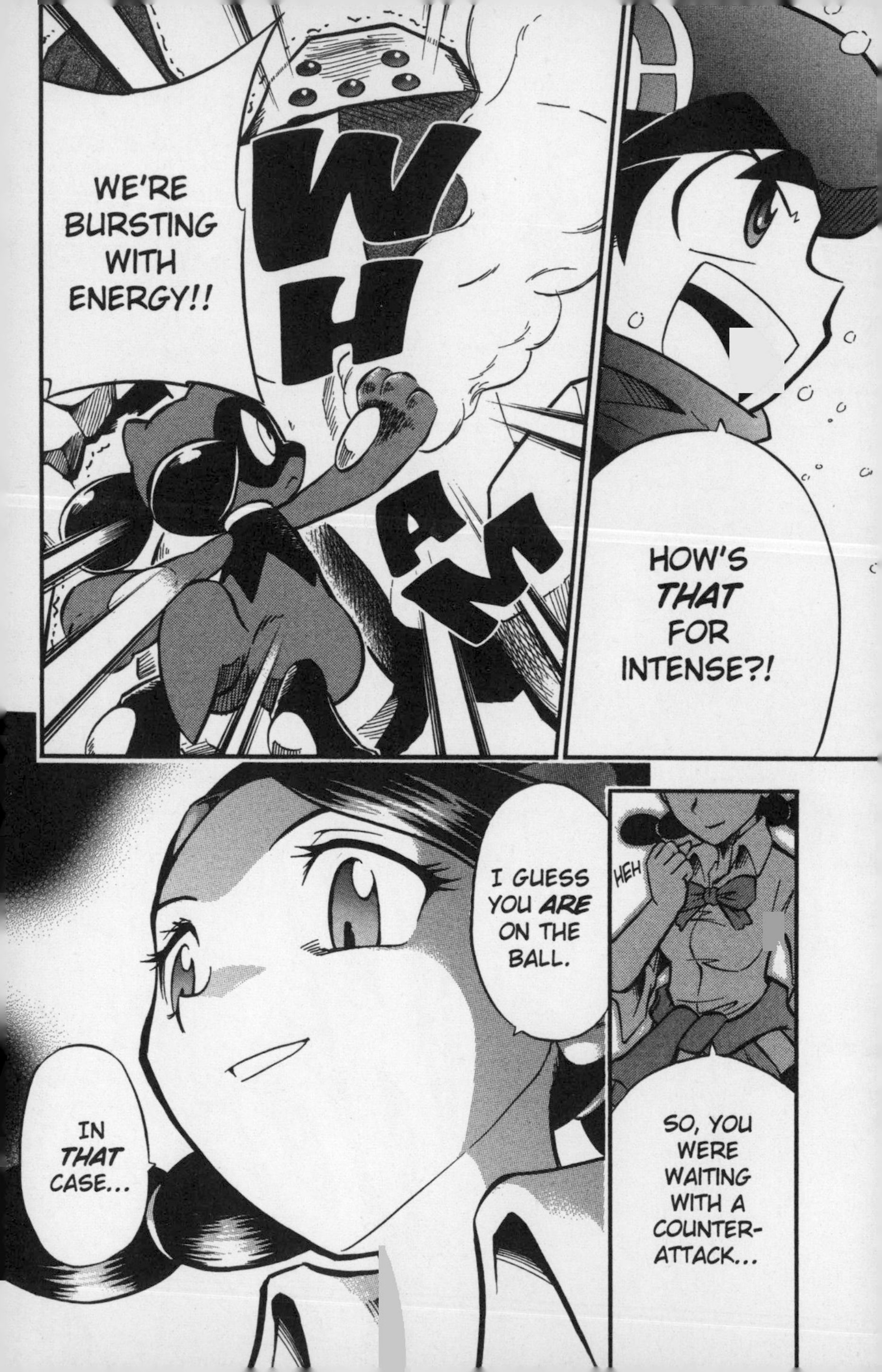
HOW'S *THAT* FOR INTENSE?!
WHAM
WE'RE BURSTING WITH ENERGY!!
HEH
SO, YOU WERE WAITING WITH A COUNTER-ATTACK...
I GUESS YOU *ARE* ON THE BALL.
IN *THAT* CASE...

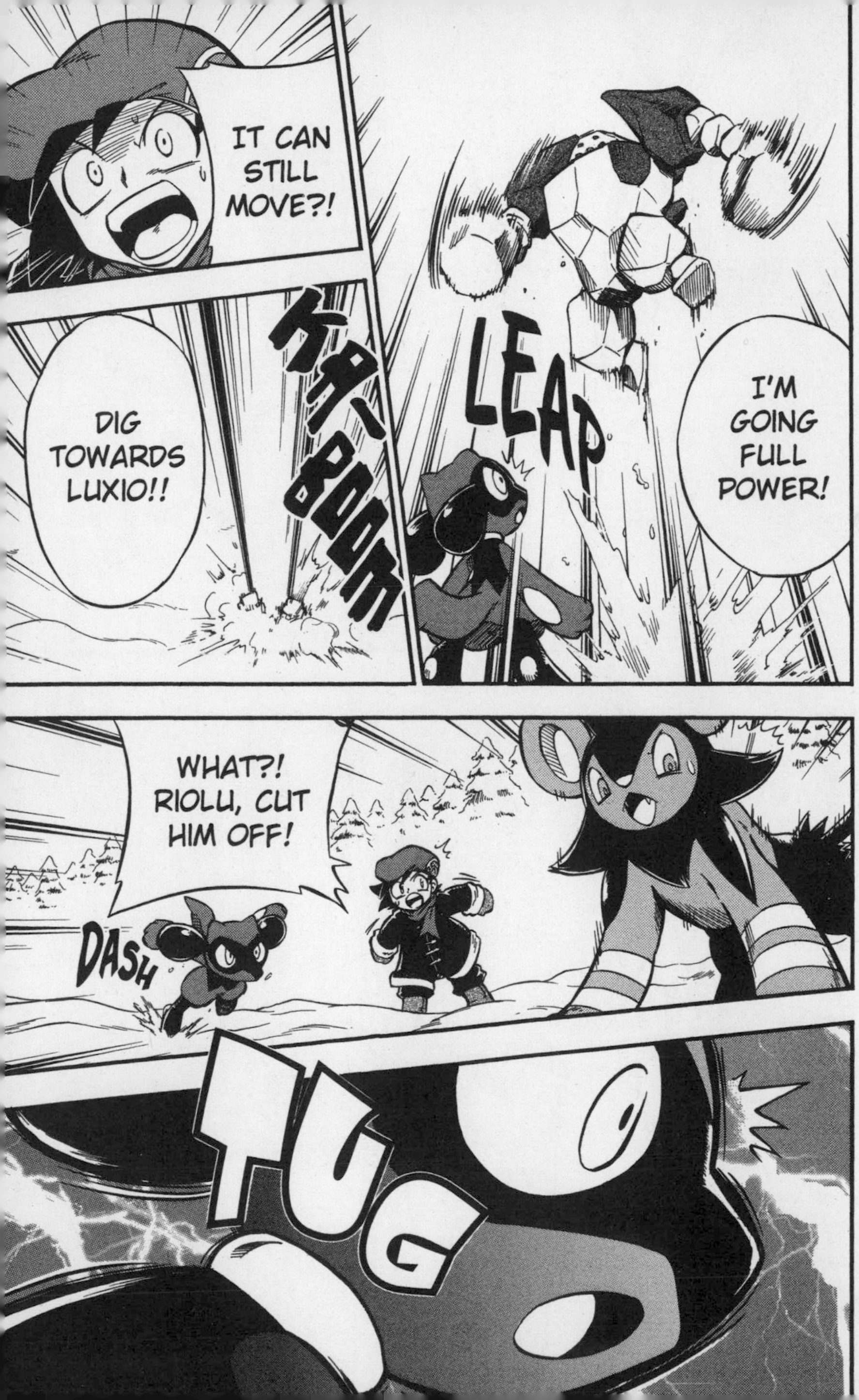
I'M GOING FULL POWER!
LEAP
IT CAN STILL MOVE?!
KA-BOOM
DIG TOWARDS LUXIO!!
WHAT?! RIOLU, CUT HIM OFF!
DASH
TUG

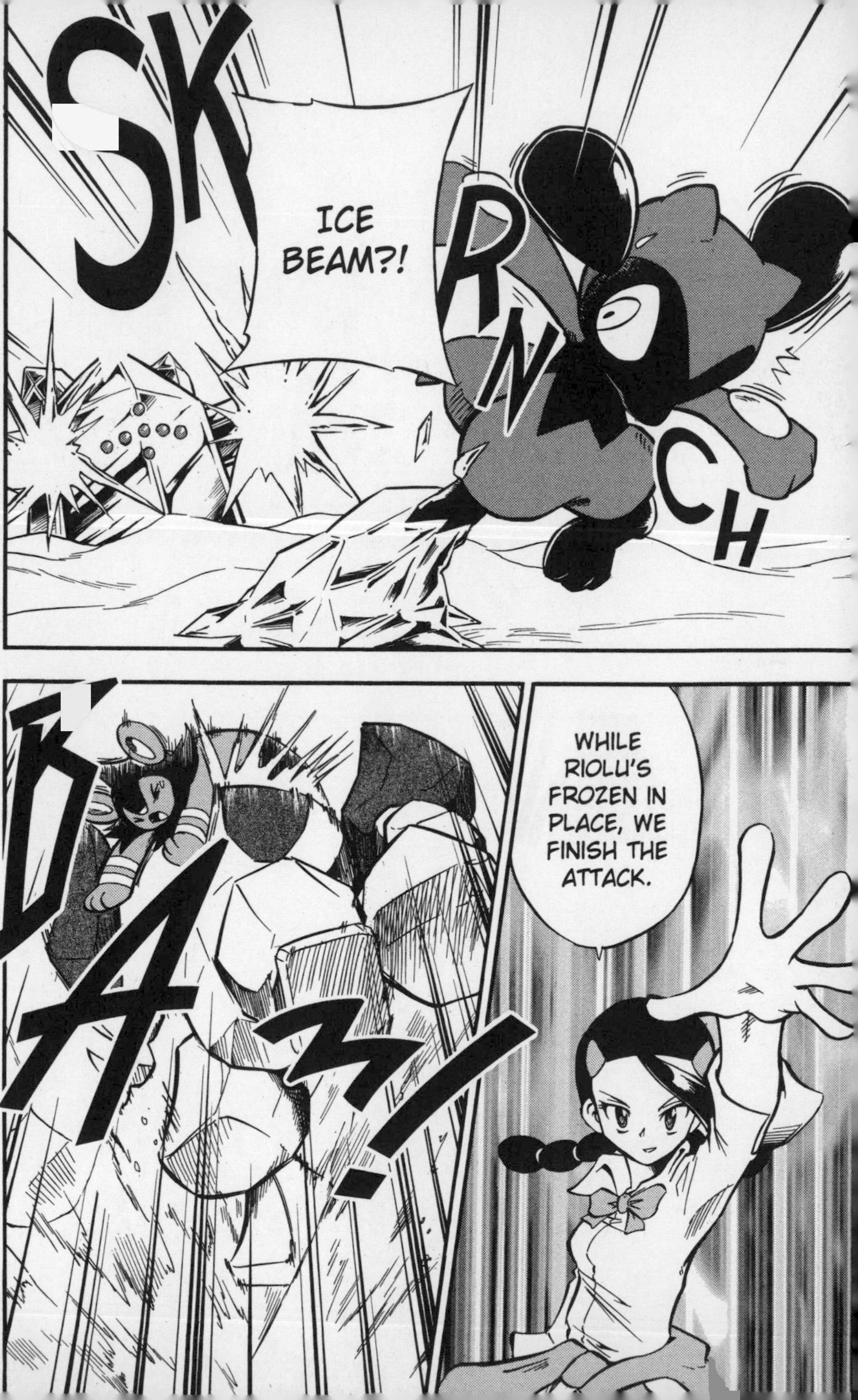
ICE BEAM?!
SKRNCH
WHILE RIOLU'S FROZEN IN PLACE, WE FINISH THE ATTACK.
DAM!

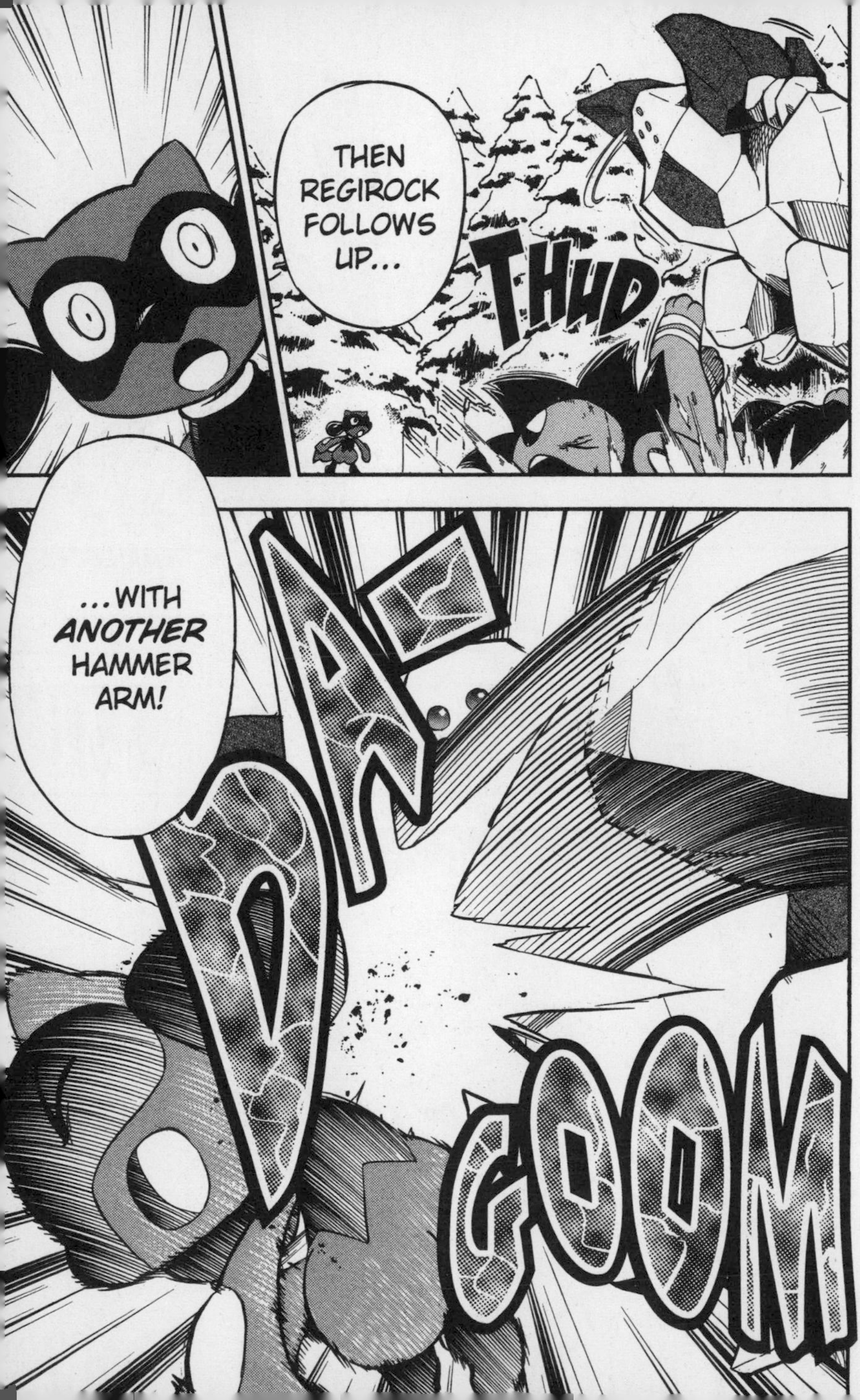
THEN REGIROCK FOLLOWS UP...
THUD
...WITH *ANOTHER* HAMMER ARM!

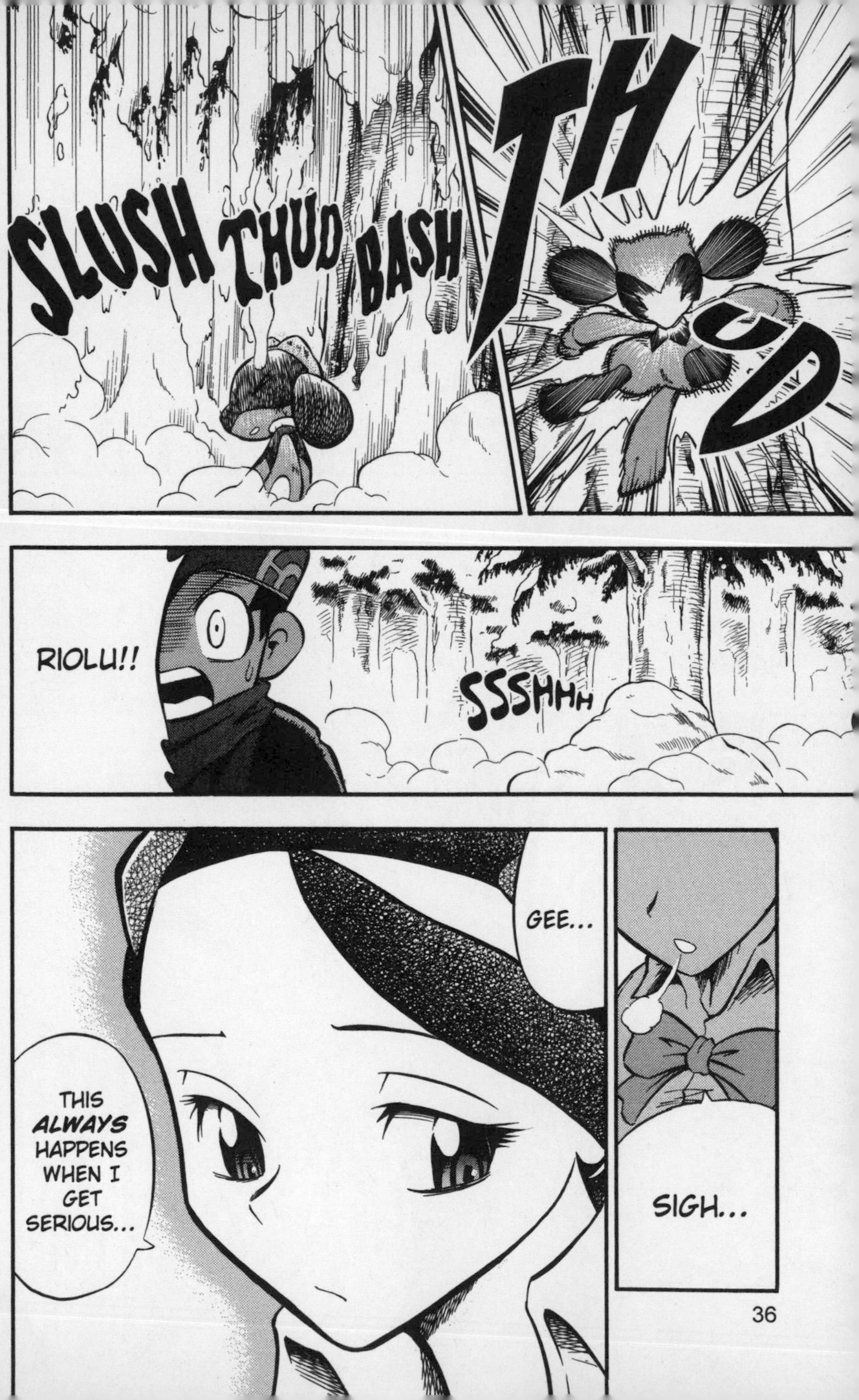
THUD
SLUSH THUD BASH
SSSHHH
RIOLU!!
SIGH...
GEE...
THIS *ALWAYS* HAPPENS WHEN I GET SERIOUS...

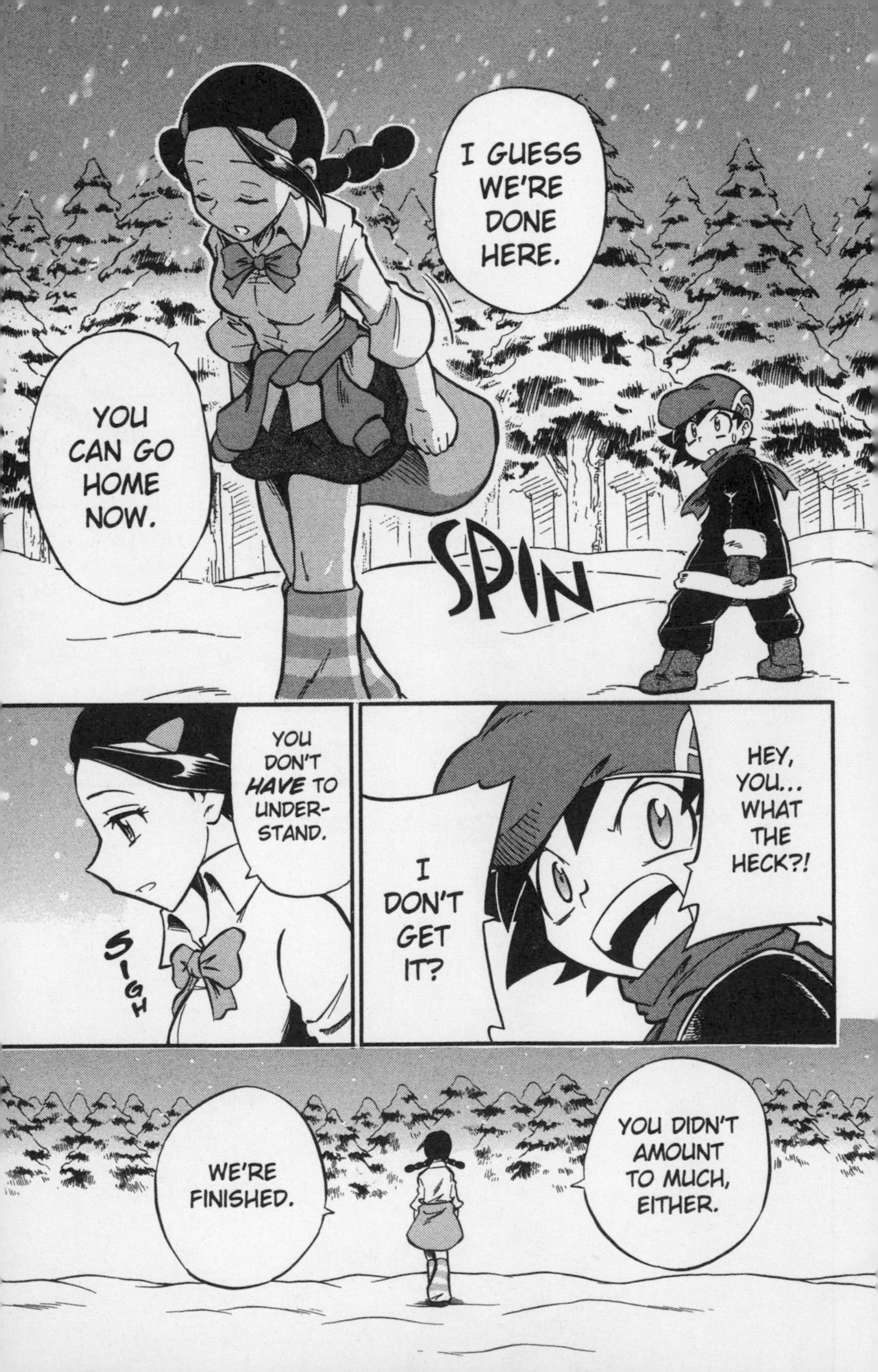
I GUESS WE'RE DONE HERE.
SPIN
YOU CAN GO HOME NOW.
HEY, YOU... WHAT THE HECK?!
I DON'T GET IT?
YOU DON'T *HAVE* TO UNDER-STAND.
SIGH
YOU DIDN'T AMOUNT TO MUCH, EITHER.
WE'RE FINISHED.

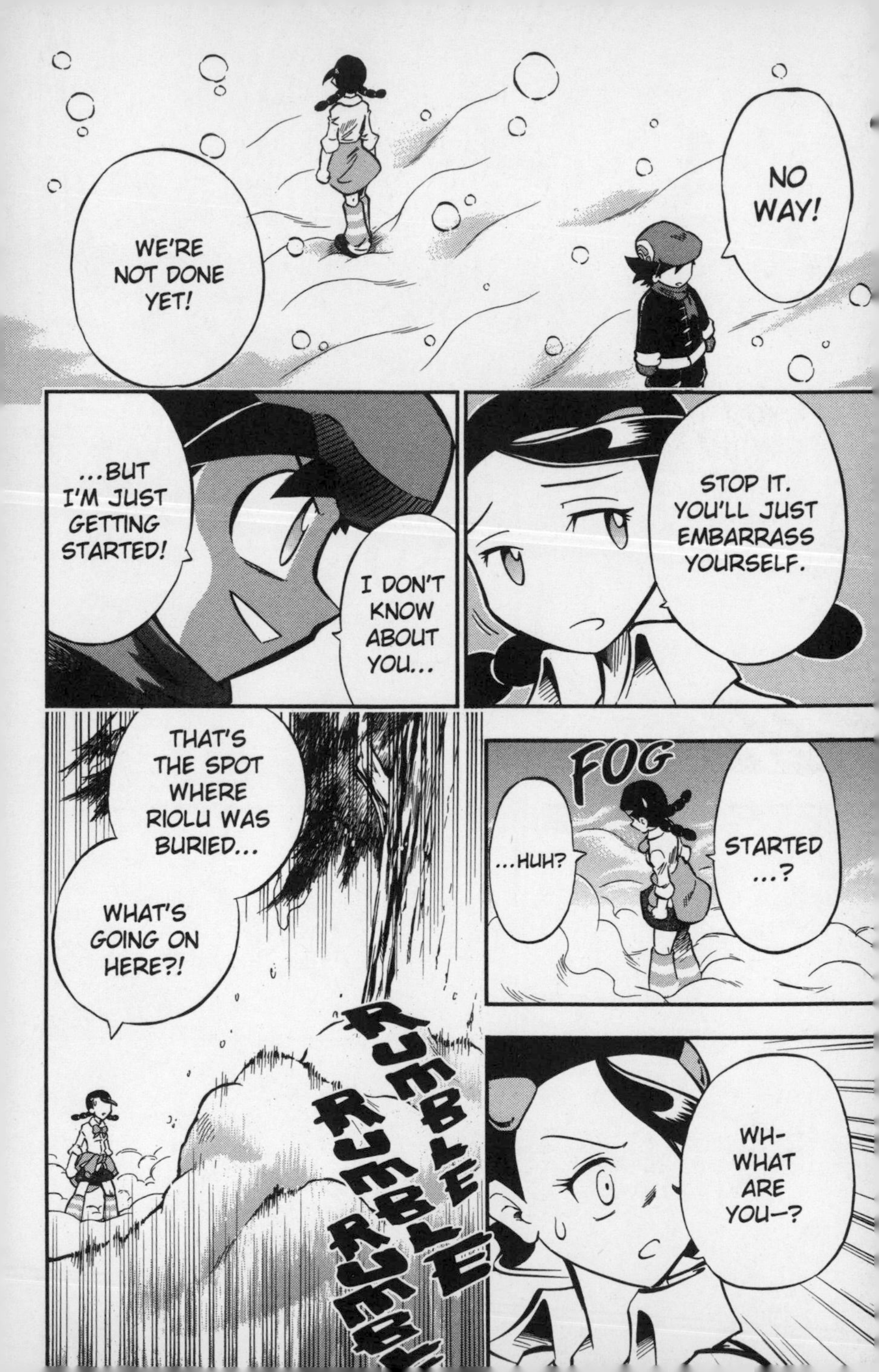
NO WAY!
WE'RE NOT DONE YET!
STOP IT. YOU'LL JUST EMBARRASS YOURSELF.
I DON'T KNOW ABOUT YOU...
...BUT I'M JUST GETTING STARTED!
FOG
STARTED...?
...HUH?
WH-WHAT ARE YOU–?
THAT'S THE SPOT WHERE RIOLU WAS BURIED...
WHAT'S GOING ON HERE?!
RUMBLE
RUMBLE
RUMBLE

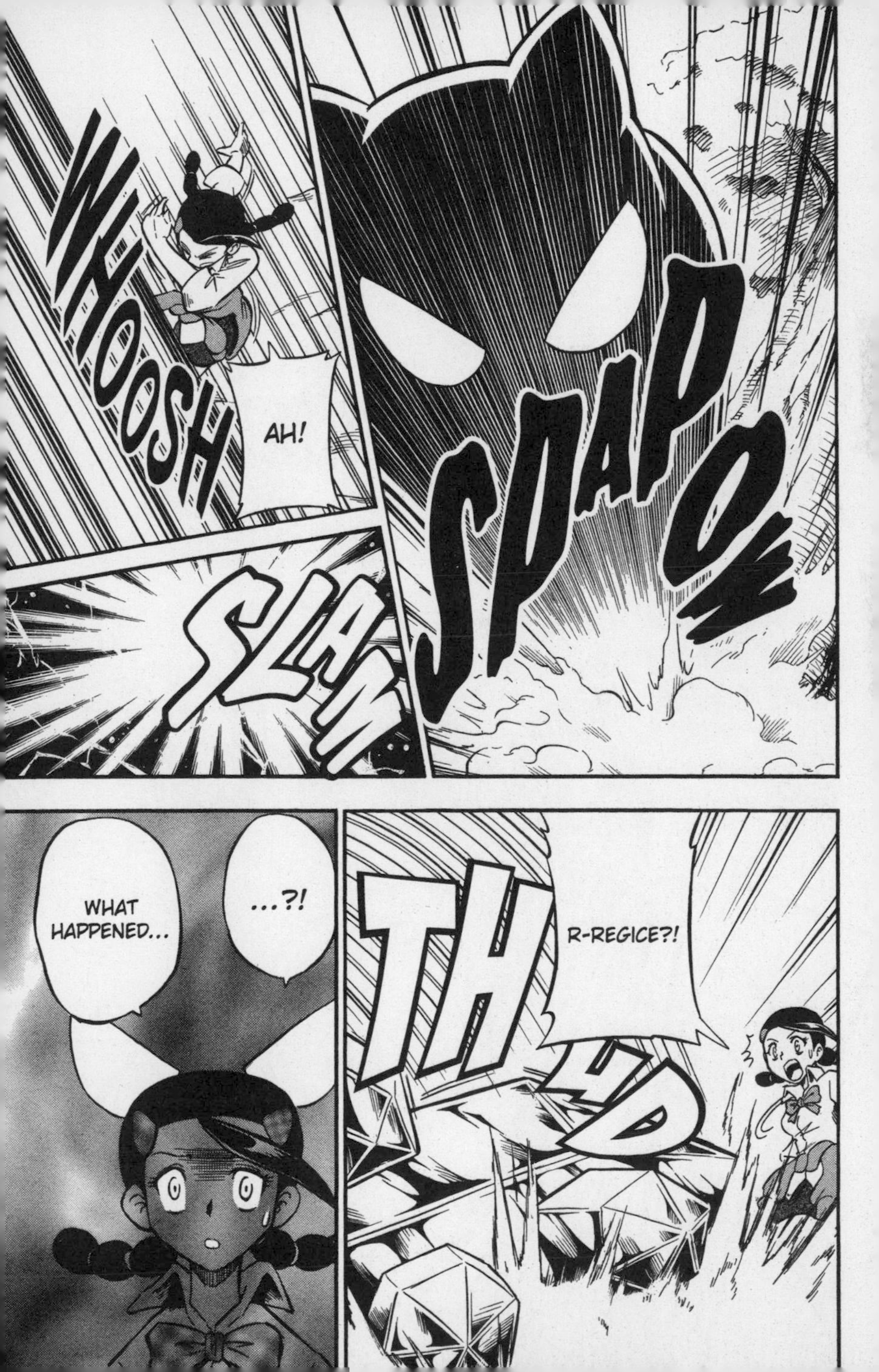
SPADOW
WHOOSH
AH!
SLAM
R-REGICE?!
THUD
...?!
WHAT HAPPENED...

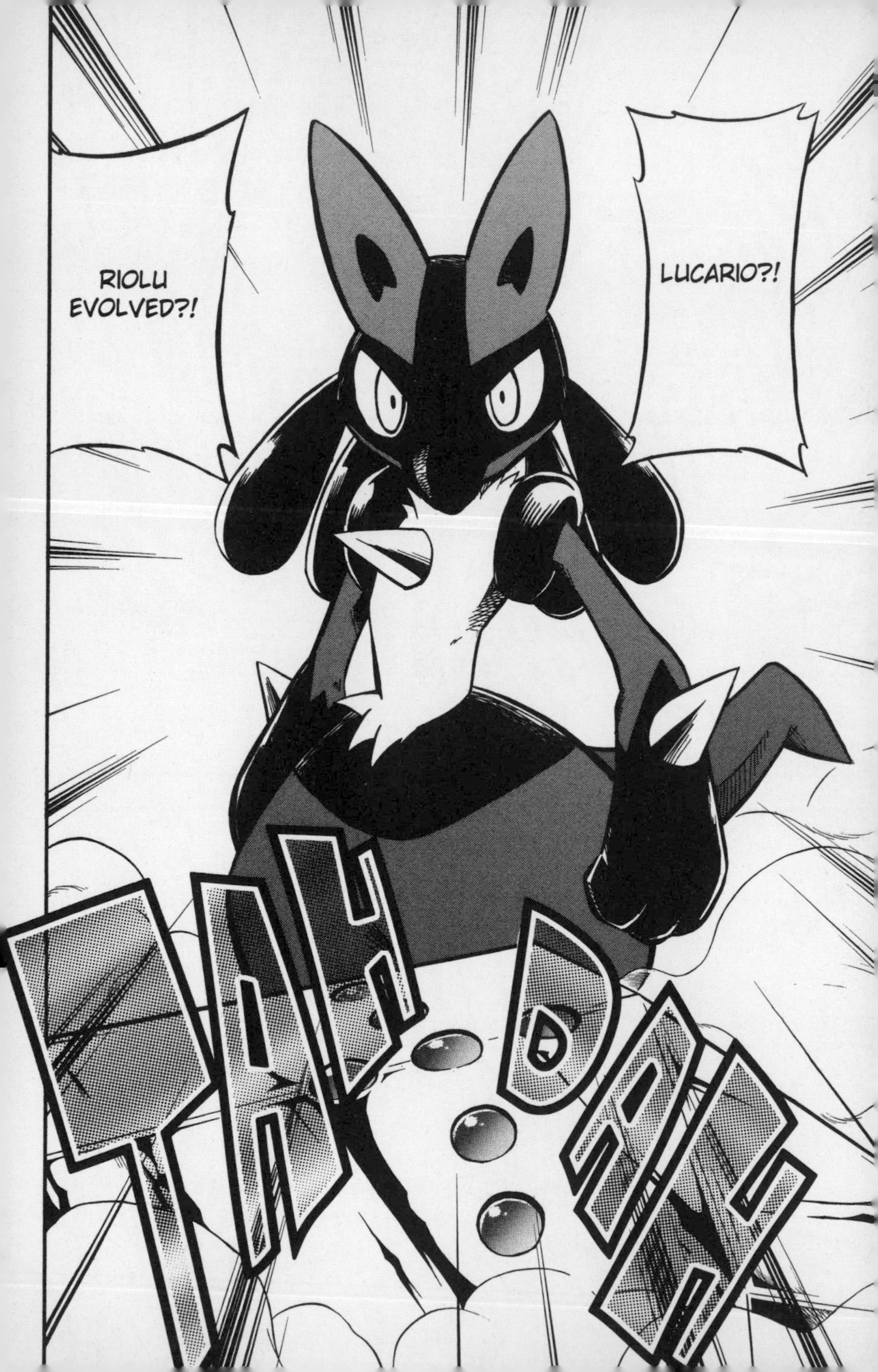
LUCARIO?!
RIOLU EVOLVED?!

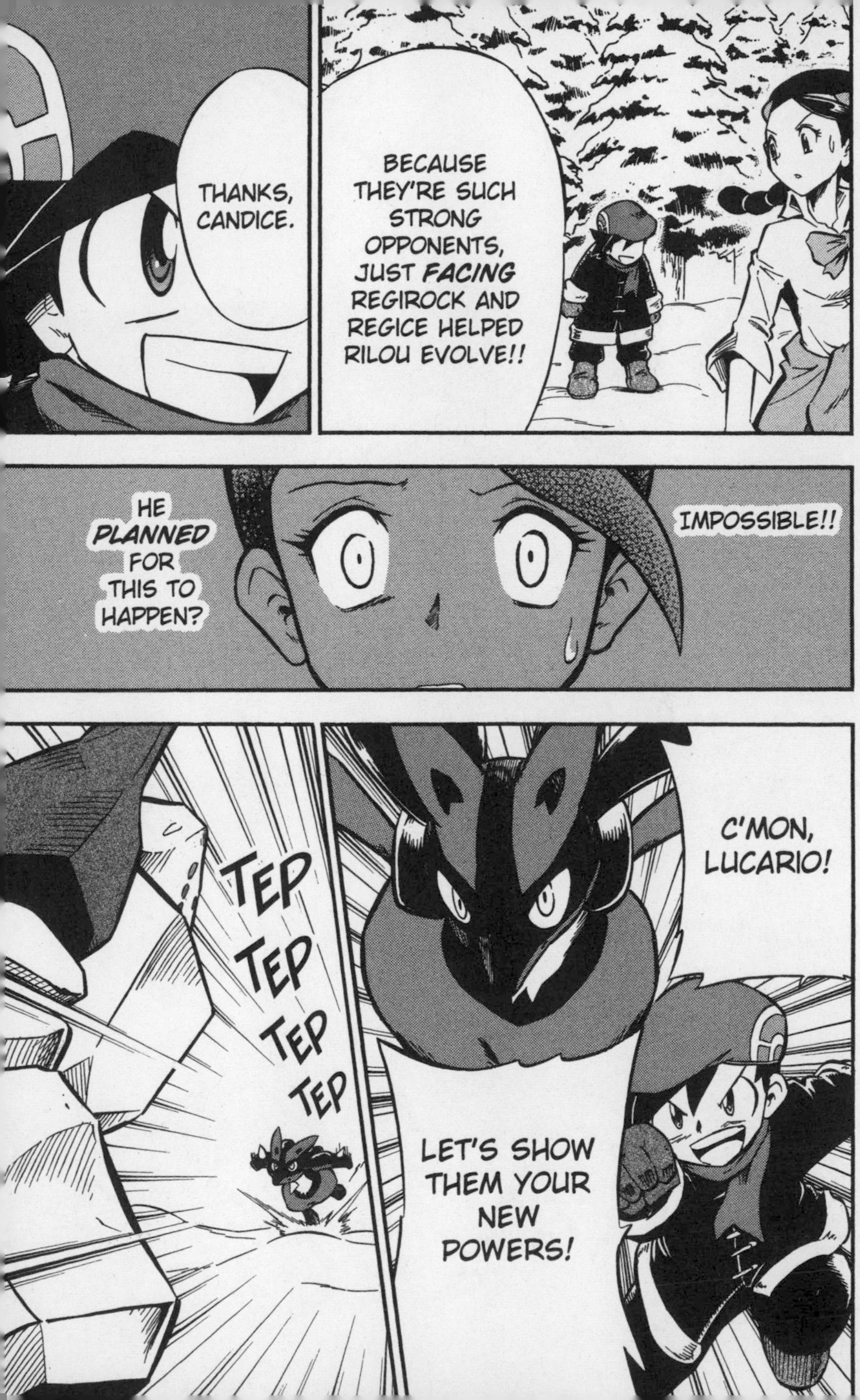
BECAUSE THEY'RE SUCH STRONG OPPONENTS, JUST *FACING* REGIROCK AND REGICE HELPED RILOU EVOLVE!!
THANKS, CANDICE.
IMPOSSIBLE!!
HE *PLANNED* FOR THIS TO HAPPEN?
C'MON, LUCARIO!
LET'S SHOW THEM YOUR NEW POWERS!
TEP TEP TEP TEP

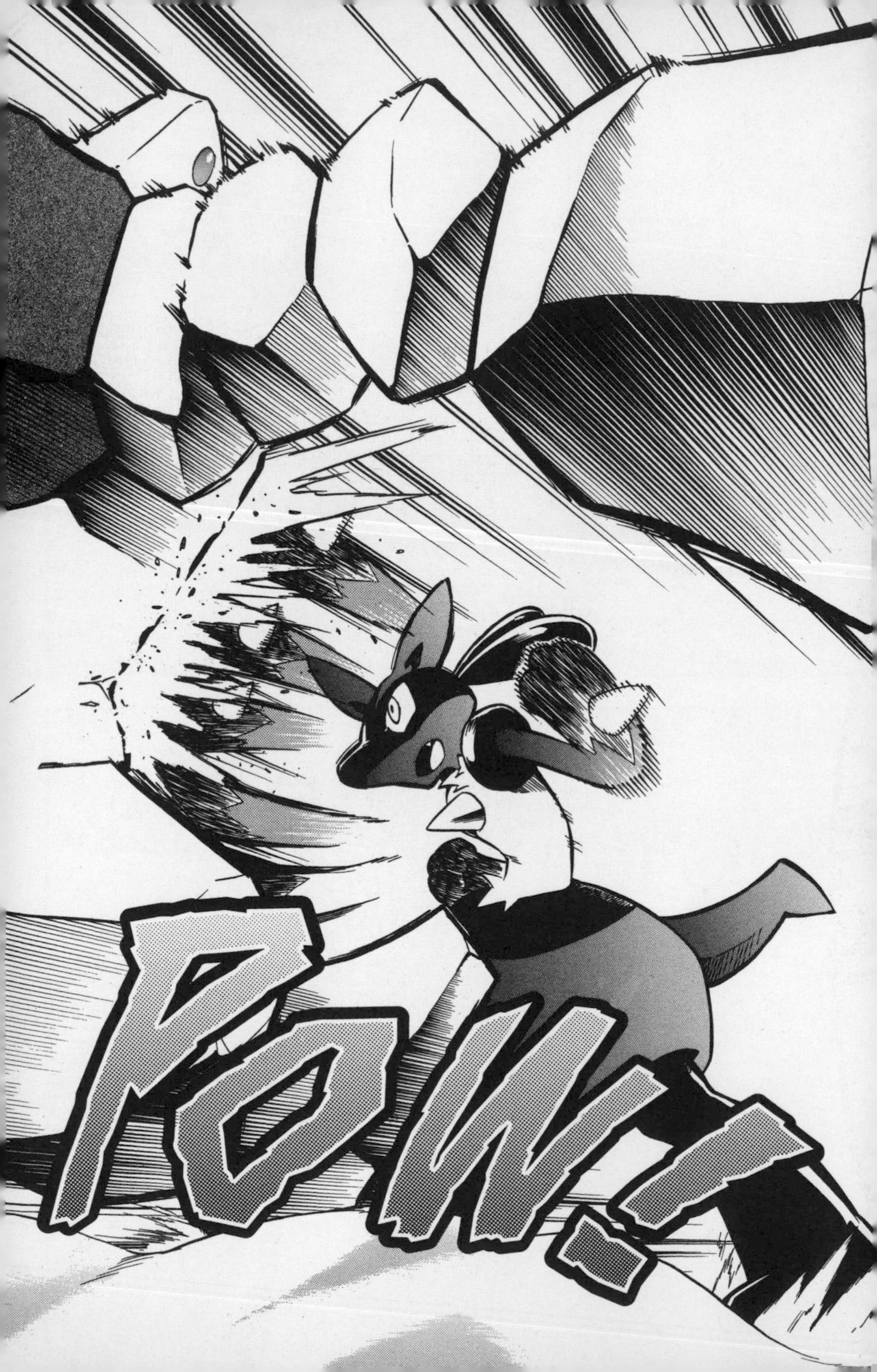
POW!!

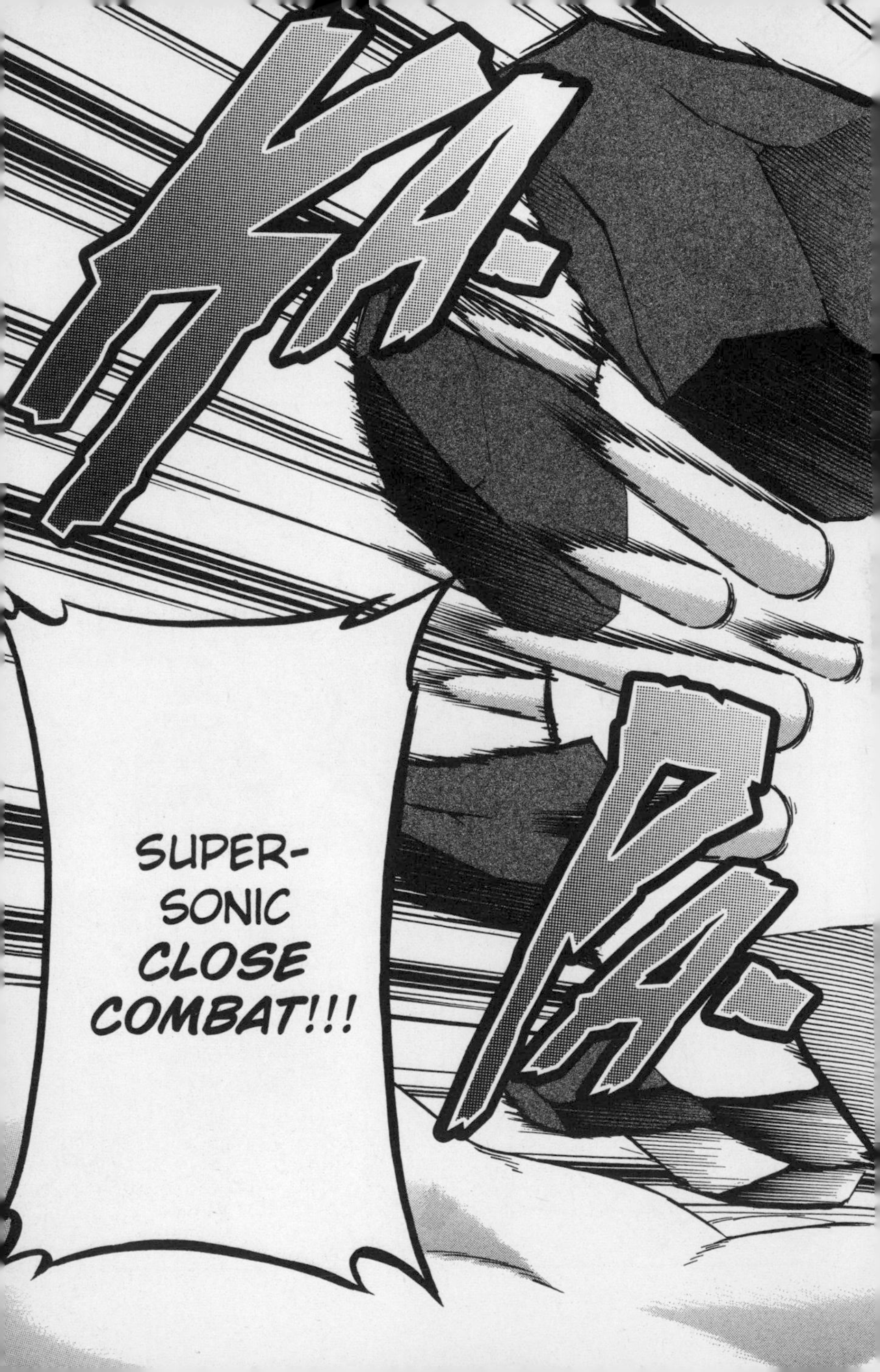
SUPER-
SONIC
CLOSE
COMBAT!!!

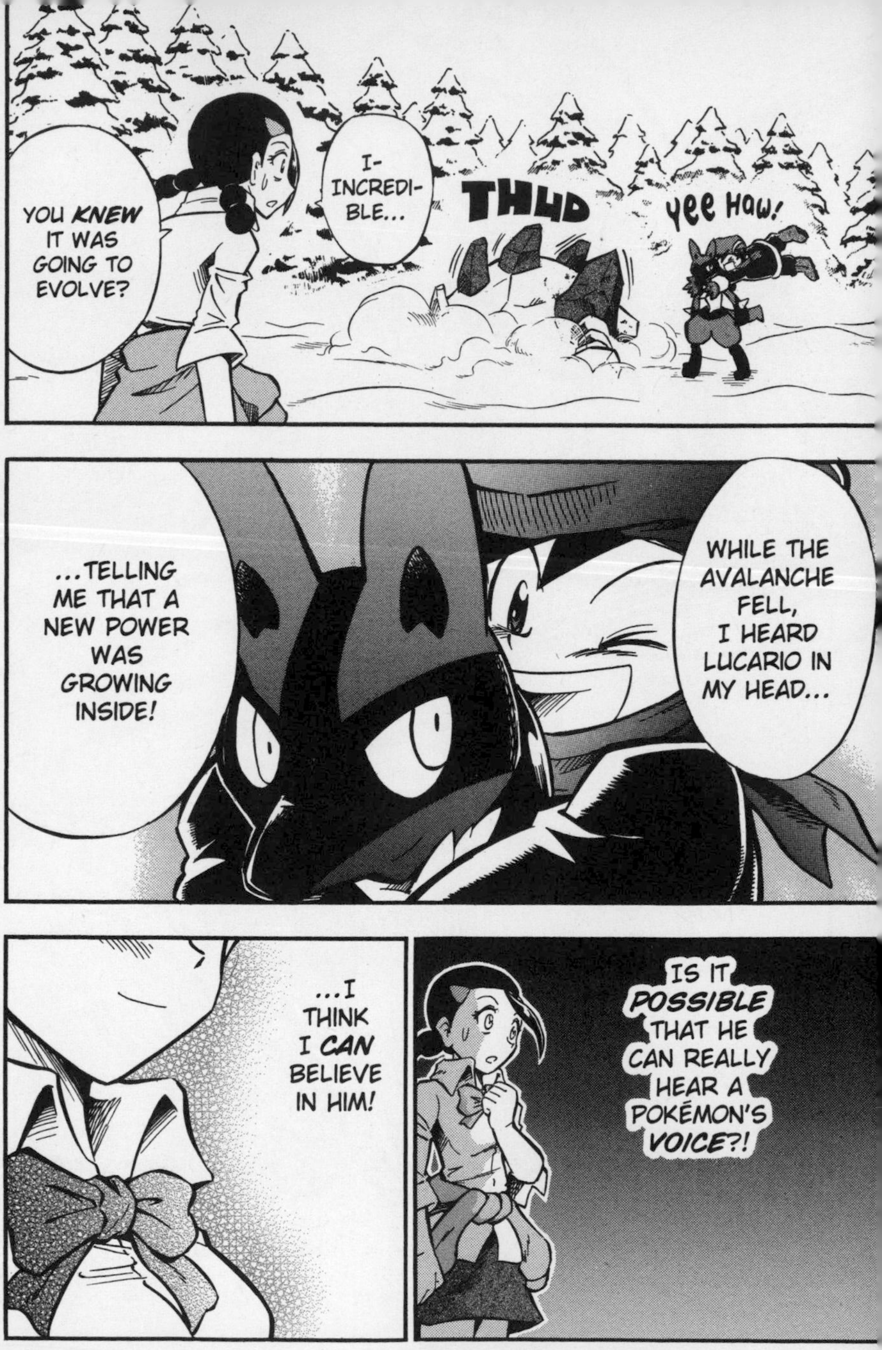
YEE HAW!
THUD
I-INCREDI-BLE...
YOU KNEW IT WAS GOING TO EVOLVE?
WHILE THE AVALANCHE FELL, I HEARD LUCARIO IN MY HEAD...
...TELLING ME THAT A NEW POWER WAS GROWING INSIDE!
IS IT POSSIBLE THAT HE CAN REALLY HEAR A POKÉMON'S VOICE?!
...I THINK I CAN BELIEVE IN HIM!

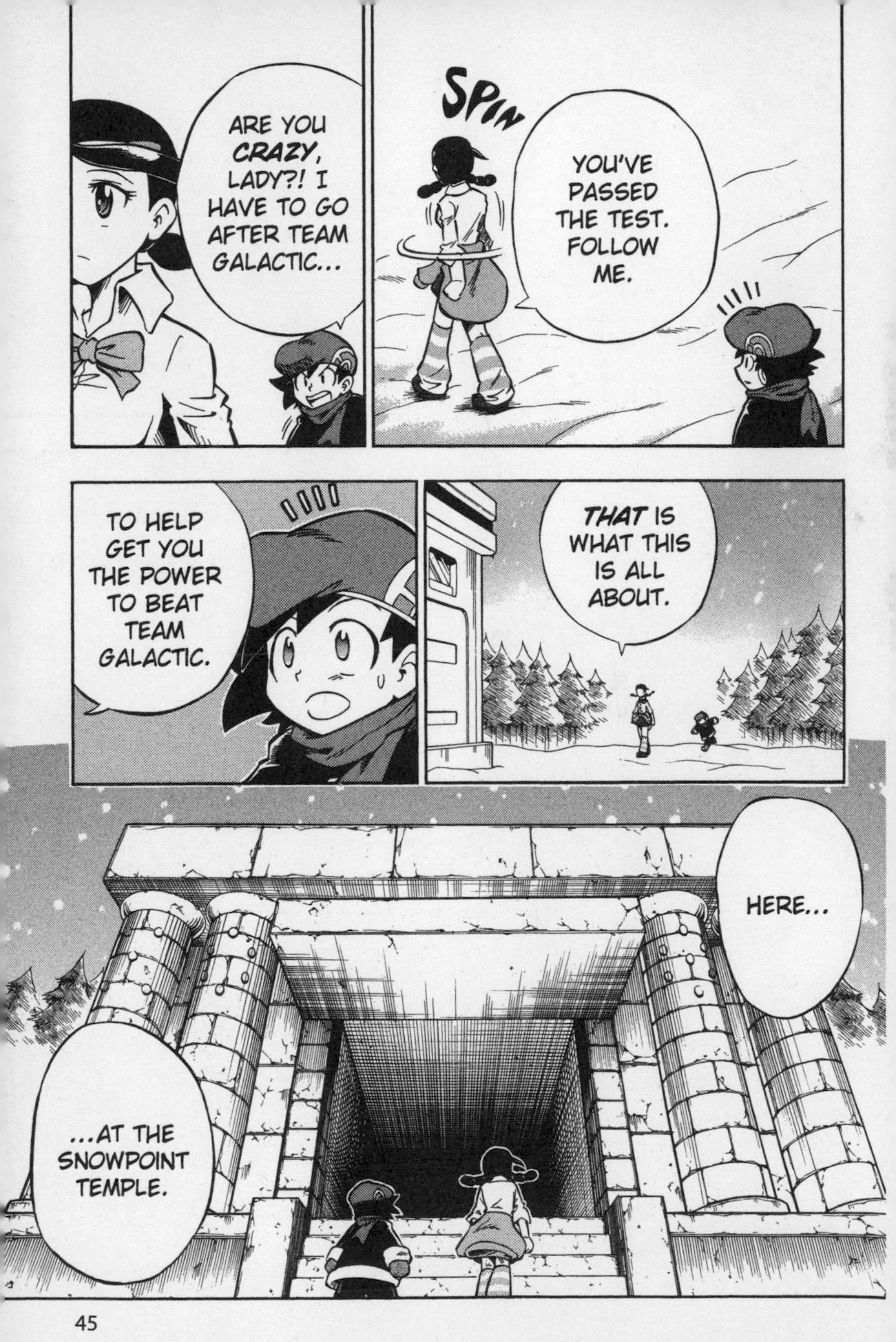
ARE YOU CRAZY, LADY?! I HAVE TO GO AFTER TEAM GALACTIC...
SPIN
YOU'VE PASSED THE TEST. FOLLOW ME.
TO HELP GET YOU THE POWER TO BEAT TEAM GALACTIC.
THAT IS WHAT THIS IS ALL ABOUT.
HERE...
...AT THE SNOWPOINT TEMPLE.

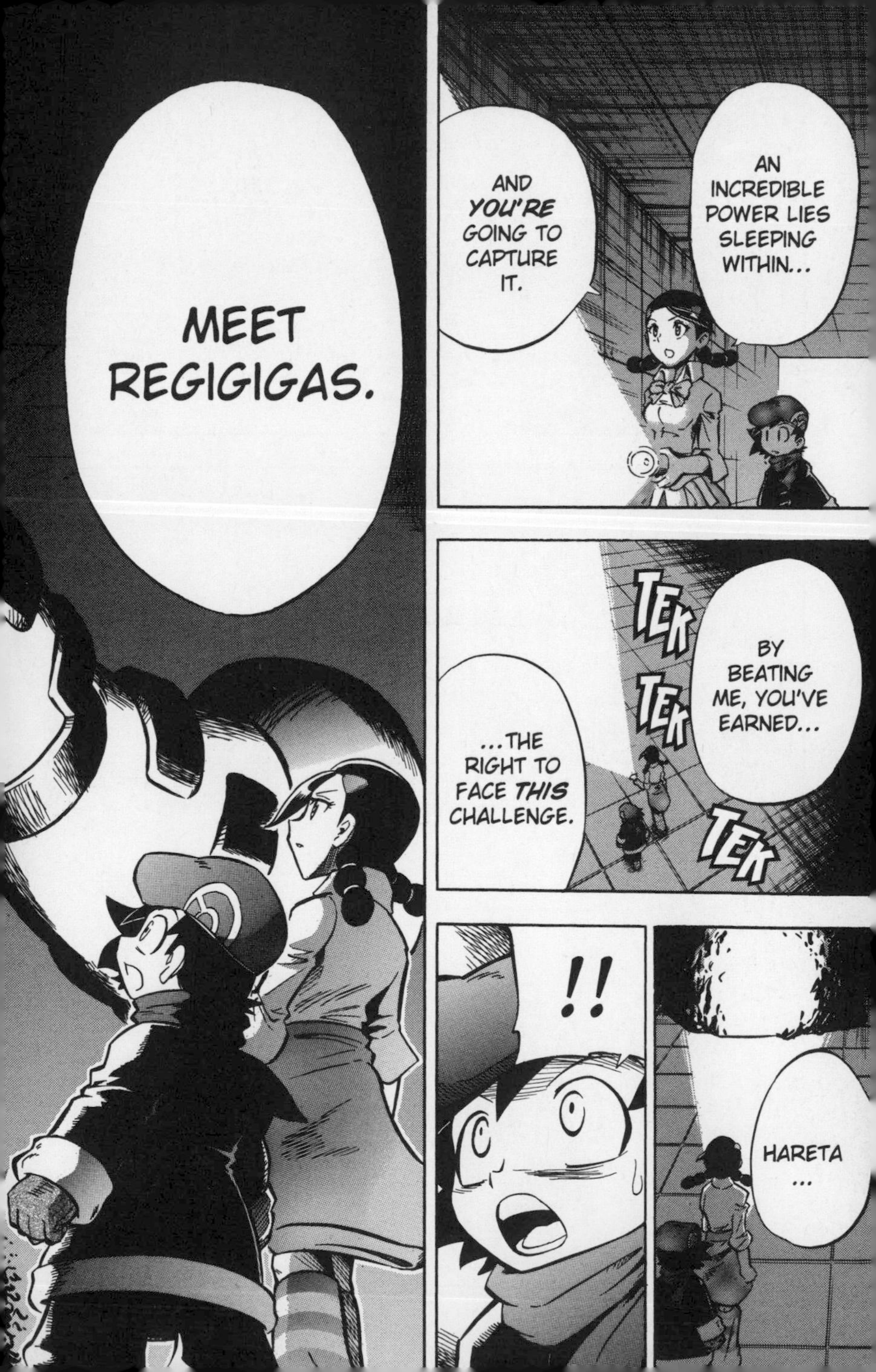
AN INCREDIBLE POWER LIES SLEEPING WITHIN...
AND *YOU'RE* GOING TO CAPTURE IT.
BY BEATING ME, YOU'VE EARNED...
TEK
TEK
TEK
...THE RIGHT TO FACE *THIS* CHALLENGE.
HARETA ...
!!
MEET REGIGIGAS.

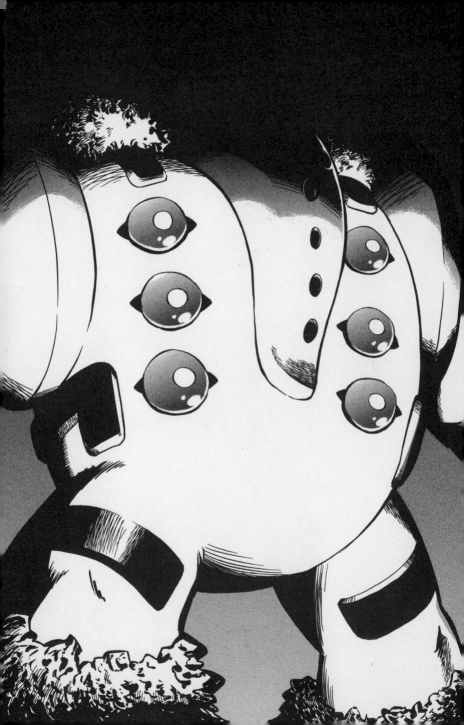

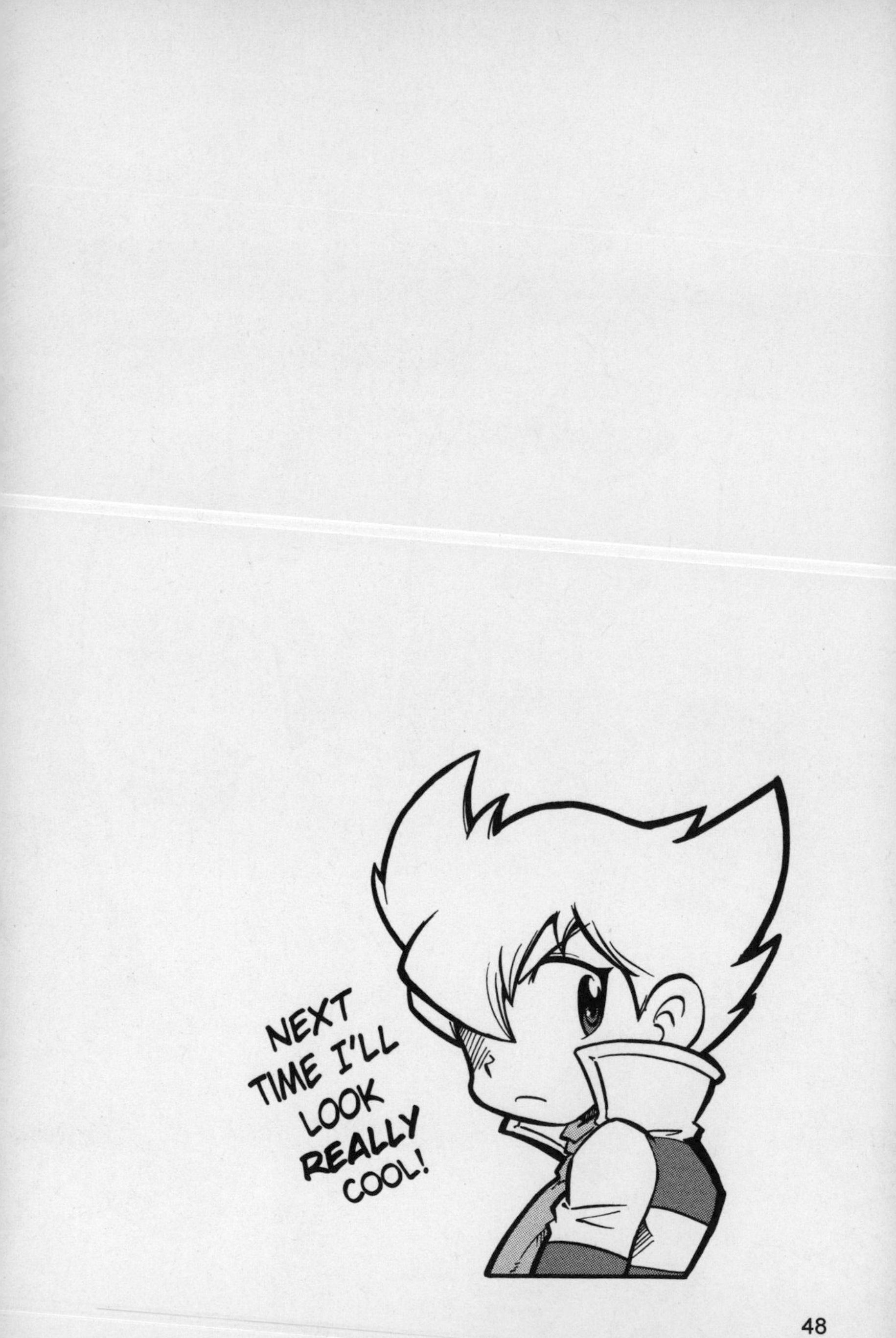
NEXT TIME I'LL LOOK **REALLY** COOL!

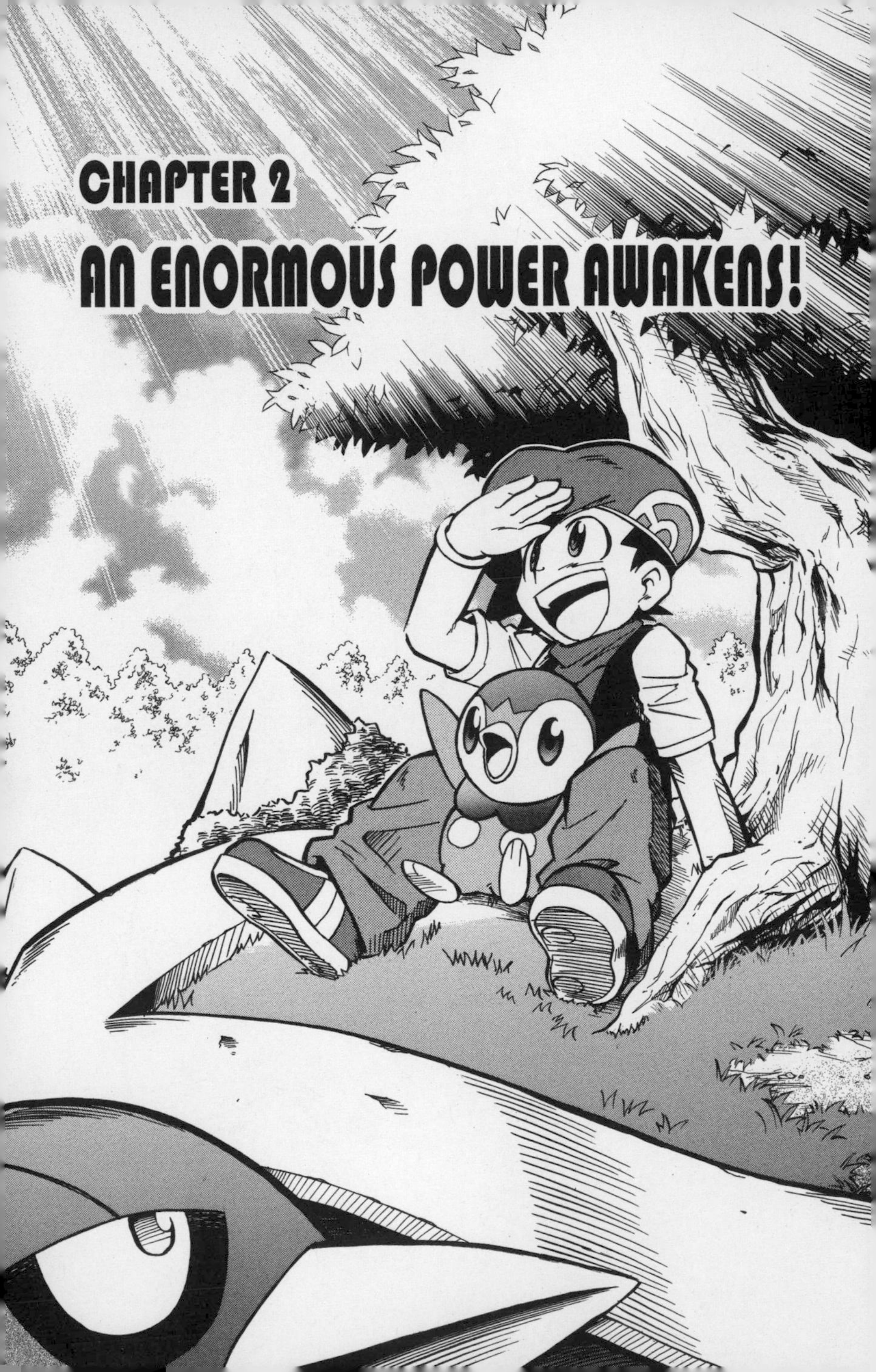
CHAPTER 2
AN ENORMOUS POWER AWAKENS!

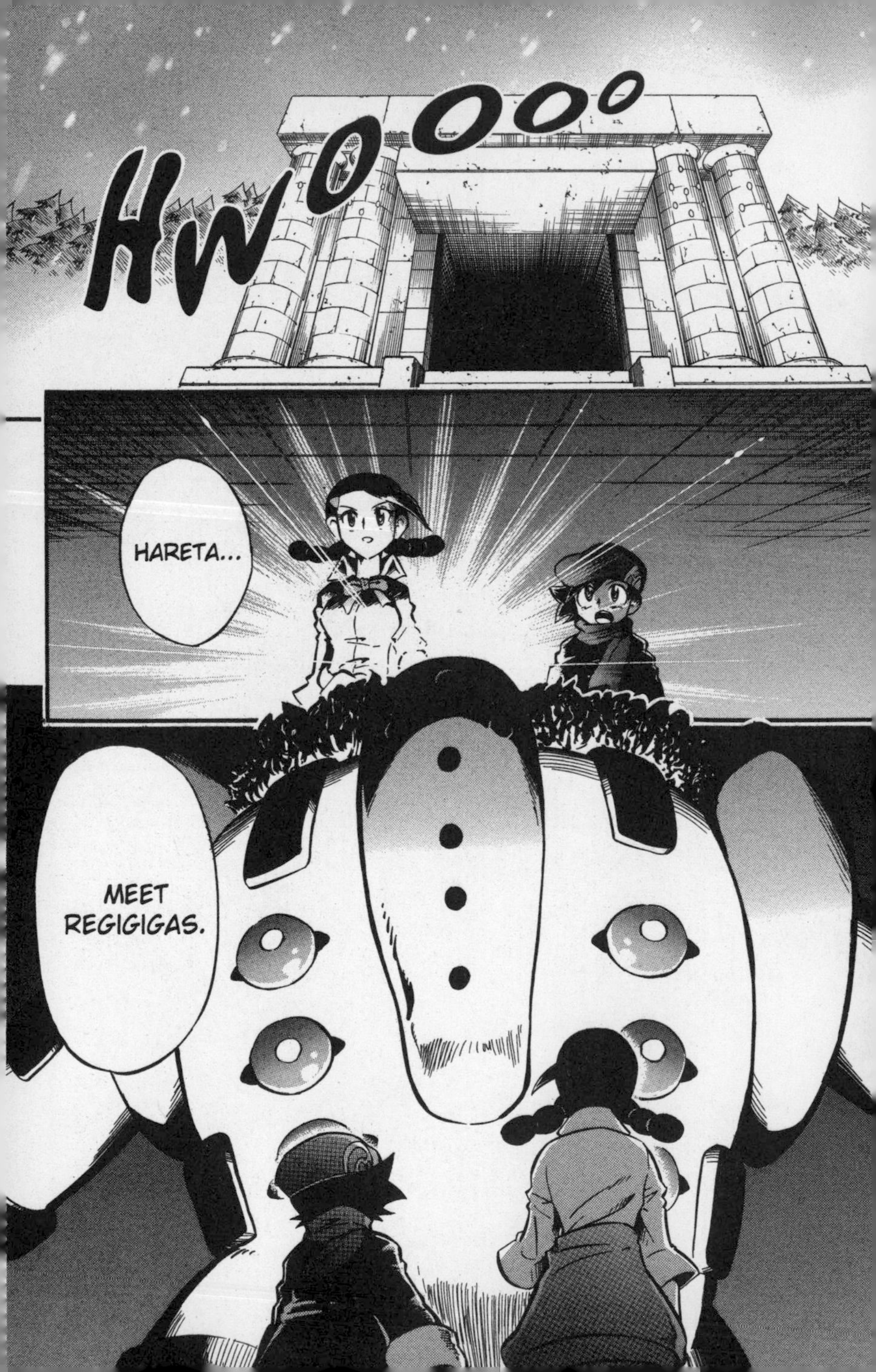
HWOOOO
HARETA...
MEET REGIGIGAS.

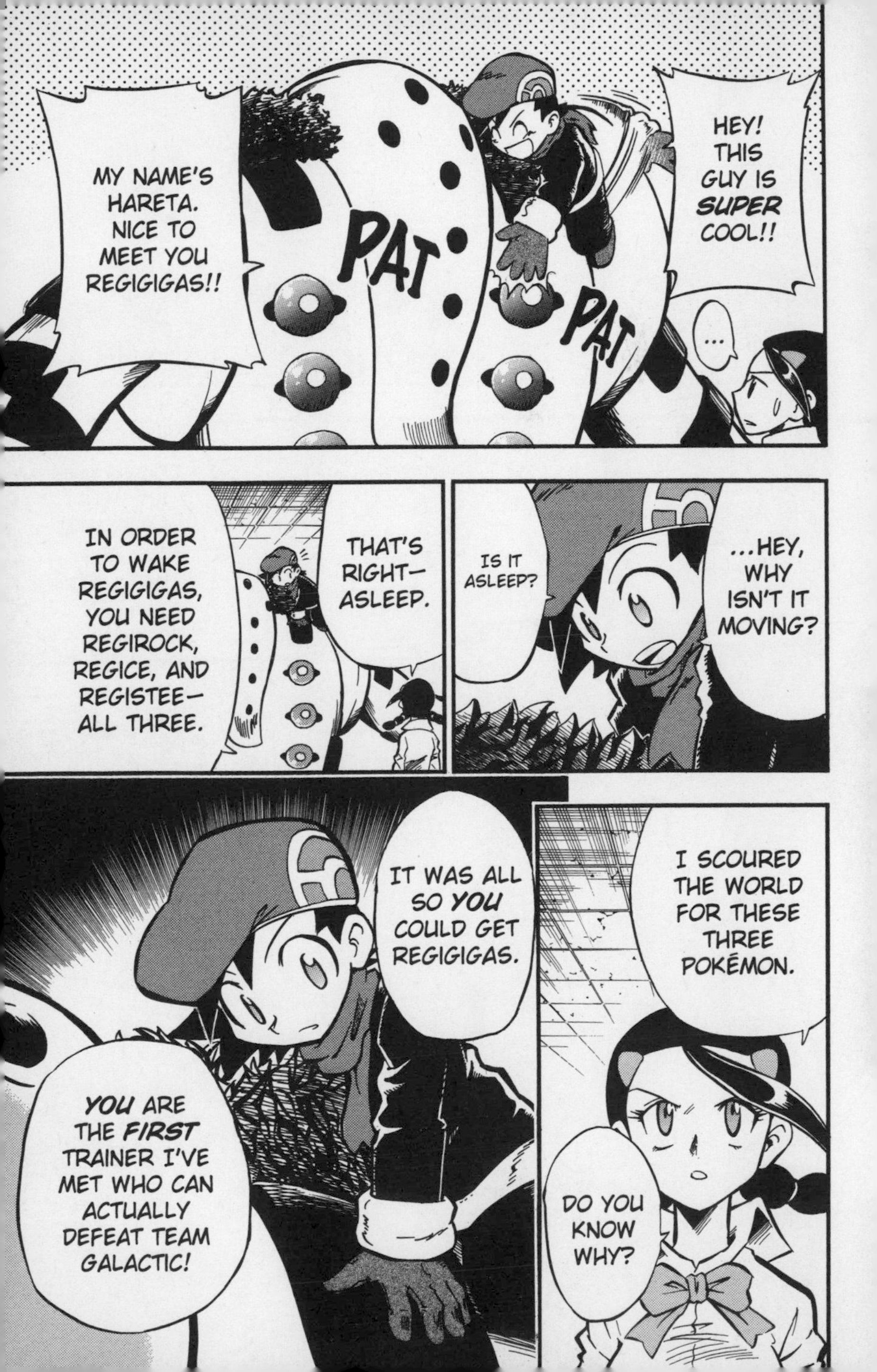
HEY! THIS GUY IS SUPER COOL!!
PAT
PAT
...
MY NAME'S HARETA. NICE TO MEET YOU REGIGIGAS!!
...HEY, WHY ISN'T IT MOVING?
IS IT ASLEEP?
THAT'S RIGHT—ASLEEP.
IN ORDER TO WAKE REGIGIGAS, YOU NEED REGIROCK, REGICE, AND REGISTEE—ALL THREE.
I SCOURED THE WORLD FOR THESE THREE POKÉMON.
DO YOU KNOW WHY?
IT WAS ALL SO YOU COULD GET REGIGIGAS.
YOU ARE THE FIRST TRAINER I'VE MET WHO CAN ACTUALLY DEFEAT TEAM GALACTIC!

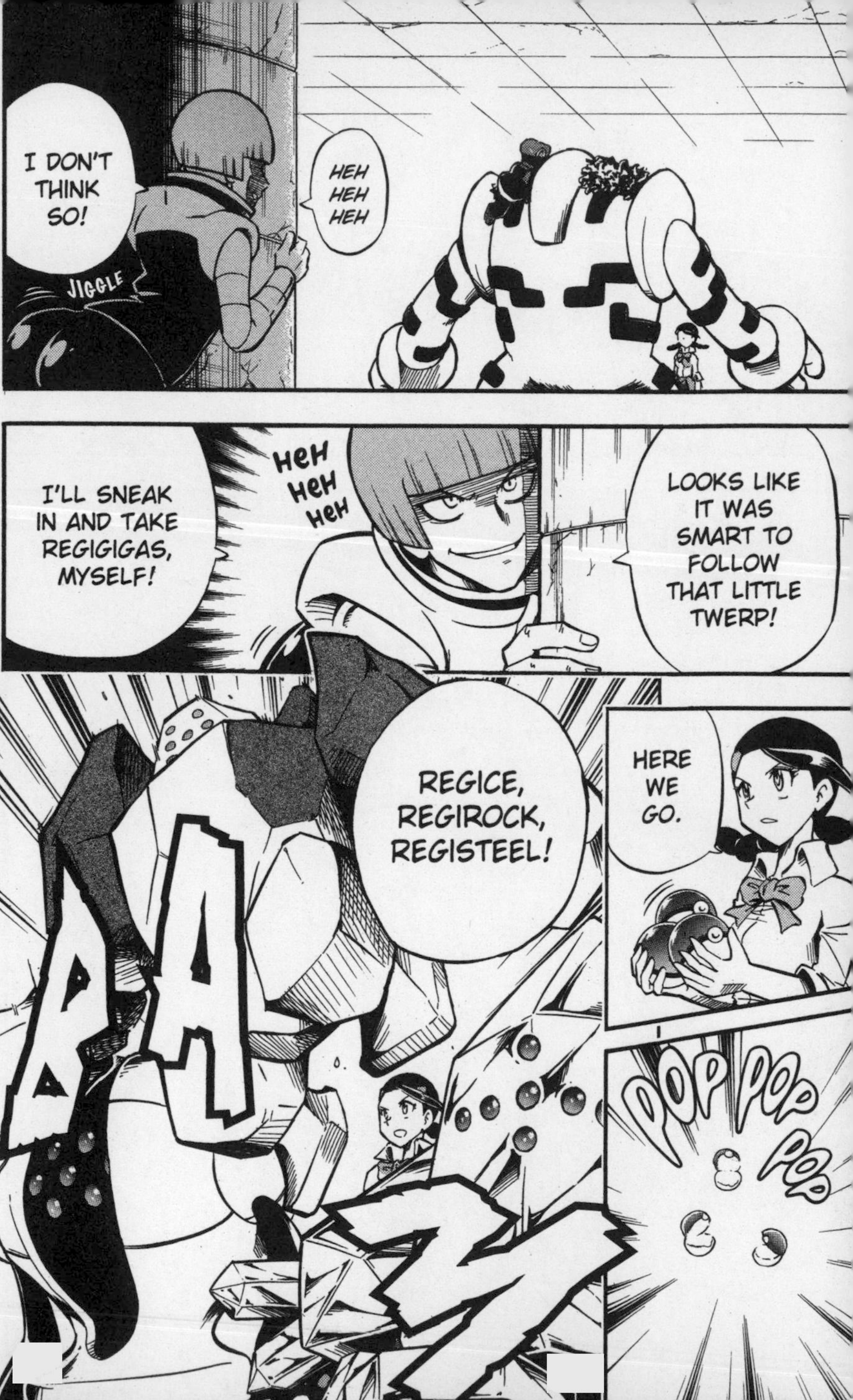
HEH HEH HEH
I DON'T THINK SO!
JIGGLE
LOOKS LIKE IT WAS SMART TO FOLLOW THAT LITTLE TWERP!
HEH HEH HEH
I'LL SNEAK IN AND TAKE REGIGIGAS, MYSELF!
HERE WE GO.
POP POP POP POP
REGICE, REGIROCK, REGISTEEL!

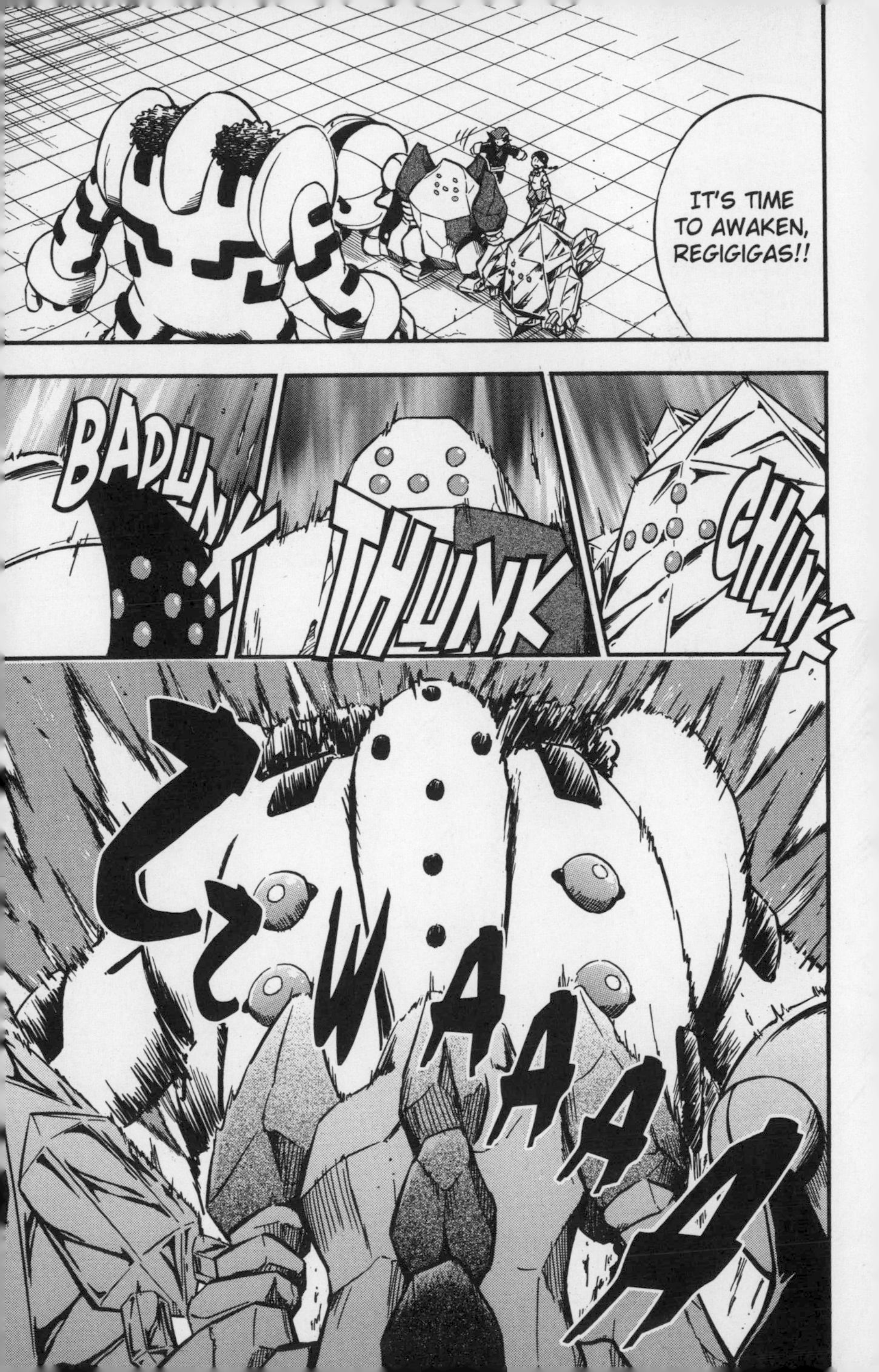
IT'S TIME TO AWAKEN, REGIGIGAS!!
CHUNK
THUNK
BADUNK
GWAAAAA

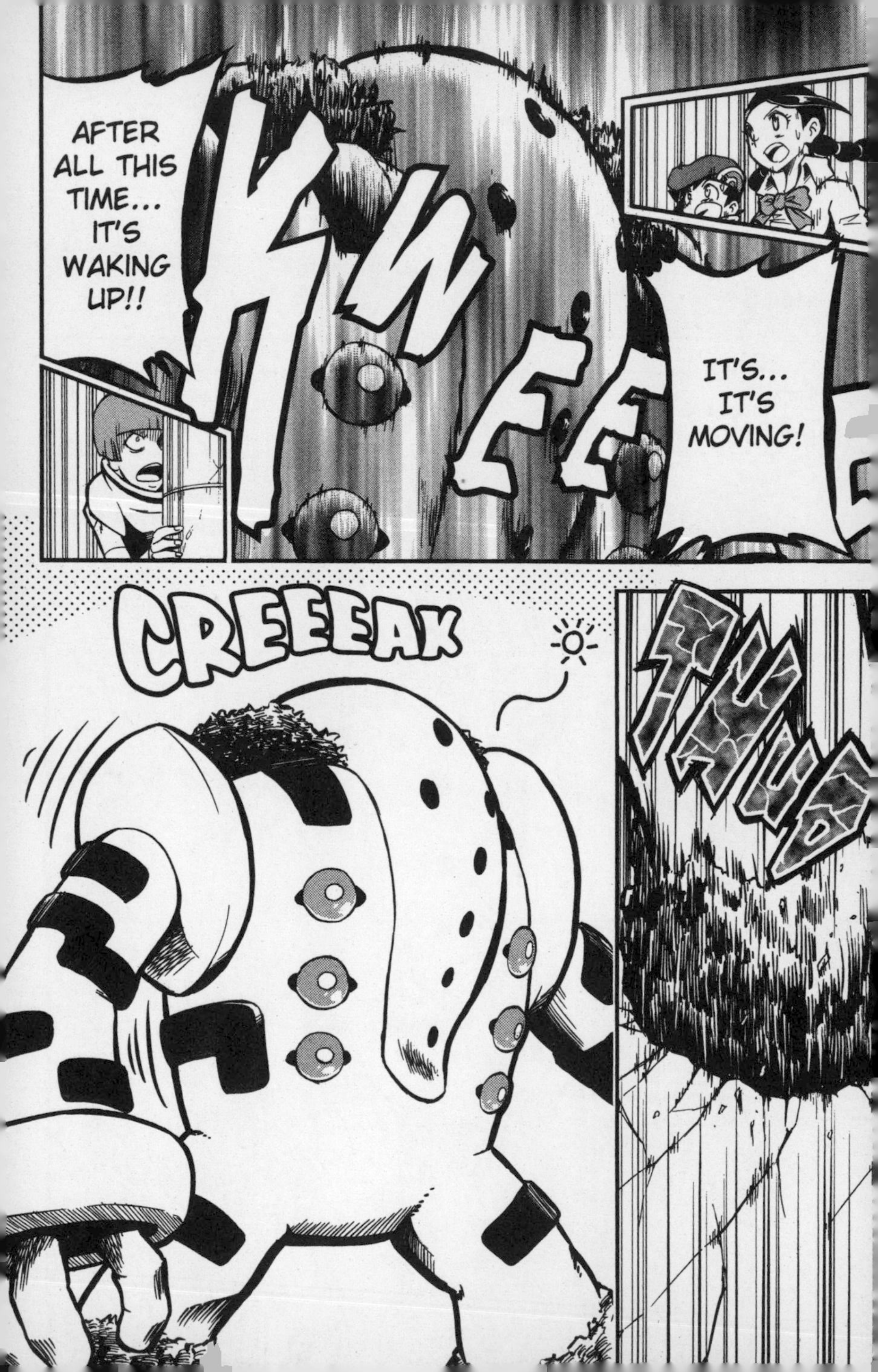
IT'S... IT'S MOVING!
AFTER ALL THIS TIME... IT'S WAKING UP!!
THUD
CREEEAK

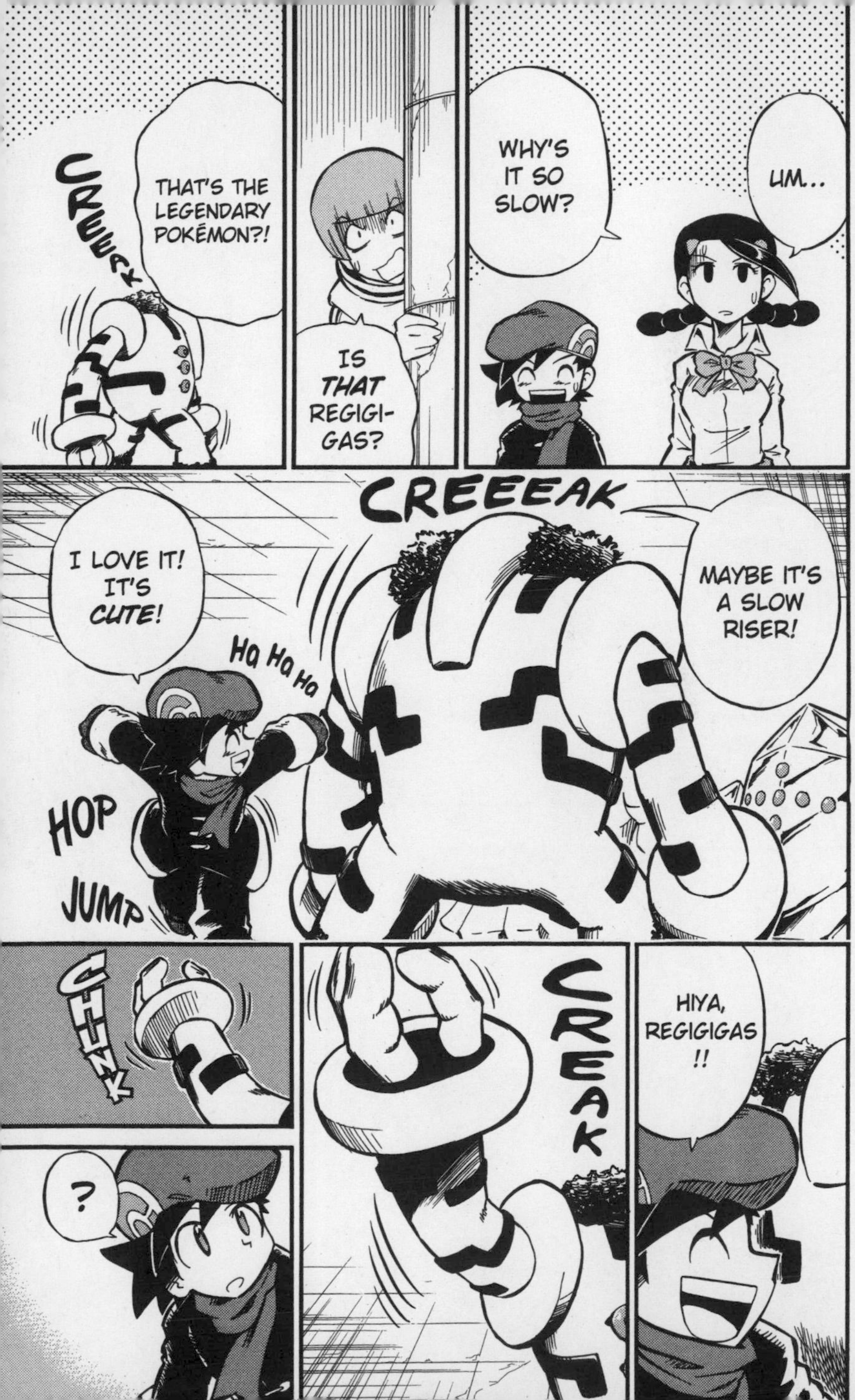
UM..
WHY'S IT SO SLOW?
IS THAT REGIGIGAS?
THAT'S THE LEGENDARY POKÉMON?!
CREEEAK
CREEEAK
MAYBE IT'S A SLOW RISER!
I LOVE IT! IT'S CUTE!
Ha Ha Ha
HOP
JUMP
HIYA, REGIGIGAS !!
CREAK
CHUNK
?

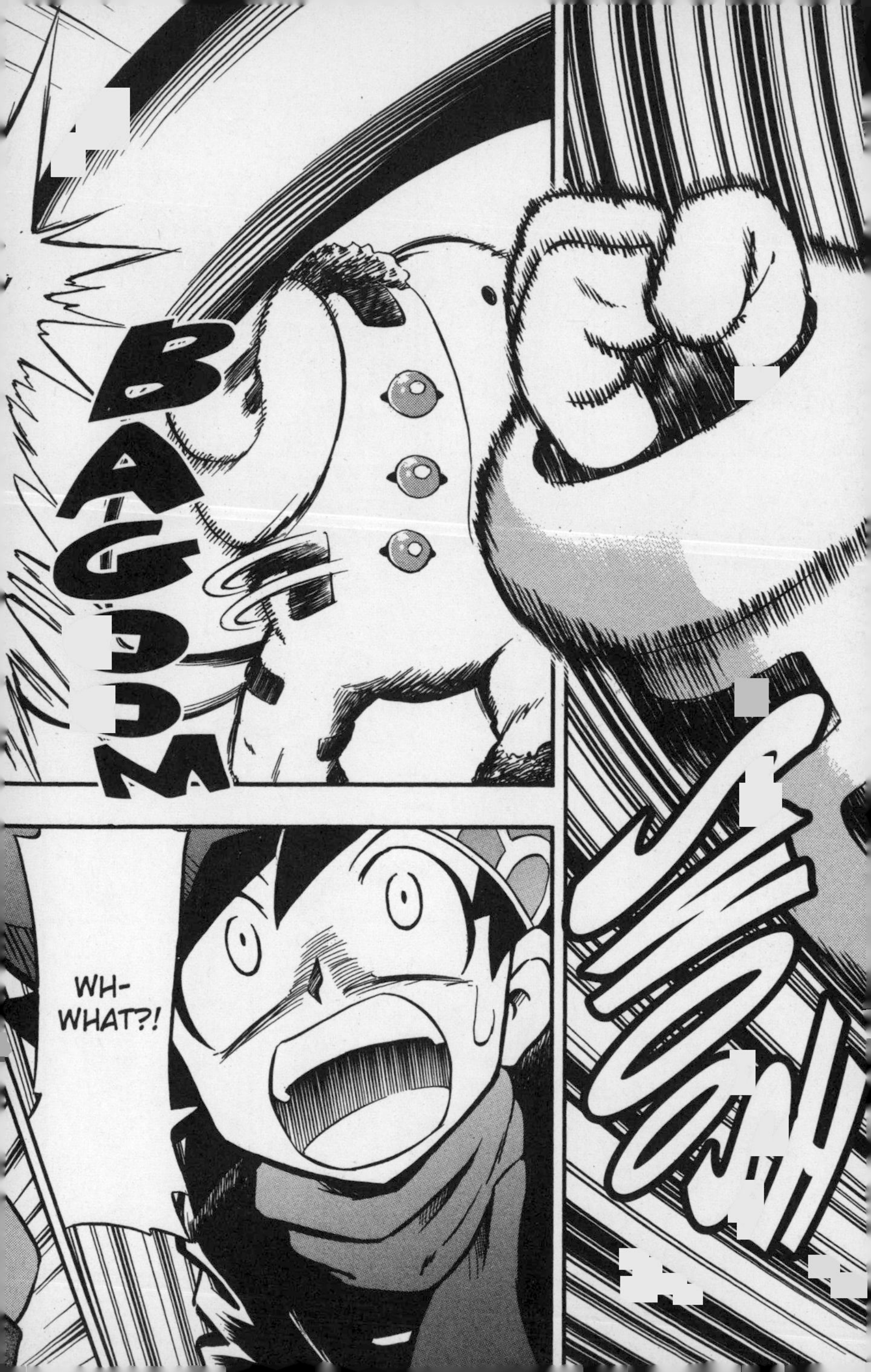
BAGOOM
WH-
WHAT?!

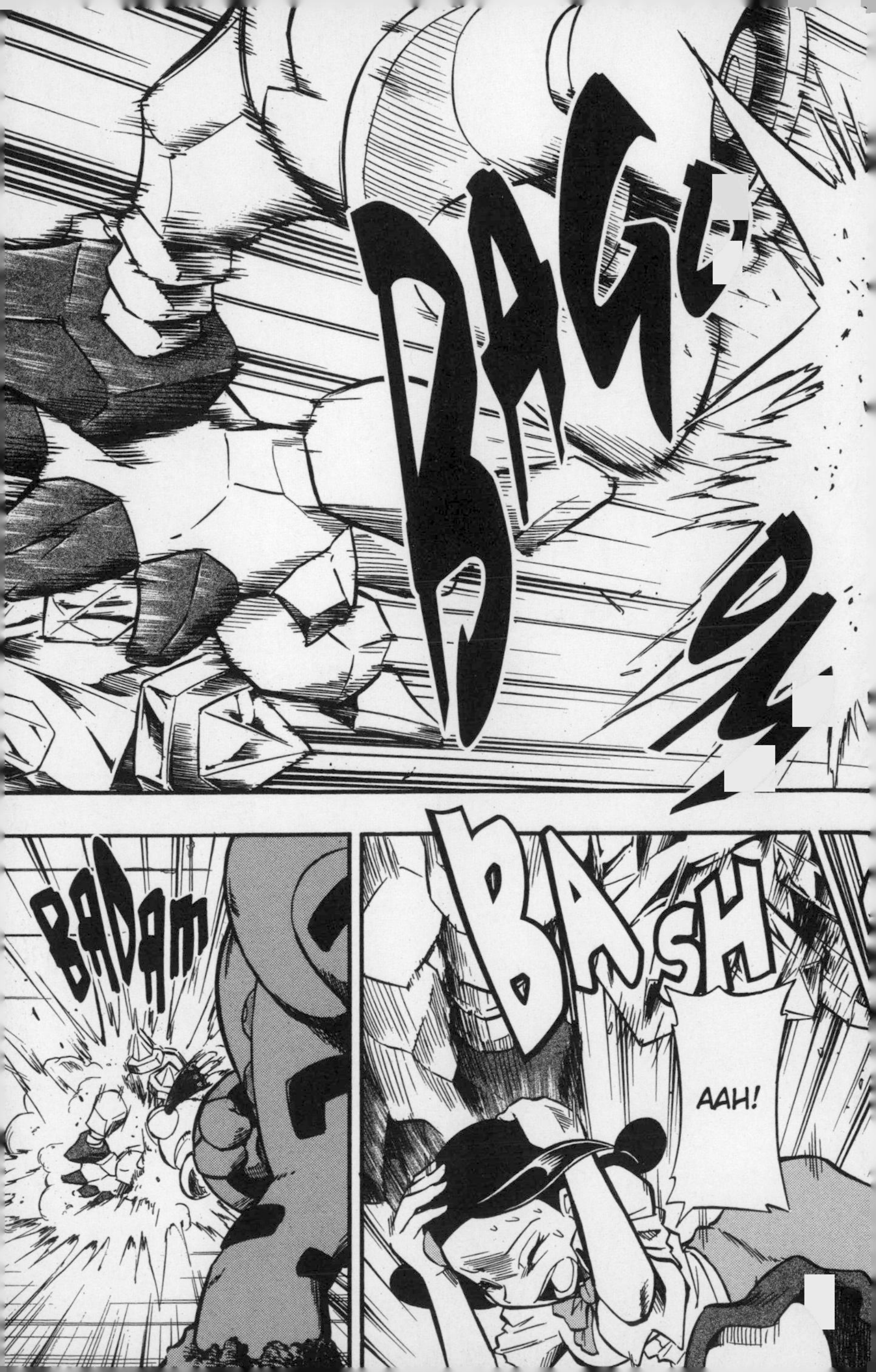
BAGOM
BASH
AAH!
BADAM

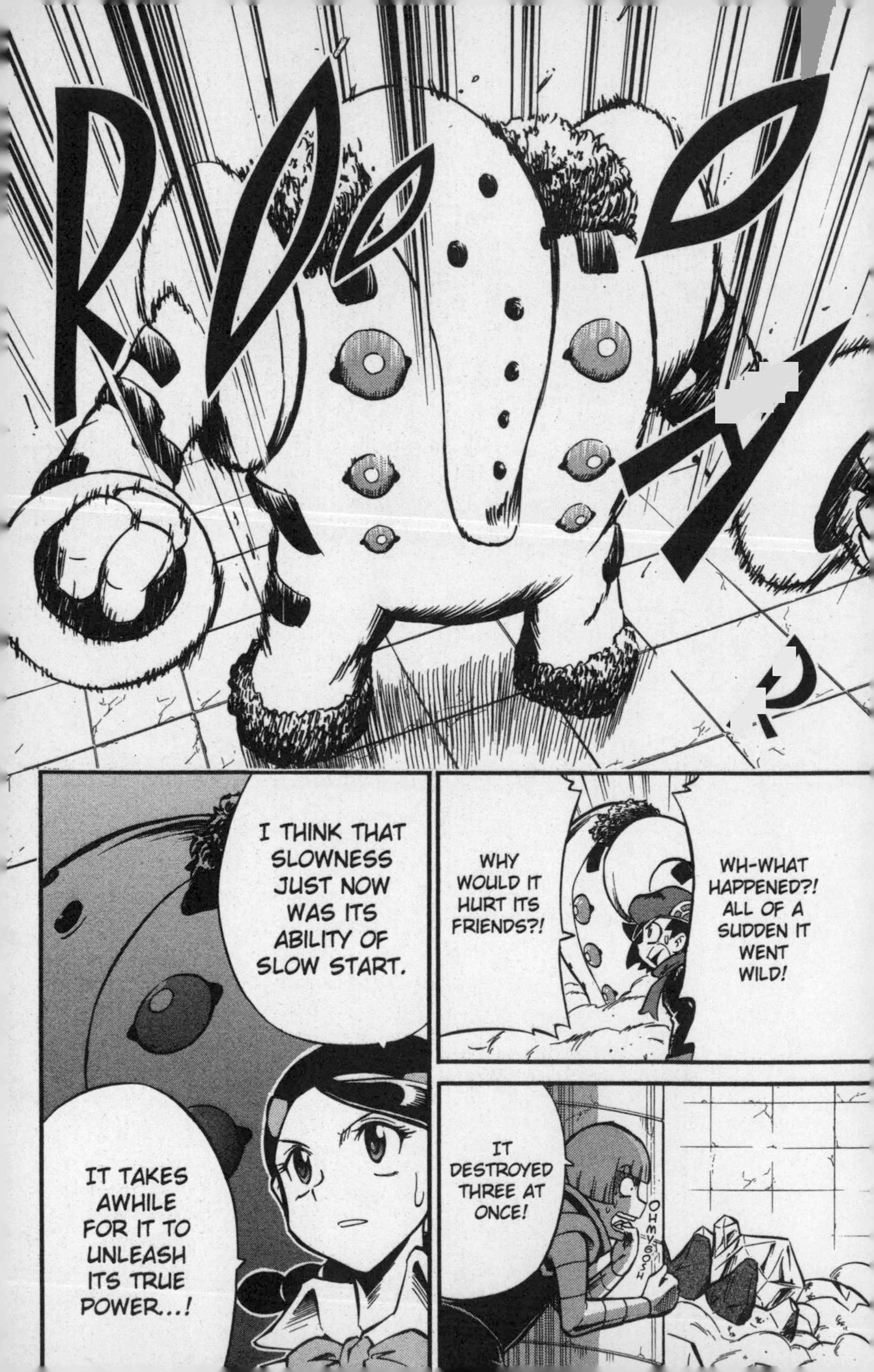
WH-WHAT HAPPENED?! ALL OF A SUDDEN IT WENT WILD!
WHY WOULD IT HURT ITS FRIENDS?!
IT DESTROYED THREE AT ONCE!
OHMYGOSH
I THINK THAT SLOWNESS JUST NOW WAS ITS ABILITY OF SLOW START.
IT TAKES AWHILE FOR IT TO UNLEASH ITS TRUE POWER...!

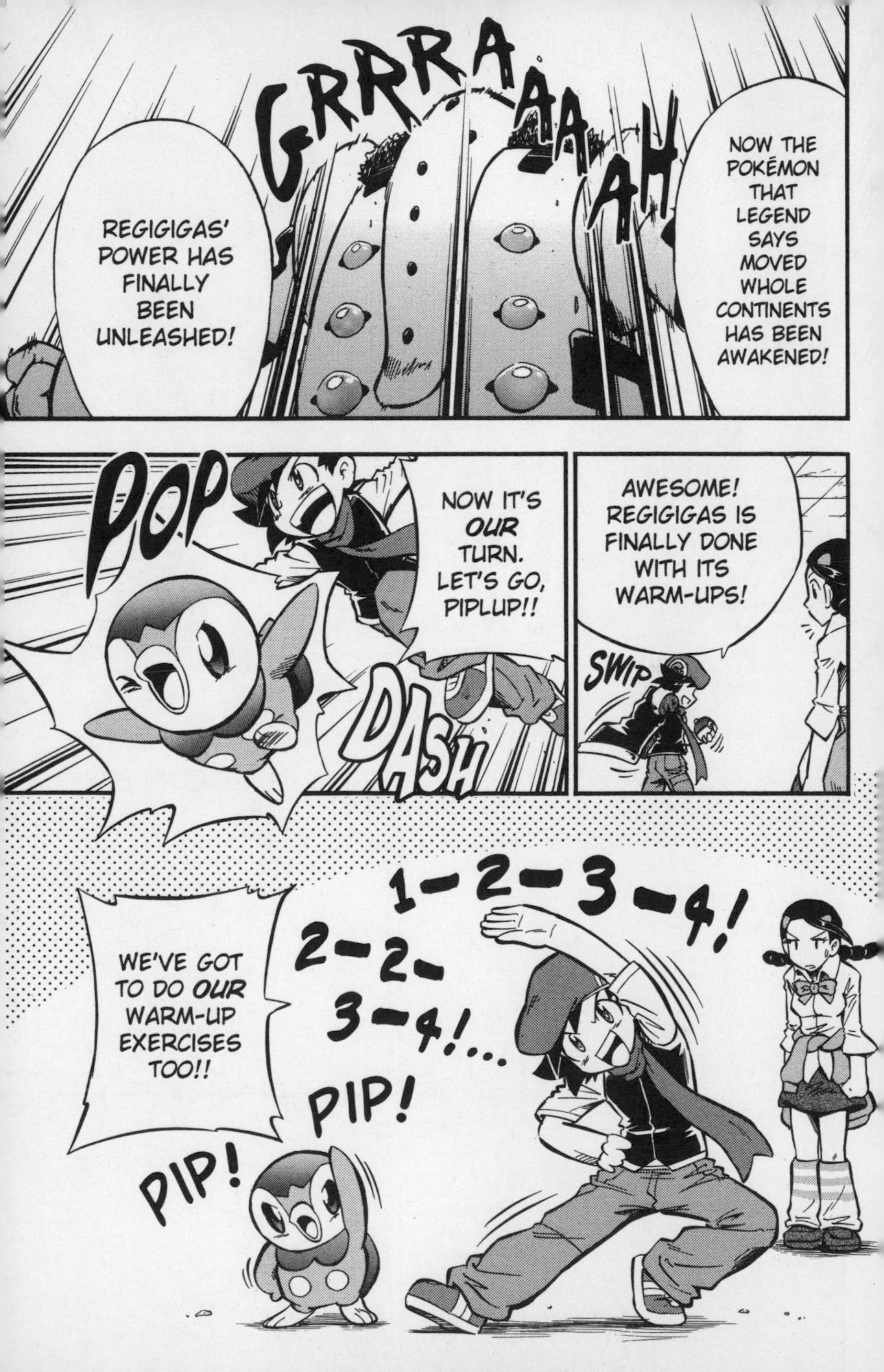
NOW THE POKÉMON THAT LEGEND SAYS MOVED WHOLE CONTINENTS HAS BEEN AWAKENED!
GRRRAAAAH
REGIGIGAS' POWER HAS FINALLY BEEN UNLEASHED!
AWESOME! REGIGIGAS IS FINALLY DONE WITH ITS WARM-UPS!
SWIP
NOW IT'S *OUR* TURN. LET'S GO, PIPLUP!!
POP
DASH
1-2-3-4!
2-2-3-4!...
WE'VE GOT TO DO *OUR* WARM-UP EXERCISES TOO!!
PIP!
PIP!

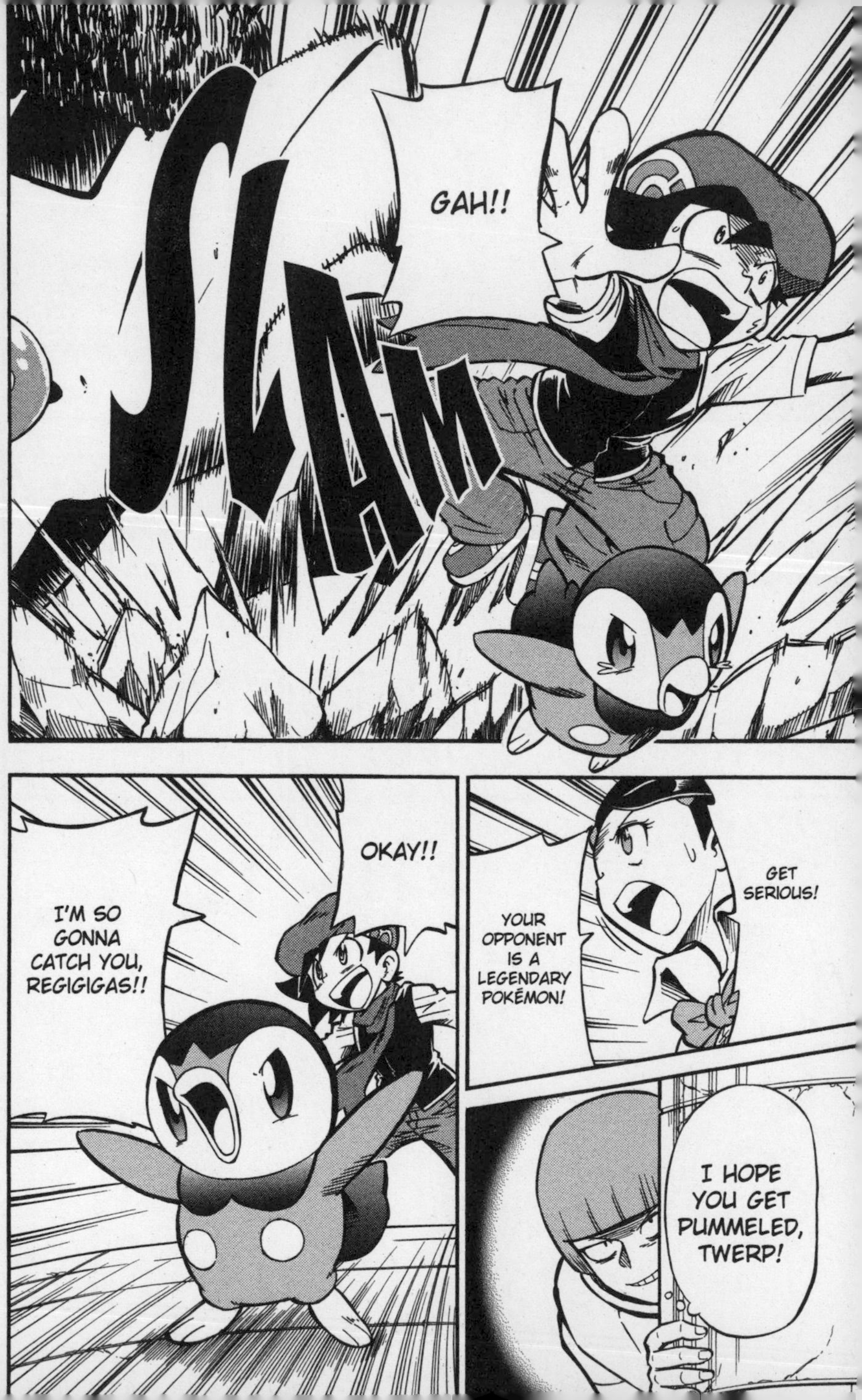
GAH!!
SLAM
GET SERIOUS!
YOUR OPPONENT IS A LEGENDARY POKÉMON!
I HOPE YOU GET PUMMELED, TWERP!
OKAY!!
I'M SO GONNA CATCH YOU, REGIGIGAS!!

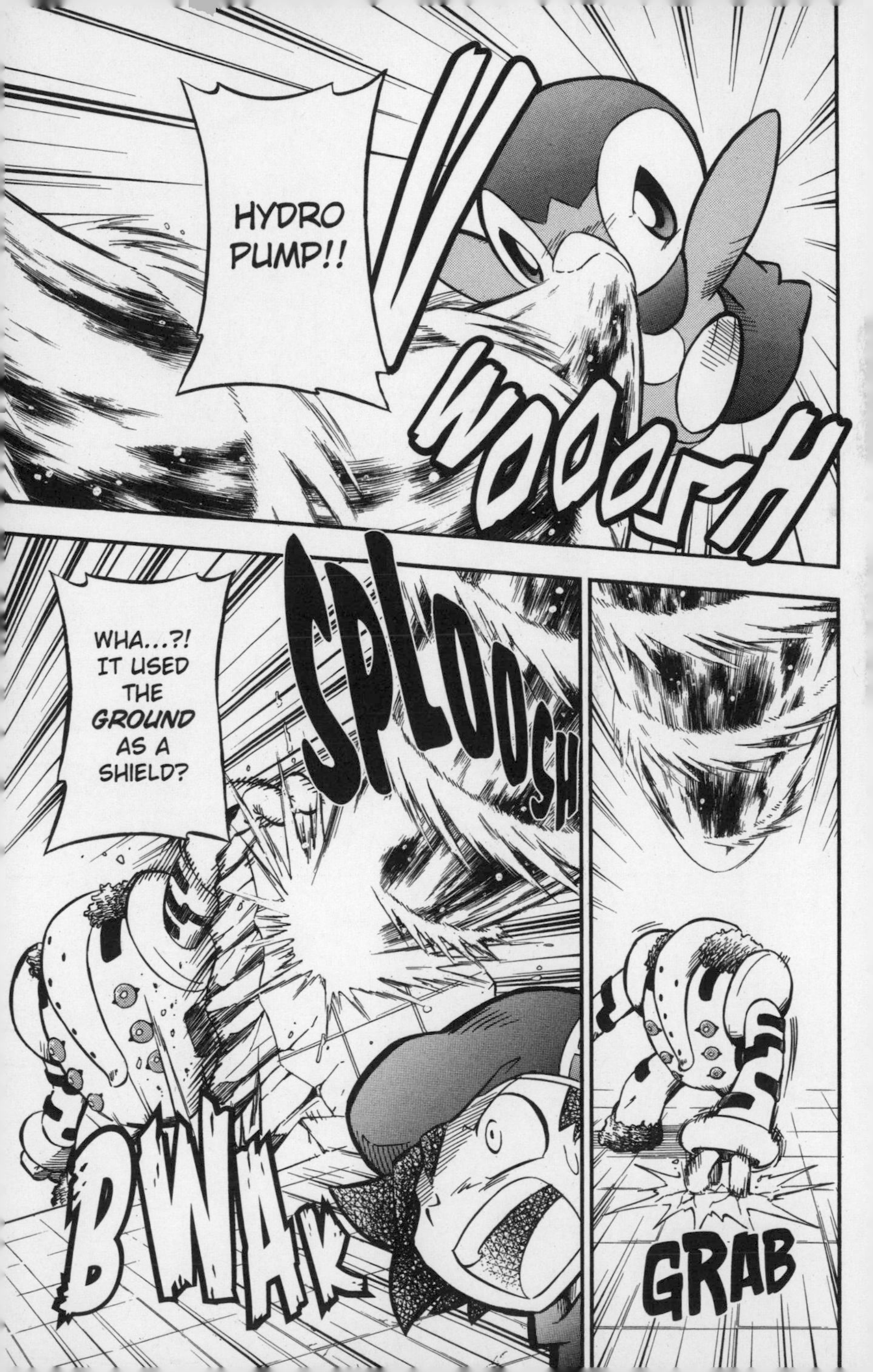
HYDRO PUMP!!
WOOOSH
GRAB
WHA...?! IT USED THE GROUND AS A SHIELD?
SPLOOSH
BWAK

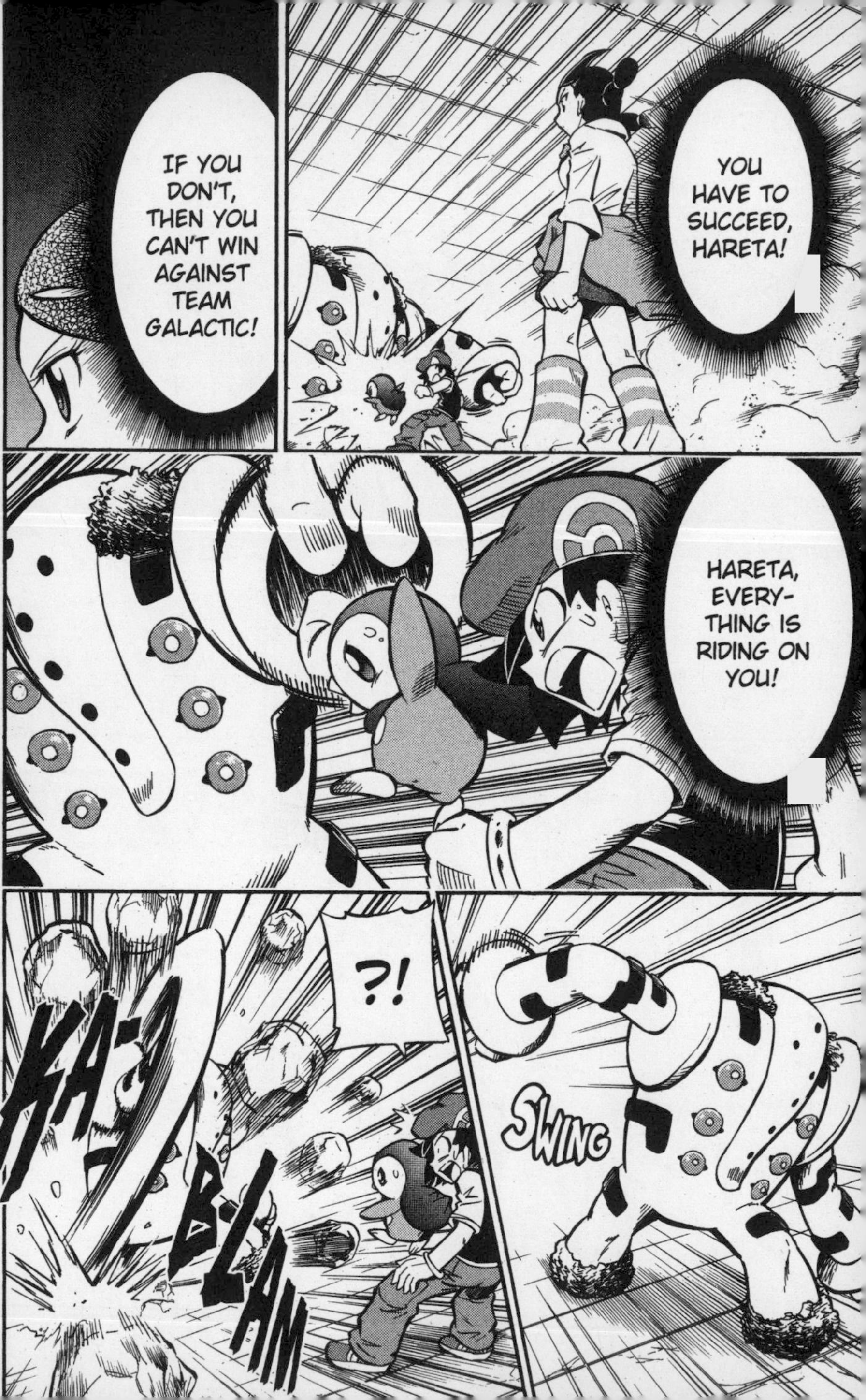
YOU HAVE TO SUCCEED, HARETA!
IF YOU DON'T, THEN YOU CAN'T WIN AGAINST TEAM GALACTIC!
HARETA, EVERY-THING IS RIDING ON YOU!
SWING
?!
KA-BLAM

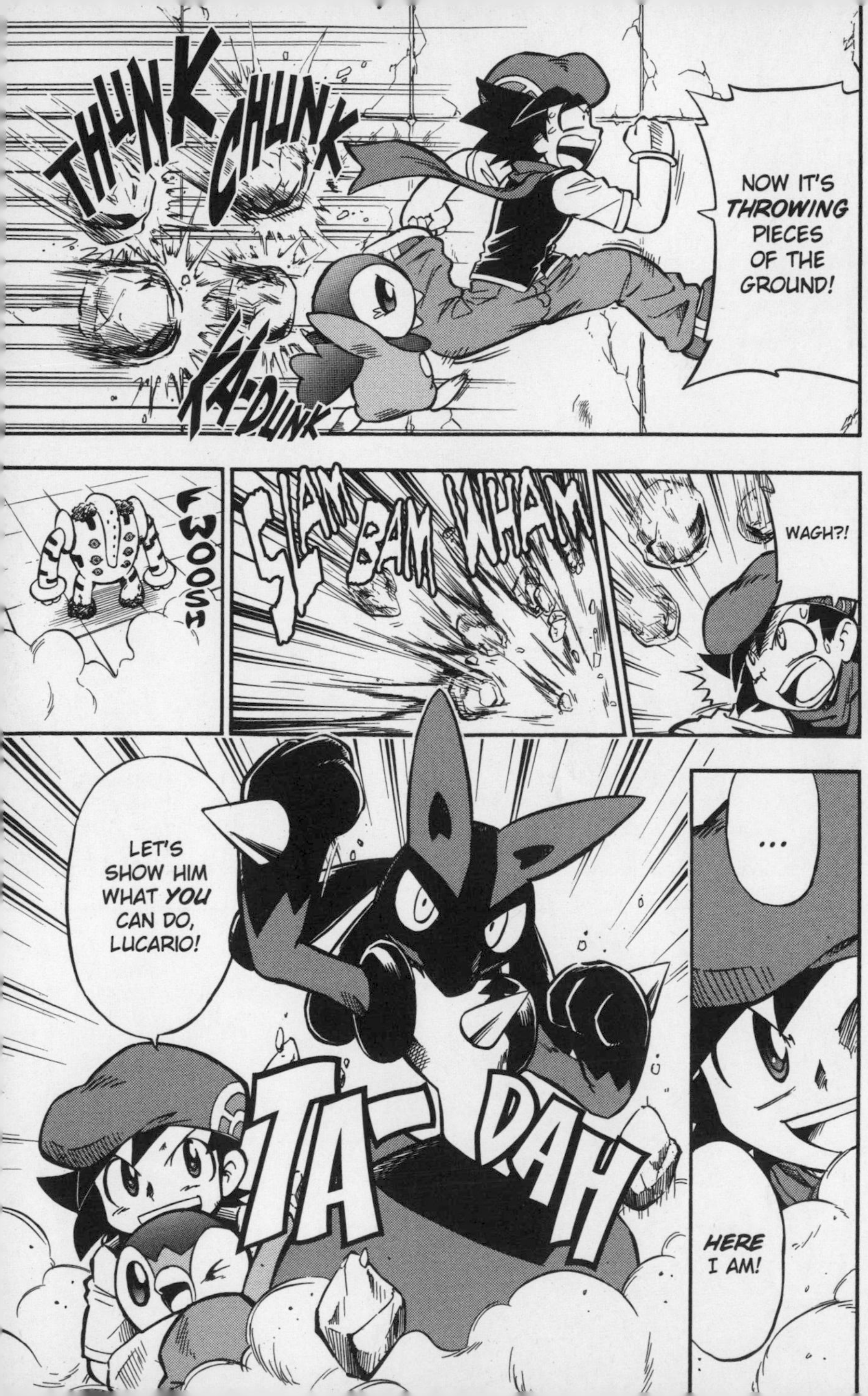
NOW IT'S *THROWING* PIECES OF THE GROUND!
CHUNK
THUNK
KA-DUNK
WAGH?!
SLAM BAM WHAM
FWOOSH
...
HERE I AM!
LET'S SHOW HIM WHAT *YOU* CAN DO, LUCARIO!
TA-DAH

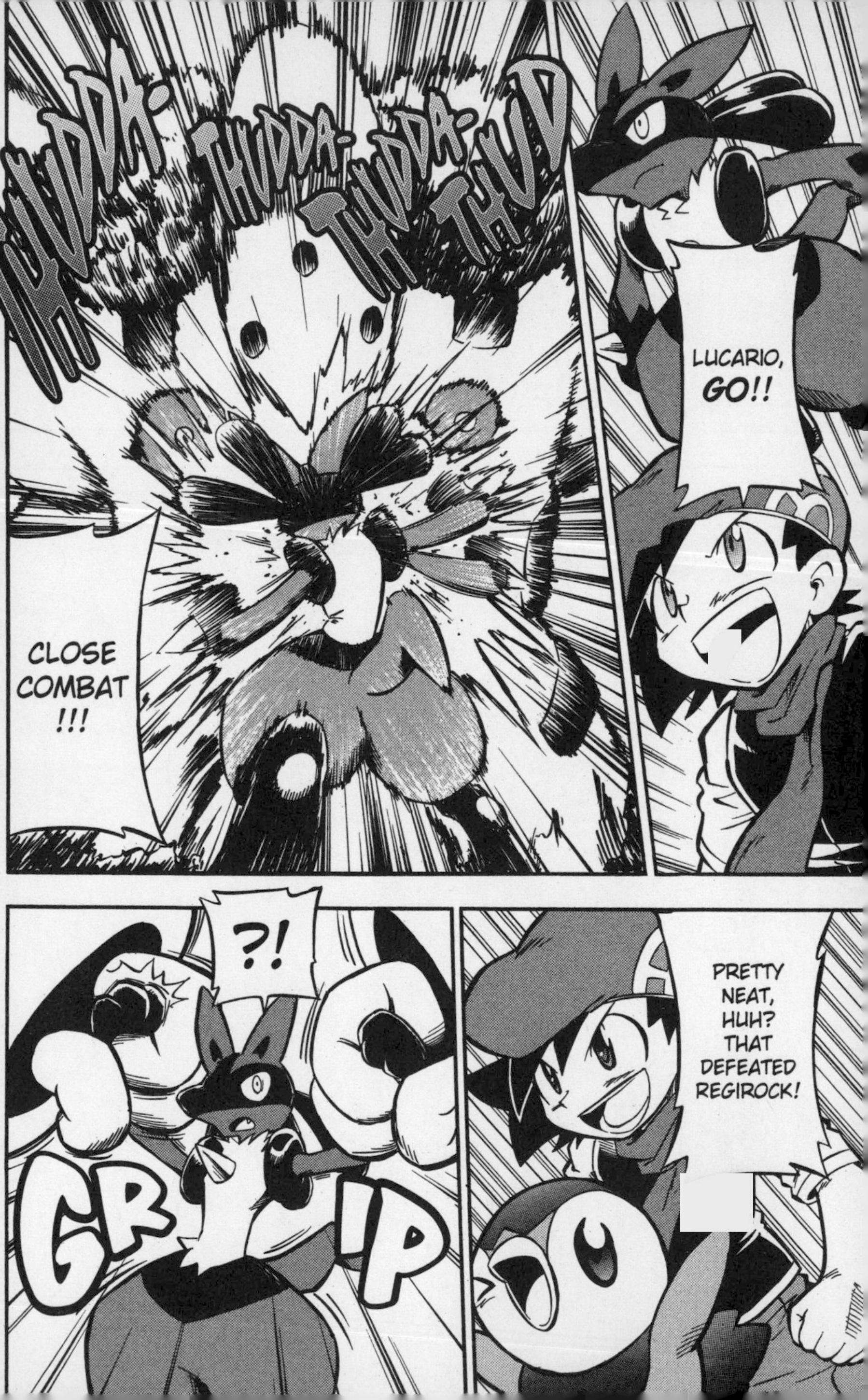
LUCARIO, GO!!
THUDDA-THUDDA-THUDDA-THUD
CLOSE COMBAT!!!
PRETTY NEAT, HUH? THAT DEFEATED REGIROCK!
?!
GRIP

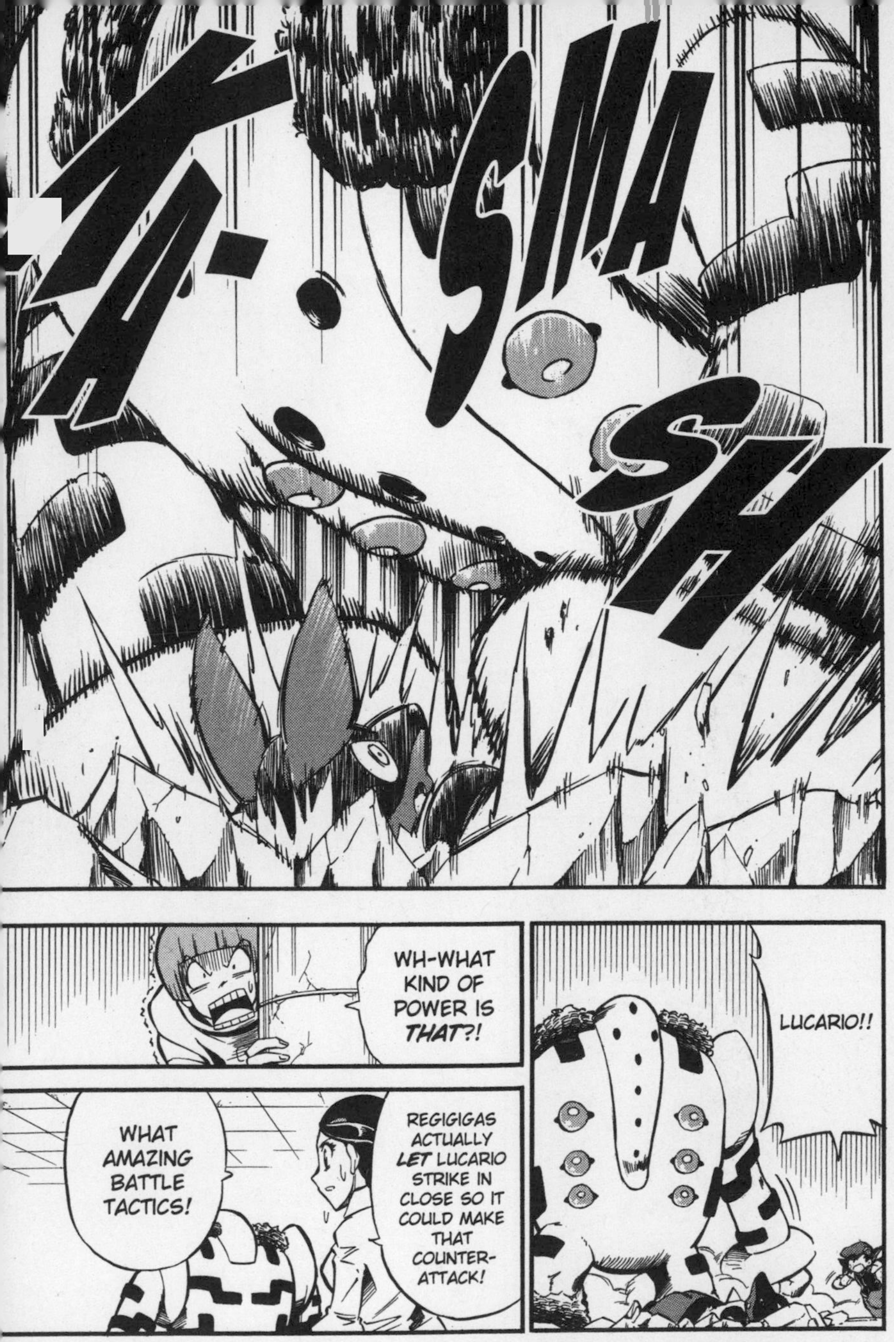
KA-SMASH
LUCARIO!!
WH-WHAT KIND OF POWER IS *THAT*?!
REGIGIGAS ACTUALLY *LET* LUCARIO STRIKE IN CLOSE SO IT COULD MAKE THAT COUNTER-ATTACK!
WHAT AMAZING BATTLE TACTICS!

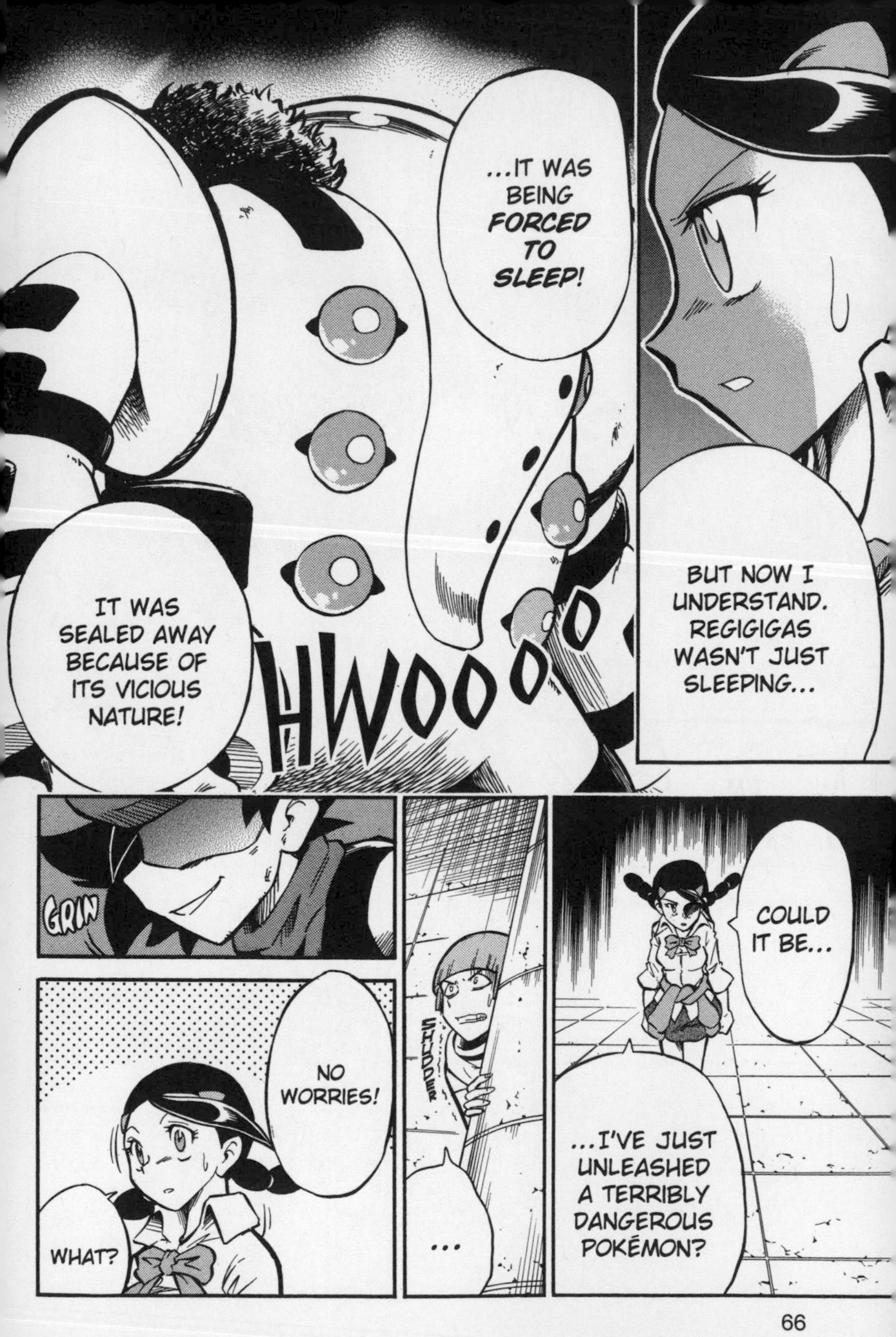
BUT NOW I UNDERSTAND. REGIGIGAS WASN'T JUST SLEEPING...
...IT WAS BEING *FORCED* TO *SLEEP!*
IT WAS SEALED AWAY BECAUSE OF ITS VICIOUS NATURE!
HWOOOO
COULD IT BE...
...I'VE JUST UNLEASHED A TERRIBLY DANGEROUS POKÉMON?
SHUDDER
...
GRIN
NO WORRIES!
WHAT?

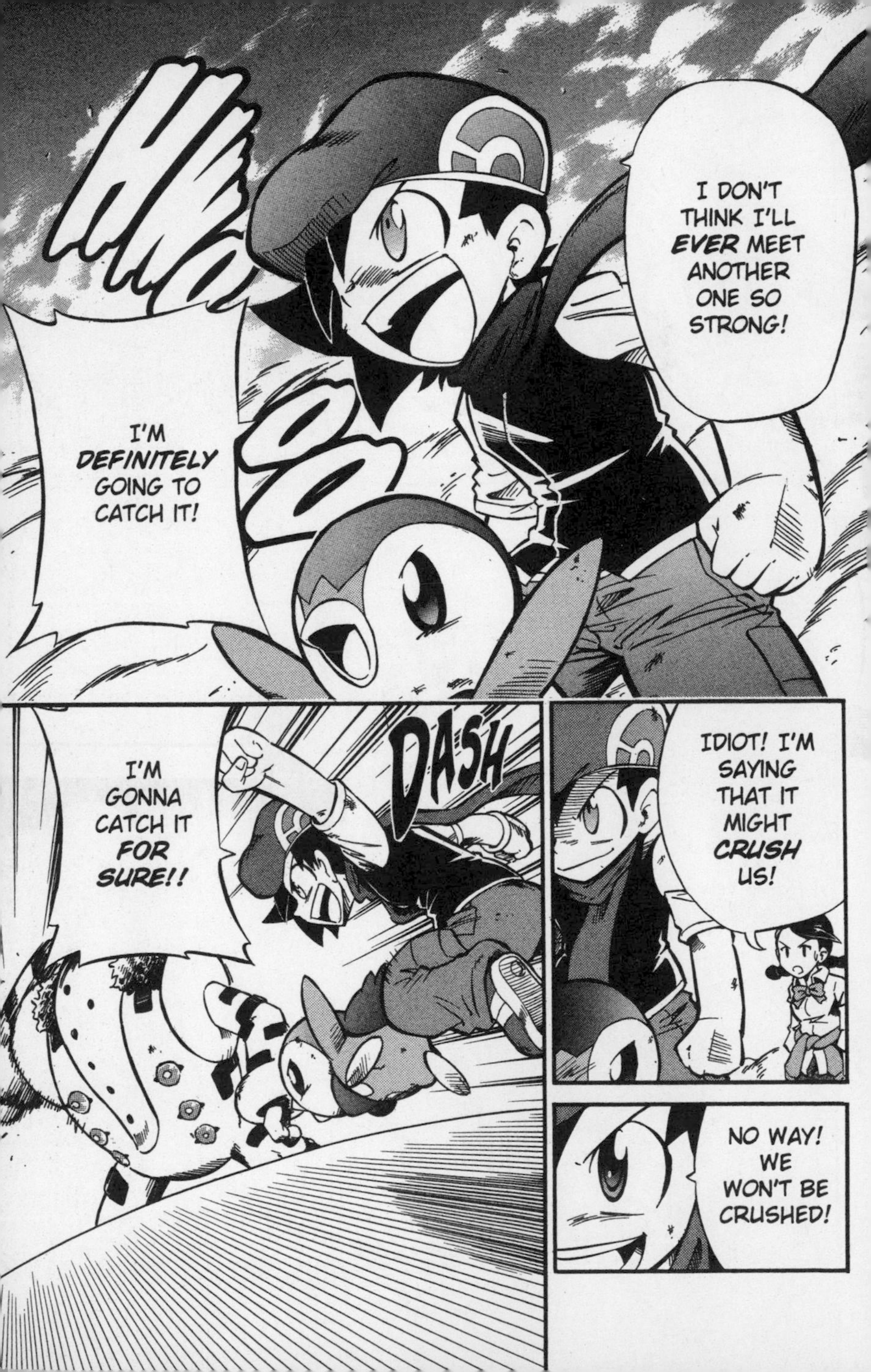
I DON'T THINK I'LL **EVER** MEET ANOTHER ONE SO STRONG!
I'M **DEFINITELY** GOING TO CATCH IT!
IDIOT! I'M SAYING THAT IT MIGHT **CRUSH** US!
NO WAY! WE WON'T BE CRUSHED!
DASH
I'M GONNA CATCH IT **FOR SURE!!**

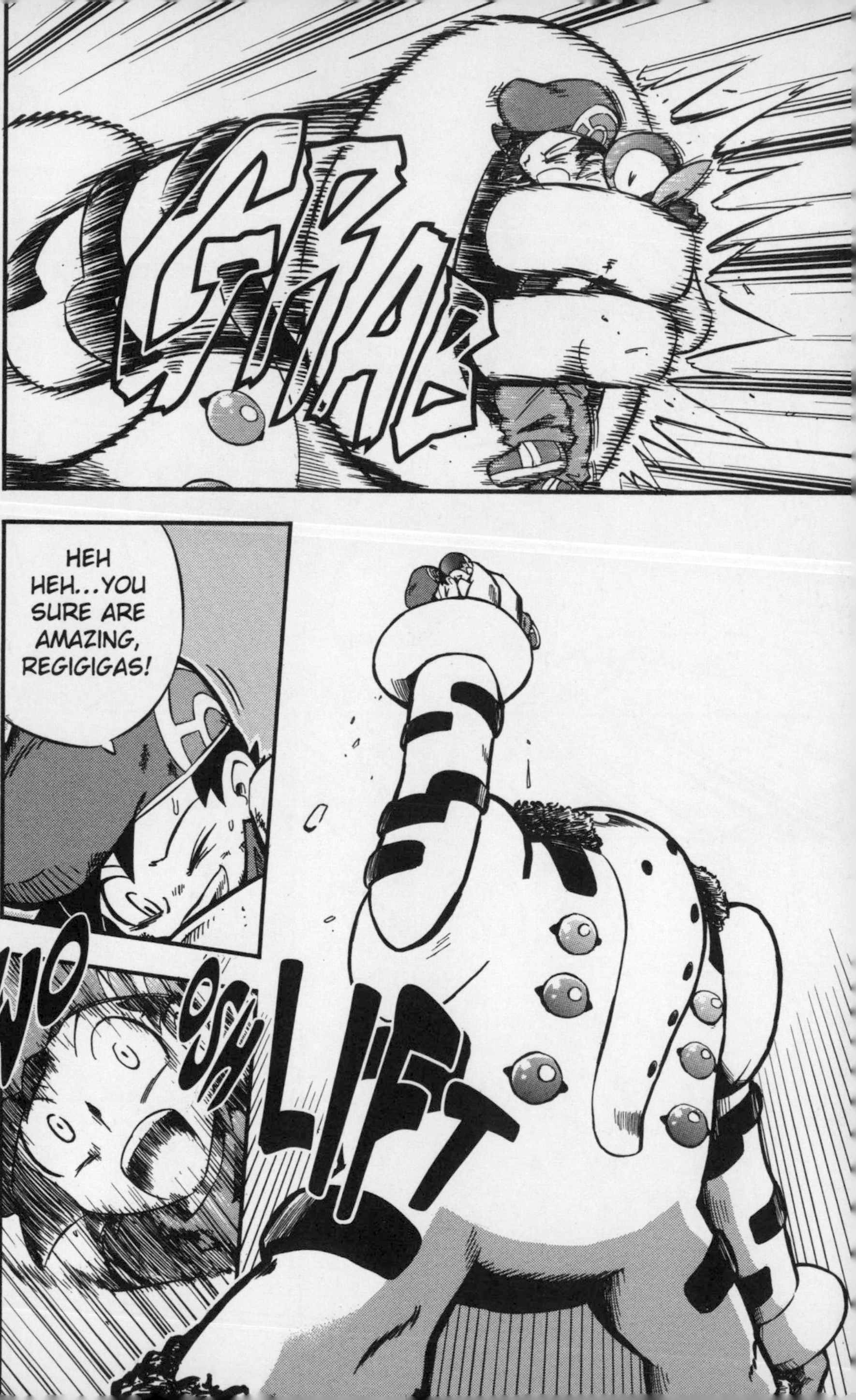
GRAB
HEH HEH...YOU SURE ARE AMAZING, REGIGIGAS!
LIFT
WOOSH

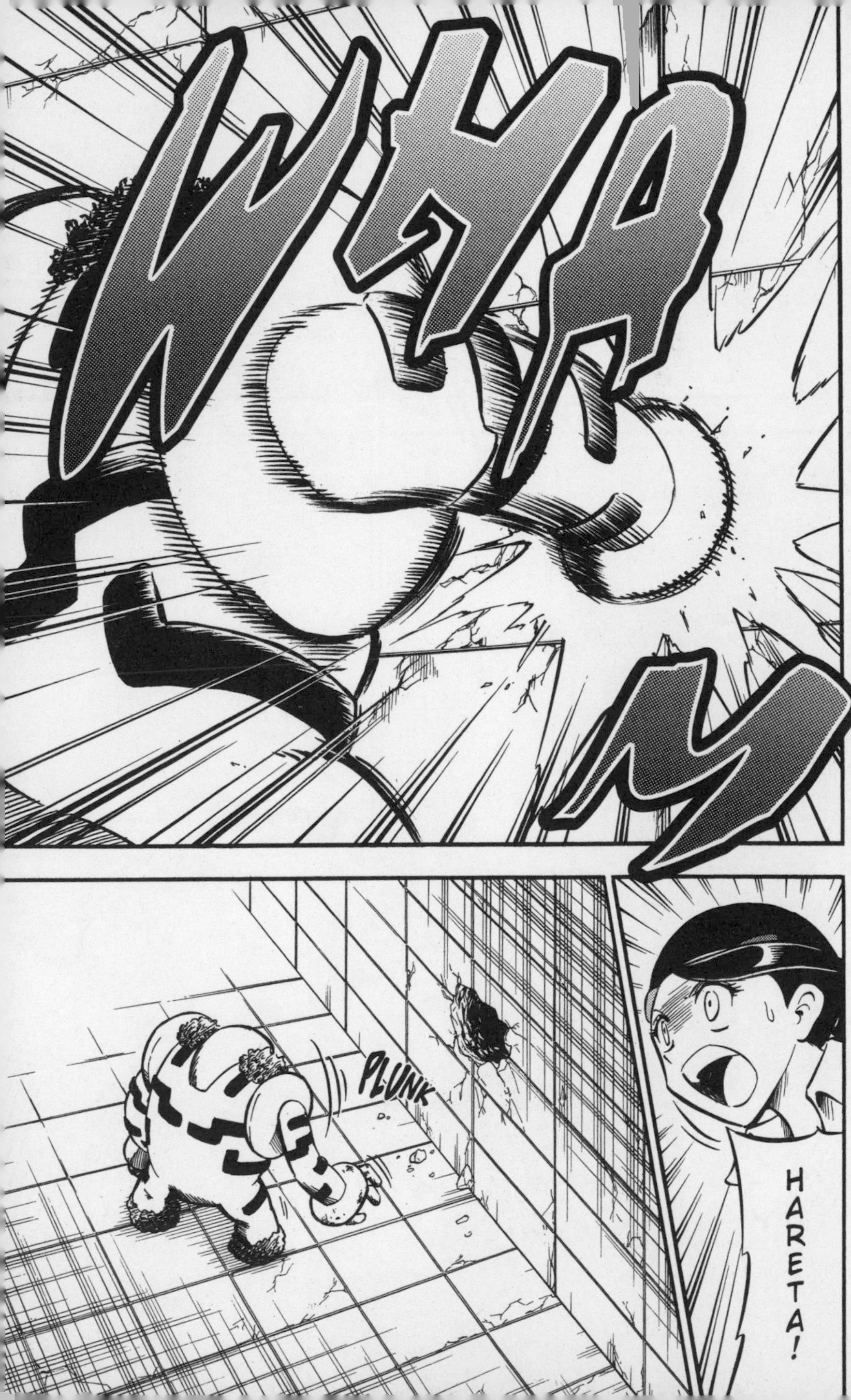
WHAM
HARETA!
PLUNK

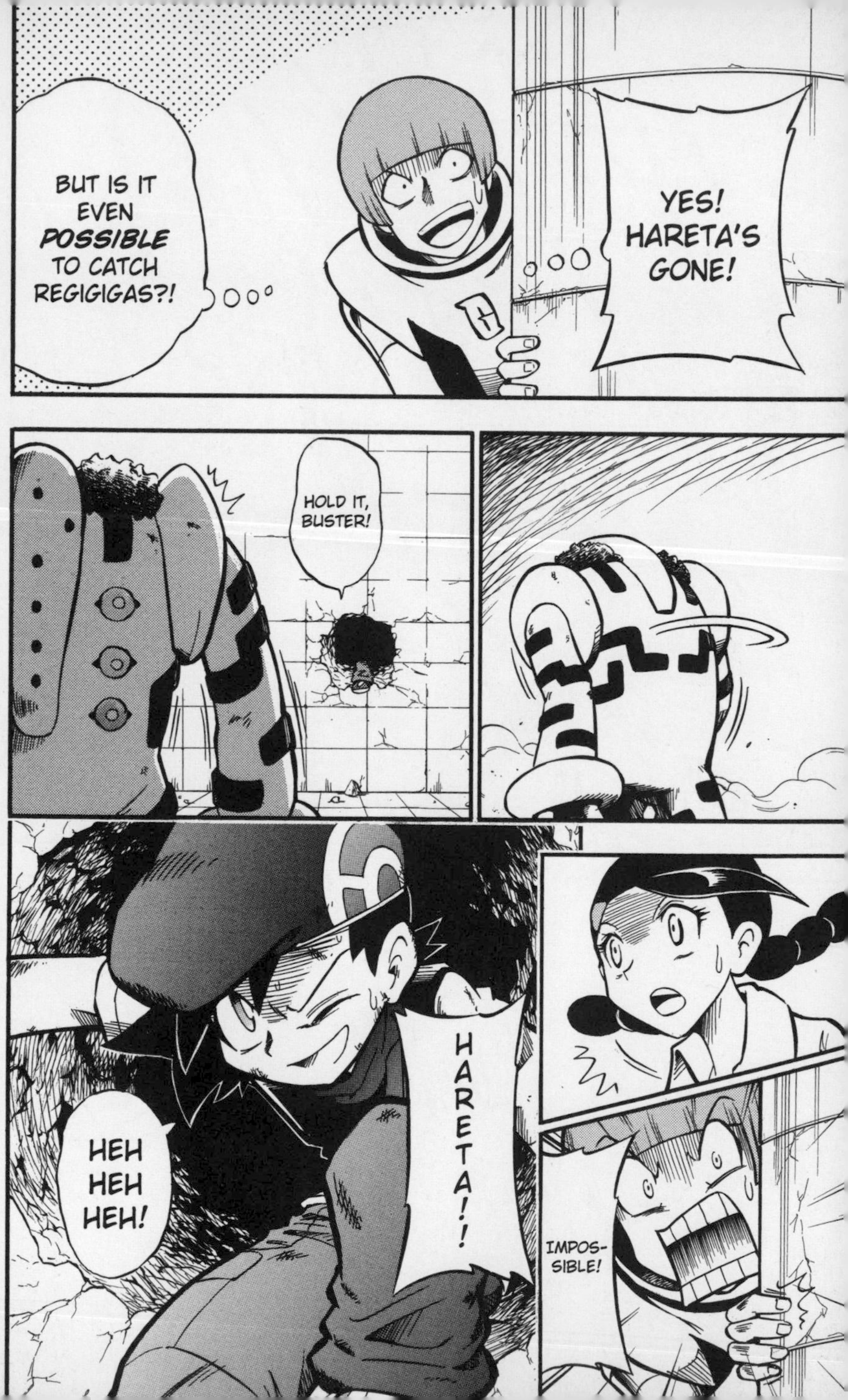
YES! HARETA'S GONE!
BUT IS IT EVEN ***POSSIBLE*** TO CATCH REGIGIGAS?!
HOLD IT, BUSTER!
IMPOS-SIBLE!
HARETA!!
HEH HEH HEH!

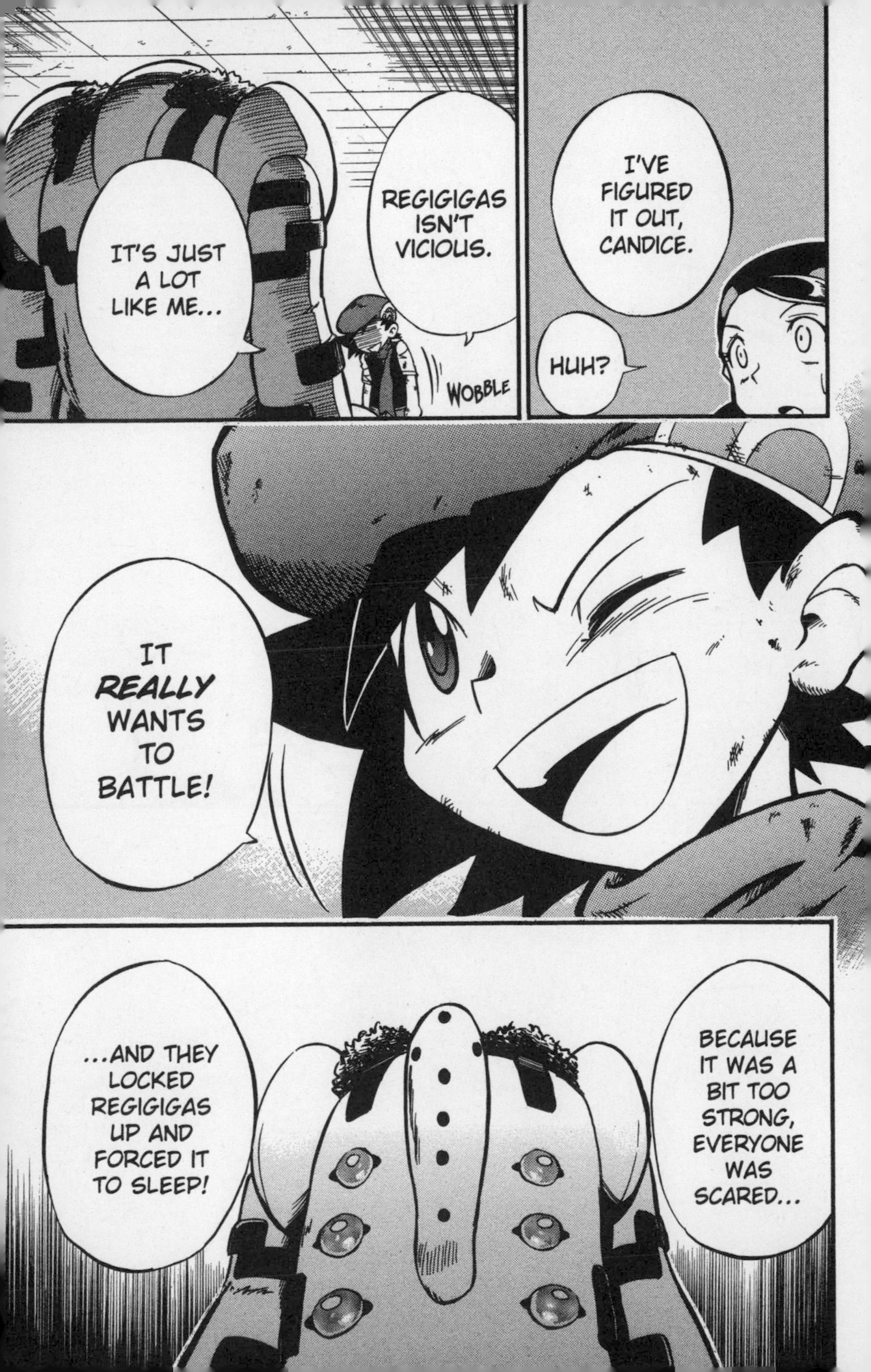
I'VE FIGURED IT OUT, CANDICE.
HUH?
REGIGIGAS ISN'T VICIOUS.
WOBBLE
IT'S JUST A LOT LIKE ME...
IT *REALLY* WANTS TO BATTLE!
BECAUSE IT WAS A BIT TOO STRONG, EVERYONE WAS SCARED...
...AND THEY LOCKED REGIGIGAS UP AND FORCED IT TO SLEEP!

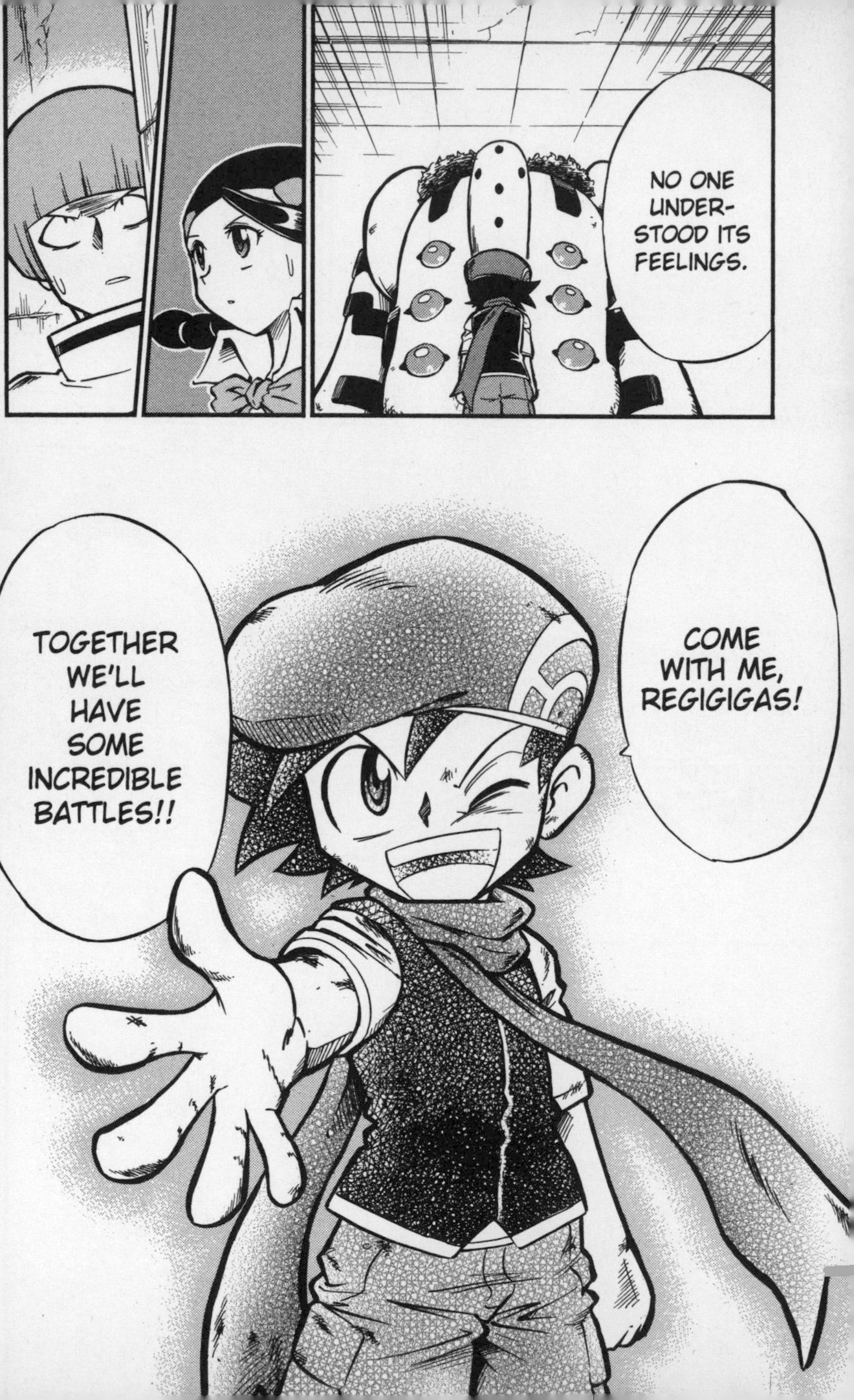
NO ONE UNDER-STOOD ITS FEELINGS.
COME WITH ME, REGIGIGAS!
TOGETHER WE'LL HAVE SOME INCREDIBLE BATTLES!!

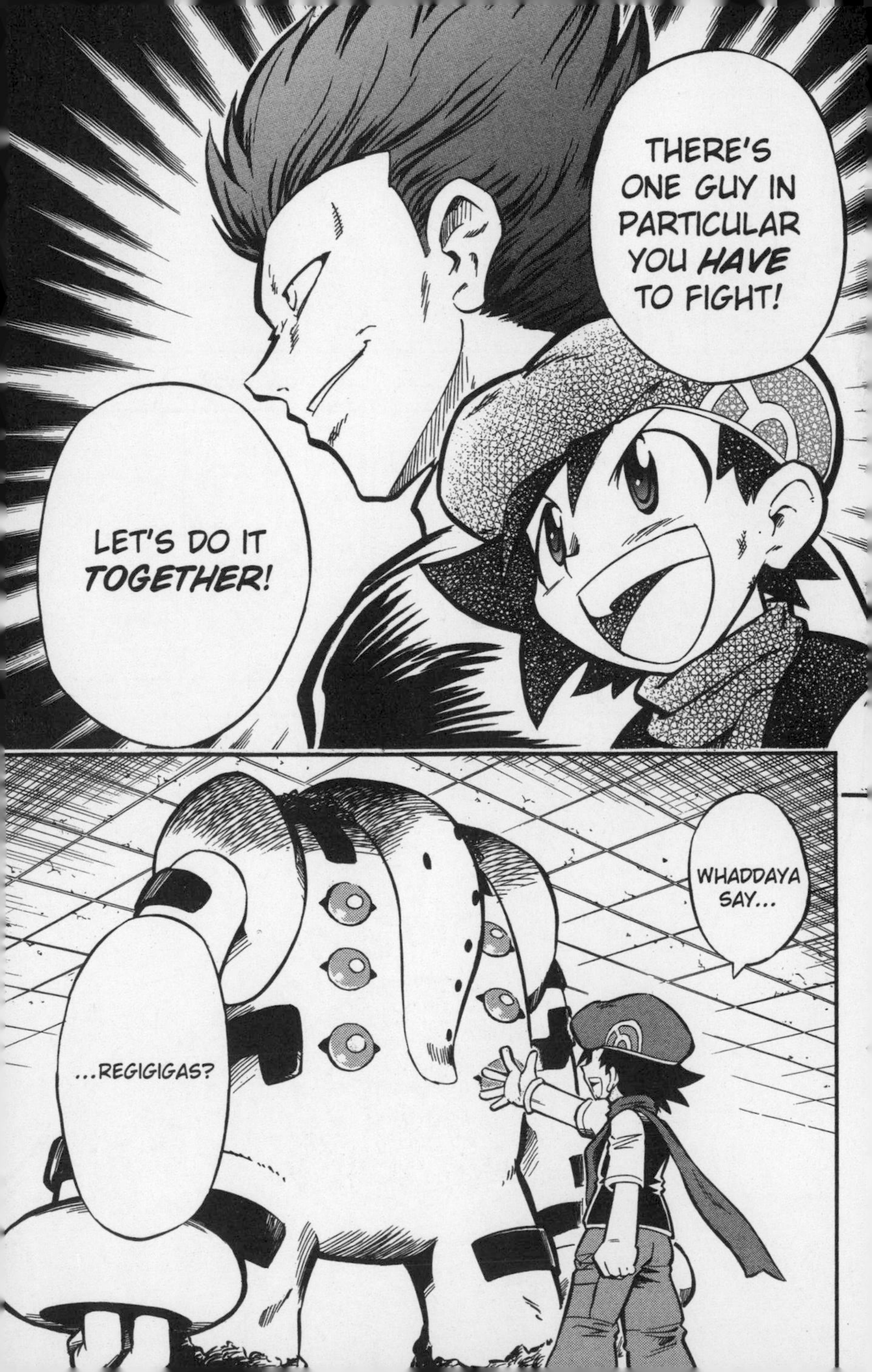
THERE'S ONE GUY IN PARTICULAR YOU *HAVE* TO FIGHT!
LET'S DO IT *TOGETHER*!
WHADDAYA SAY...
...REGIGIGAS?

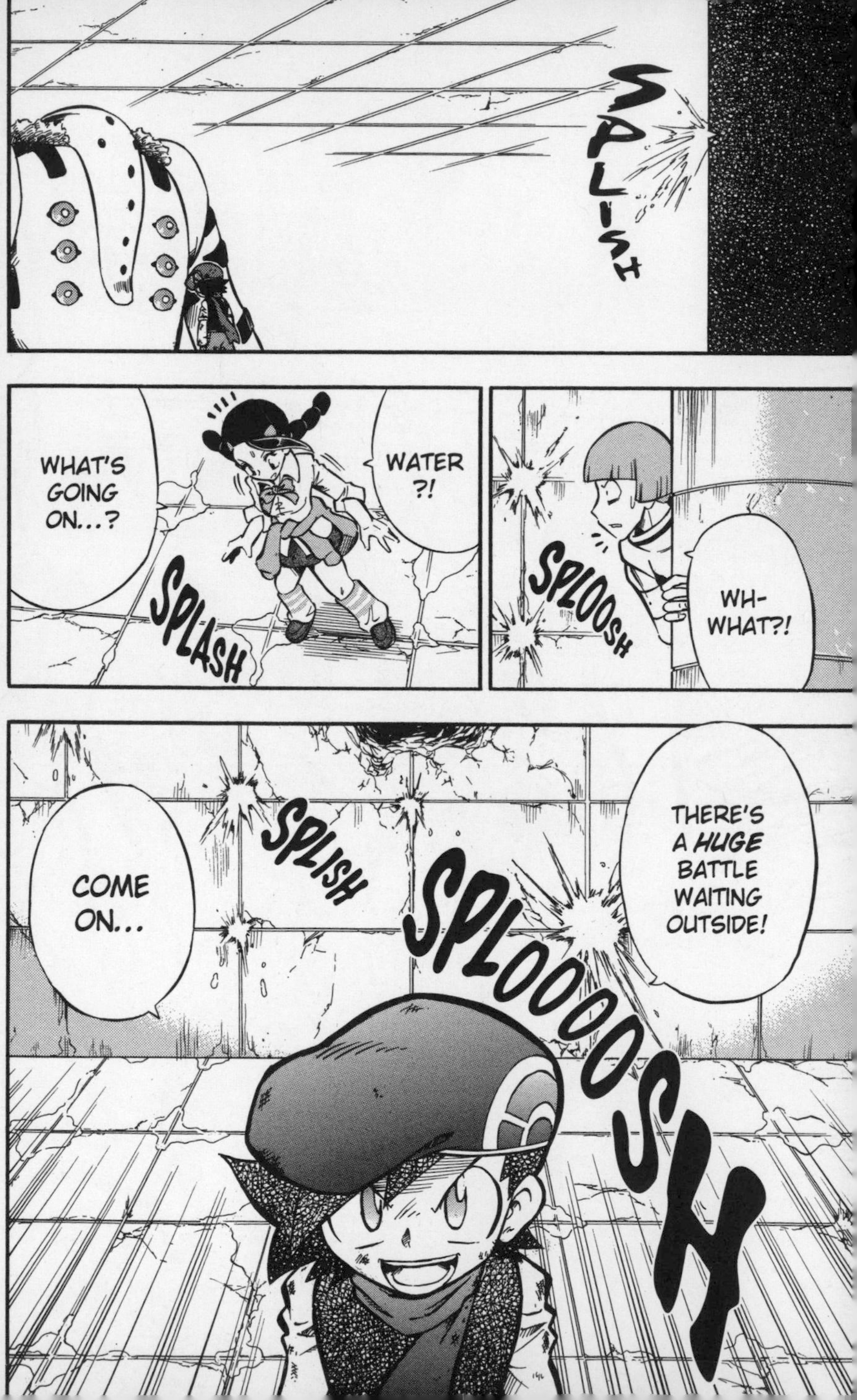
SPLISH
SPLOOSH
WH-WHAT?!
WATER?!
WHAT'S GOING ON...?
SPLASH
THERE'S A *HUGE* BATTLE WAITING OUTSIDE!
SPLOOOOSH
SPLISH
COME ON...

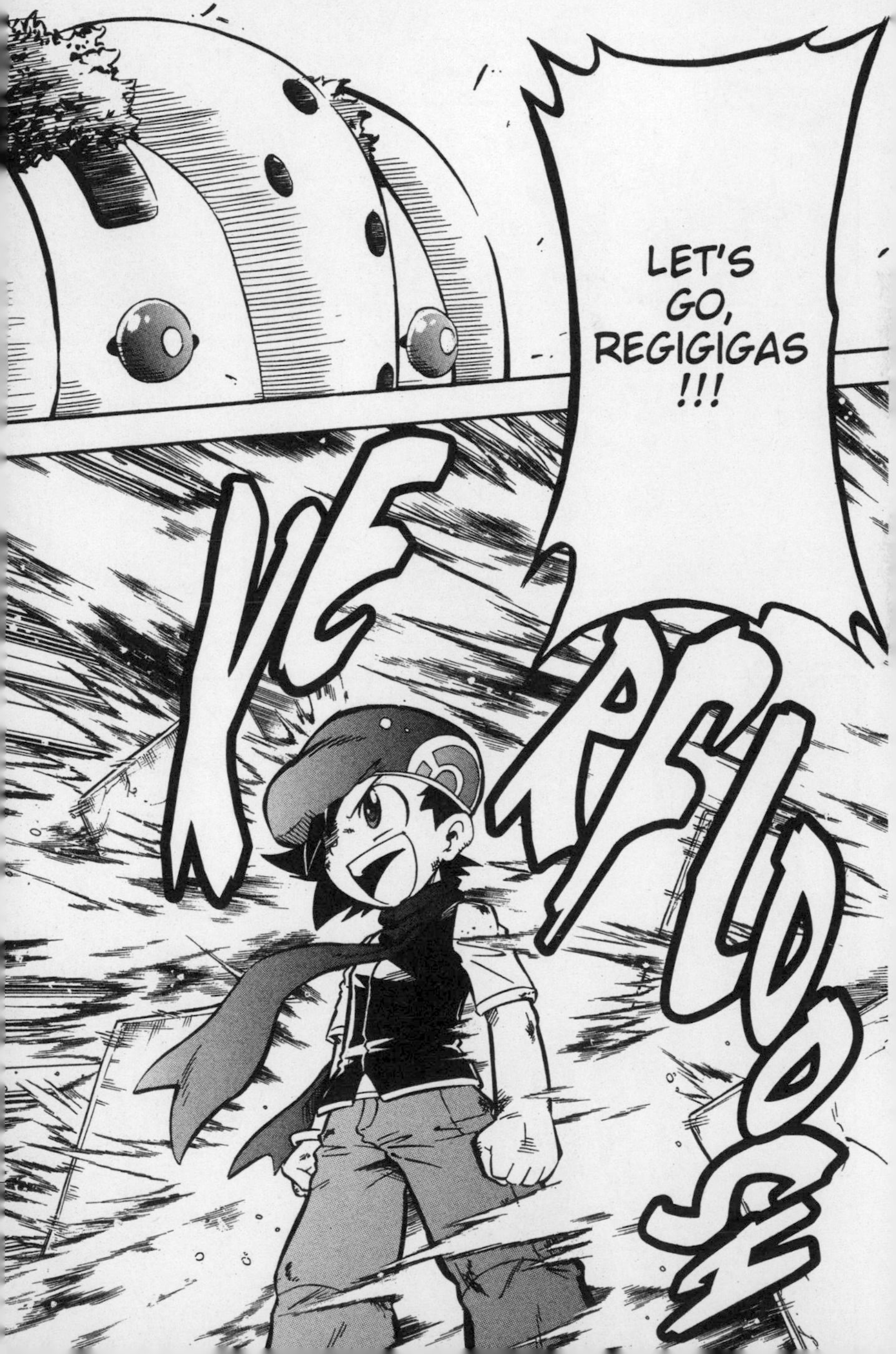
LET'S GO, REGIGIGAS!!!

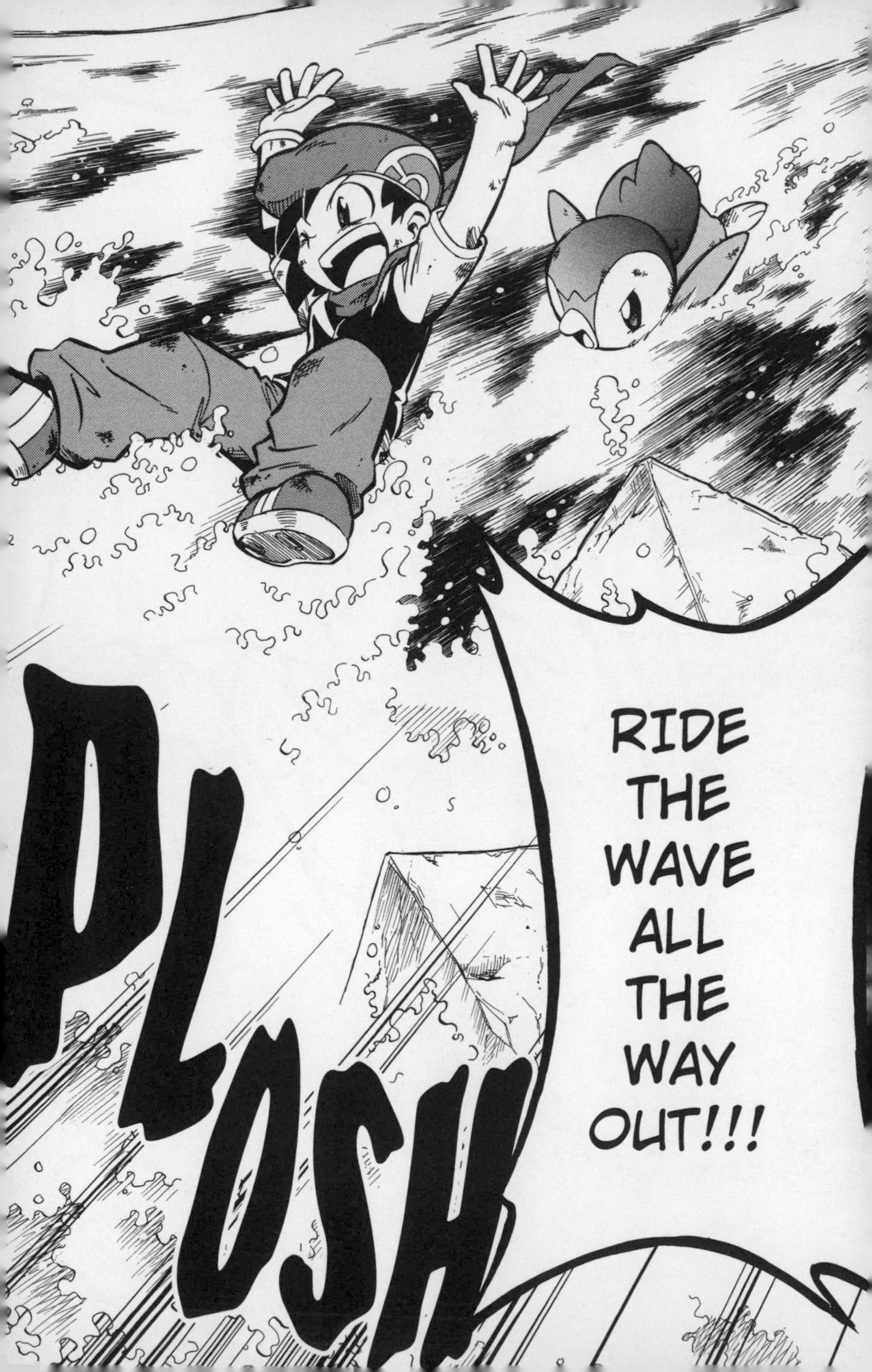
RIDE THE WAVE ALL THE WAY OUT!!!
PLOSH

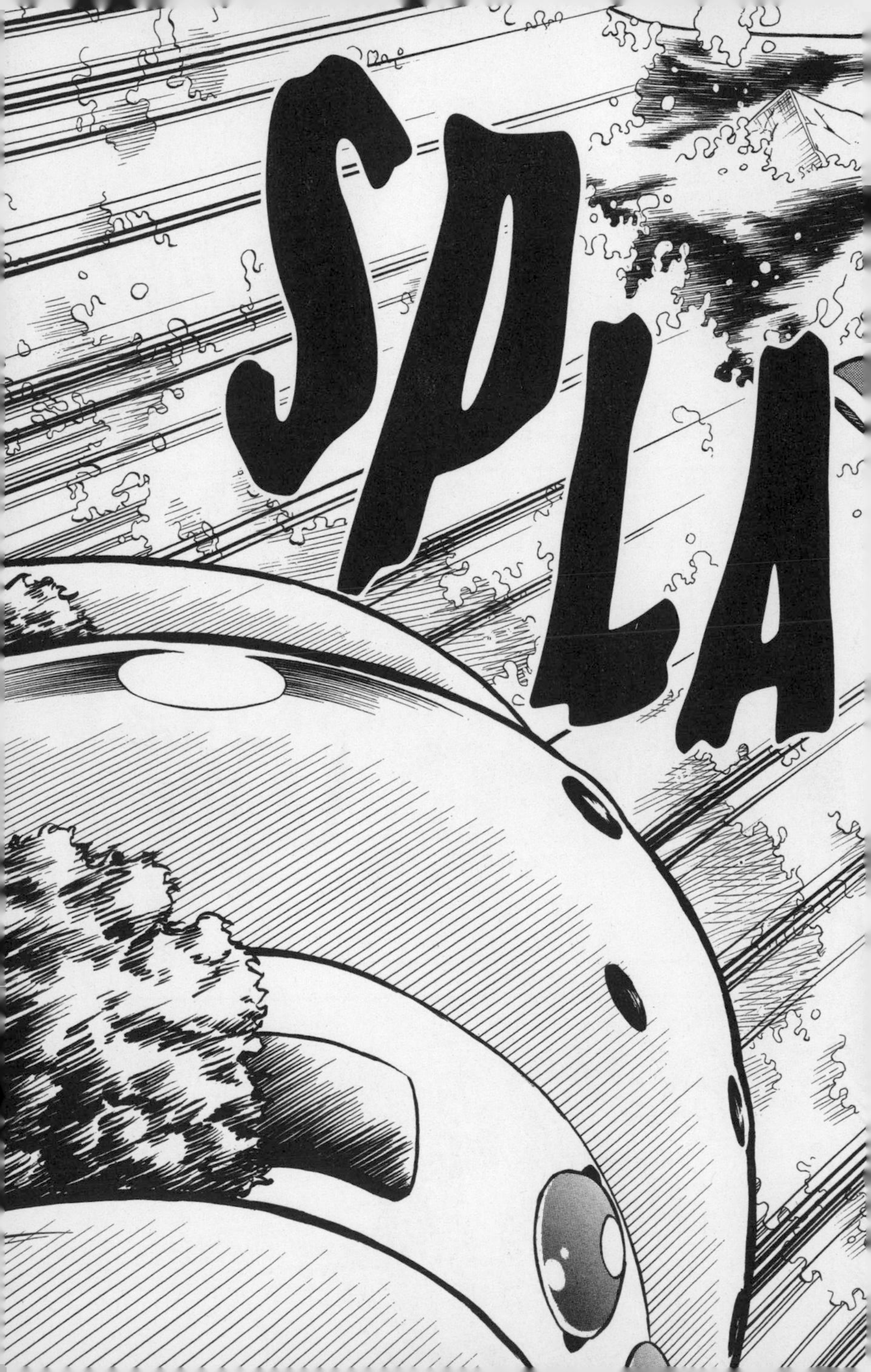
SPLA

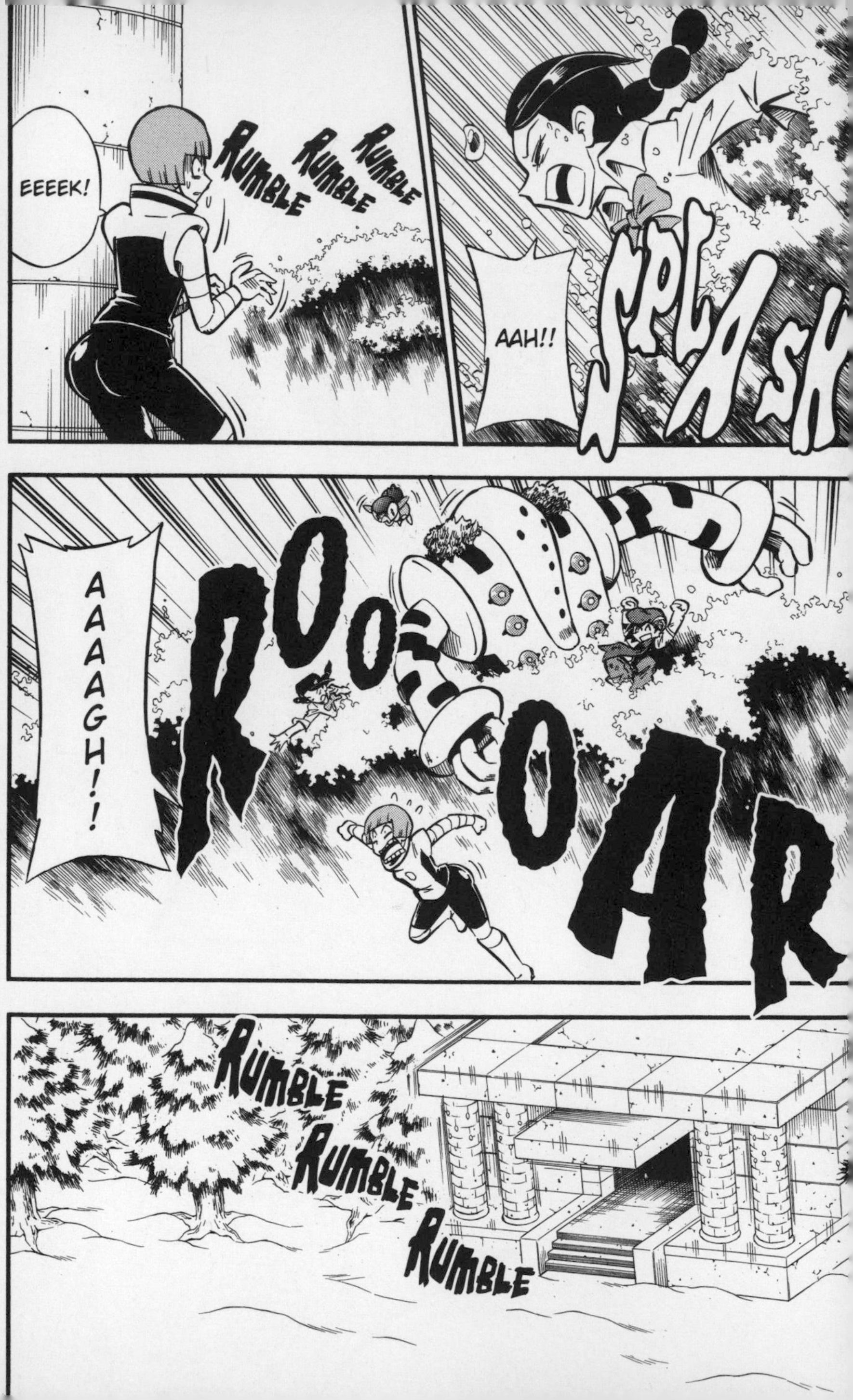
AAH!!
SPLASH
RUMBLE RUMBLE RUMBLE
EEEEK!
AAAAGH!!
ROOOOAR
RUMBLE RUMBLE RUMBLE

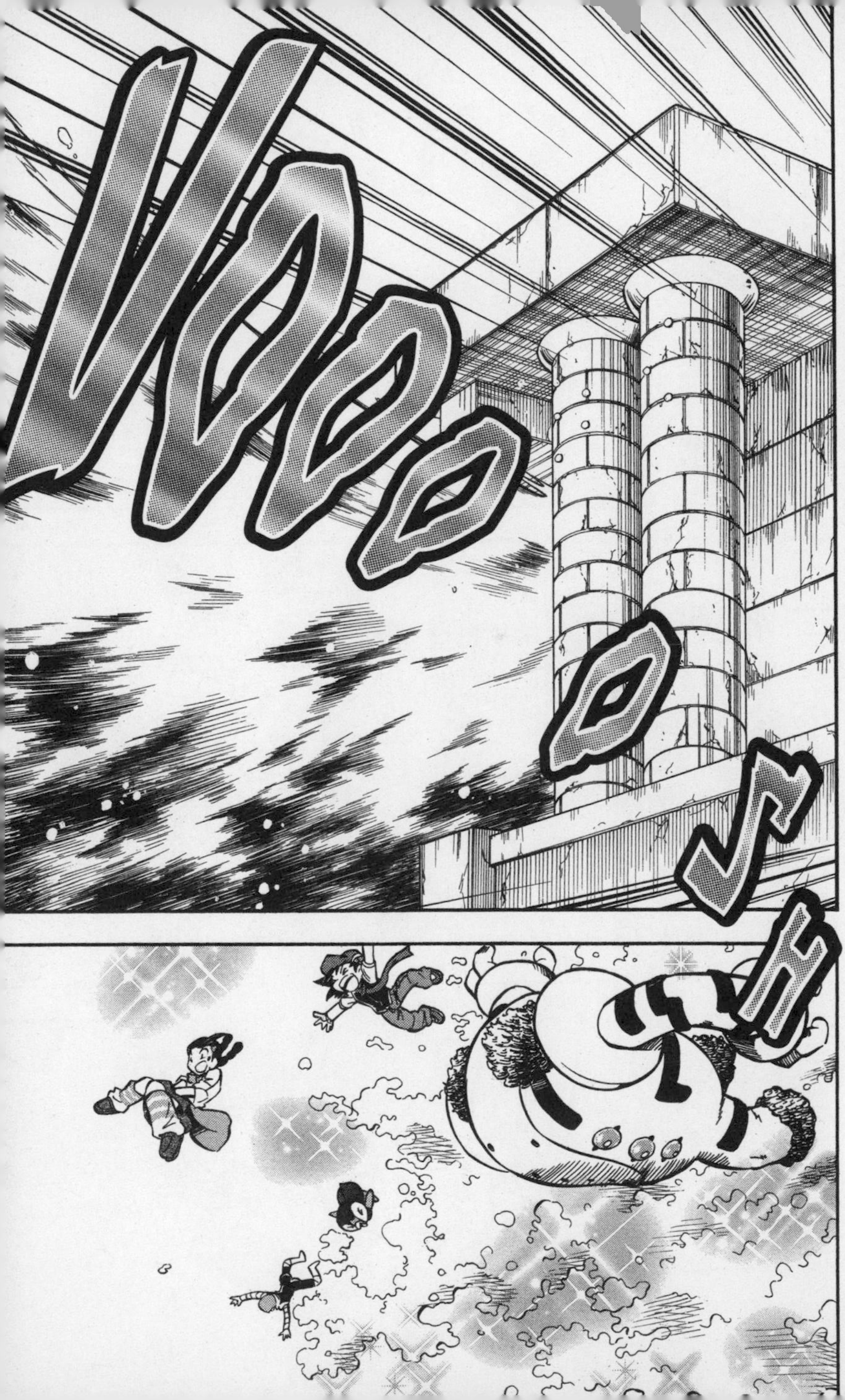
WOOOOSH

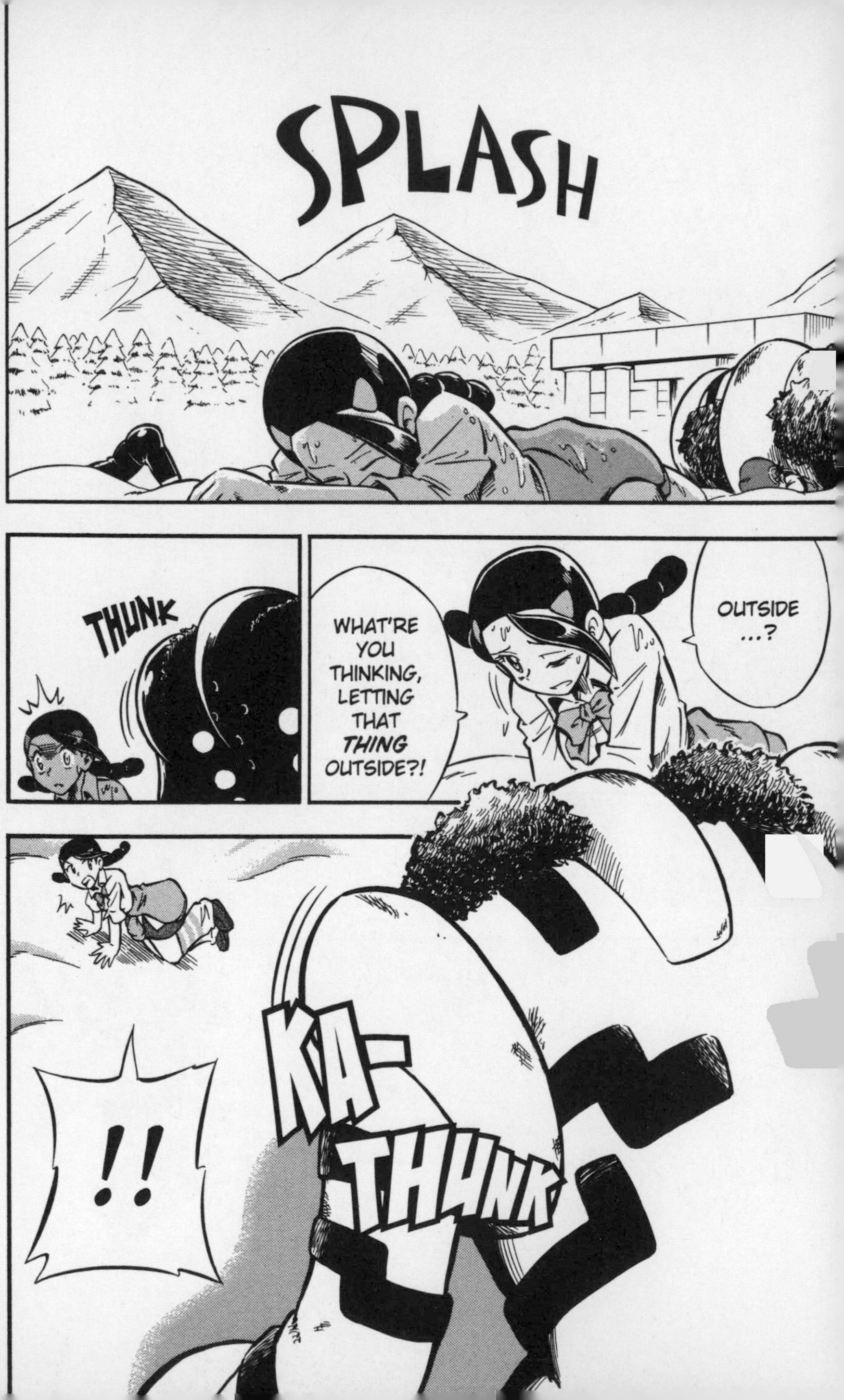
SPLASH
OUTSIDE ...?
WHAT'RE YOU THINKING, LETTING THAT *THING* OUTSIDE?!
THUNK
KA-THUNK
!!

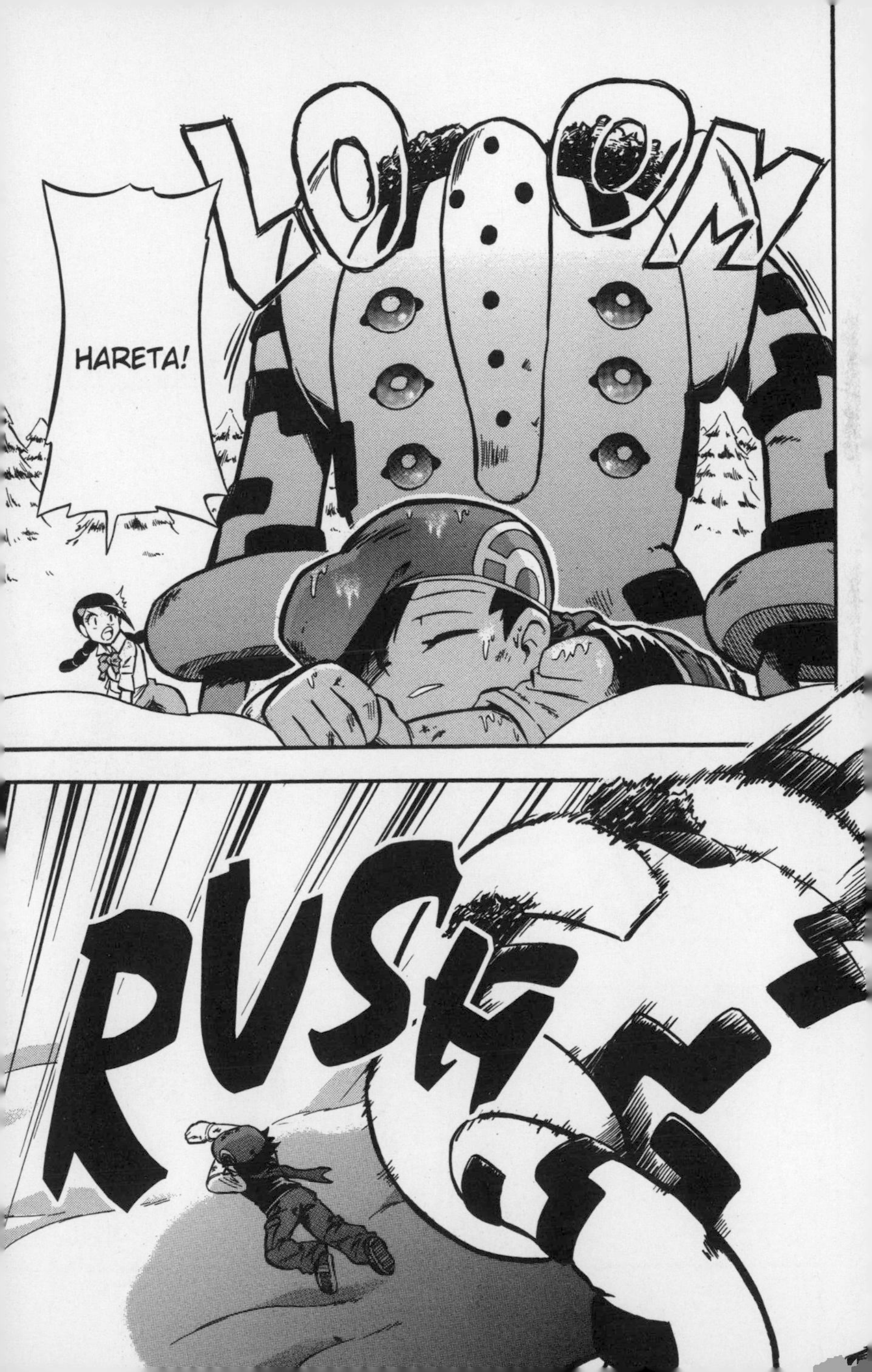
LOOOOM
HARETA!
RUSH

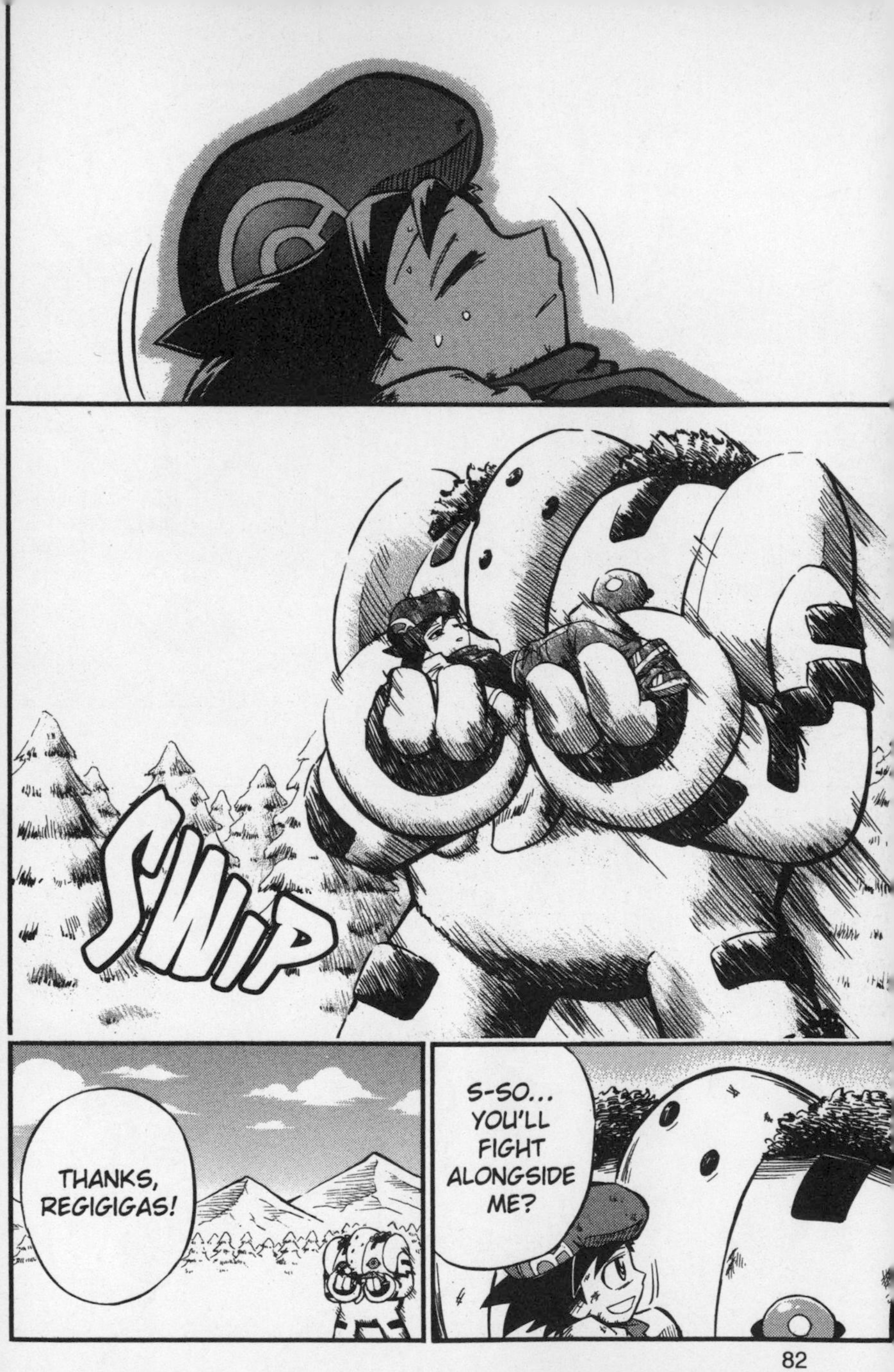
SWIP
S-SO... YOU'LL FIGHT ALONGSIDE ME?
THANKS, REGIGIGAS!

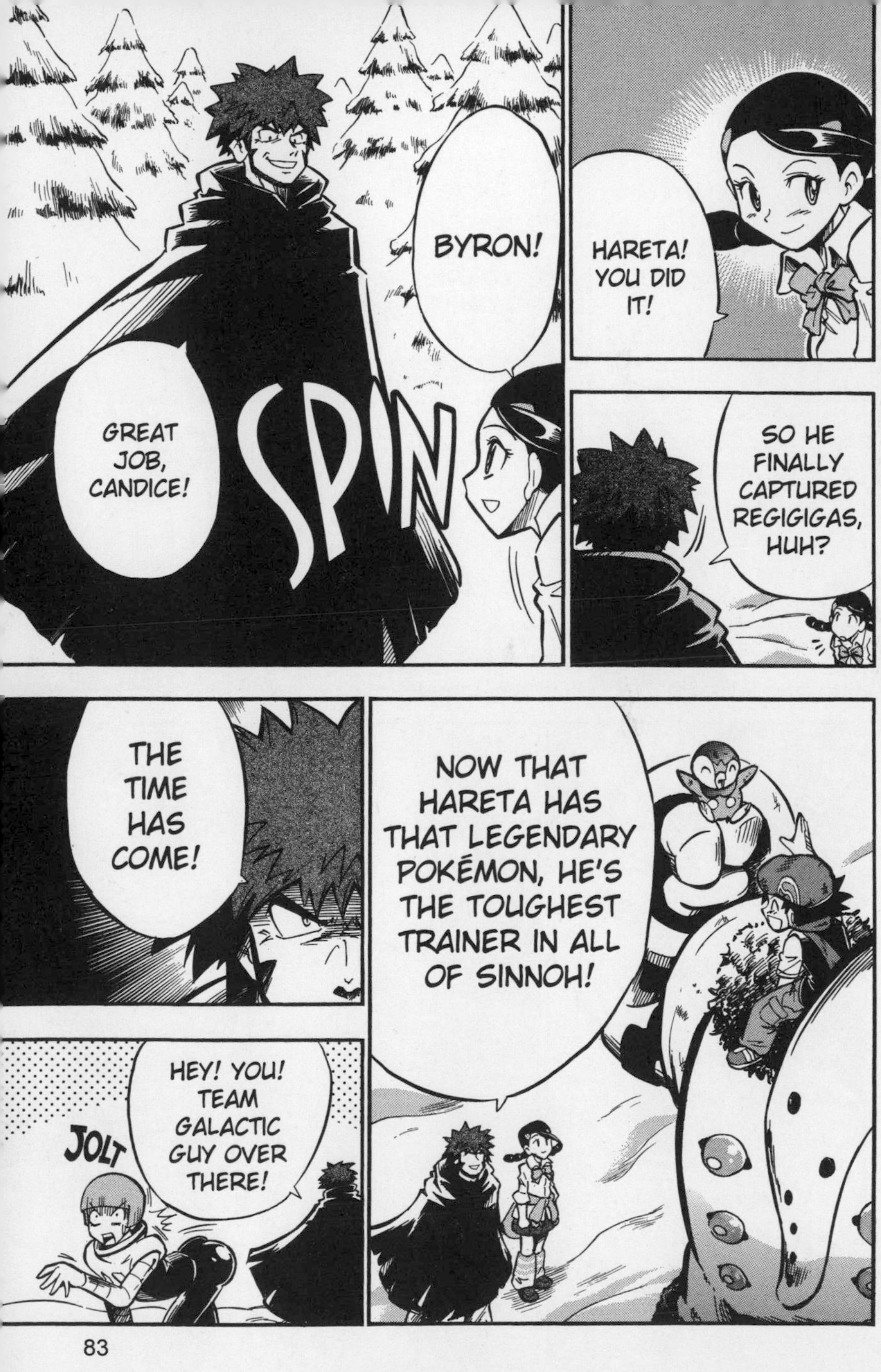
HARETA! YOU DID IT!
SO HE FINALLY CAPTURED REGIGIGAS, HUH?
BYRON!
SPIN
GREAT JOB, CANDICE!
NOW THAT HARETA HAS THAT LEGENDARY POKÉMON, HE'S THE TOUGHEST TRAINER IN ALL OF SINNOH!
THE TIME HAS COME!
HEY! YOU! TEAM GALACTIC GUY OVER THERE!
JOLT

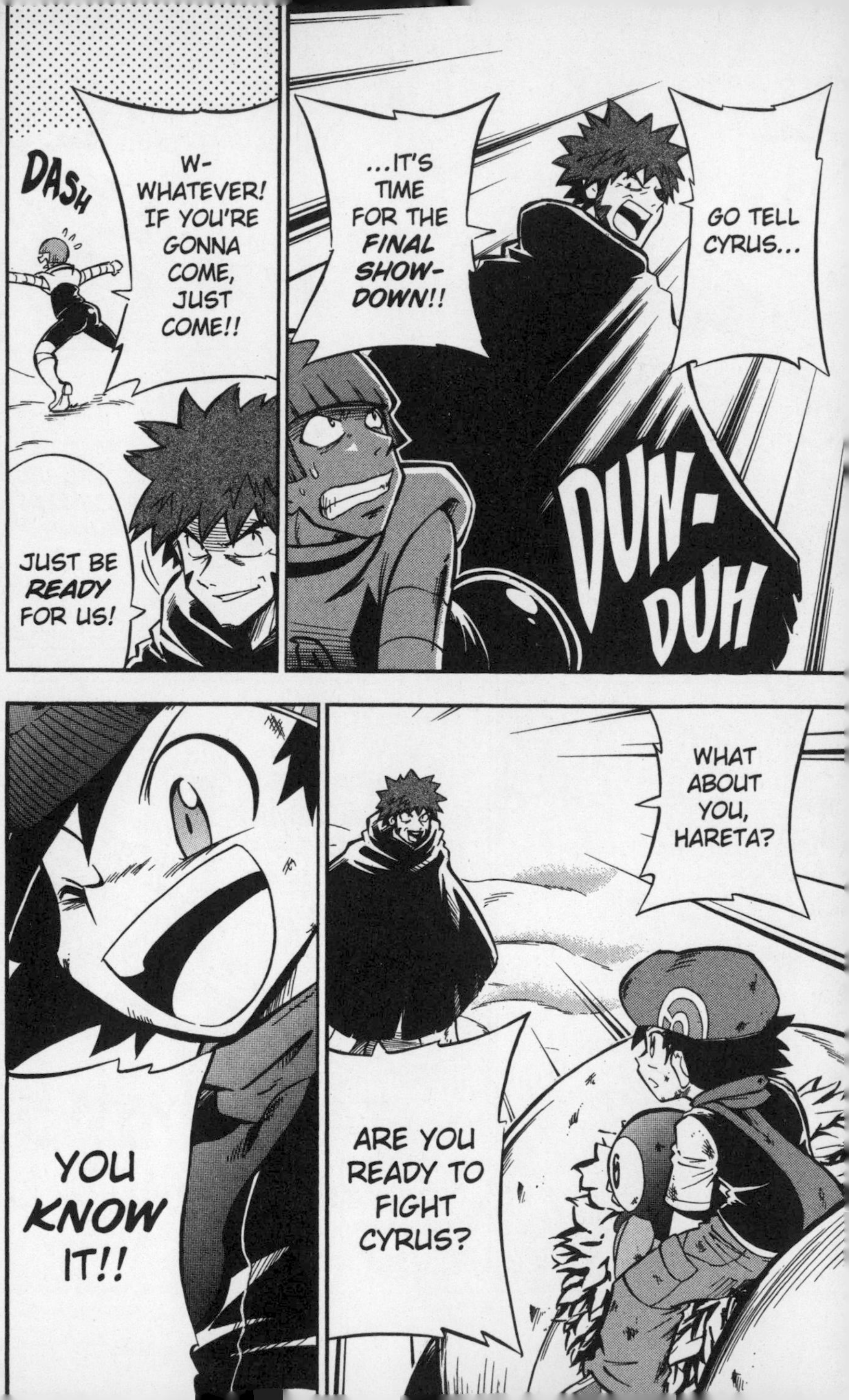
GO TELL CYRUS...
...IT'S TIME FOR THE *FINAL SHOW-DOWN*!!
DUN-DUH
DASH
W-WHATEVER! IF YOU'RE GONNA COME, JUST COME!!
JUST BE *READY* FOR US!
WHAT ABOUT YOU, HARETA?
ARE YOU READY TO FIGHT CYRUS?
YOU *KNOW* IT!!

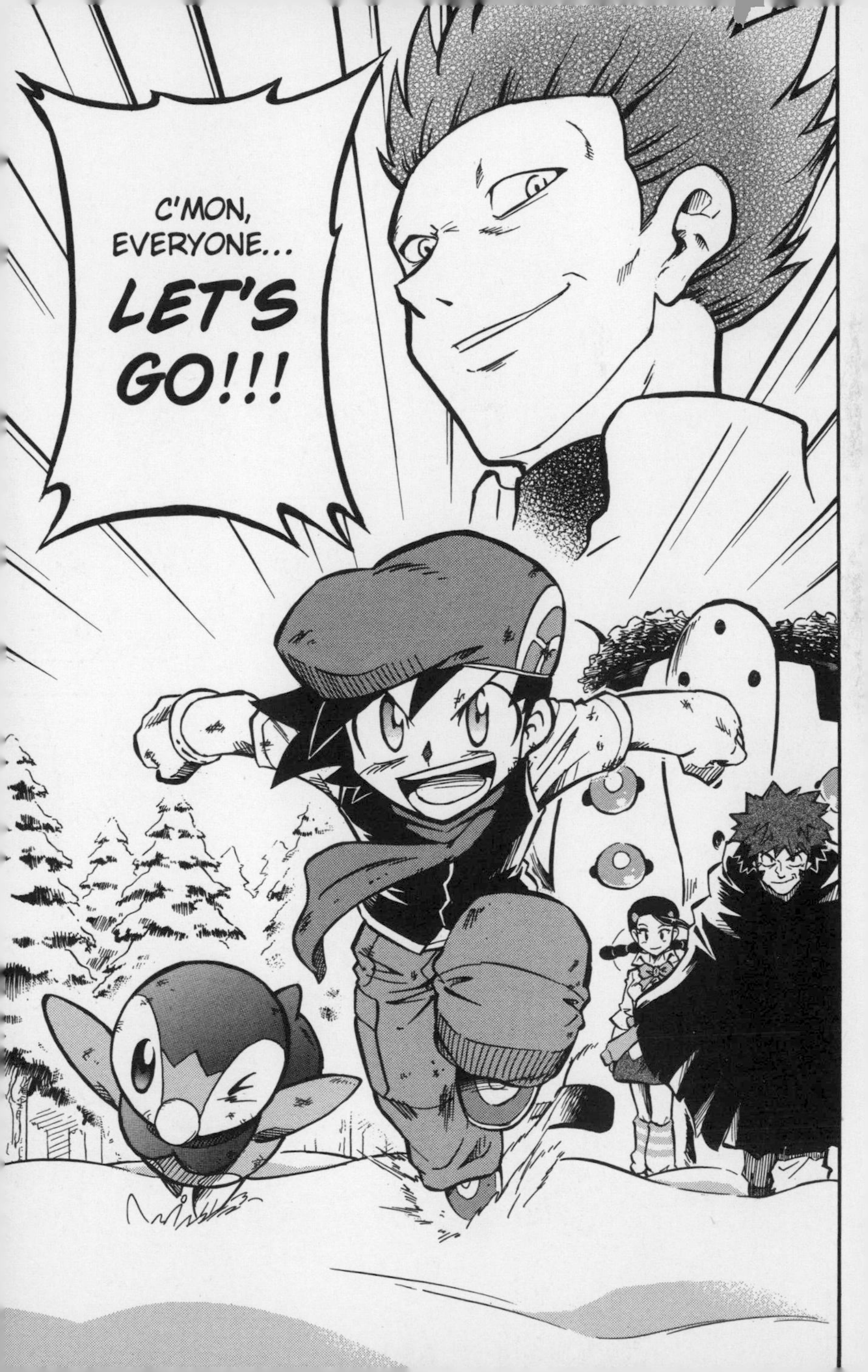
C'MON, EVERYONE... LET'S GO!!!

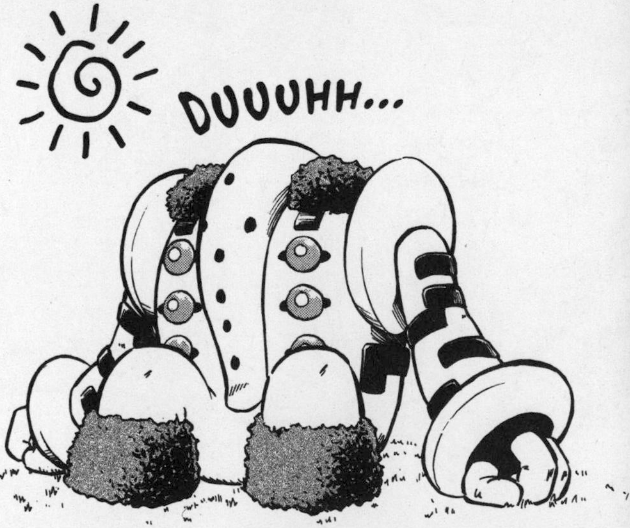
DUUUHH...

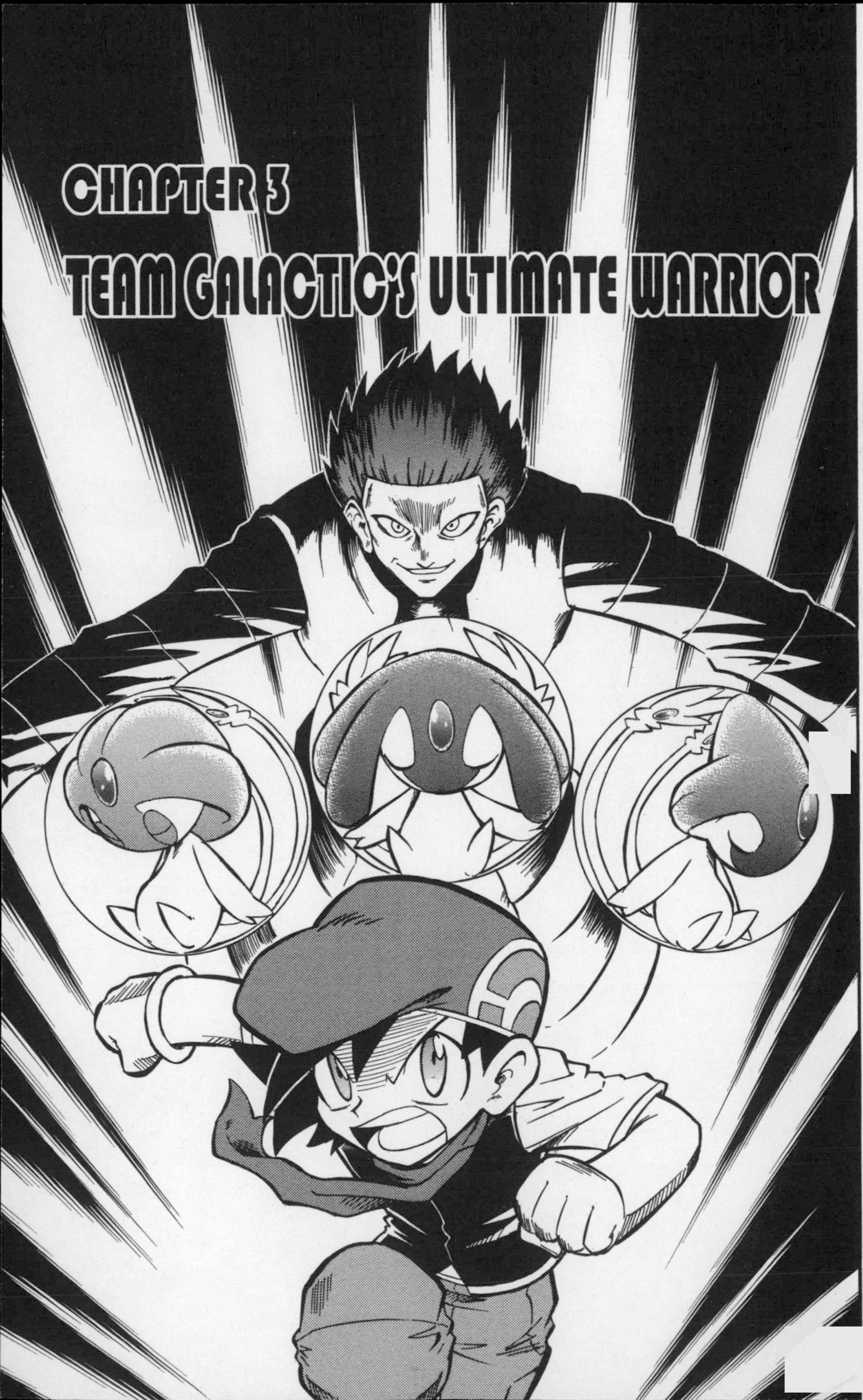
CHAPTER 3
TEAM GALACTIC'S ULTIMATE WARRIOR

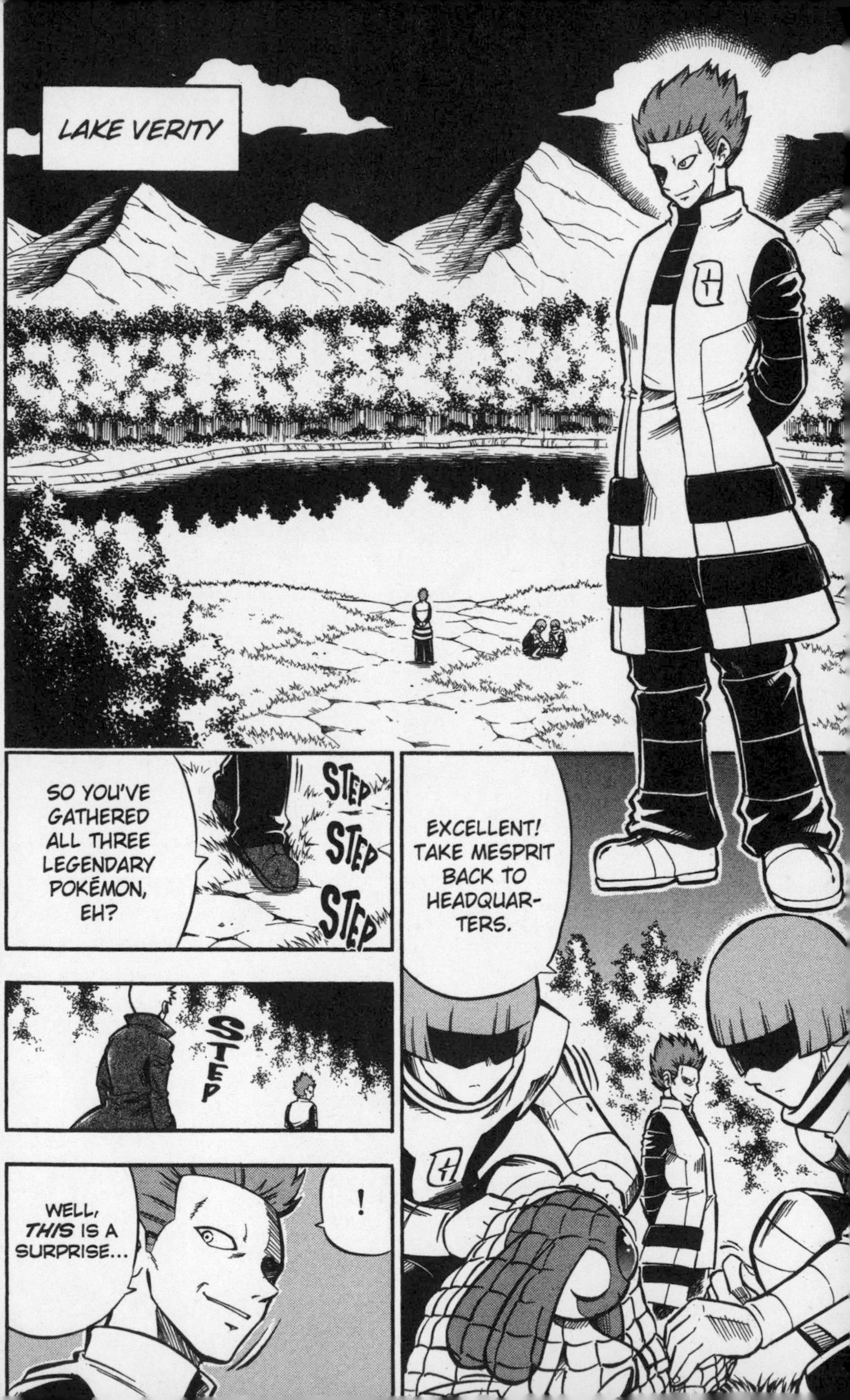
LAKE VERITY
EXCELLENT! TAKE MESPRIT BACK TO HEADQUARTERS.
SO YOU'VE GATHERED ALL THREE LEGENDARY POKÉMON, EH?
STEP
STEP
STEP
STEP
!
WELL, *THIS* IS A SURPRISE...

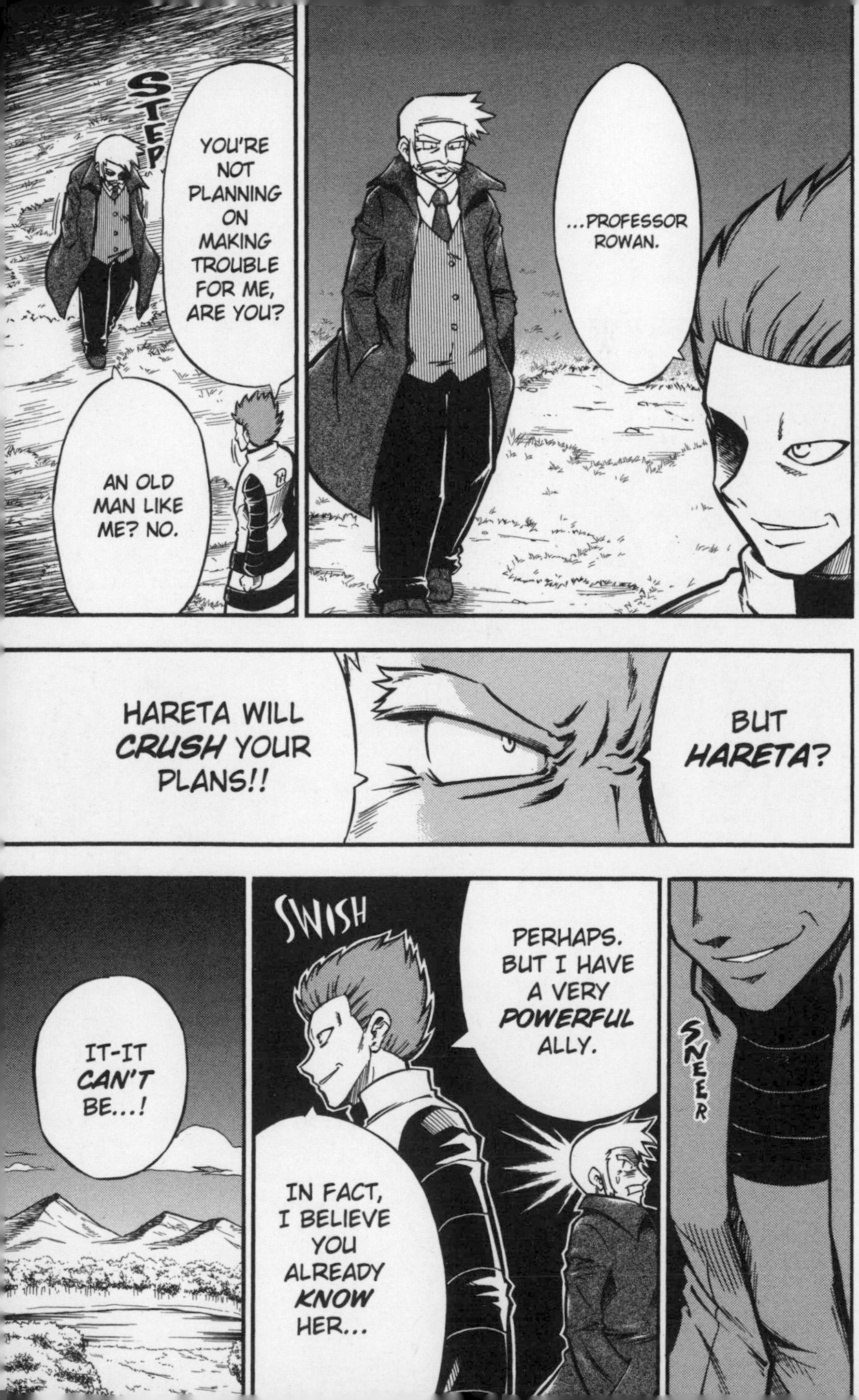
...PROFESSOR ROWAN.
STEP
YOU'RE NOT PLANNING ON MAKING TROUBLE FOR ME, ARE YOU?
AN OLD MAN LIKE ME? NO.
BUT *HARETA*?
HARETA WILL *CRUSH* YOUR PLANS!!
SNEER
SWISH
PERHAPS. BUT I HAVE A VERY *POWERFUL* ALLY.
IN FACT, I BELIEVE YOU ALREADY *KNOW* HER...
IT-IT *CAN'T* BE...!

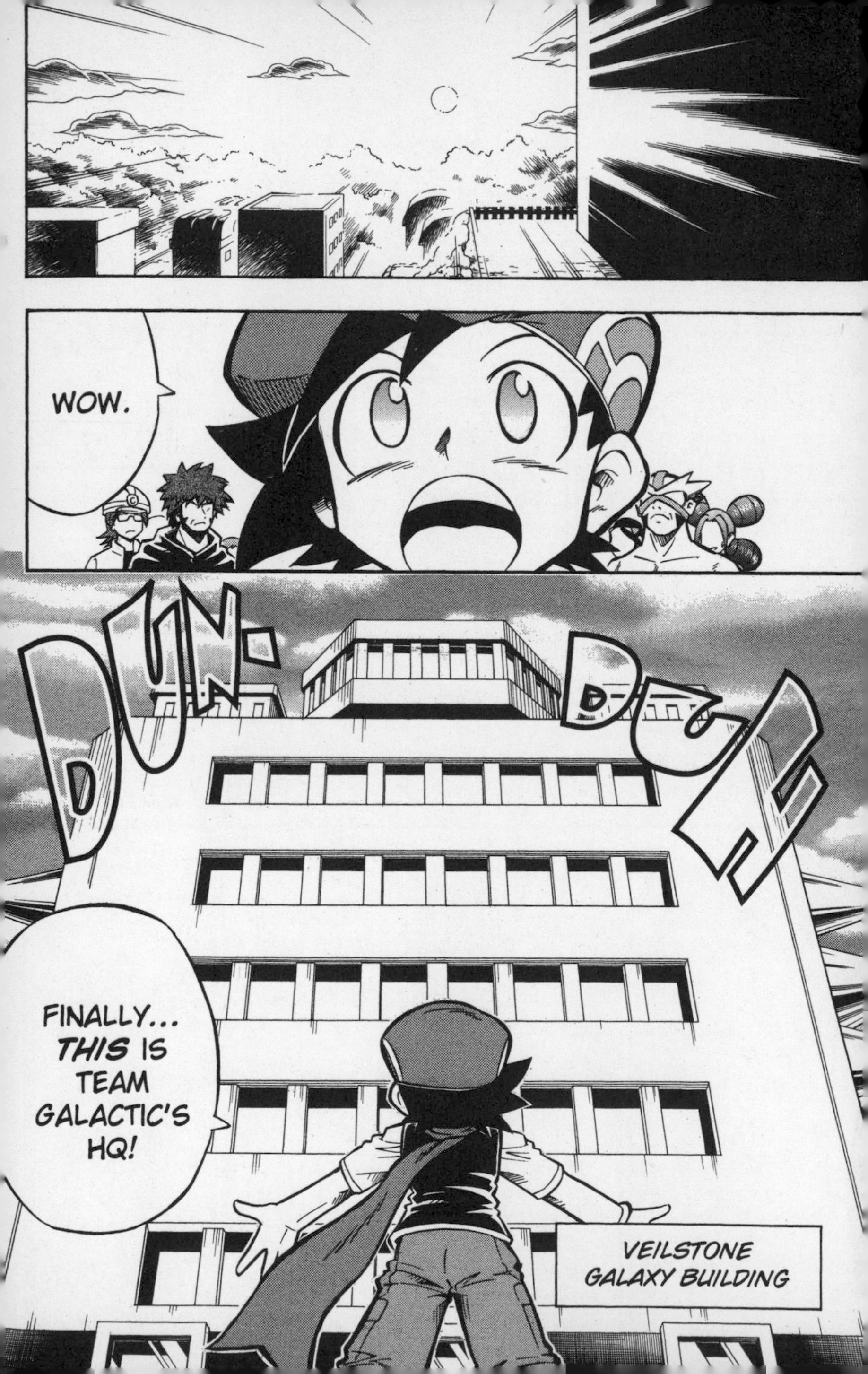
WOW.
DUN-DUN
FINALLY... THIS IS TEAM GALACTIC'S HQ!
VEILSTONE GALAXY BUILDING

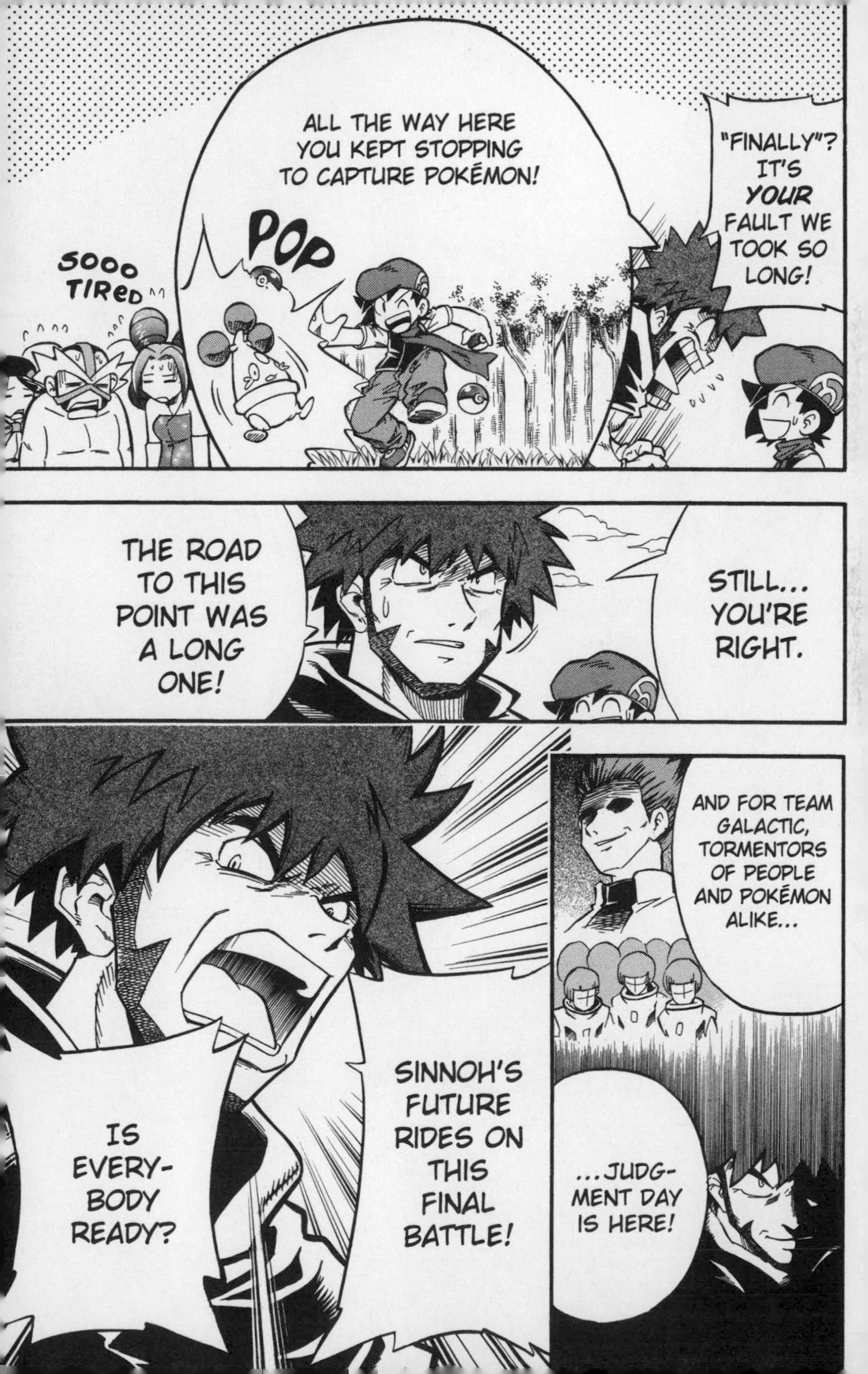
"FINALLY"? IT'S ***YOUR*** FAULT WE TOOK SO LONG!
ALL THE WAY HERE YOU KEPT STOPPING TO CAPTURE POKÉMON!
POP
SOOO TIRED
STILL... YOU'RE RIGHT.
THE ROAD TO THIS POINT WAS A LONG ONE!
AND FOR TEAM GALACTIC, TORMENTORS OF PEOPLE AND POKÉMON ALIKE...
...JUDG-MENT DAY IS HERE!
SINNOH'S FUTURE RIDES ON THIS FINAL BATTLE!
IS EVERY-BODY READY?

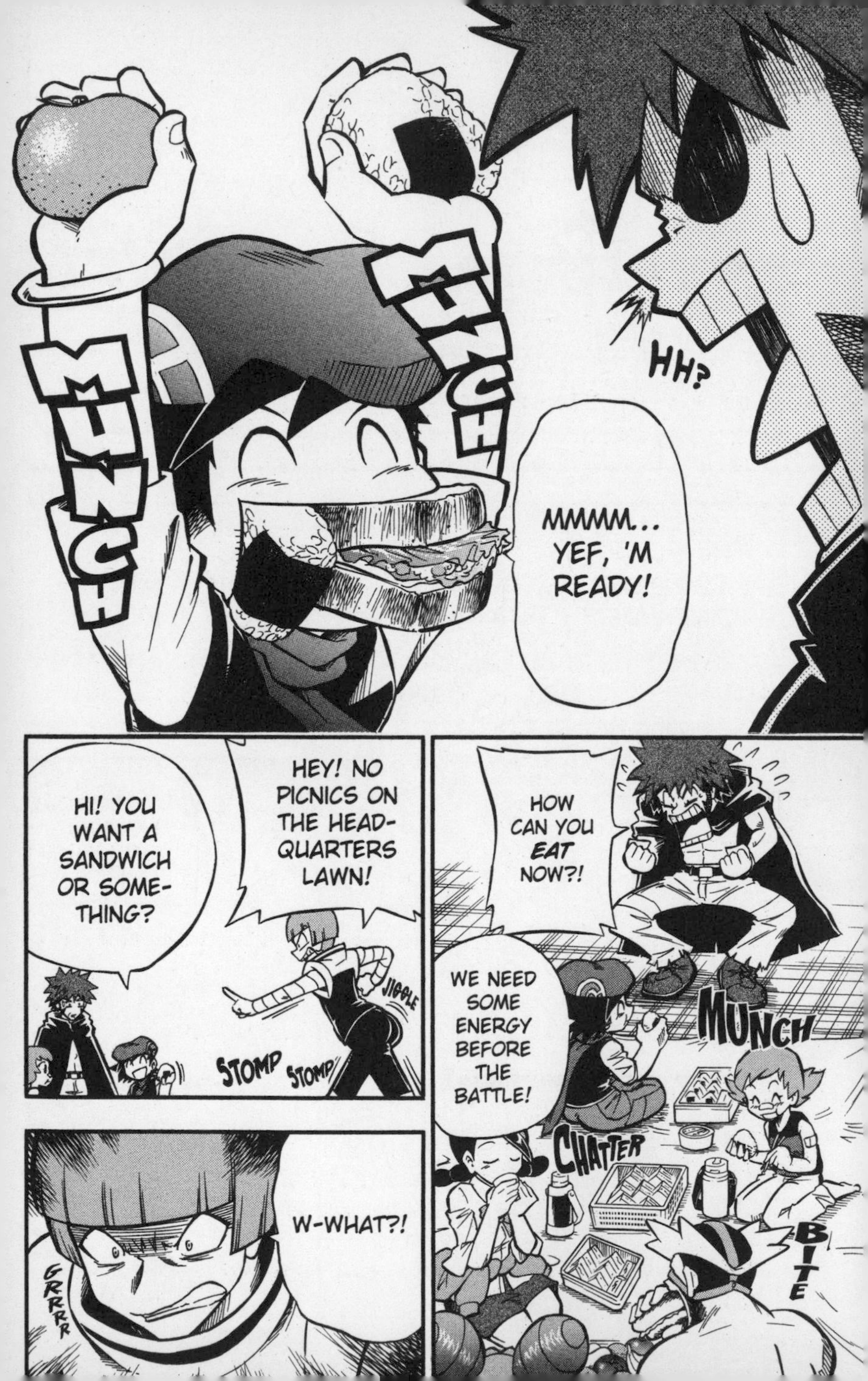
HH?
MMMM... YEF, 'M READY!
MUNCH
MUNCH
HOW CAN YOU EAT NOW?!
WE NEED SOME ENERGY BEFORE THE BATTLE!
MUNCH
CHATTER
BITE
HEY! NO PICNICS ON THE HEAD-QUARTERS LAWN!
HI! YOU WANT A SANDWICH OR SOME-THING?
JIGGLE
STOMP STOMP
W-WHAT?!
GRRRR

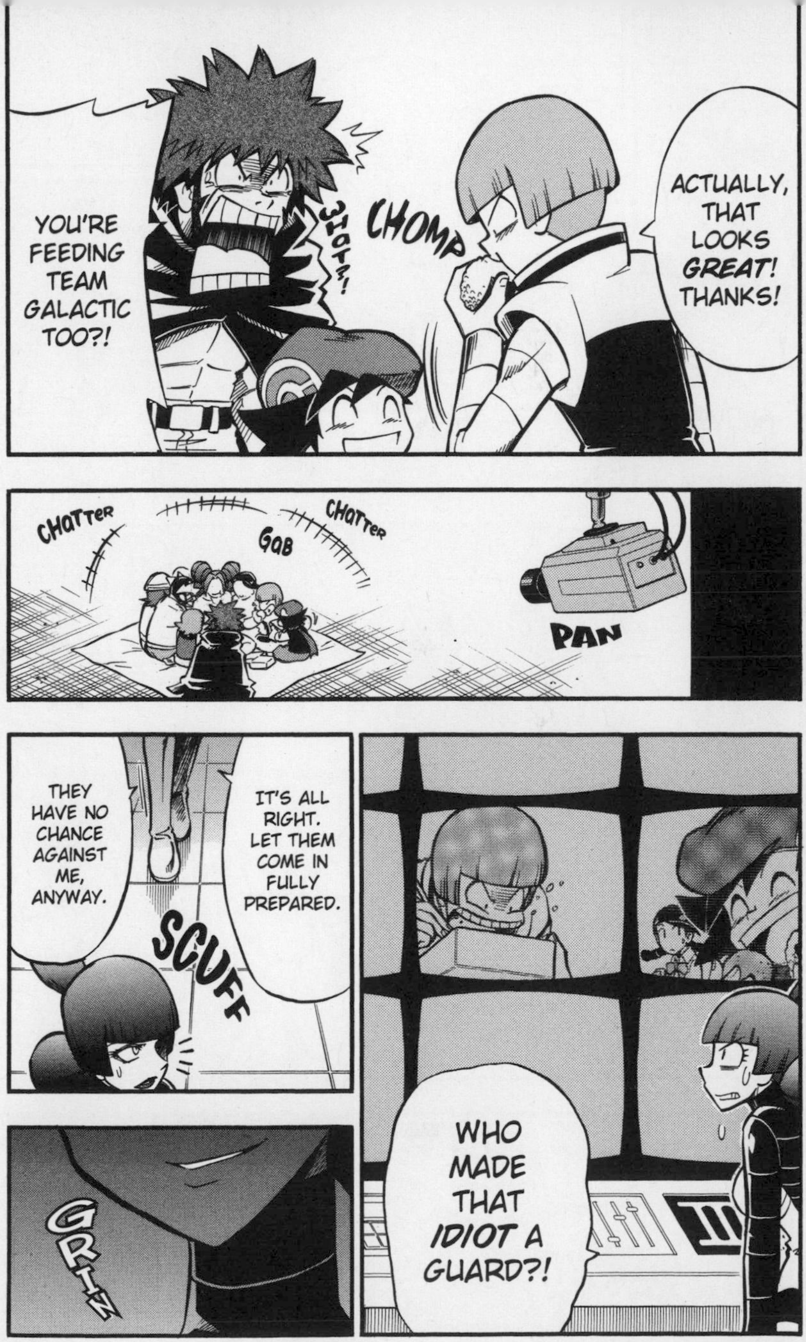
ACTUALLY, THAT LOOKS *GREAT*! THANKS!
CHOMP
WHAT?!
YOU'RE FEEDING TEAM GALACTIC TOO?!
PAN
CHATTER
GAB
CHATTER
WHO MADE THAT *IDIOT* A GUARD?!
IT'S ALL RIGHT. LET THEM COME IN FULLY PREPARED.
THEY HAVE NO CHANCE AGAINST ME, ANYWAY.
SCUFF
GRIN

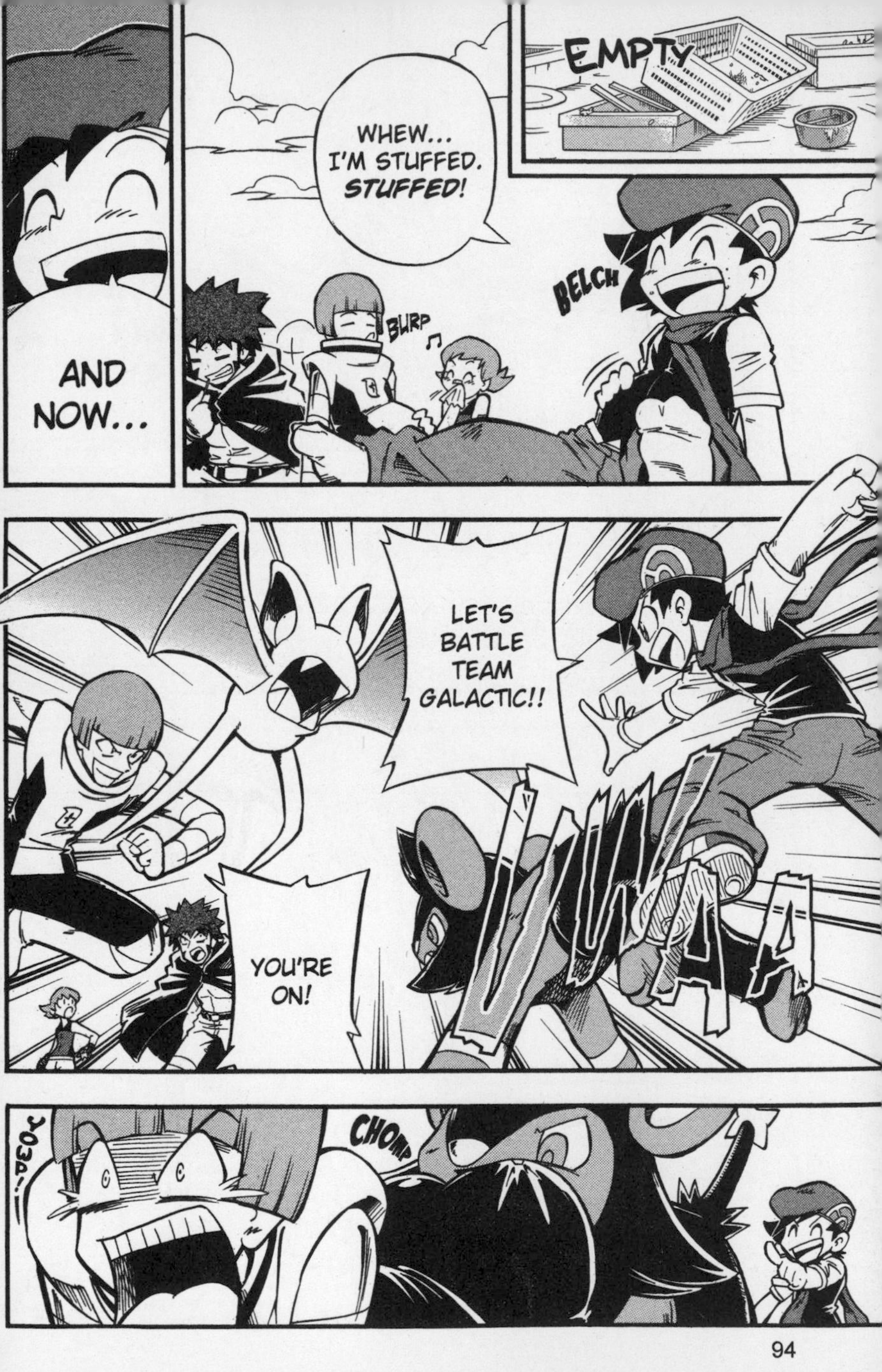

EMPTY
BELCH
WHEW... I'M STUFFED. STUFFED!
BURP ♪
AND NOW...
LET'S BATTLE TEAM GALACTIC!!
YOU'RE ON!
CHOMP
YOWP!!

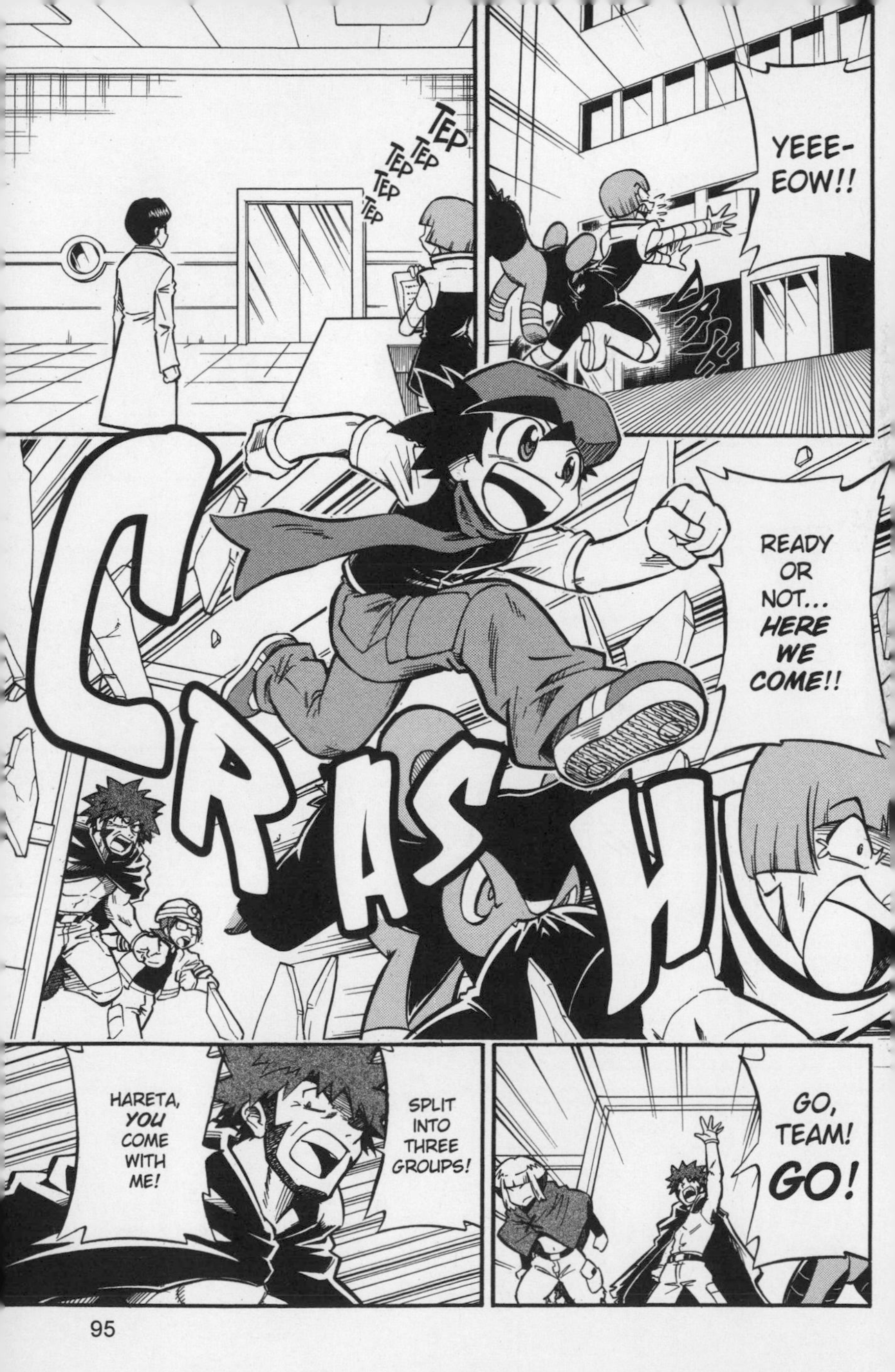
YEEE-EOW!!
DASH
TEP TEP TEP TEP TEP
READY OR NOT... HERE WE COME!!
CRASH
GO, TEAM! GO!
SPLIT INTO THREE GROUPS!
HARETA, YOU COME WITH ME!

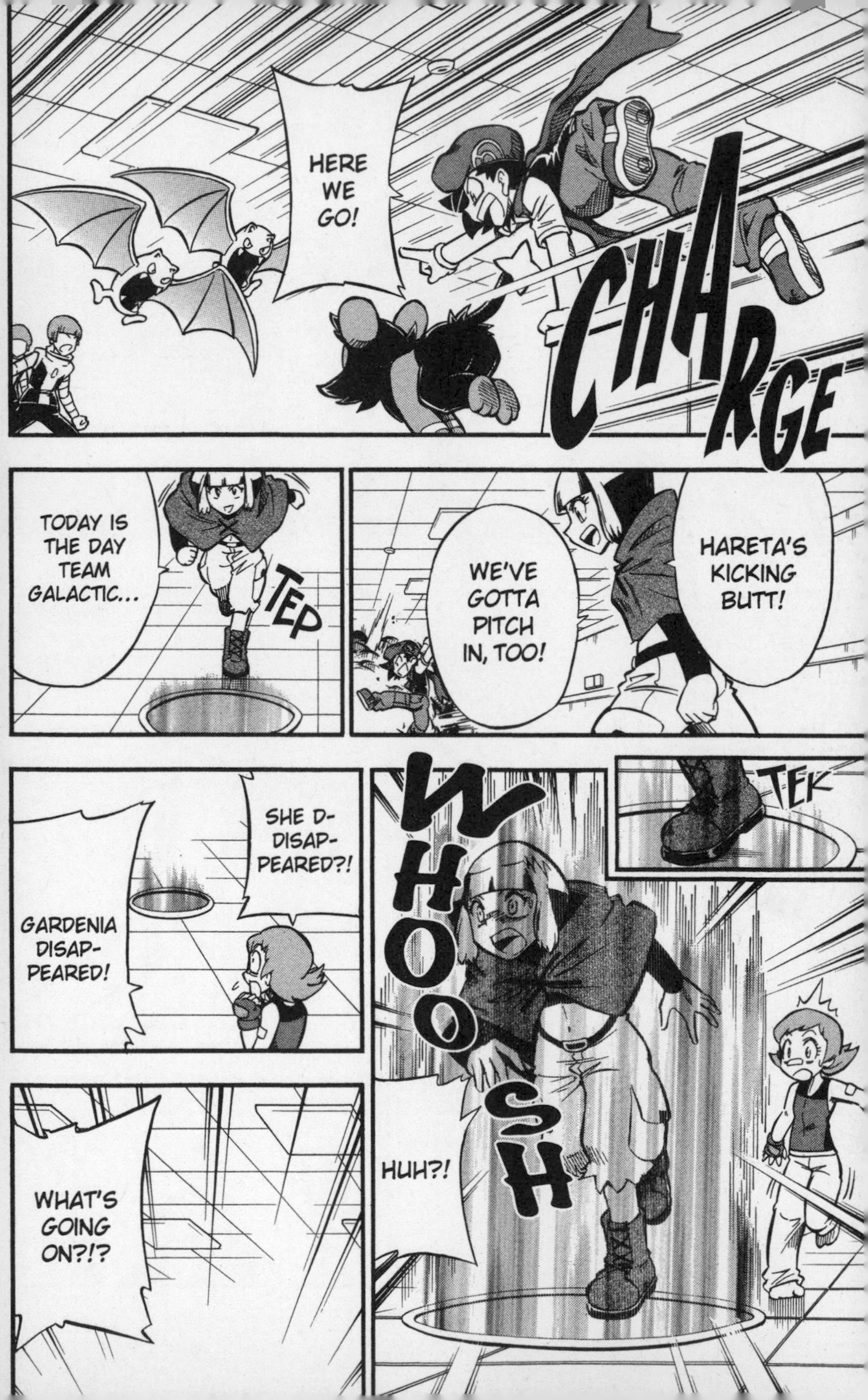
HERE WE GO!
CHARGE
HARETA'S KICKING BUTT!
WE'VE GOTTA PITCH IN, TOO!
TODAY IS THE DAY TEAM GALACTIC...
TEP
TEK
WHOOSH
HUH?!
SHE D-DISAP-PEARED?!
GARDENIA DISAP-PEARED!
WHAT'S GOING ON?!?

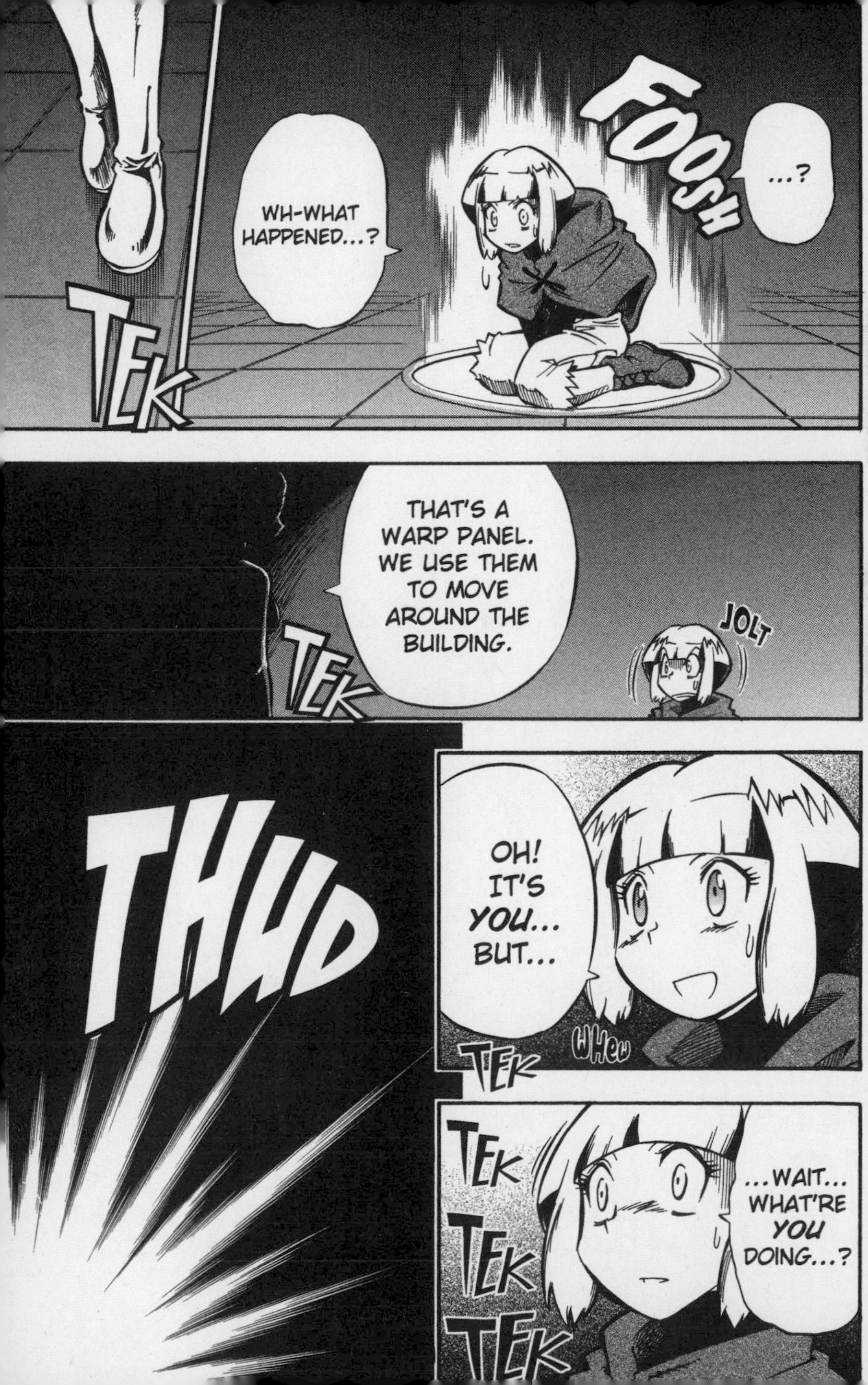
...?
FOOSH
WH-WHAT HAPPENED...?
TEK
JOLT
THAT'S A WARP PANEL. WE USE THEM TO MOVE AROUND THE BUILDING.
TEK
OH! IT'S *YOU*... BUT...
WHEW
TEK
...WAIT... WHAT'RE *YOU* DOING...?
TEK
TEK
TEK
THUD

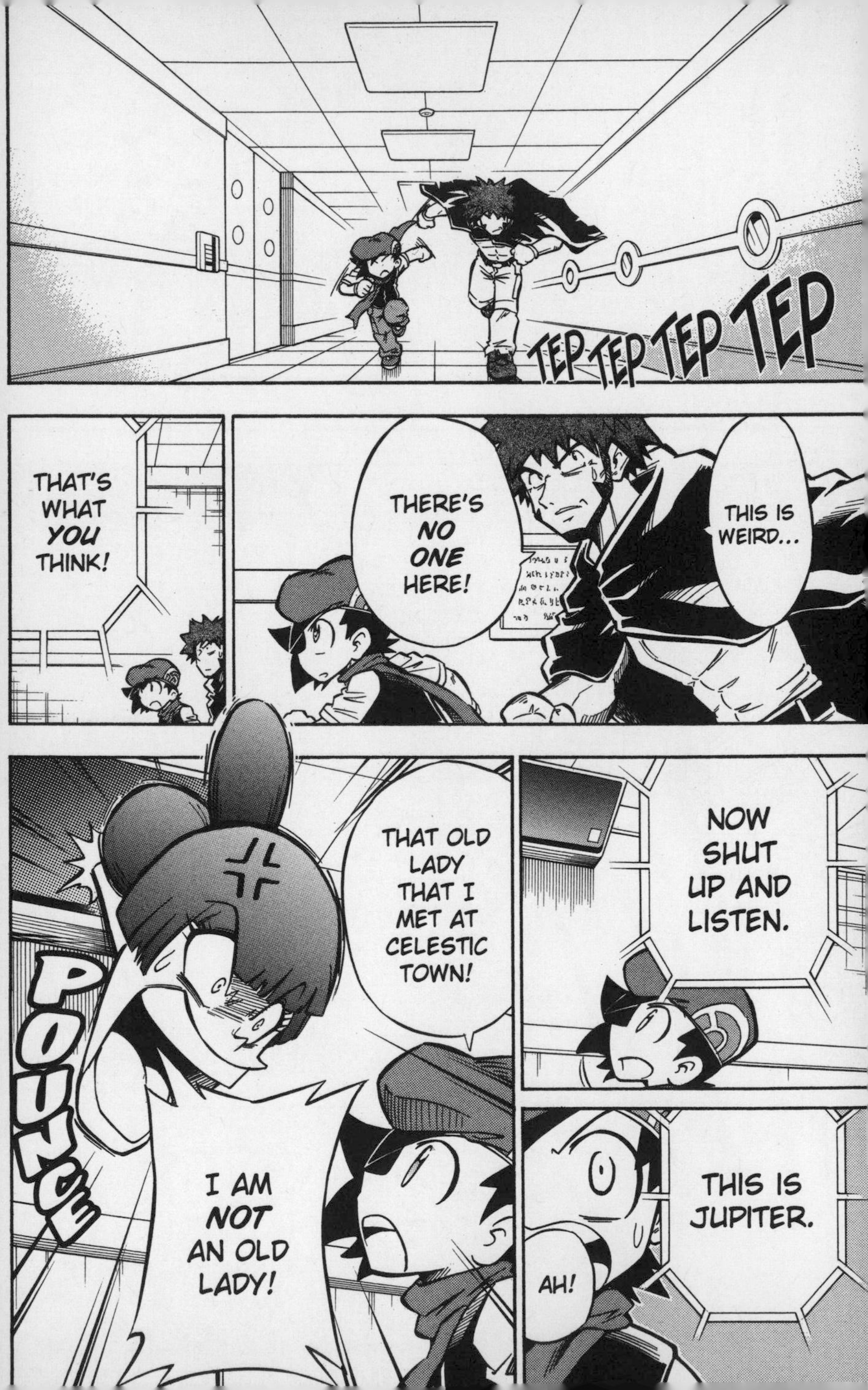
TEP TEP TEP TEP
THIS IS WEIRD...
THERE'S *NO ONE* HERE!
THAT'S WHAT *YOU* THINK!
NOW SHUT UP AND LISTEN.
THIS IS JUPITER.
AH!
THAT OLD LADY THAT I MET AT CELESTIC TOWN!
POUNCE
I AM *NOT* AN OLD LADY!

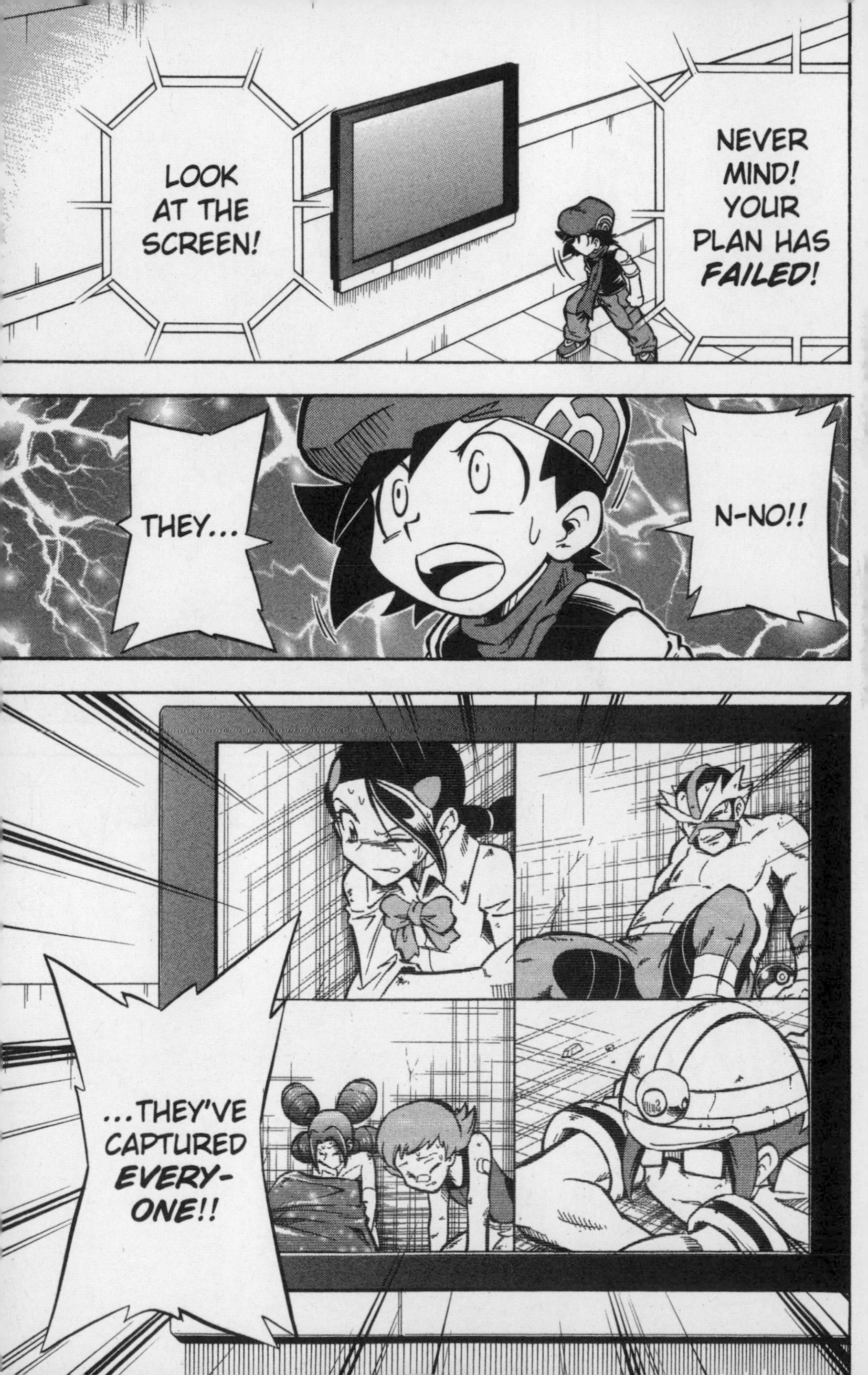
NEVER MIND! YOUR PLAN HAS FAILED!
LOOK AT THE SCREEN!
N-NO!!
THEY...
...THEY'VE CAPTURED EVERY-ONE!!

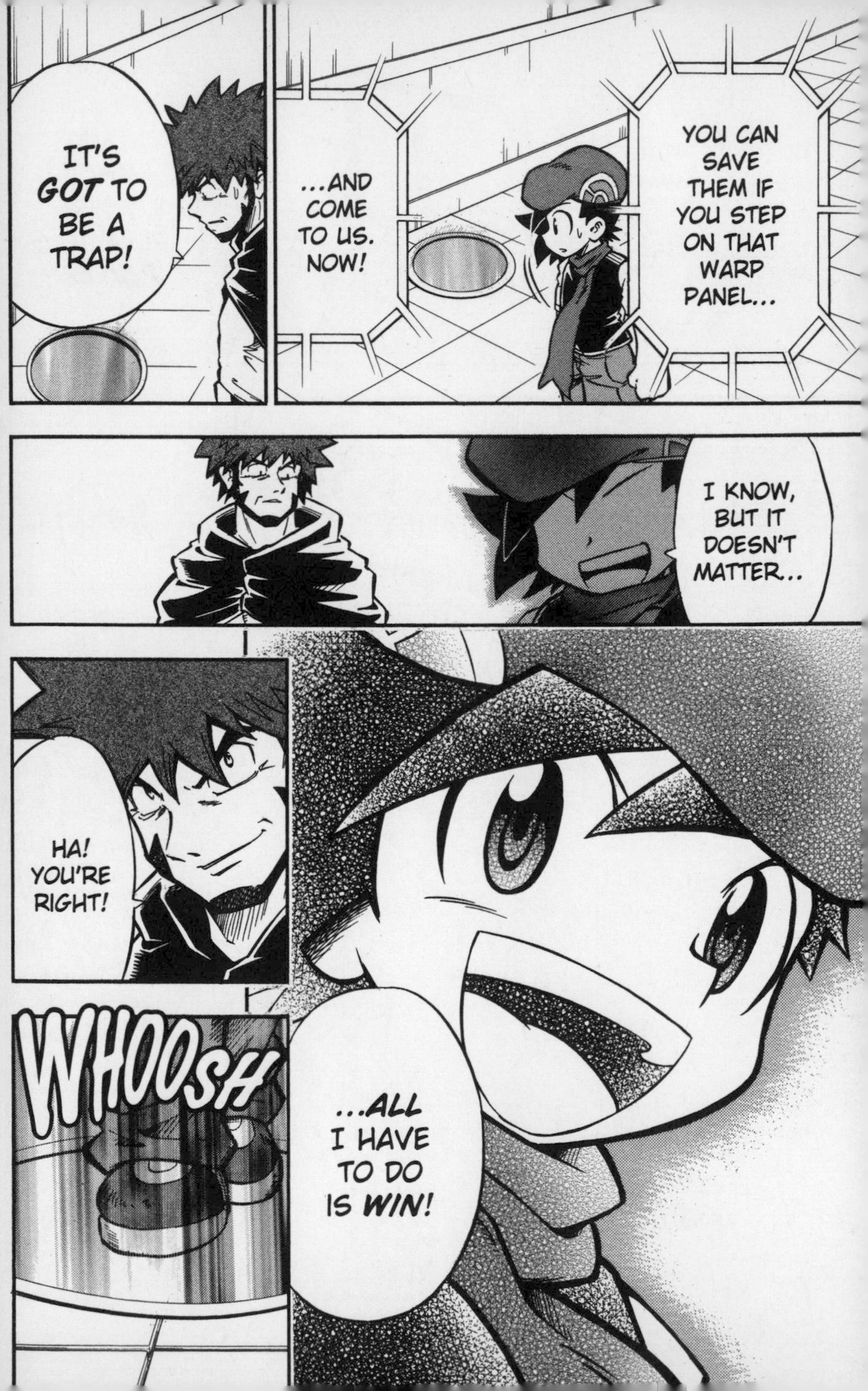
YOU CAN SAVE THEM IF YOU STEP ON THAT WARP PANEL...
...AND COME TO US. NOW!
IT'S GOT TO BE A TRAP!
I KNOW, BUT IT DOESN'T MATTER...
...ALL I HAVE TO DO IS WIN!
HA! YOU'RE RIGHT!
WHOOSH

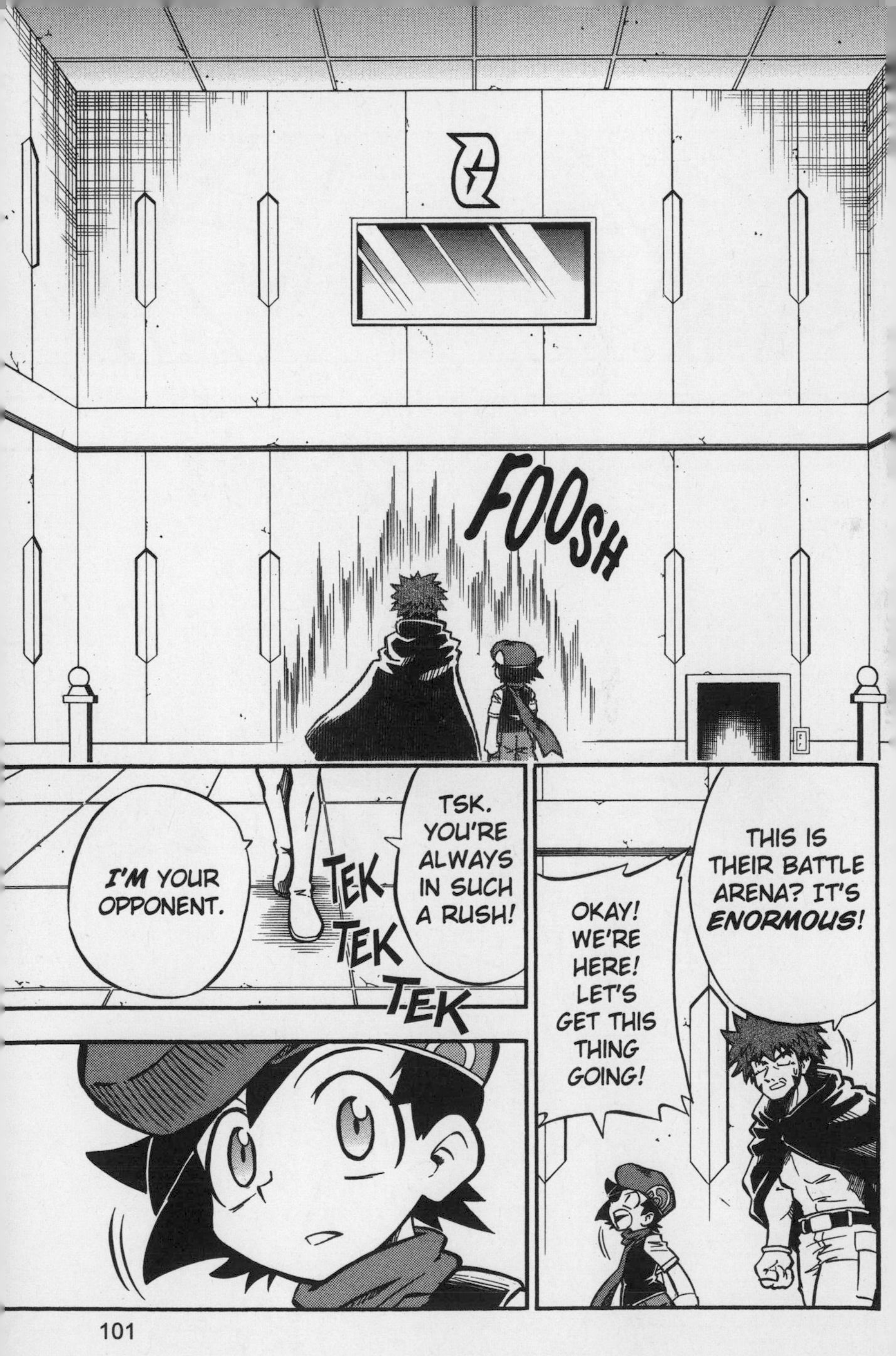
FOOSH
THIS IS THEIR BATTLE ARENA? IT'S ENORMOUS!
OKAY! WE'RE HERE! LET'S GET THIS THING GOING!
TSK. YOU'RE ALWAYS IN SUCH A RUSH!
TEK TEK TEK
I'M YOUR OPPONENT.

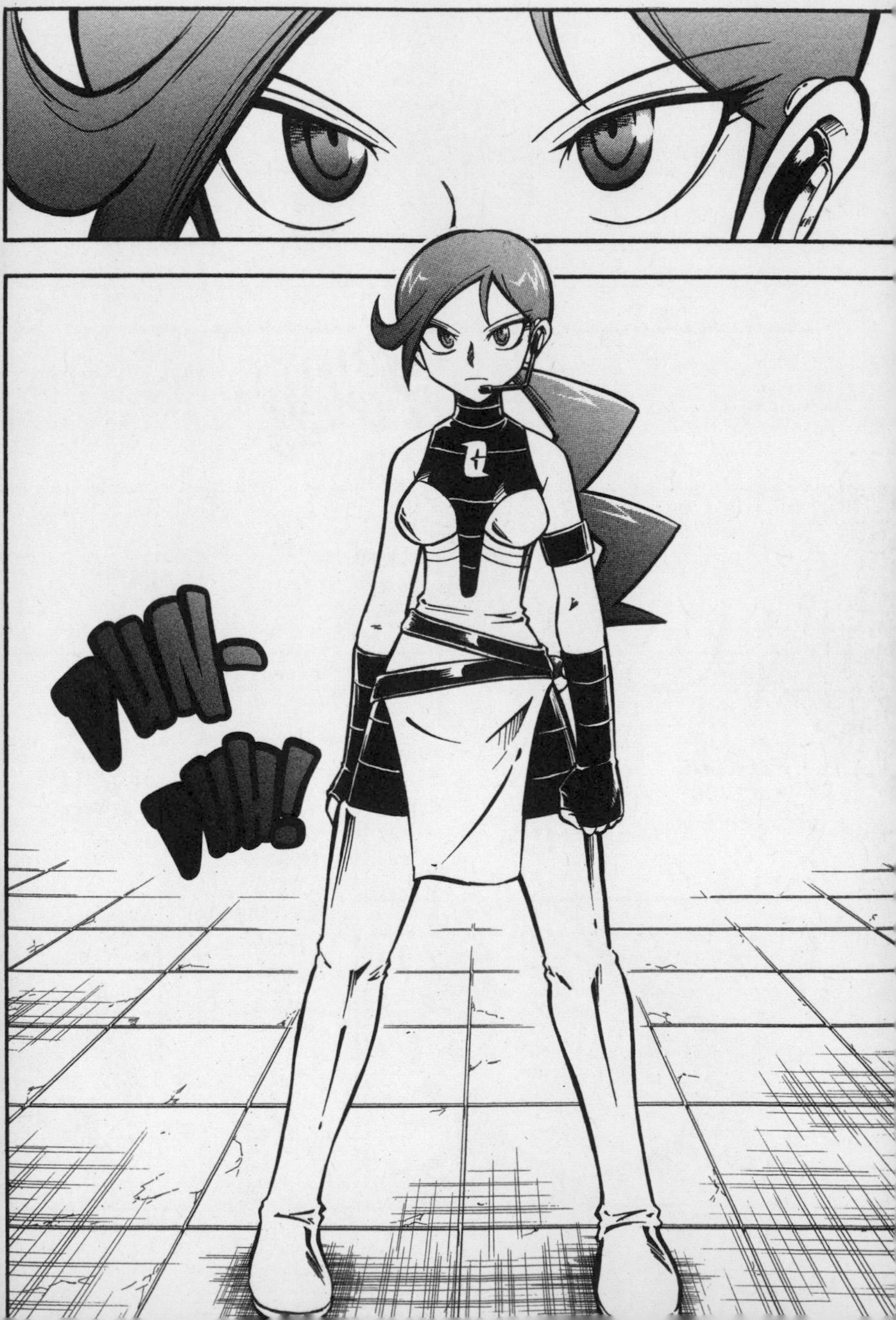

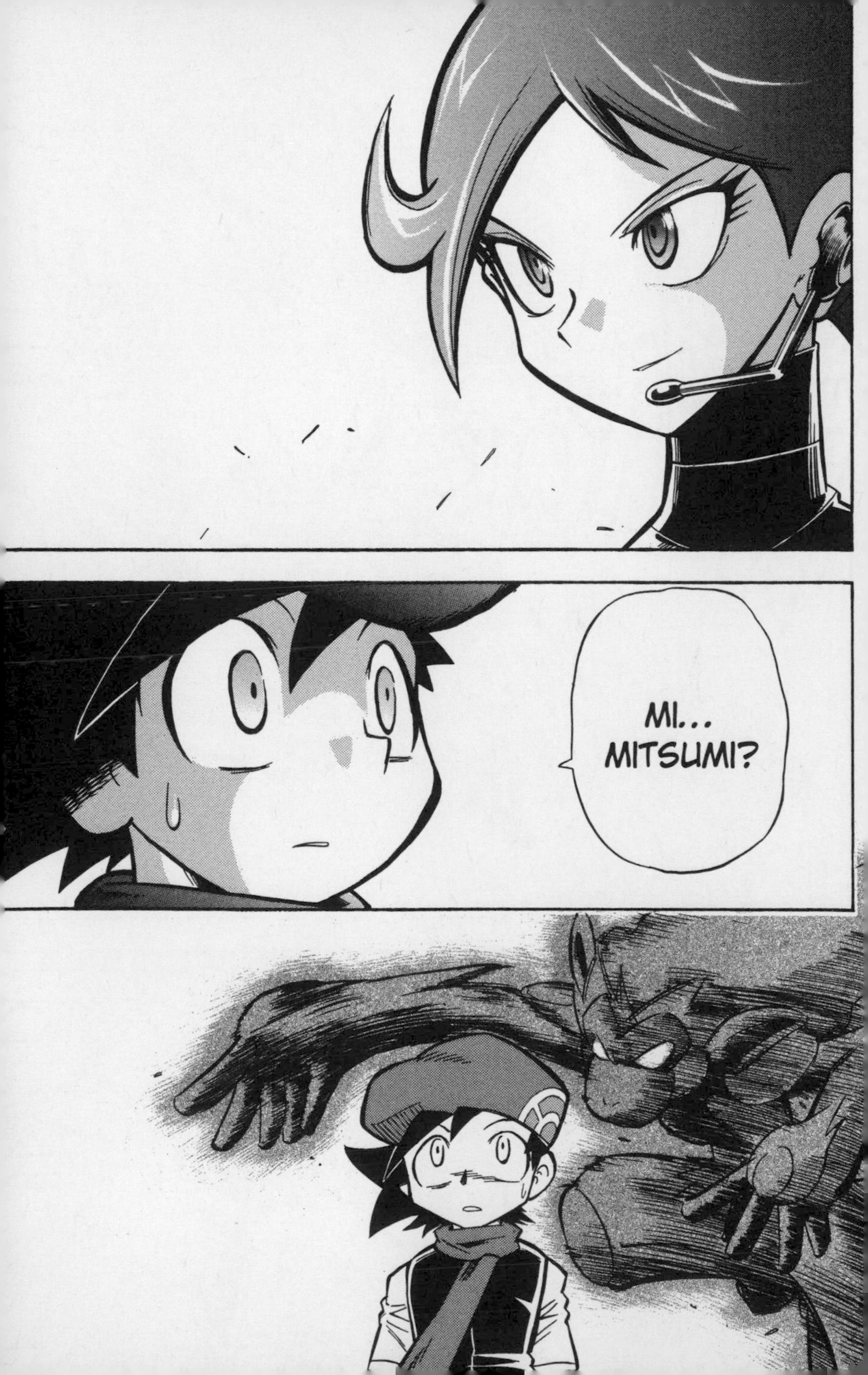
MI... MITSUMI?

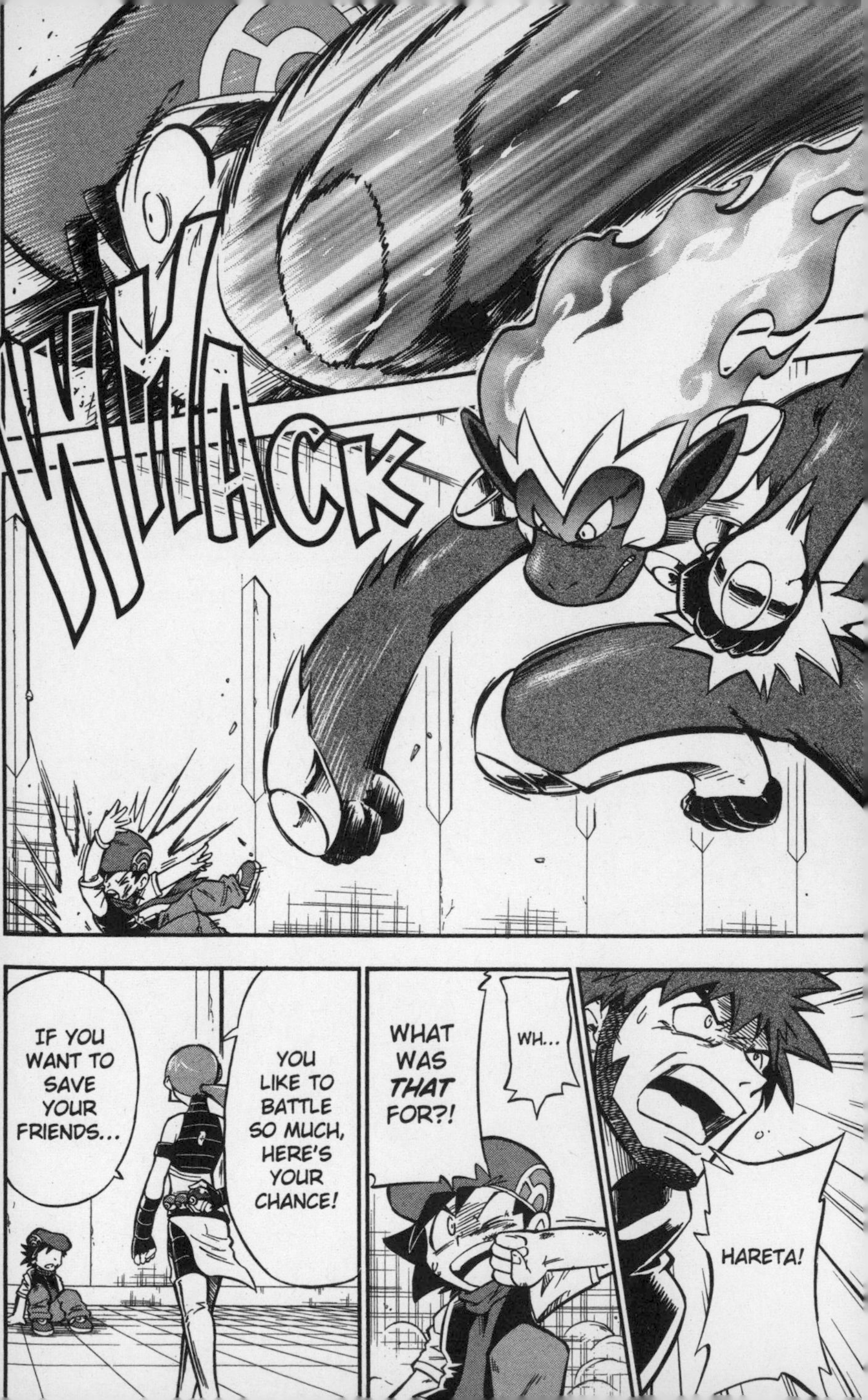
WHACK
HARETA!
WH...
WHAT WAS *THAT* FOR?!
YOU LIKE TO BATTLE SO MUCH, HERE'S YOUR CHANCE!
IF YOU WANT TO SAVE YOUR FRIENDS...

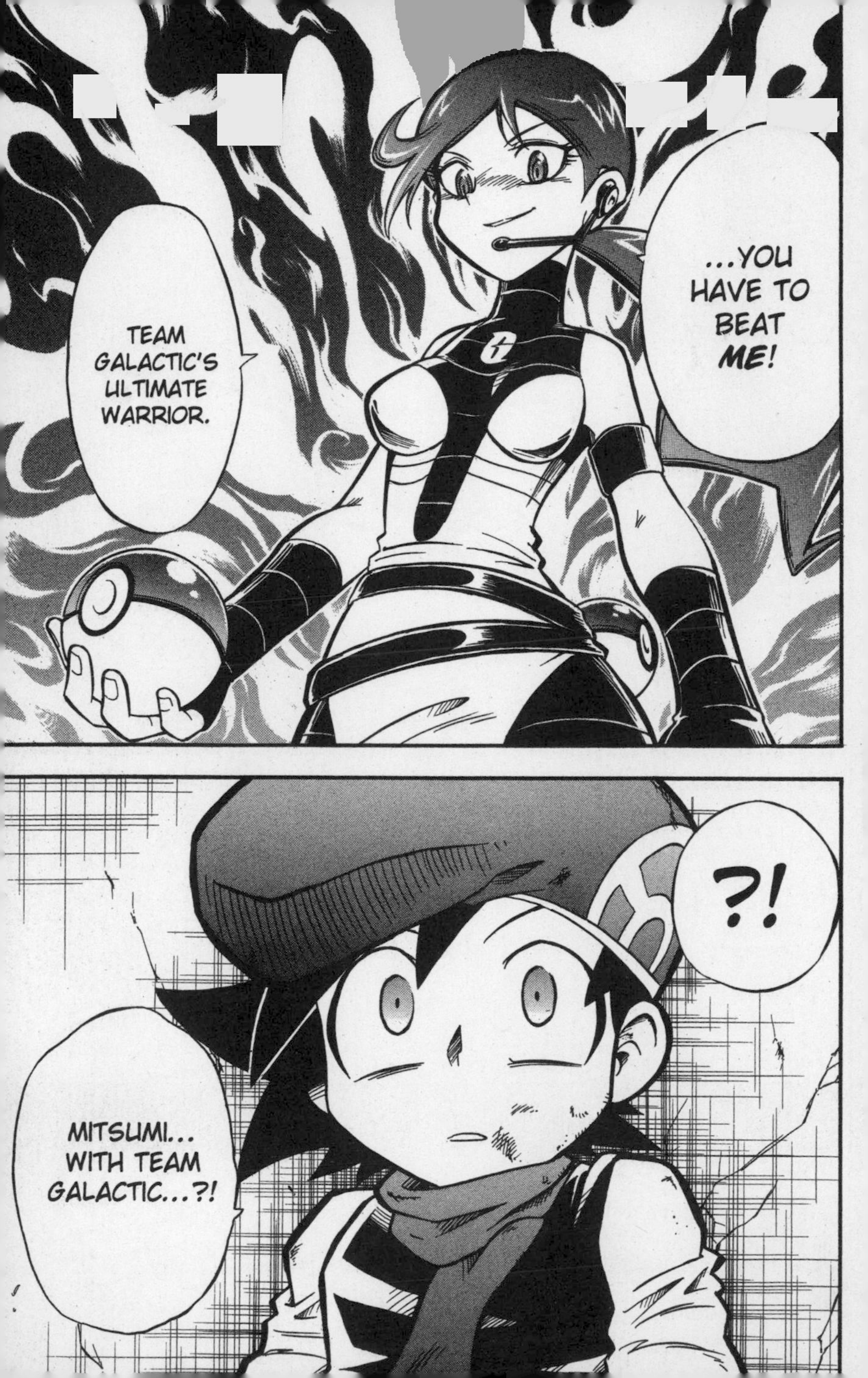
...YOU HAVE TO BEAT ME!
TEAM GALACTIC'S ULTIMATE WARRIOR.
?!
MITSUMI... WITH TEAM GALACTIC...?!

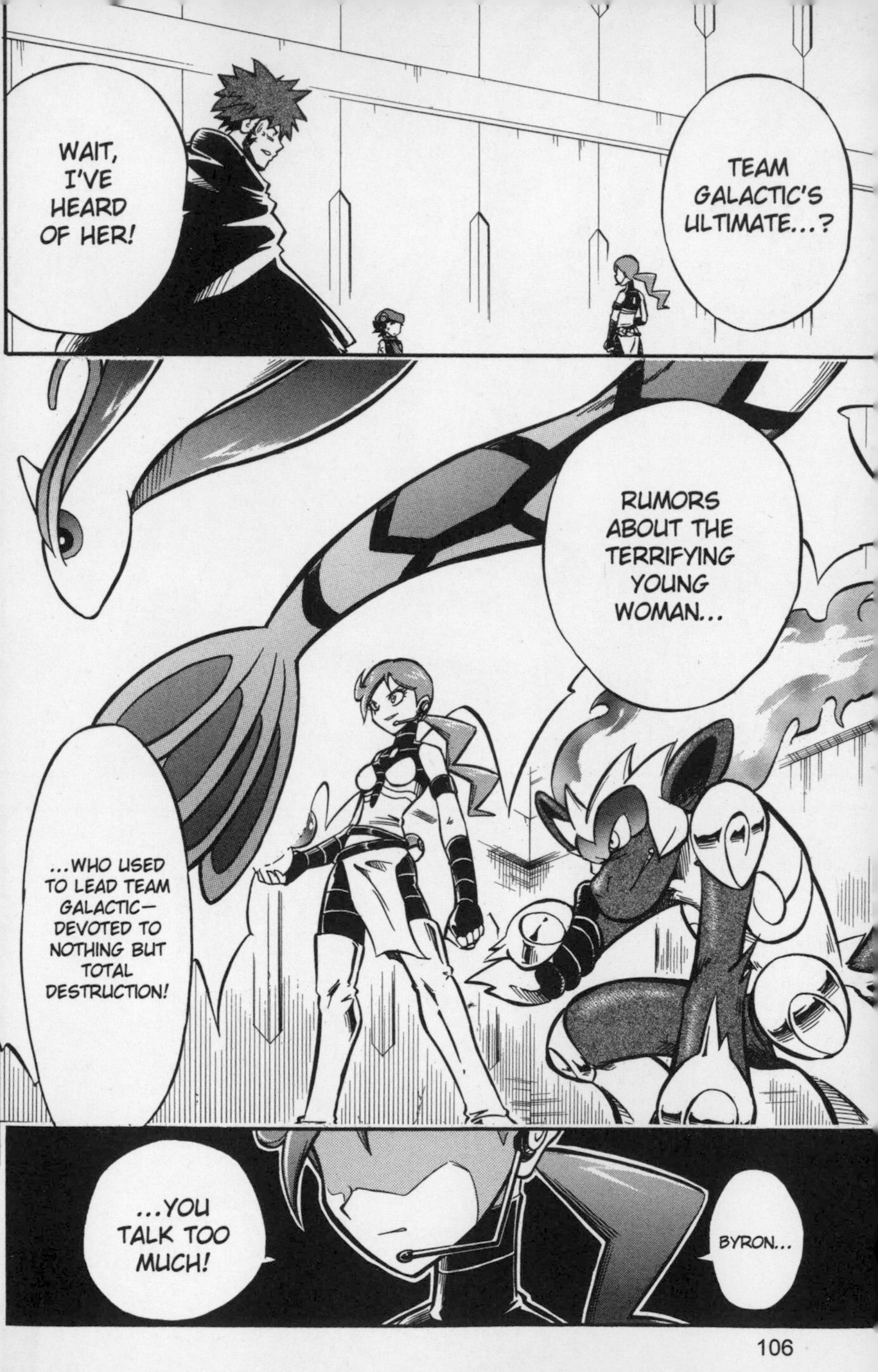
TEAM GALACTIC'S ULTIMATE...?
WAIT, I'VE HEARD OF HER!
RUMORS ABOUT THE TERRIFYING YOUNG WOMAN...
...WHO USED TO LEAD TEAM GALACTIC—DEVOTED TO NOTHING BUT TOTAL DESTRUCTION!
BYRON...
...YOU TALK TOO MUCH!

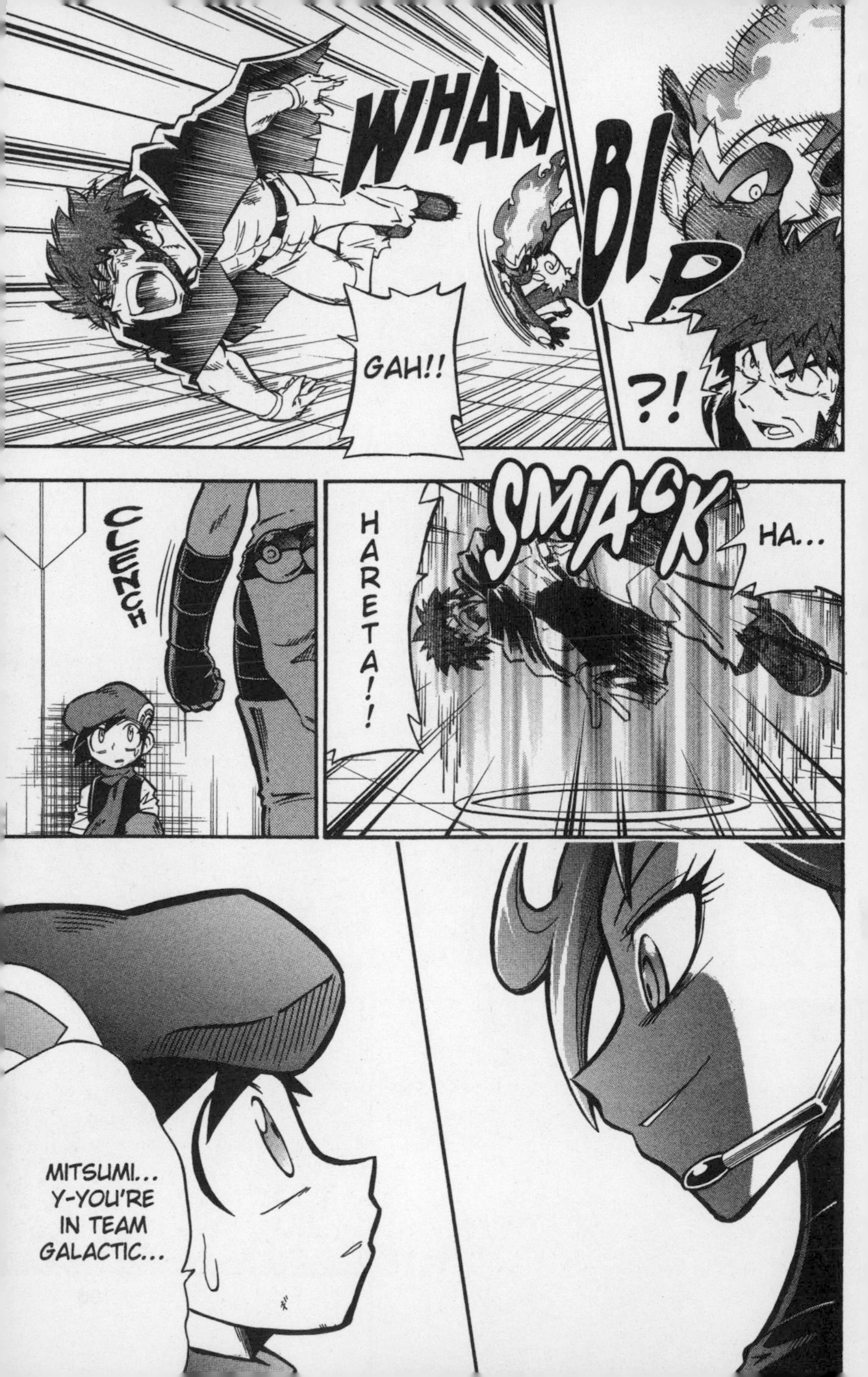
BIP
?!
WHAM
GAH!!
SMACK
HA...
HARETA!!
CLENCH
MITSUMI... Y-YOU'RE IN TEAM GALACTIC...

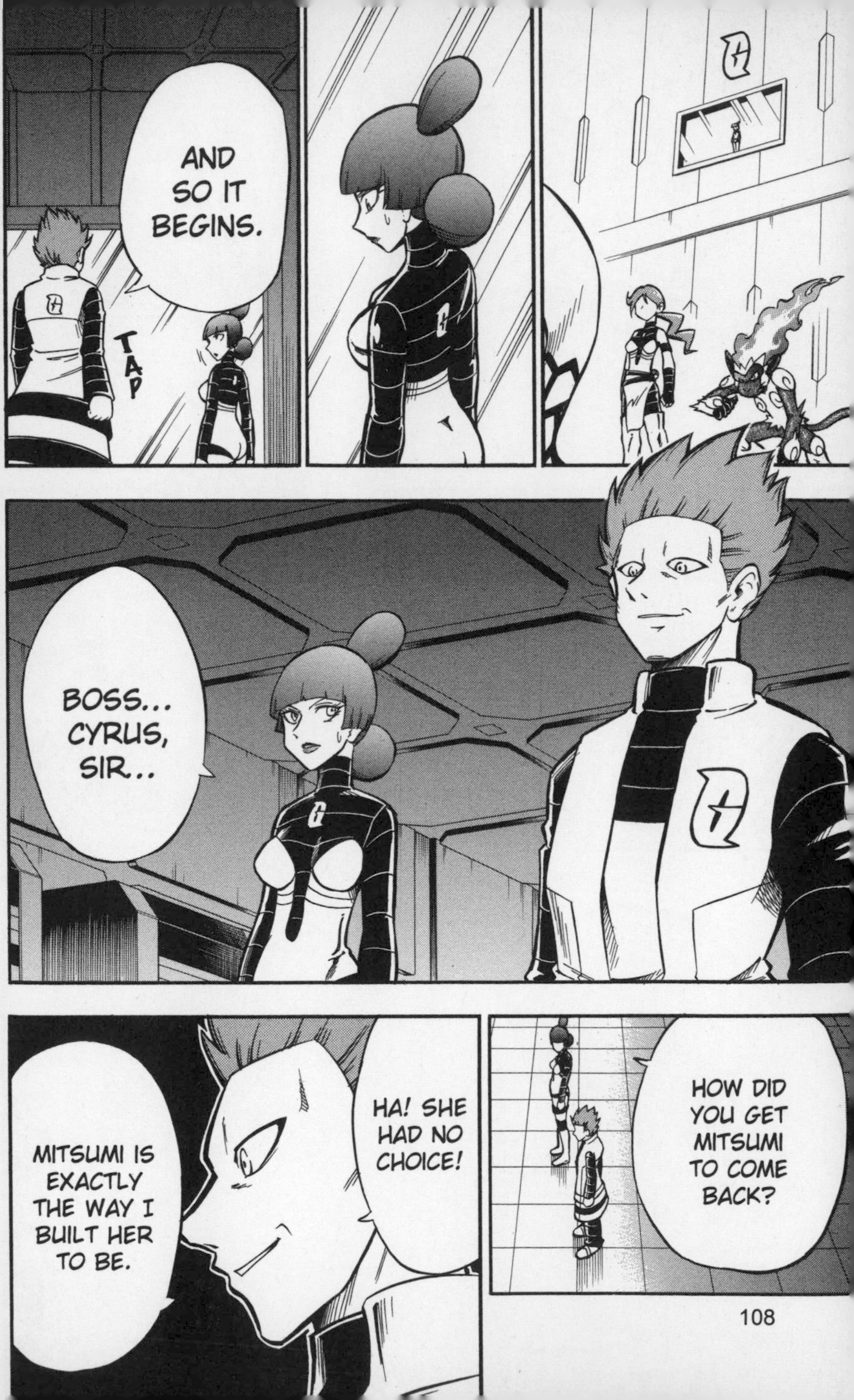
AND SO IT BEGINS.
TAP
BOSS... CYRUS, SIR...
HOW DID YOU GET MITSUMI TO COME BACK?
HA! SHE HAD NO CHOICE!
MITSUMI IS EXACTLY THE WAY I BUILT HER TO BE.

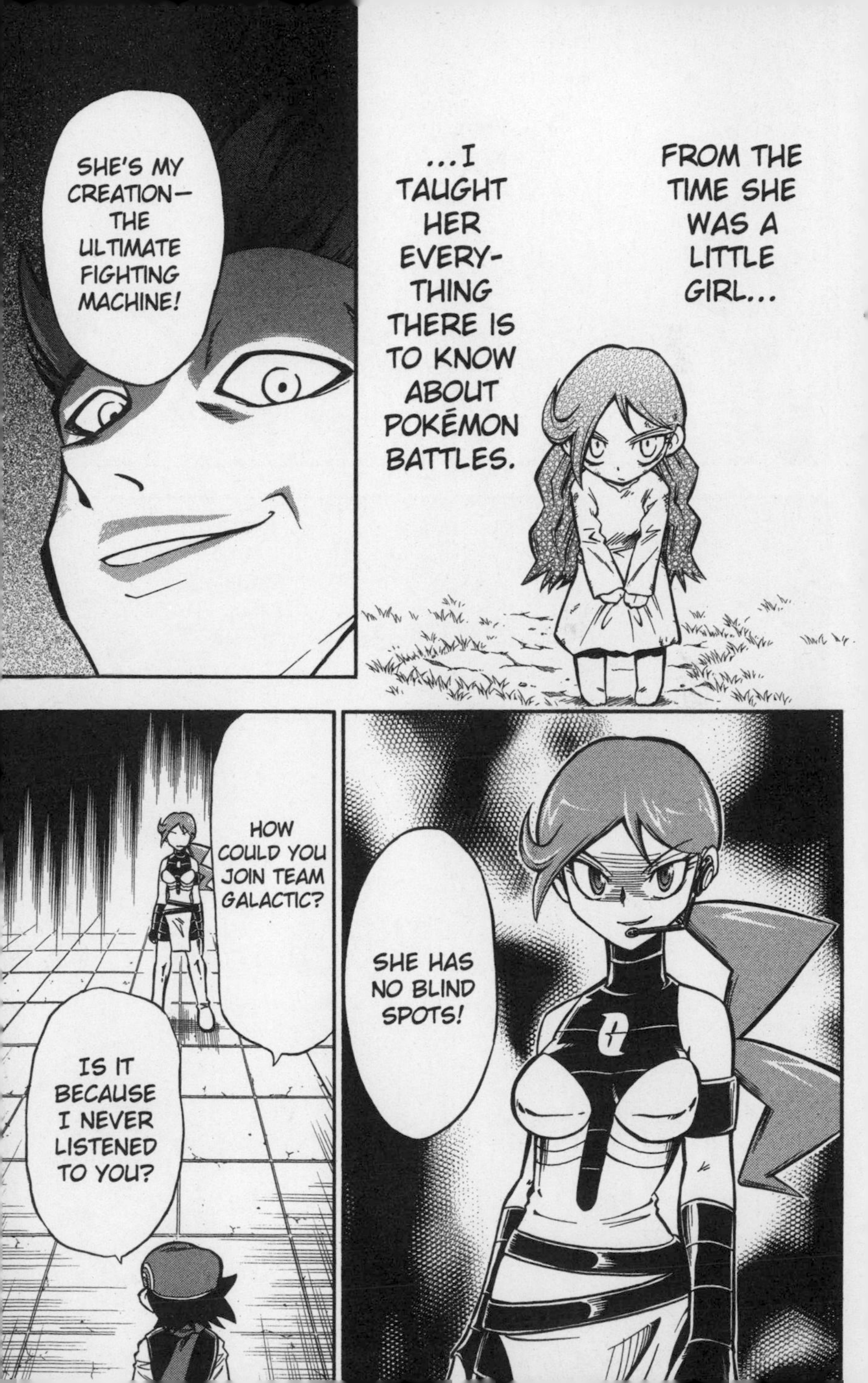
FROM THE TIME SHE WAS A LITTLE GIRL...
...I TAUGHT HER EVERYTHING THERE IS TO KNOW ABOUT POKÉMON BATTLES.
SHE'S MY CREATION—THE ULTIMATE FIGHTING MACHINE!
SHE HAS NO BLIND SPOTS!
HOW COULD YOU JOIN TEAM GALACTIC?
IS IT BECAUSE I NEVER LISTENED TO YOU?

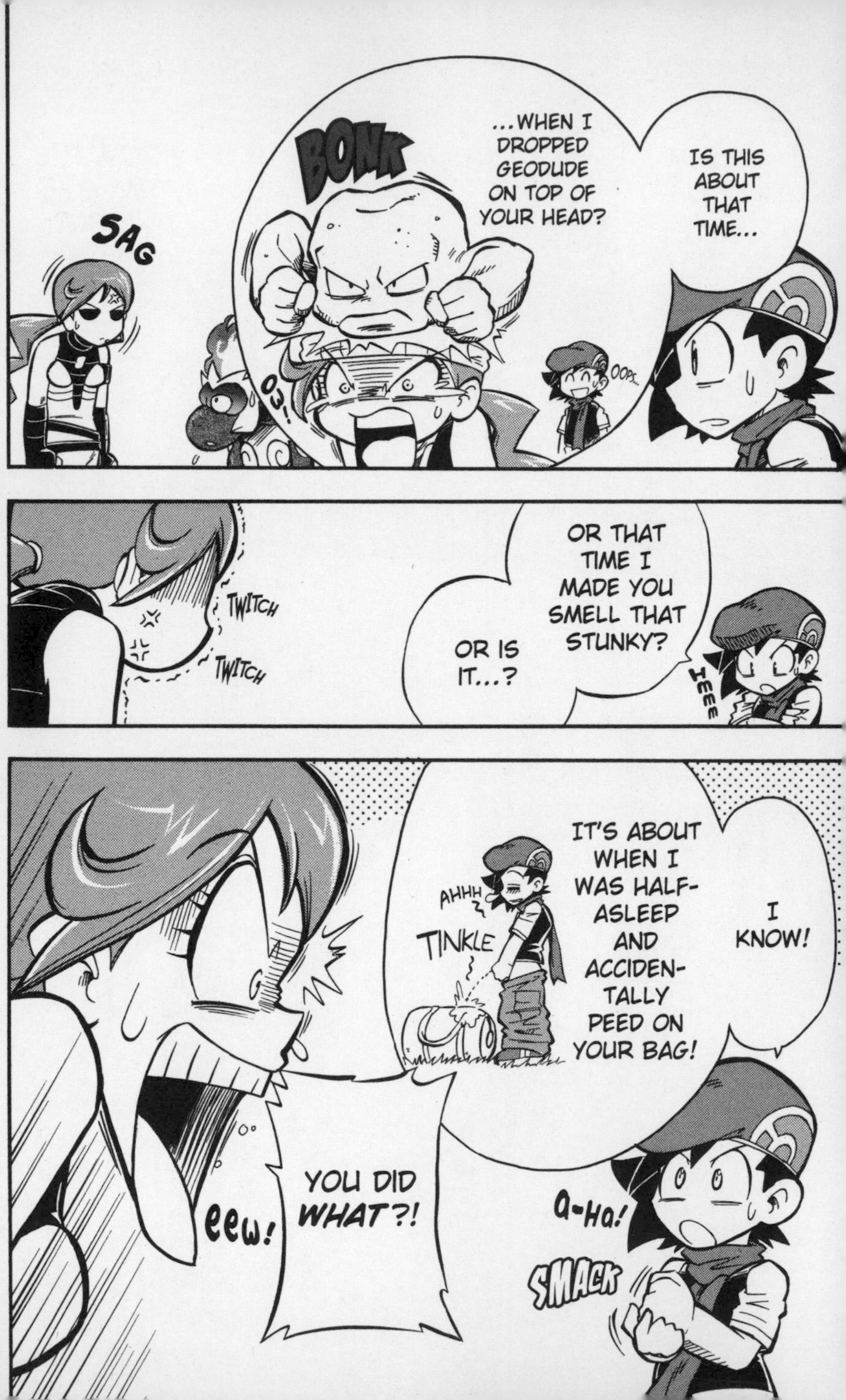
IS THIS ABOUT THAT TIME...
...WHEN I DROPPED GEODUDE ON TOP OF YOUR HEAD?
BONK
OOPS...
O3!
SAG
OR THAT TIME I MADE YOU SMELL THAT STUNKY?
OR IS IT...?
HEEE
TWITCH
TWITCH
I KNOW!
IT'S ABOUT WHEN I WAS HALF-ASLEEP AND ACCIDENTALLY PEED ON YOUR BAG!
AHHH
TINKLE
A-HA!
SMACK
YOU DID *WHAT*?!
EEW!

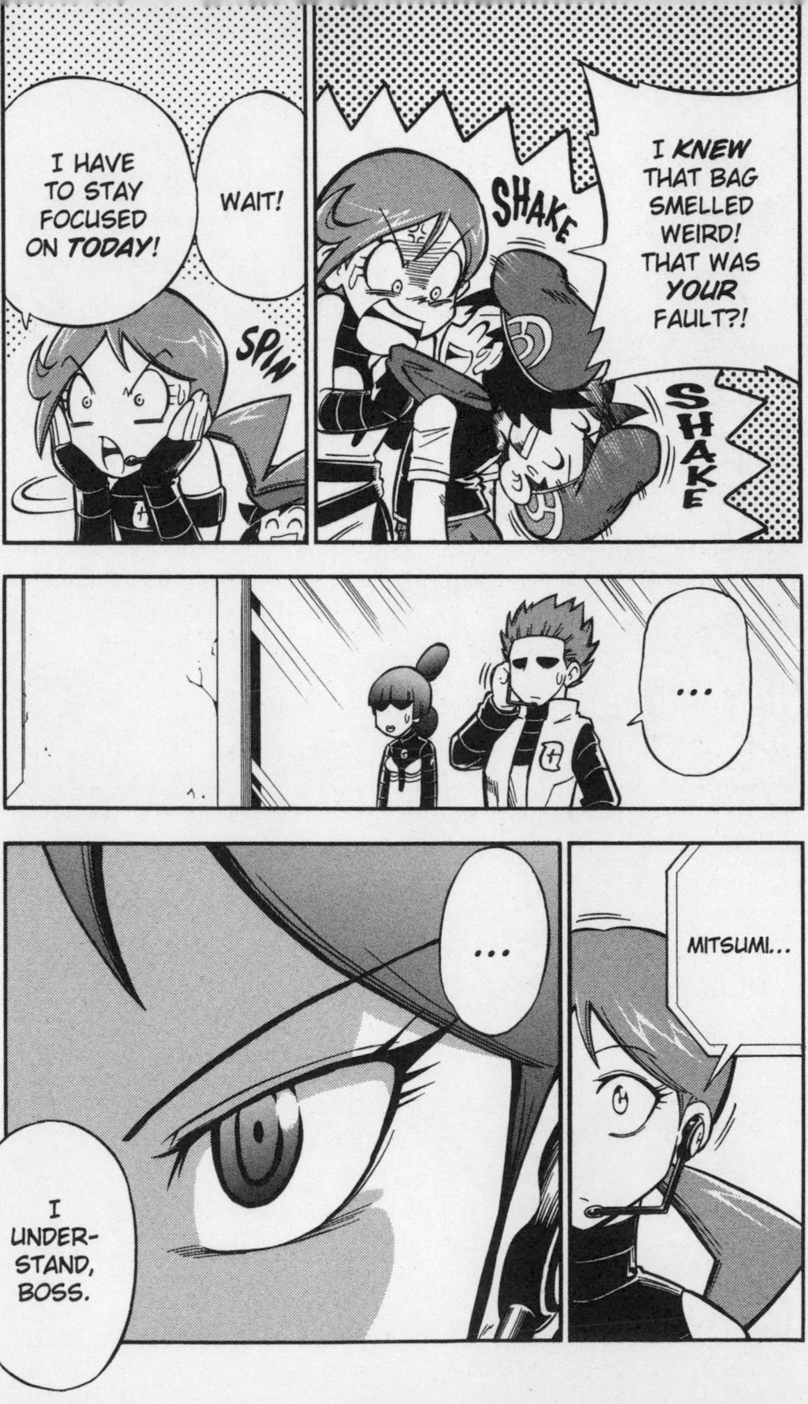
I KNEW THAT BAG SMELLED WEIRD! THAT WAS YOUR FAULT?!
SHAKE
SHAKE
WAIT!
I HAVE TO STAY FOCUSED ON TODAY!
SPIN
...
MITSUMI...
...
I UNDER-STAND, BOSS.

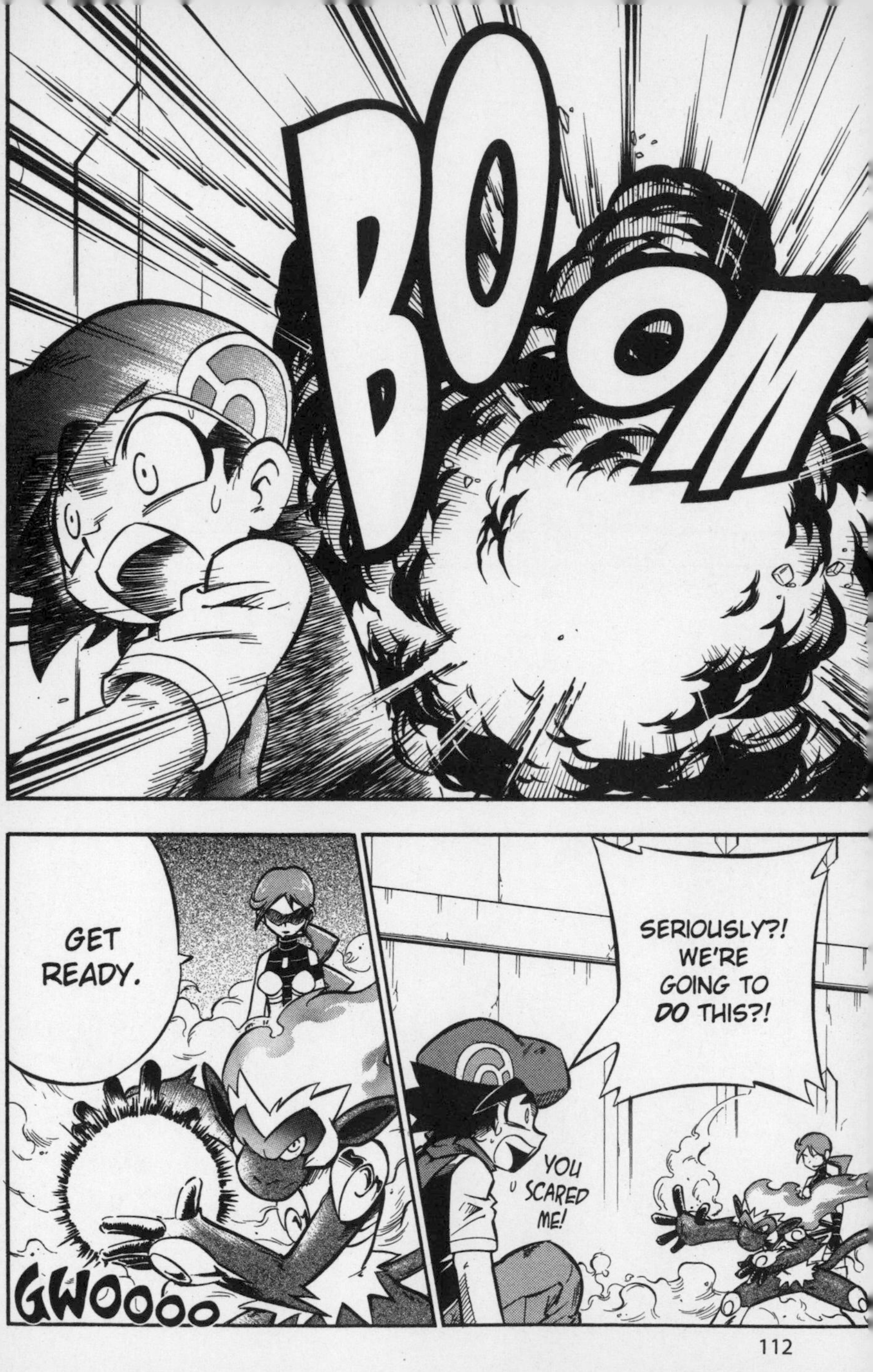
BOOM
SERIOUSLY?! WE'RE GOING TO DO THIS?!
YOU SCARED ME!
GET READY.
GWOOOO

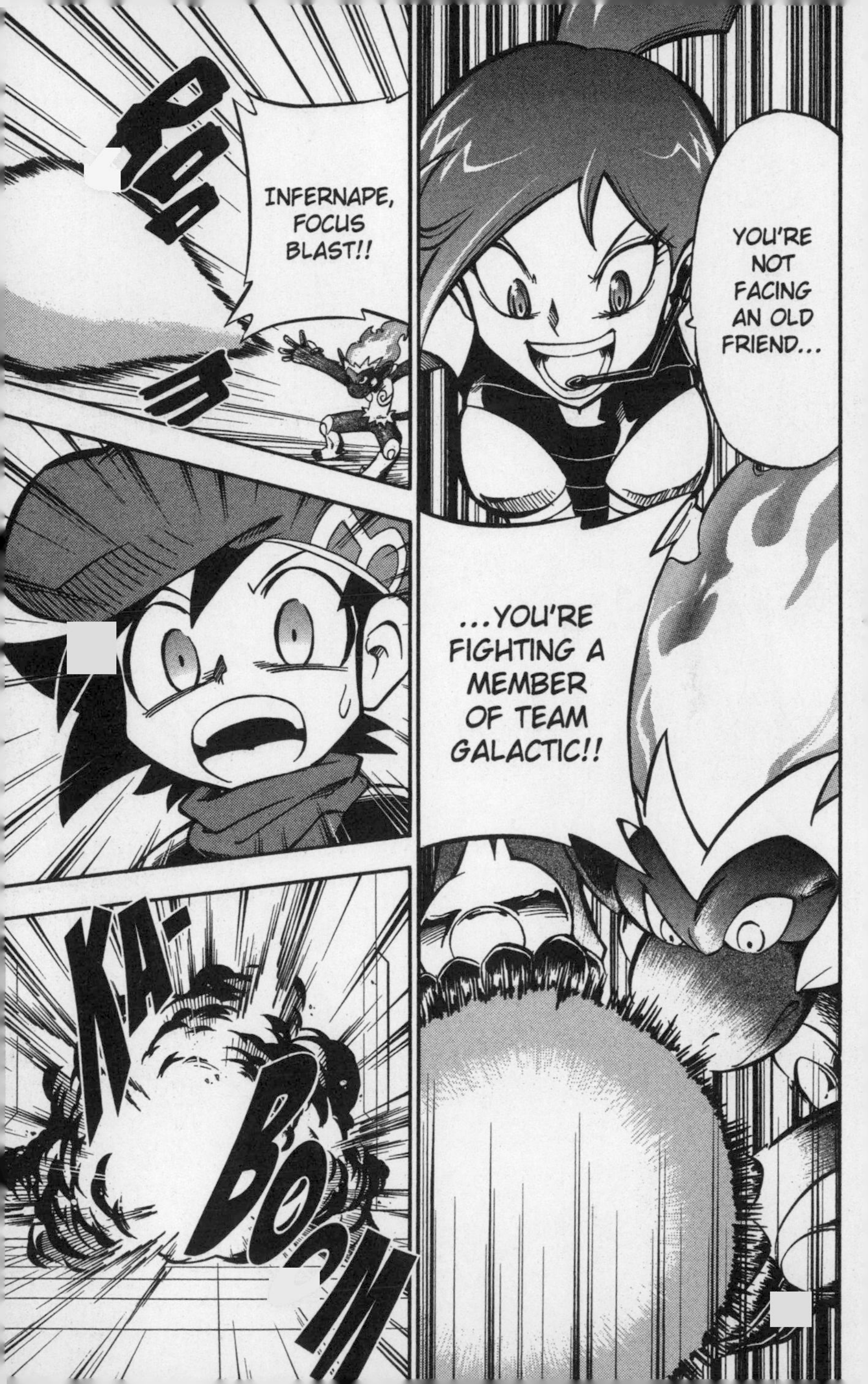
YOU'RE NOT FACING AN OLD FRIEND...
...YOU'RE FIGHTING A MEMBER OF TEAM GALACTIC!!
INFERNAPE, FOCUS BLAST!!
KA-BOOM

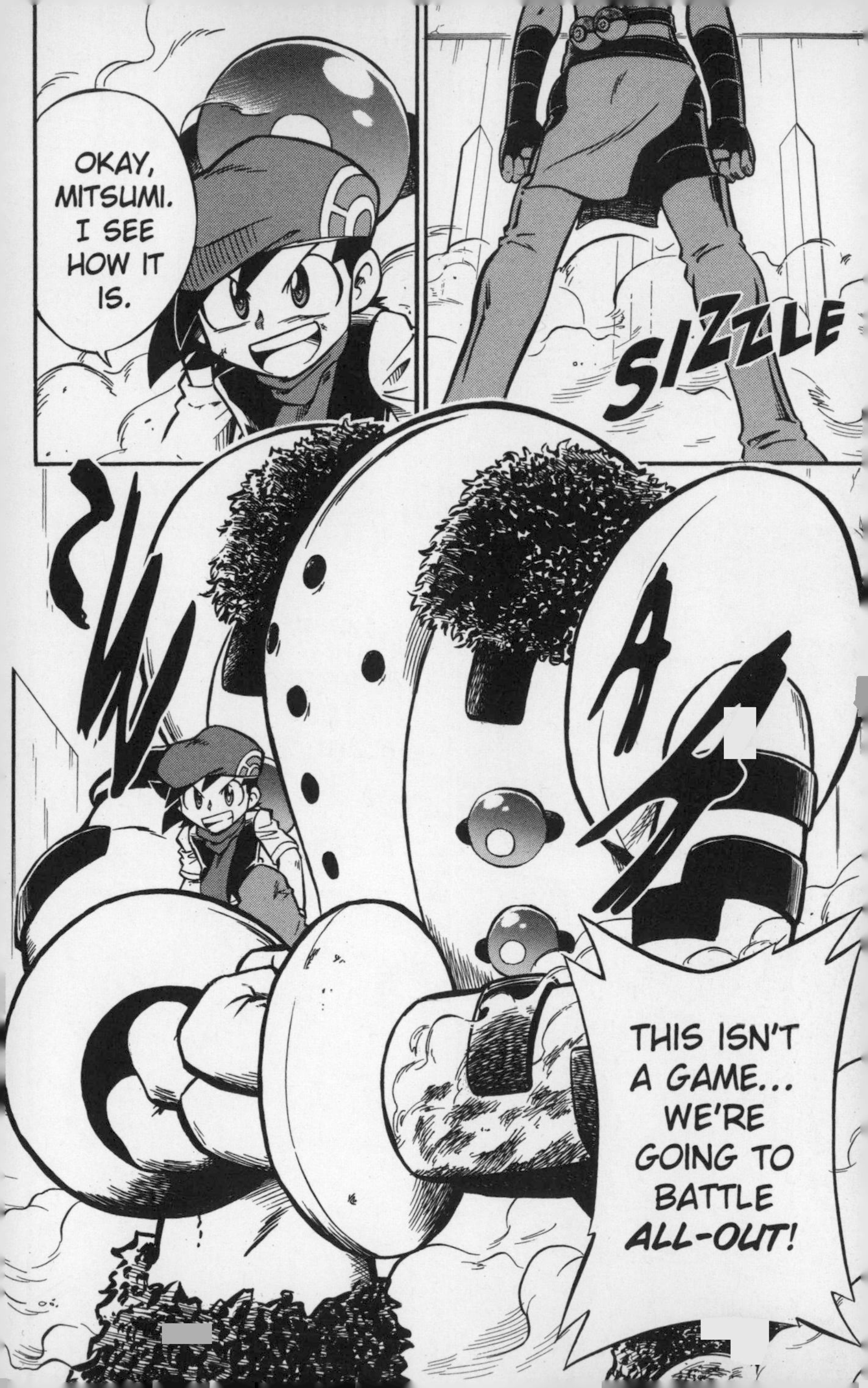
SIZZLE
OKAY, MITSUMI. I SEE HOW IT IS.
THIS ISN'T A GAME... WE'RE GOING TO BATTLE ALL-OUT!

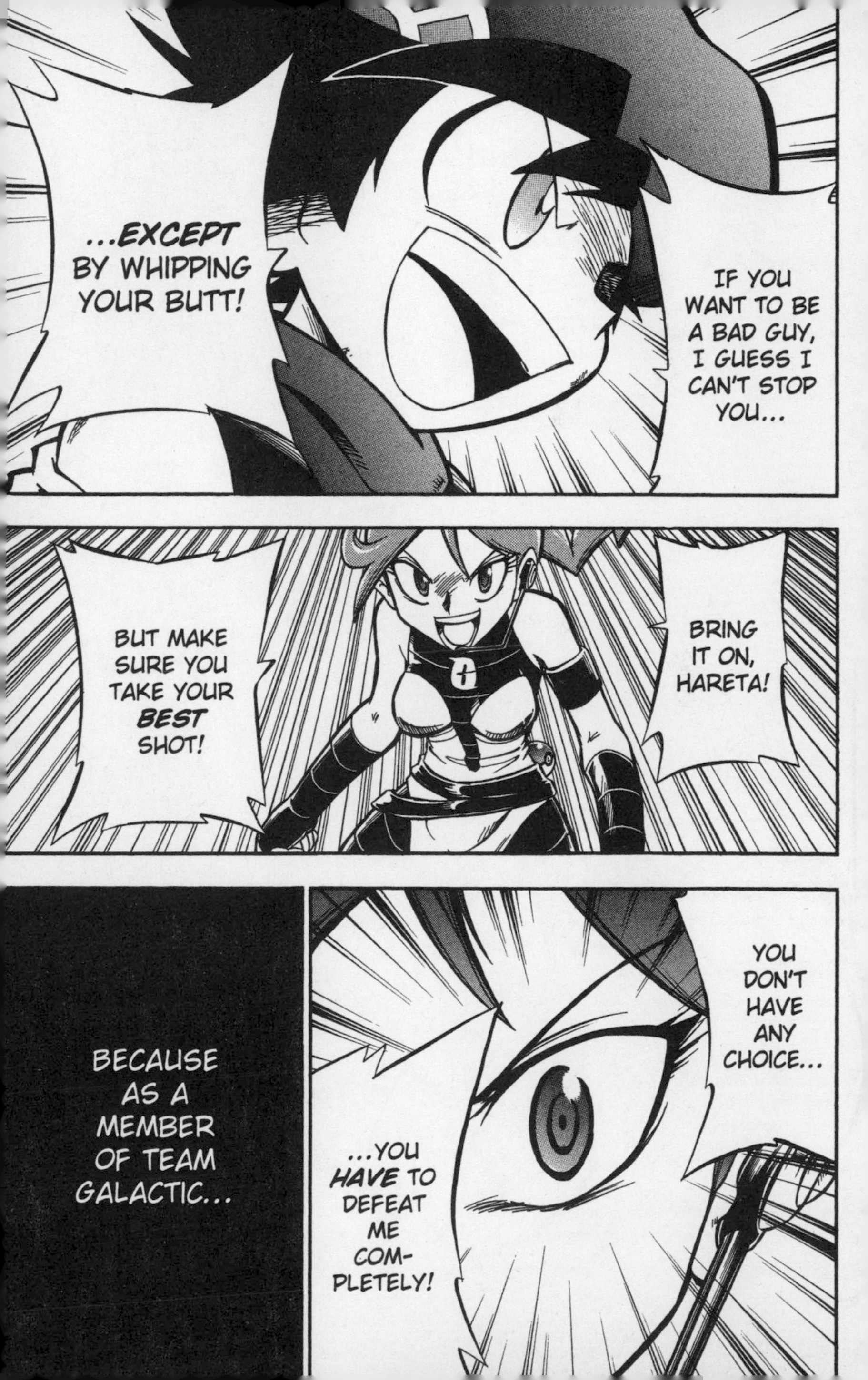
IF YOU WANT TO BE A BAD GUY, I GUESS I CAN'T STOP YOU...
...*EXCEPT* BY WHIPPING YOUR BUTT!
BRING IT ON, HARETA!
BUT MAKE SURE YOU TAKE YOUR *BEST* SHOT!
YOU DON'T HAVE ANY CHOICE...
...YOU *HAVE* TO DEFEAT ME COM-PLETELY!
BECAUSE AS A MEMBER OF TEAM GALACTIC...

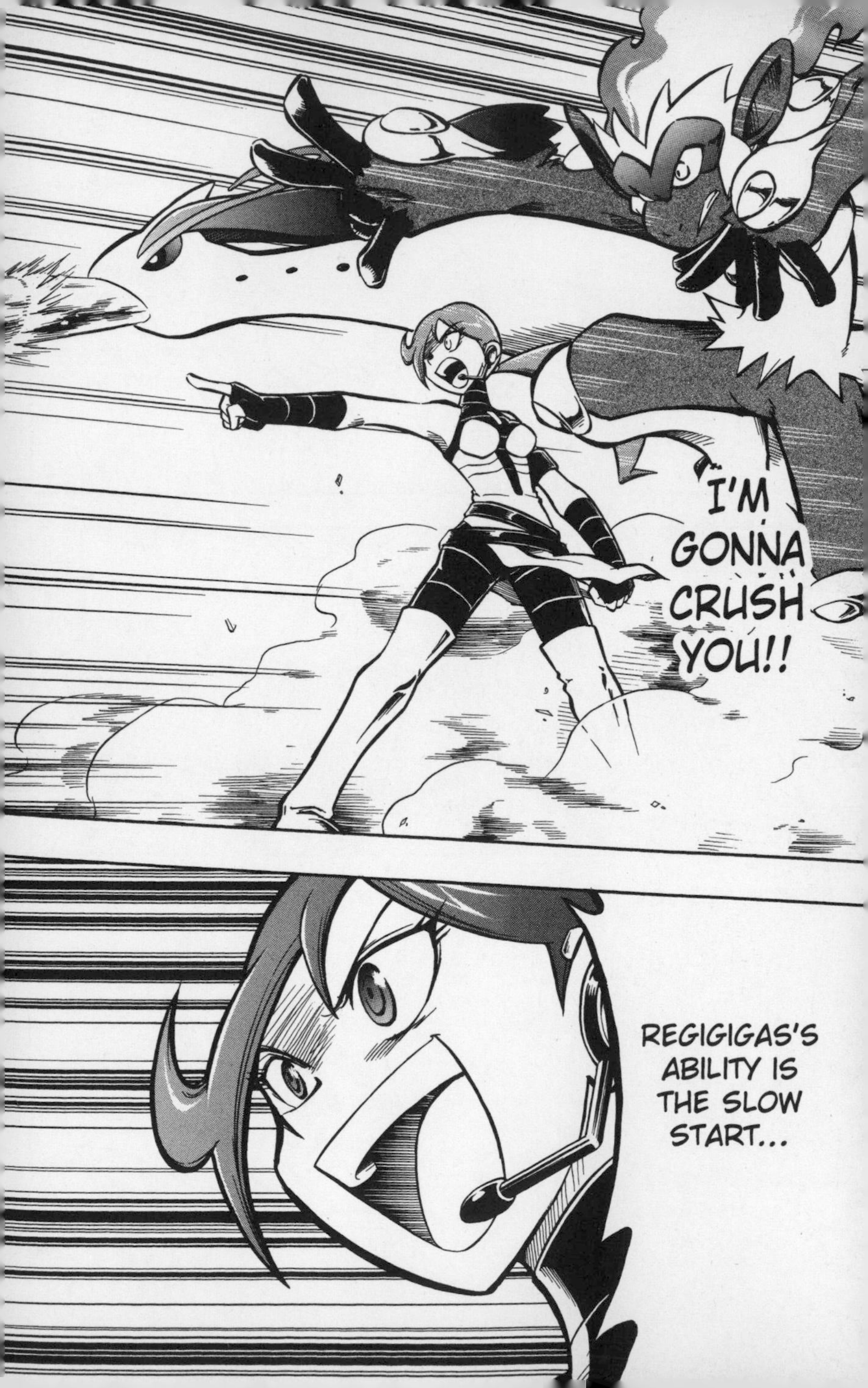
I'M GONNA CRUSH YOU!!
REGIGIGAS'S ABILITY IS THE SLOW START...

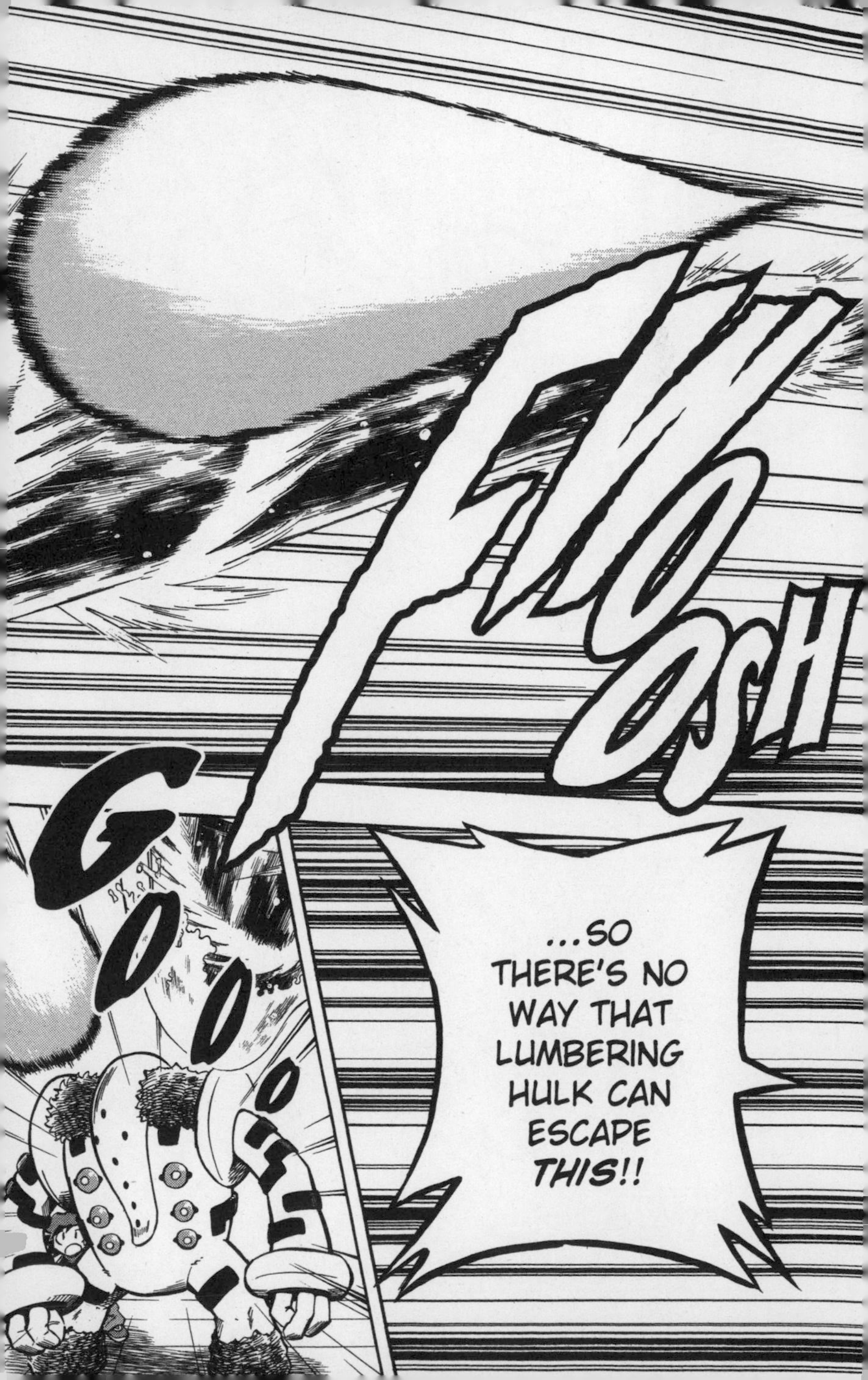
...SO THERE'S NO WAY THAT LUMBERING HULK CAN ESCAPE *THIS*!!

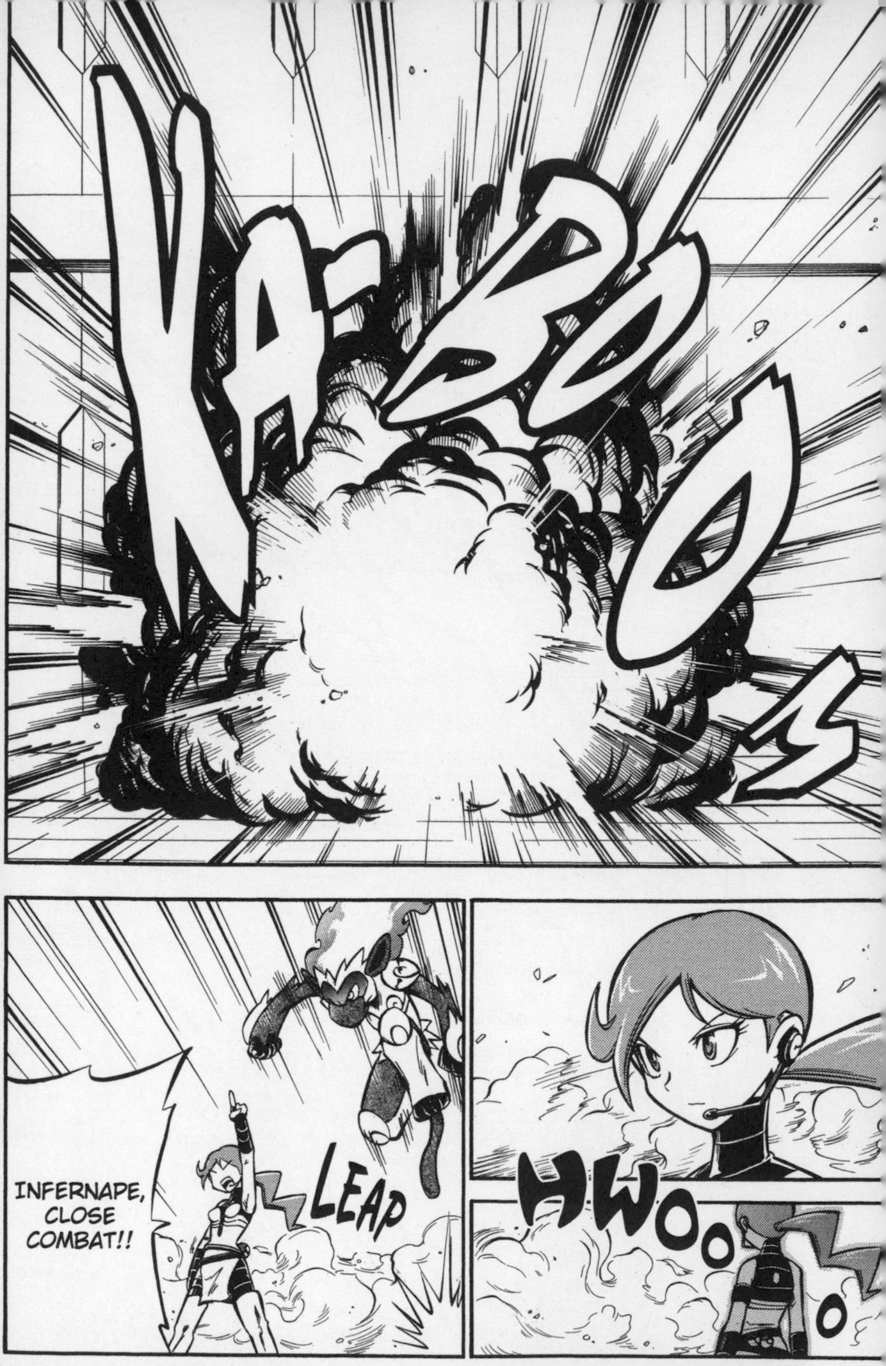
KA-BOOM
HWOOO
INFERNAPE, CLOSE COMBAT!!
LEAP

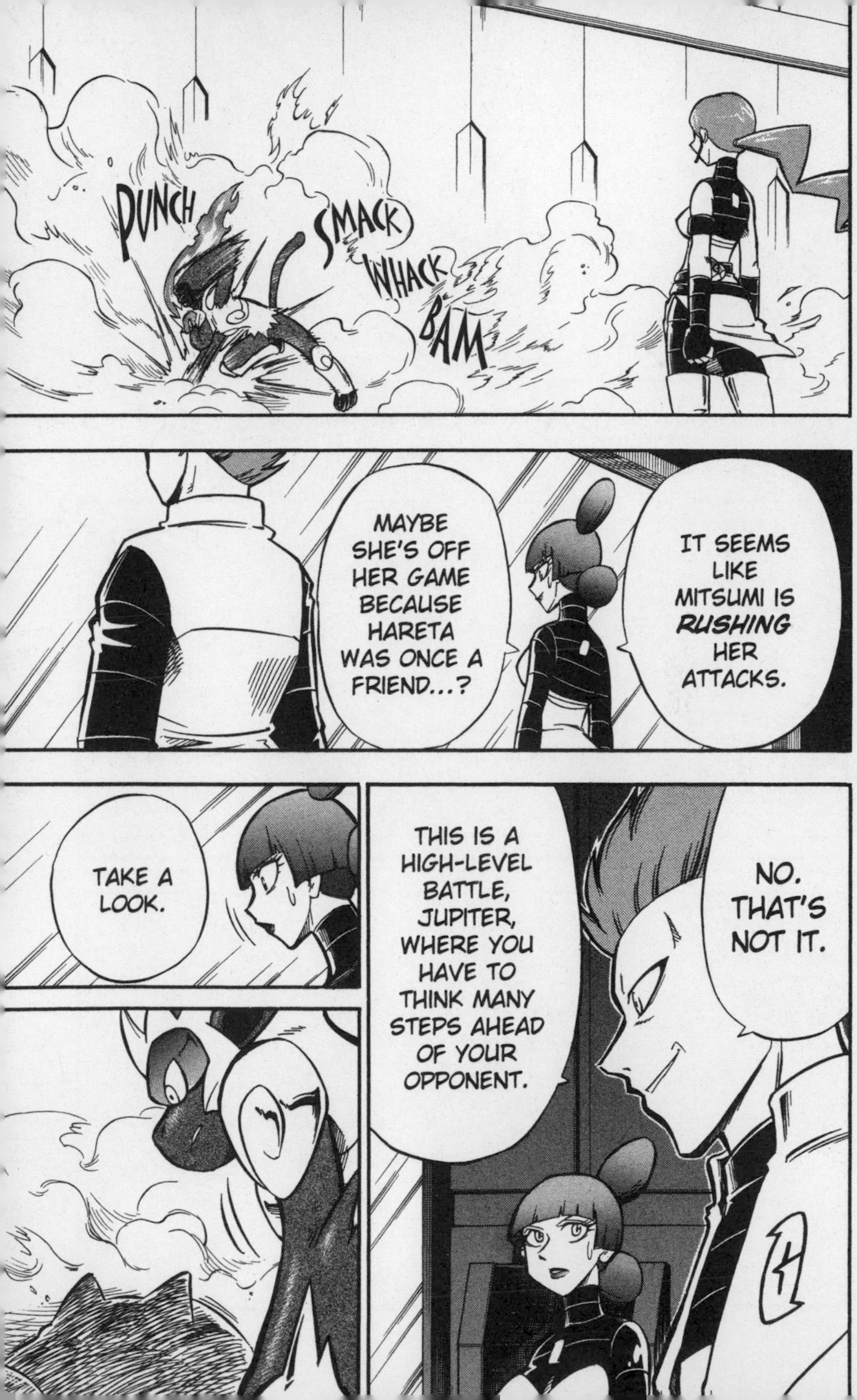
SMACK
WHACK
BAM
PUNCH
IT SEEMS LIKE MITSUMI IS RUSHING HER ATTACKS.
MAYBE SHE'S OFF HER GAME BECAUSE HARETA WAS ONCE A FRIEND...?
NO. THAT'S NOT IT.
THIS IS A HIGH-LEVEL BATTLE, JUPITER, WHERE YOU HAVE TO THINK MANY STEPS AHEAD OF YOUR OPPONENT.
TAKE A LOOK.

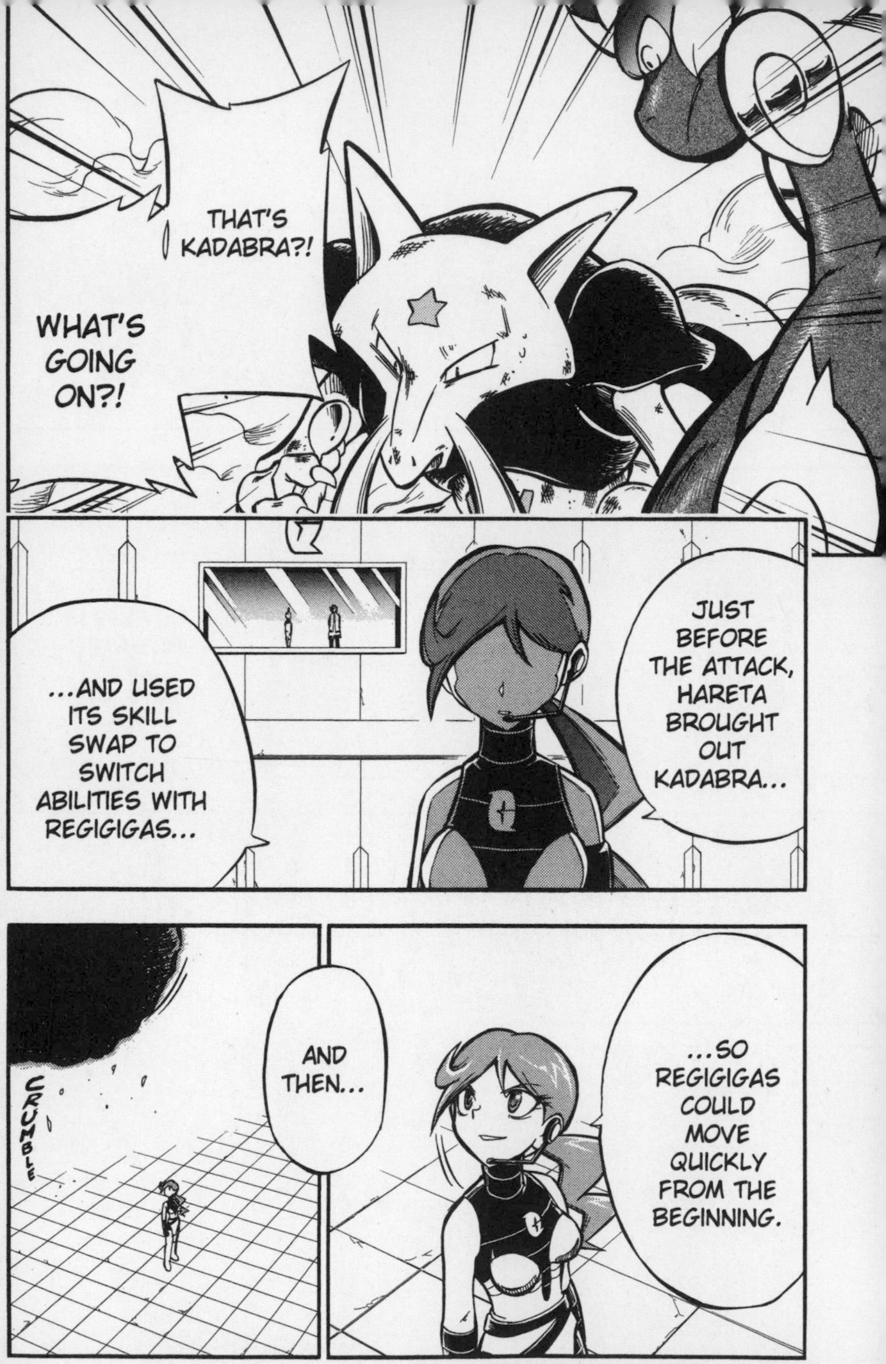
THAT'S KADABRA?!
WHAT'S GOING ON?!
JUST BEFORE THE ATTACK, HARETA BROUGHT OUT KADABRA...
...AND USED ITS SKILL SWAP TO SWITCH ABILITIES WITH REGIGIGAS...
...SO REGIGIGAS COULD MOVE QUICKLY FROM THE BEGINNING.
AND THEN...
CRUMBLE

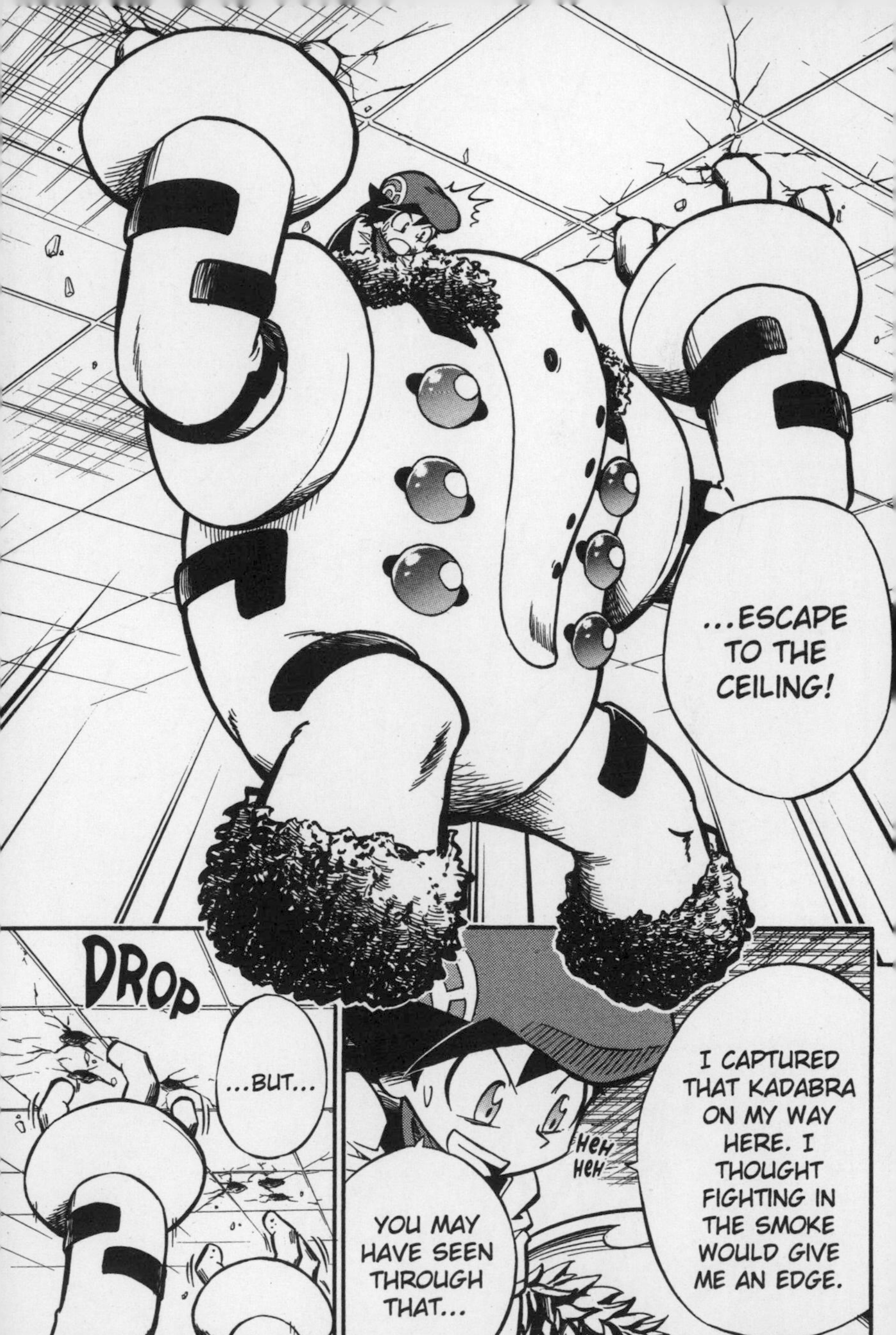
...ESCAPE TO THE CEILING!
I CAPTURED THAT KADABRA ON MY WAY HERE. I THOUGHT FIGHTING IN THE SMOKE WOULD GIVE ME AN EDGE.
HEH HEH
YOU MAY HAVE SEEN THROUGH THAT...
DROP
...BUT...

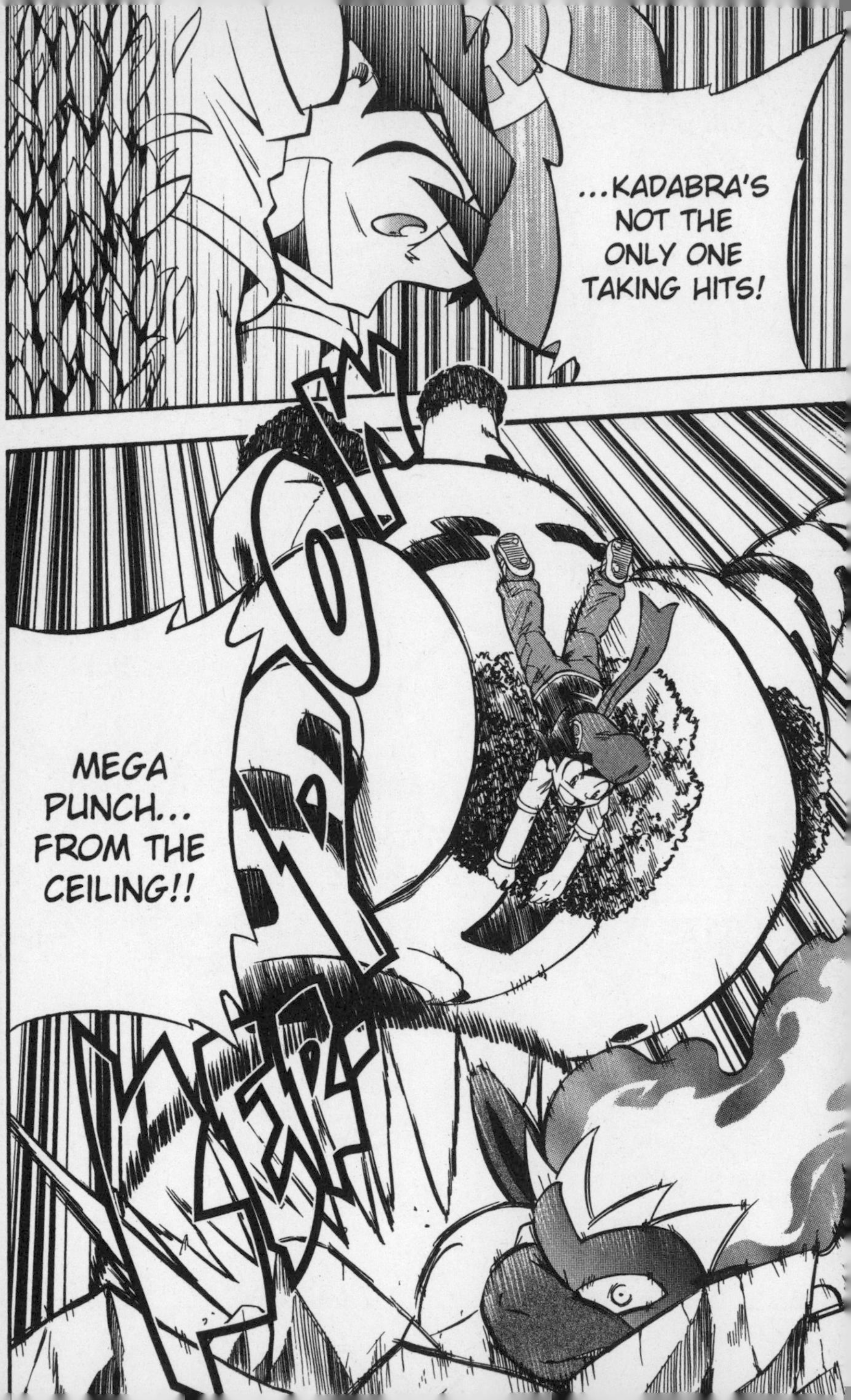
...KADABRA'S NOT THE ONLY ONE TAKING HITS!
MEGA PUNCH... FROM THE CEILING!!

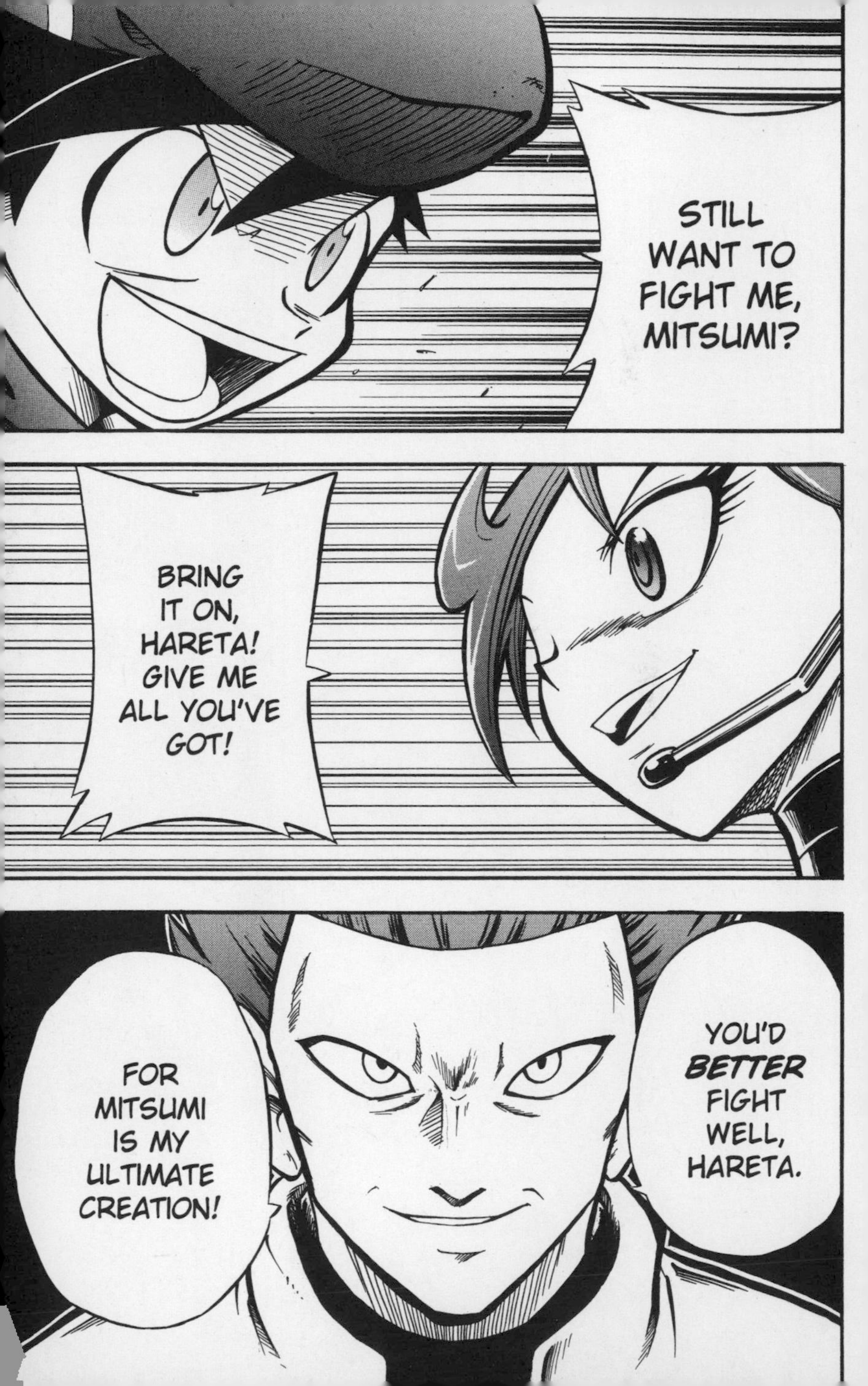
STILL WANT TO FIGHT ME, MITSUMI?
BRING IT ON, HARETA! GIVE ME ALL YOU'VE GOT!
YOU'D *BETTER* FIGHT WELL, HARETA.
FOR MITSUMI IS MY ULTIMATE CREATION!

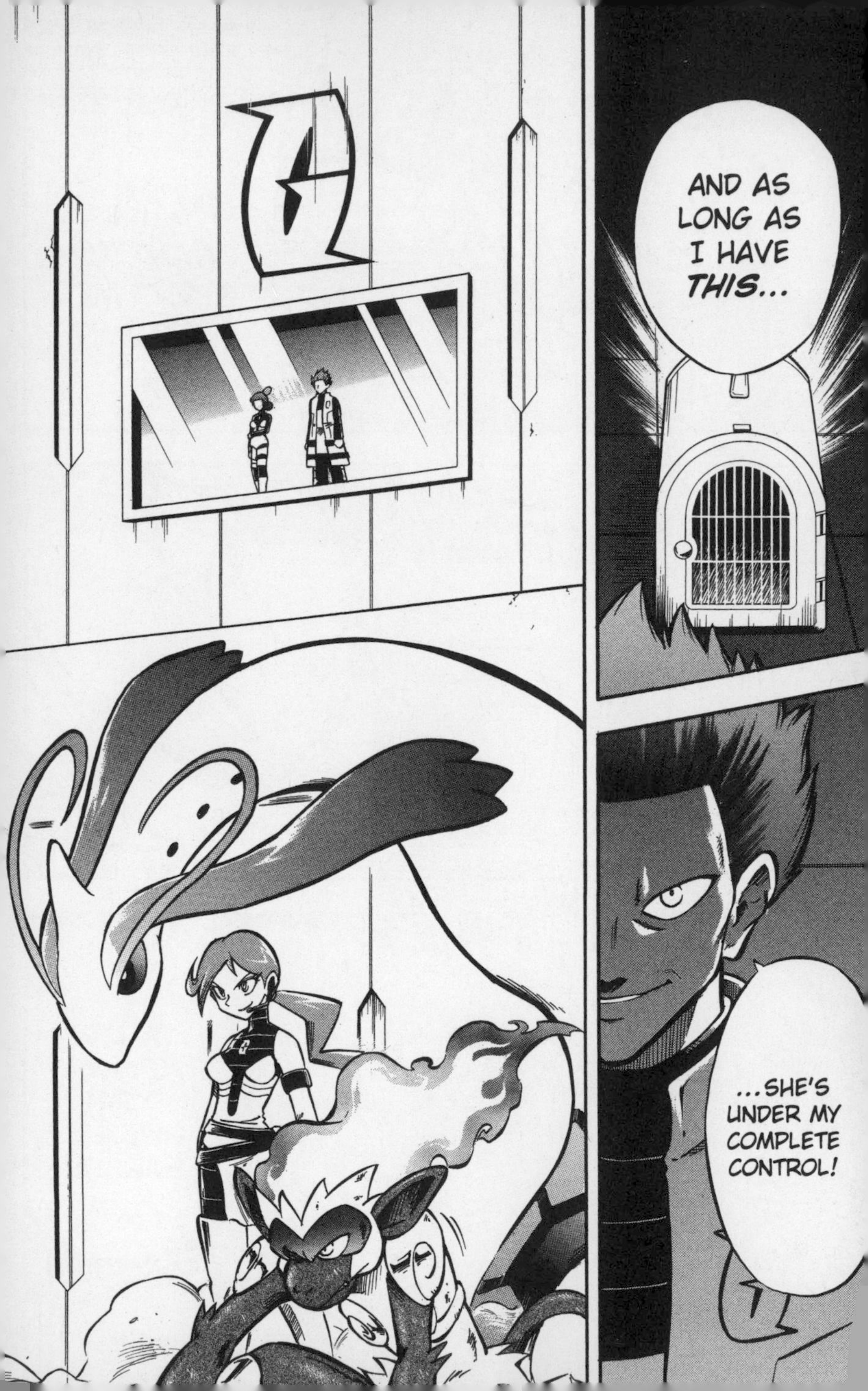
AND AS LONG AS I HAVE THIS...
...SHE'S UNDER MY COMPLETE CONTROL!

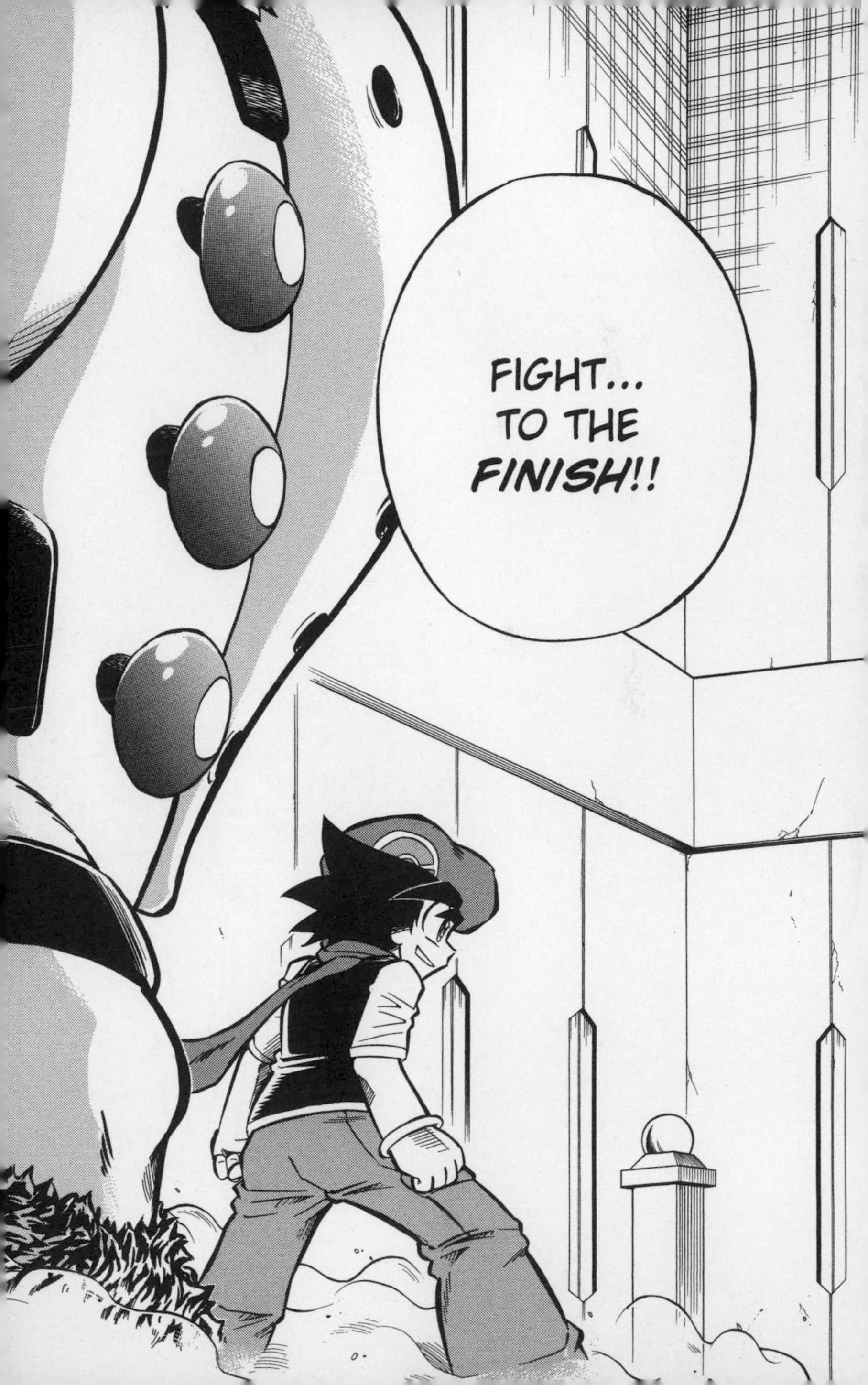
FIGHT... TO THE FINISH!!

I'M
SERIOUS
THIS
TIME.

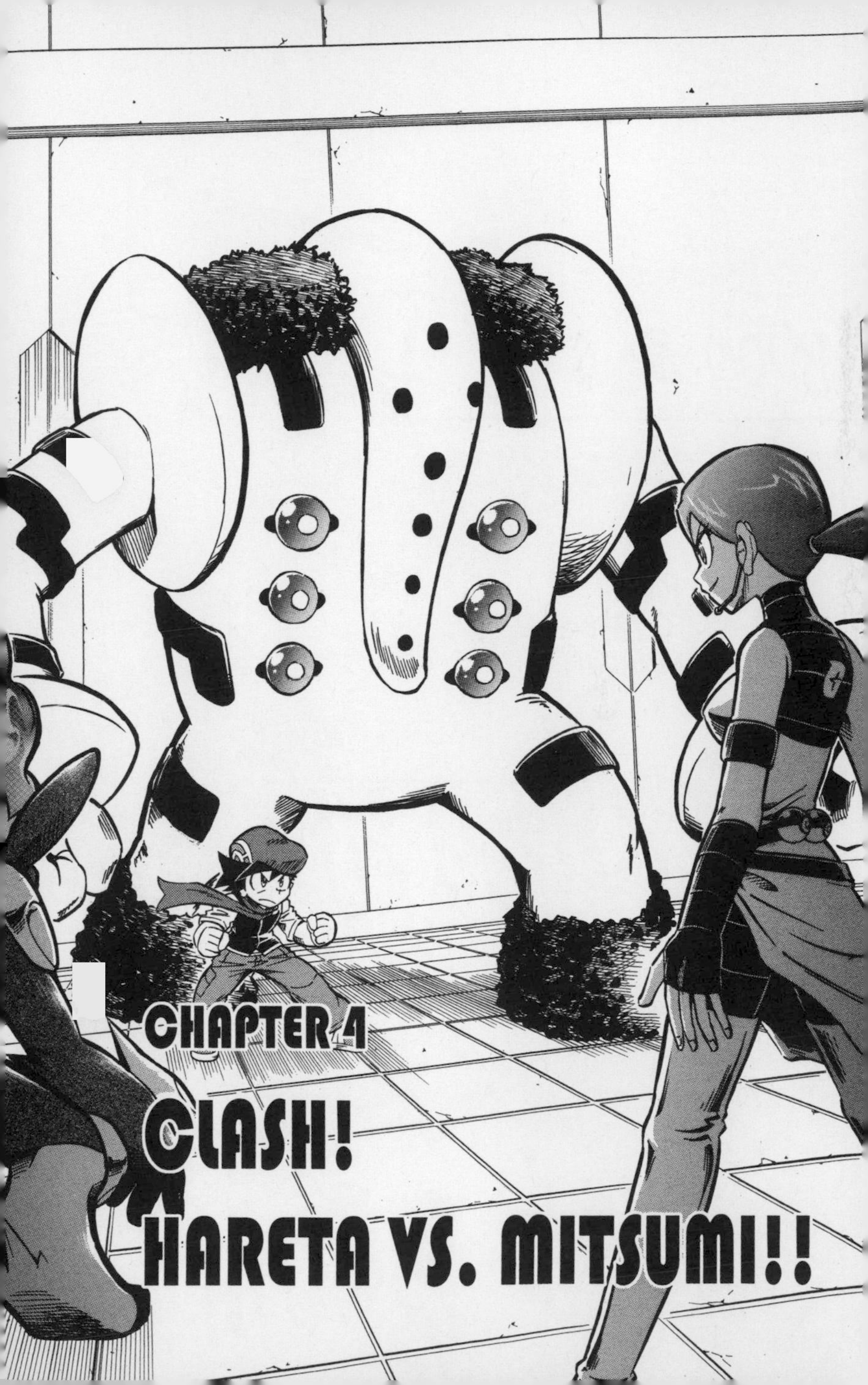
CHAPTER 4
CLASH!
HARETA VS. MITSUMI!!

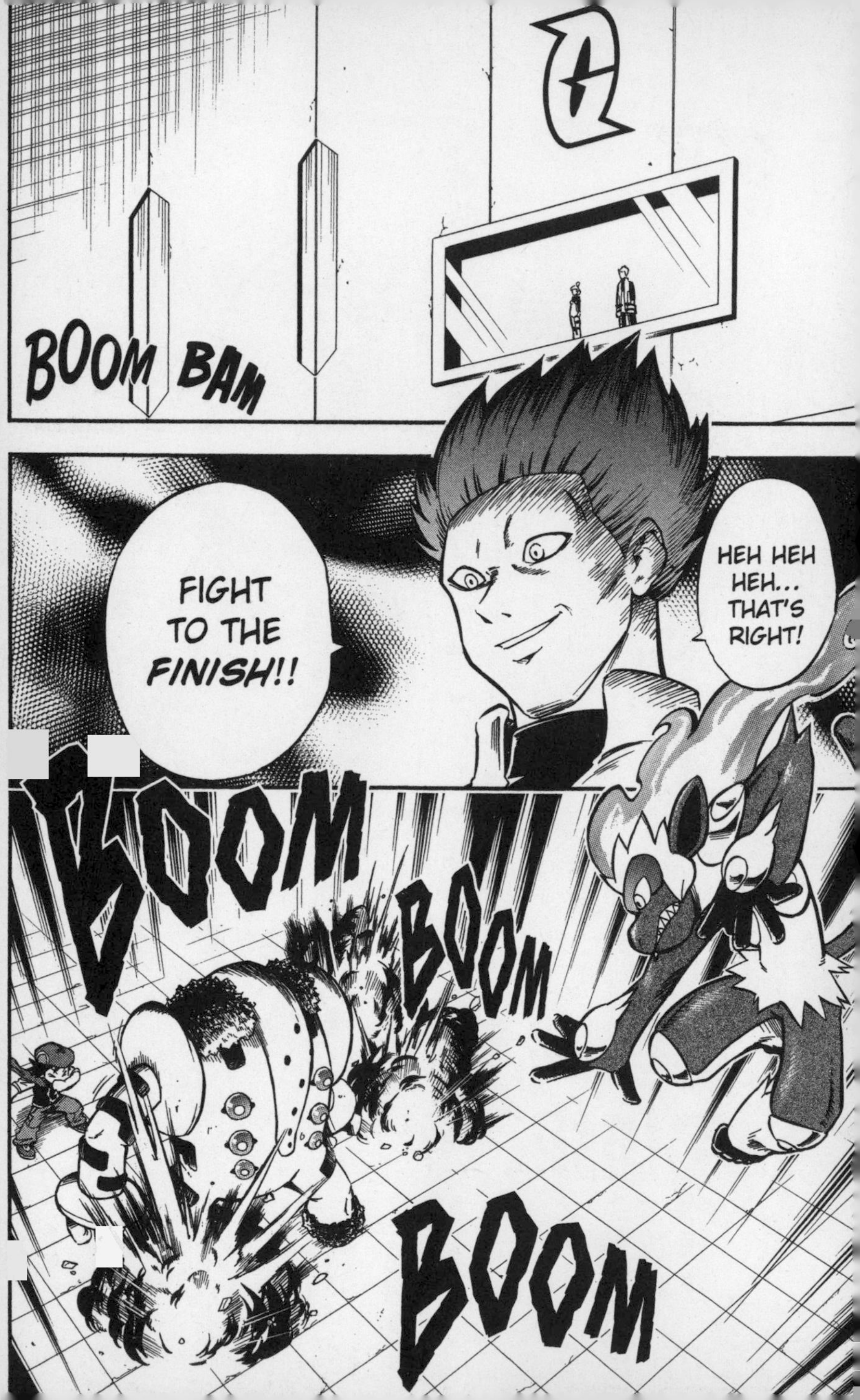
BOOM BAM
HEH HEH HEH... THAT'S RIGHT!
FIGHT TO THE *FINISH!!*
BOOM
BOOM
BOOM

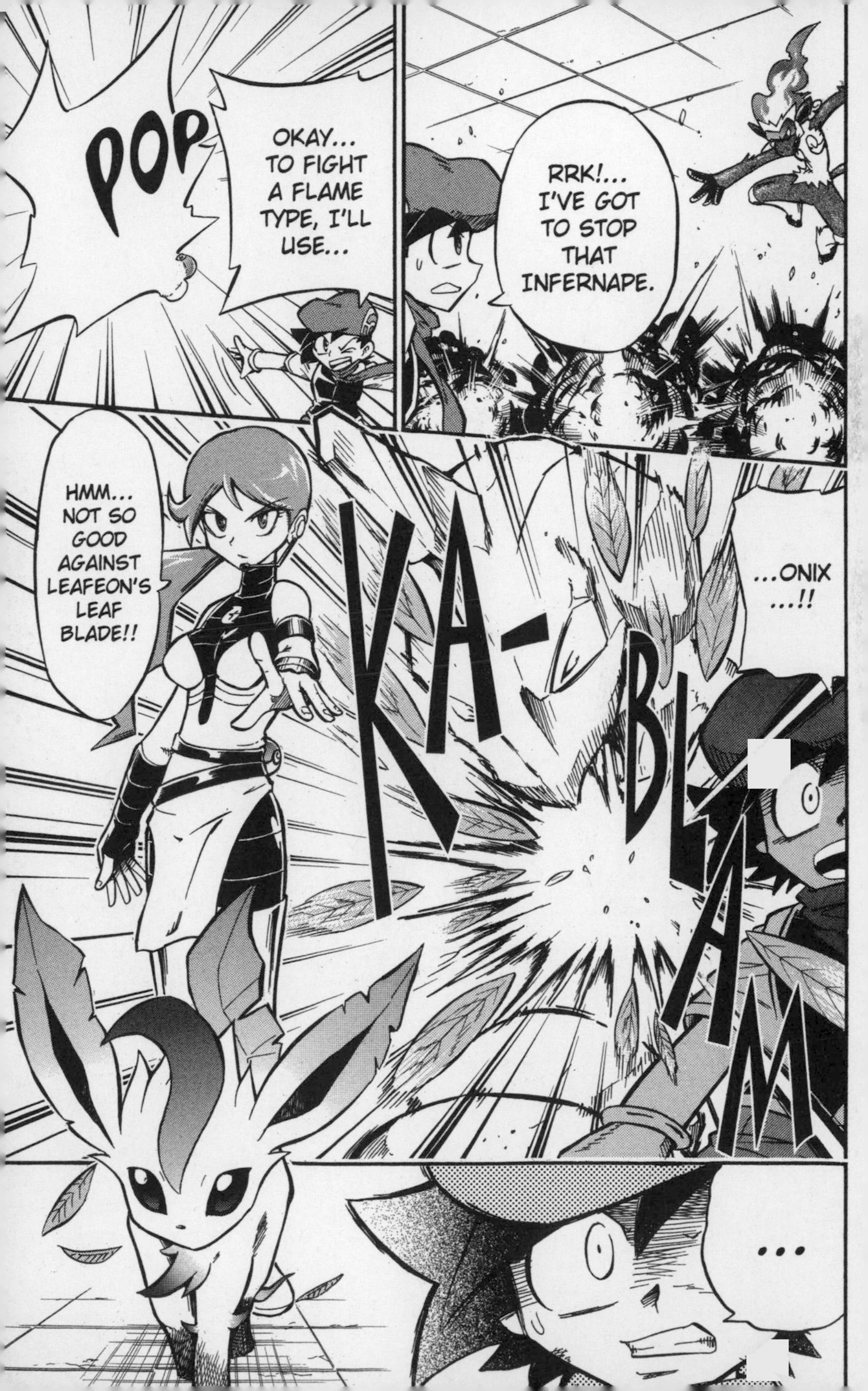
RRK!... I'VE GOT TO STOP THAT INFERNAPE.
POP
OKAY... TO FIGHT A FLAME TYPE, I'LL USE...
...ONIX ...!!
KA-BLAM
HMM... NOT SO GOOD AGAINST LEAFEON'S LEAF BLADE!!
...

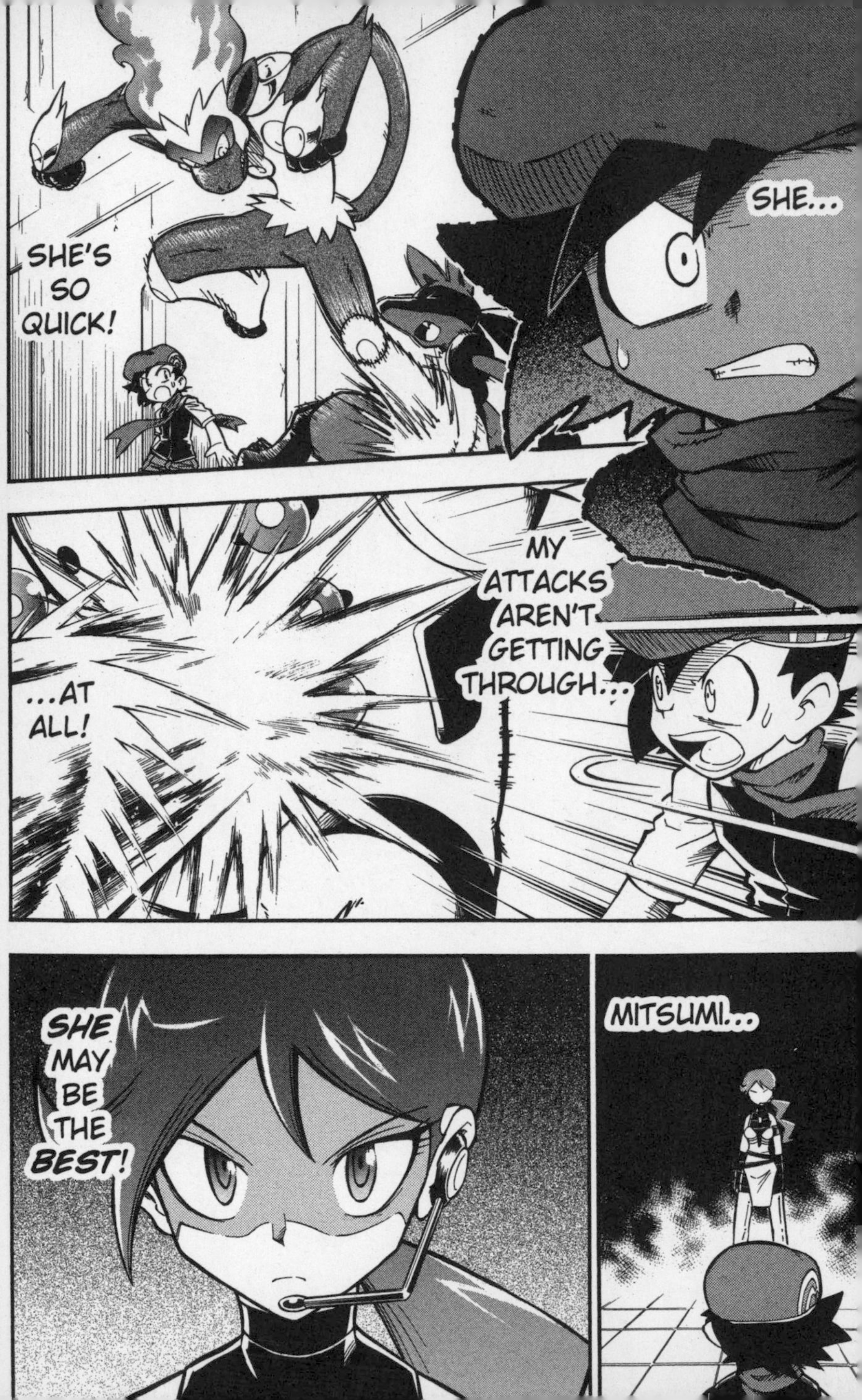
SHE...
SHE'S SO QUICK!
MY ATTACKS AREN'T GETTING THROUGH...
...AT ALL!
MITSUMI...
SHE MAY BE THE BEST!

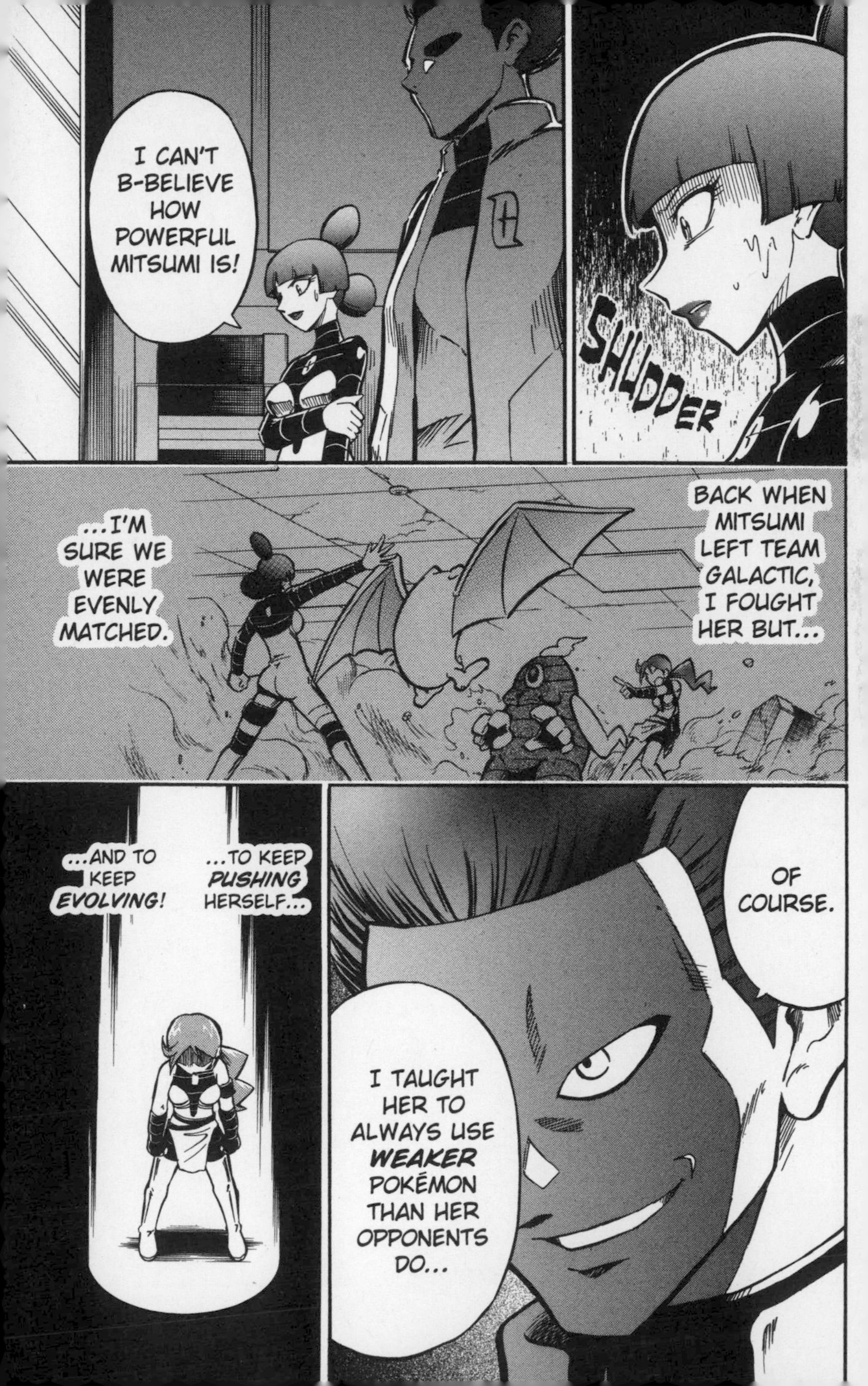
SHUDDER
I CAN'T B-BELIEVE HOW POWERFUL MITSUMI IS!
BACK WHEN MITSUMI LEFT TEAM GALACTIC, I FOUGHT HER BUT...
...I'M SURE WE WERE EVENLY MATCHED.
OF COURSE.
I TAUGHT HER TO ALWAYS USE *WEAKER* POKÉMON THAN HER OPPONENTS DO...
...TO KEEP *PUSHING* HERSELF...
...AND TO KEEP *EVOLVING*!

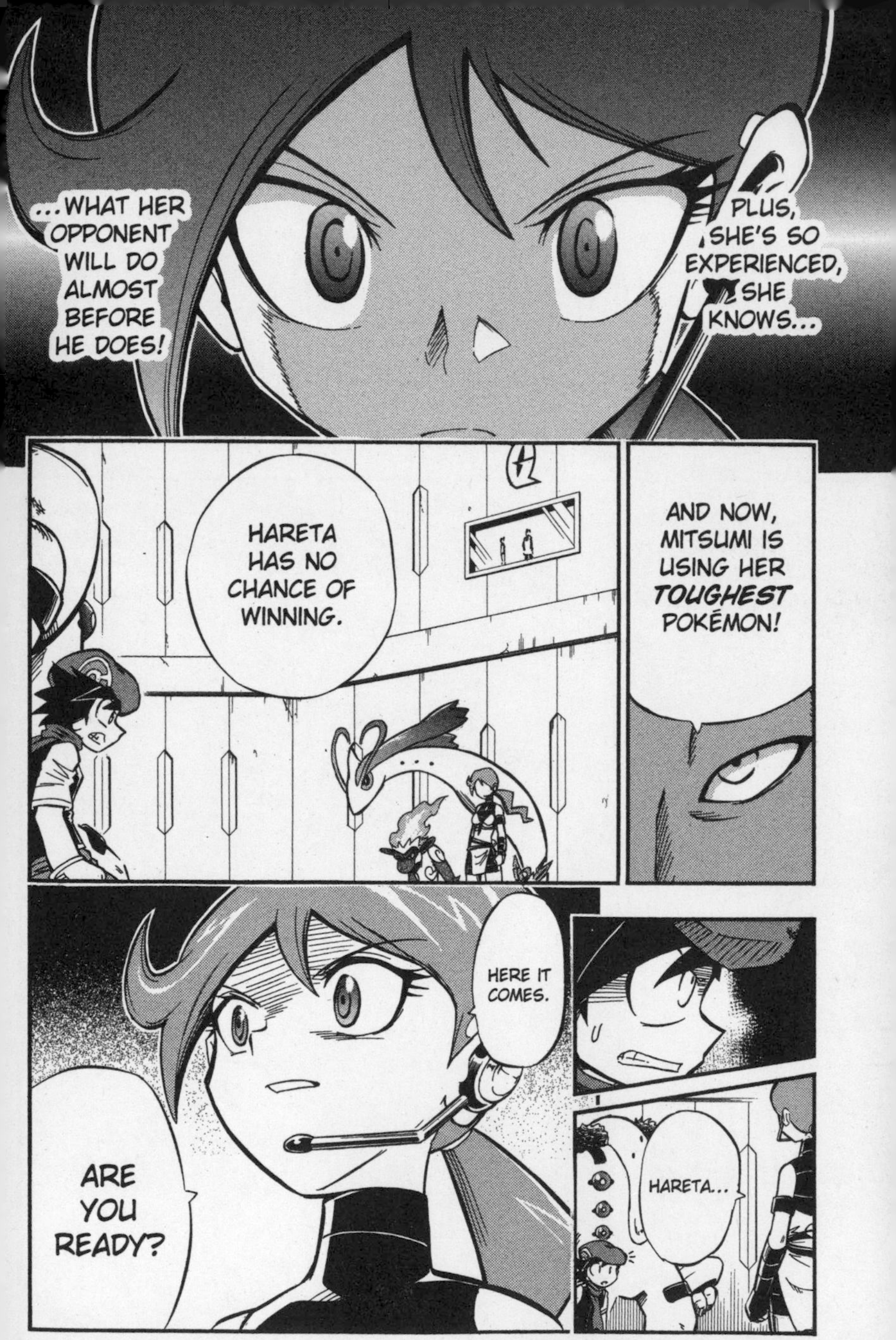
PLUS, SHE'S SO EXPERIENCED, SHE KNOWS...
...WHAT HER OPPONENT WILL DO ALMOST BEFORE HE DOES!
AND NOW, MITSUMI IS USING HER *TOUGHEST* POKÉMON!
HARETA HAS NO CHANCE OF WINNING.
HARETA...
HERE IT COMES.
ARE YOU READY?

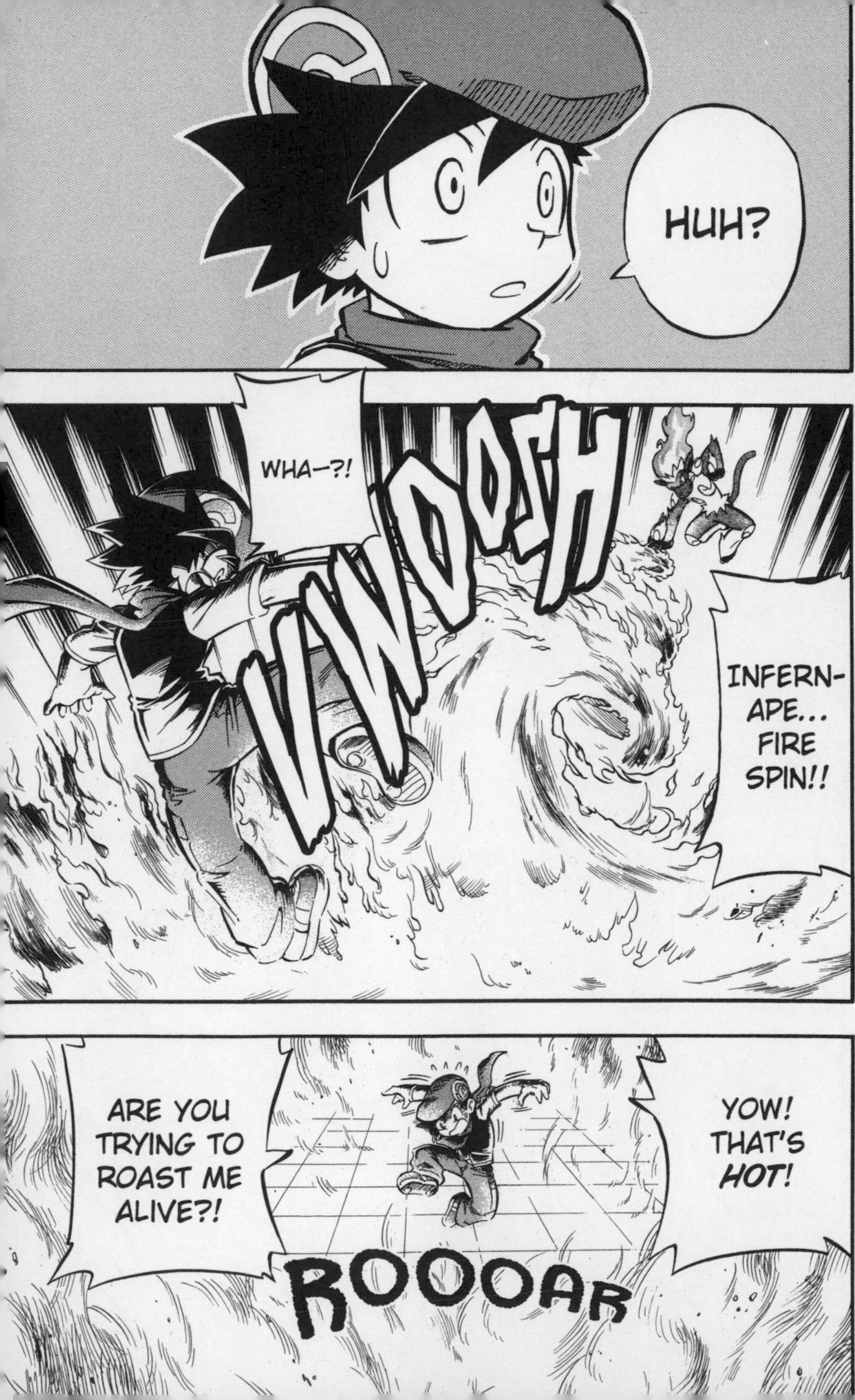
HUH?
INFERN-APE... FIRE SPIN!!
WHA--?!
VWOOSH
YOW! THAT'S *HOT*!
ARE YOU TRYING TO ROAST ME ALIVE?!
ROOOAR

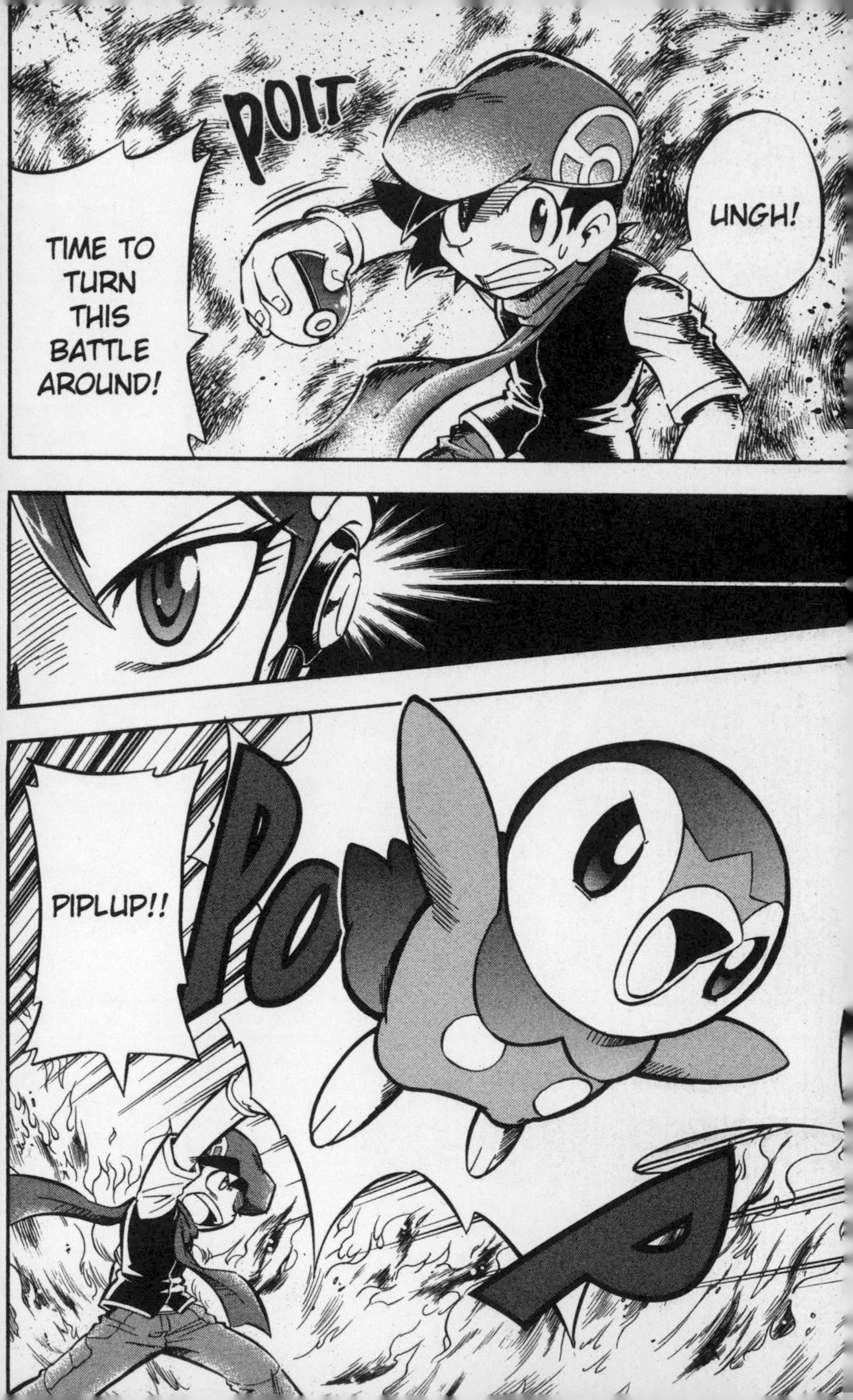
UNGH!
POIT
TIME TO TURN THIS BATTLE AROUND!
POP
PIPLUP!!

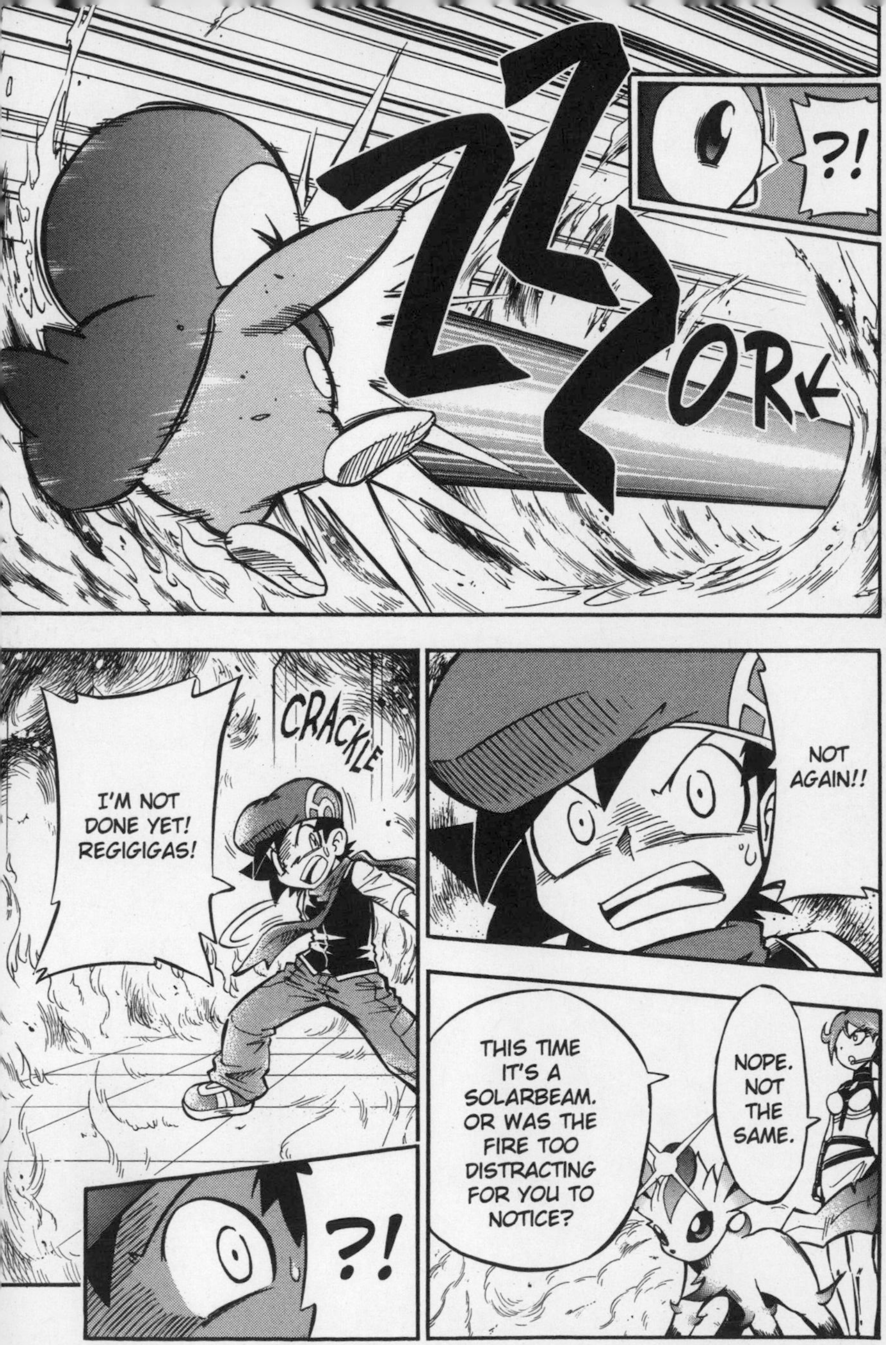
?!
ZZZORK
NOT AGAIN!!
NOPE. NOT THE SAME.
THIS TIME IT'S A SOLARBEAM. OR WAS THE FIRE TOO DISTRACTING FOR YOU TO NOTICE?
CRACKLE
I'M NOT DONE YET! REGIGIGAS!
?!

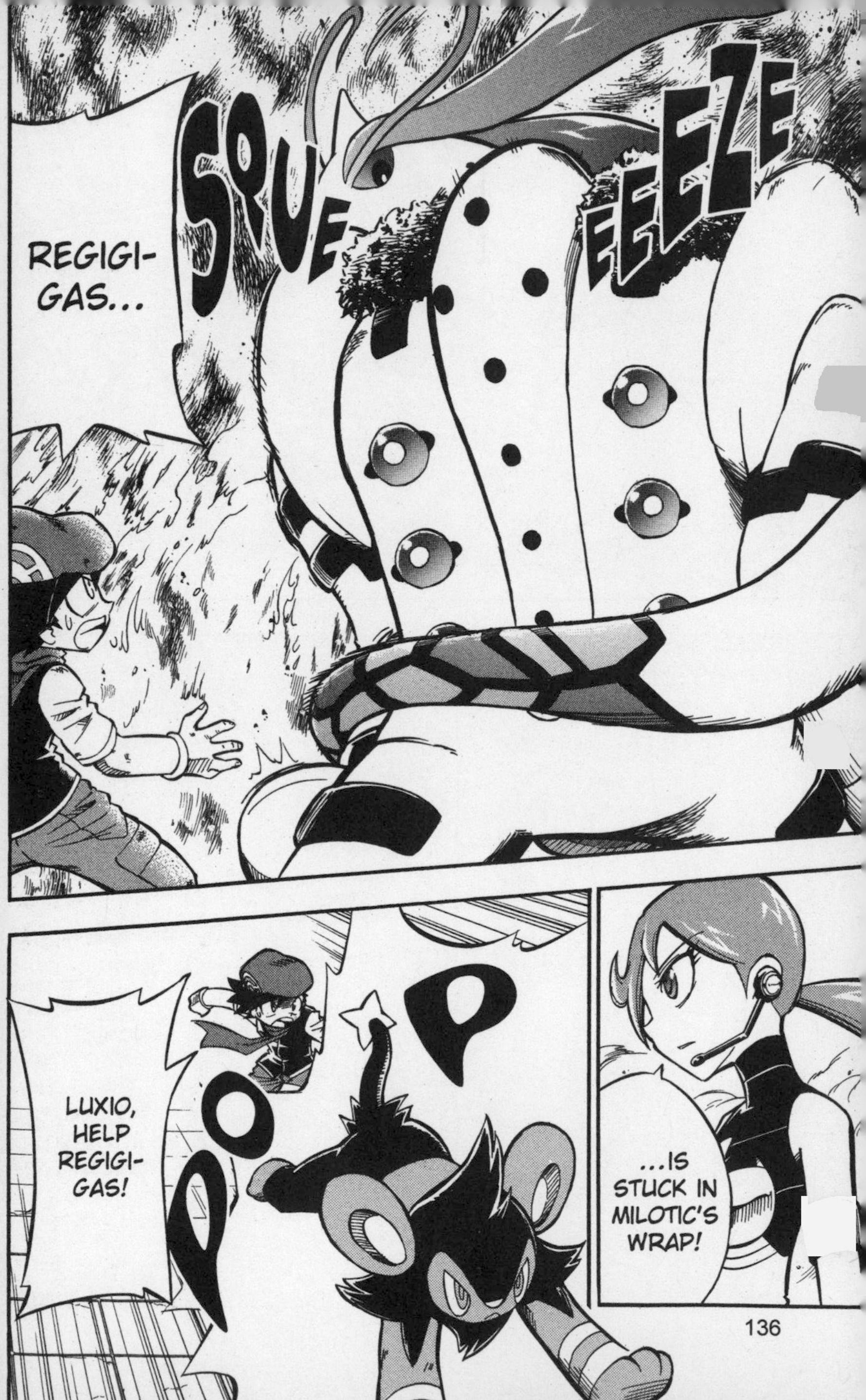
SQUE-EEEZE
REGIGI-GAS...
...IS STUCK IN MILOTIC'S WRAP!
POP
LUXIO, HELP REGIGI-GAS!

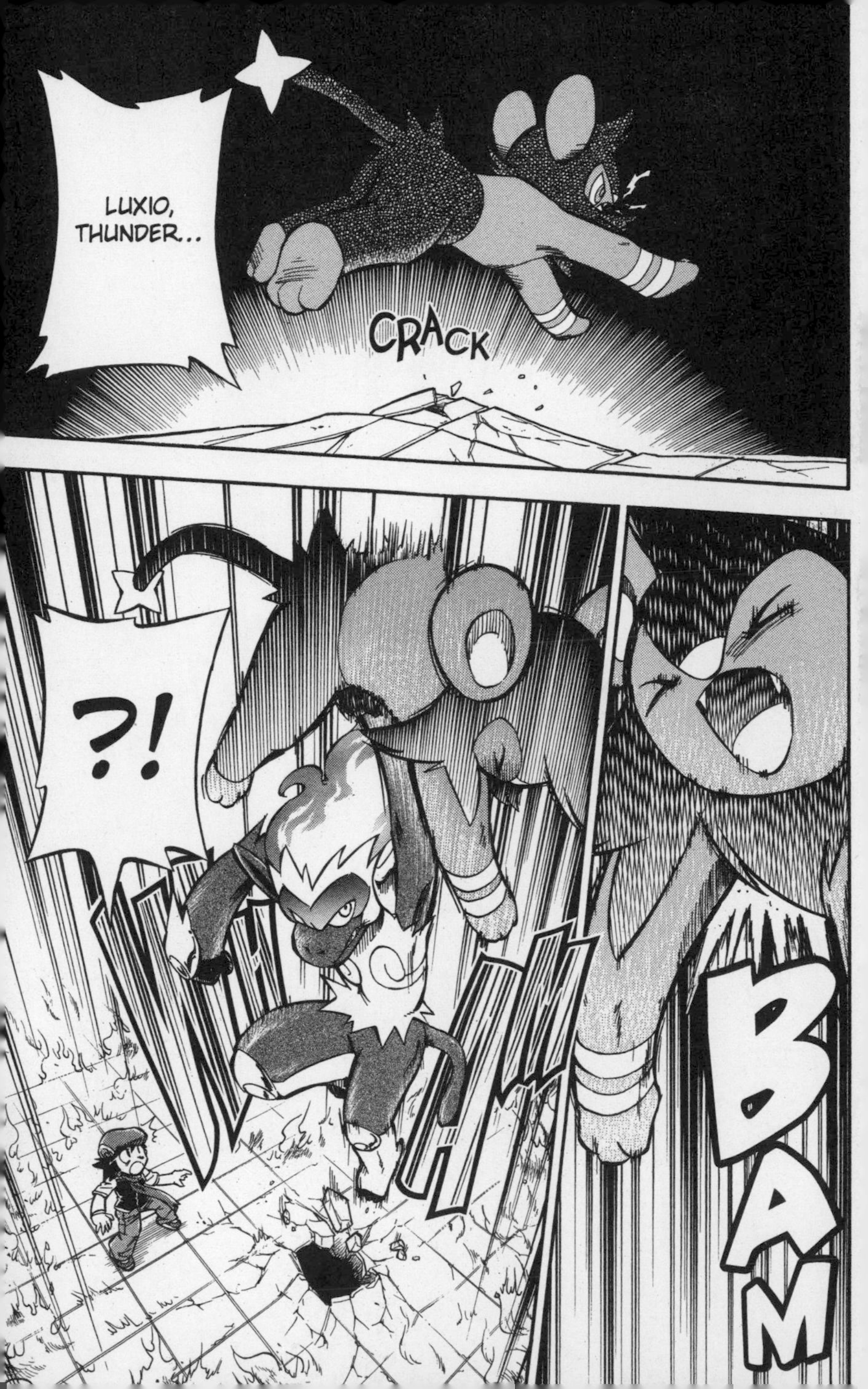
LUXIO, THUNDER...
CRACK
?!
BAM

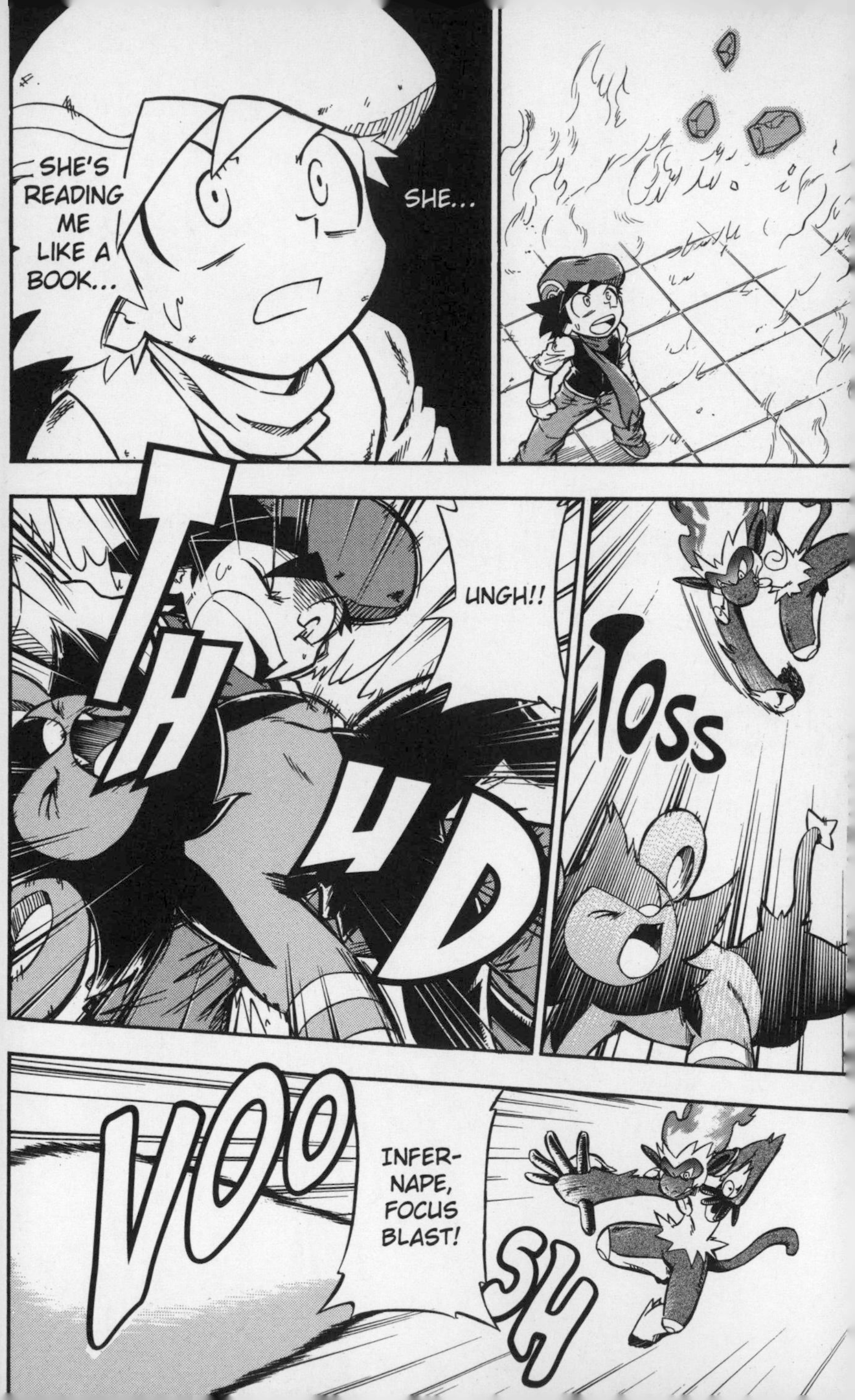
SHE...
SHE'S READING ME LIKE A BOOK...
TOSS
UNGH!!
THUD
INFERNAPE, FOCUS BLAST!
VOO
SH

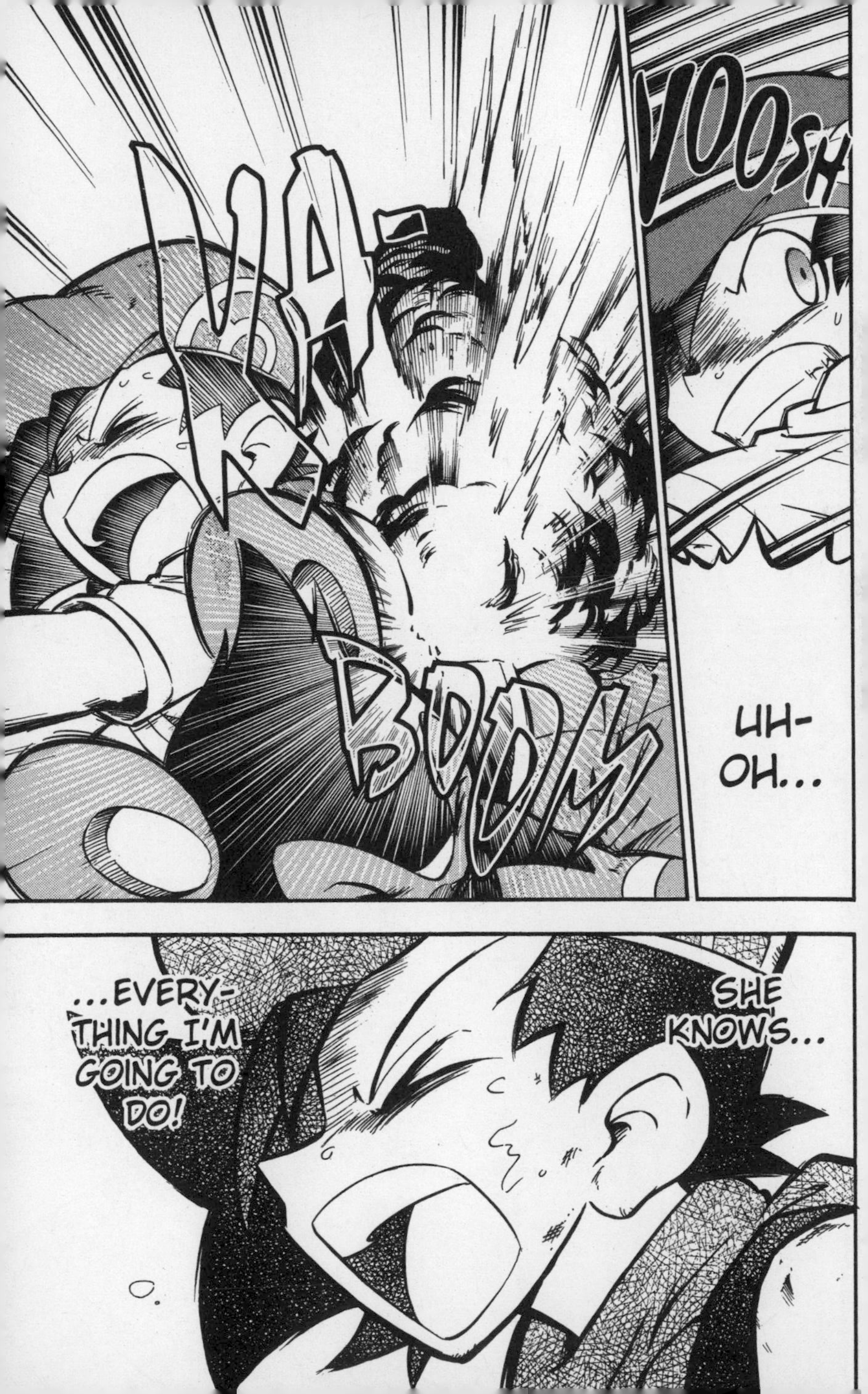
VOOSH
UH-OH...
BOOM
SHE KNOWS...
...EVERYTHING I'M GOING TO DO!

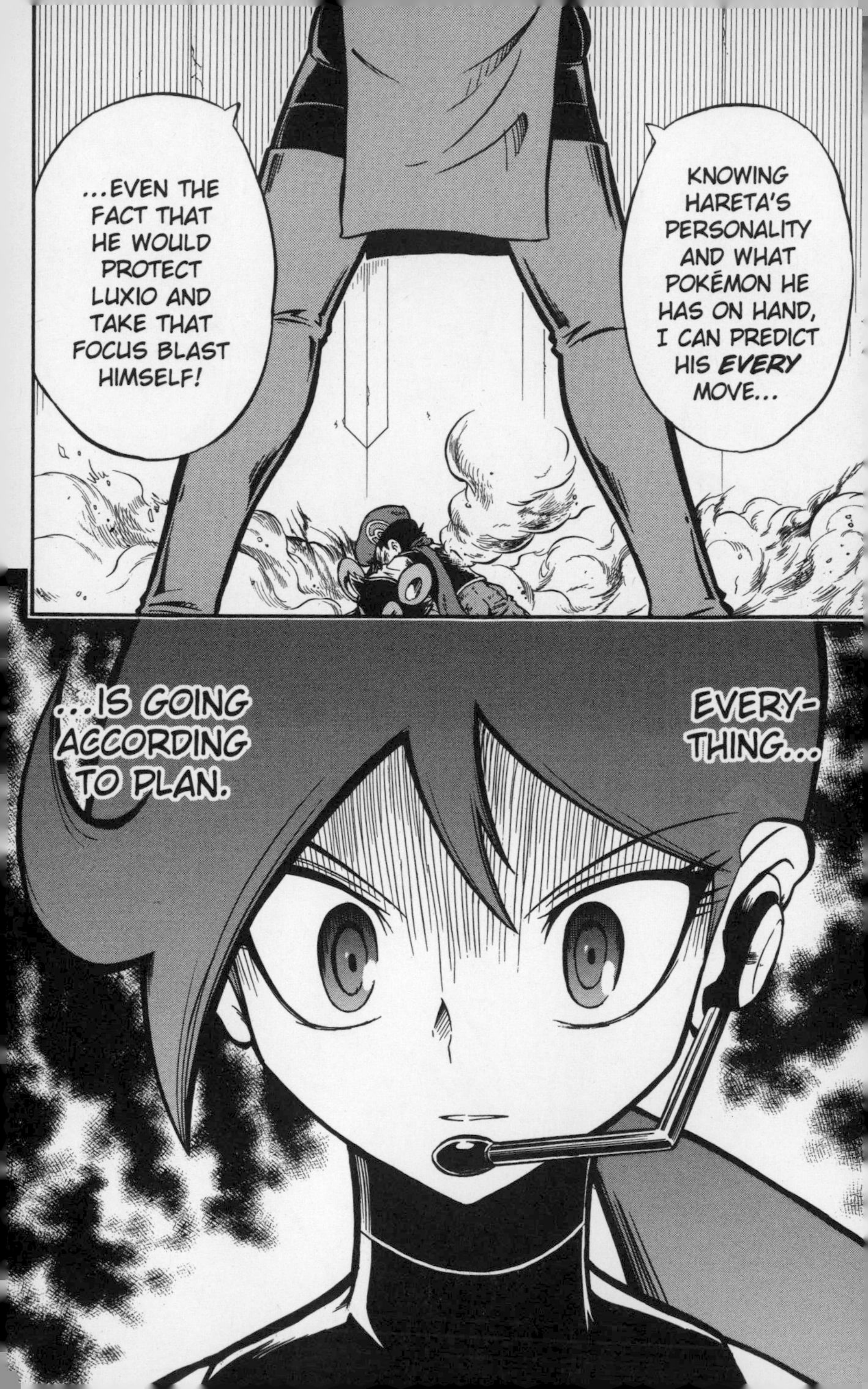
KNOWING HARETA'S PERSONALITY AND WHAT POKÉMON HE HAS ON HAND, I CAN PREDICT HIS *EVERY* MOVE...
...EVEN THE FACT THAT HE WOULD PROTECT LUXIO AND TAKE THAT FOCUS BLAST HIMSELF!
EVERY-THING...
...IS GOING ACCORDING TO PLAN.

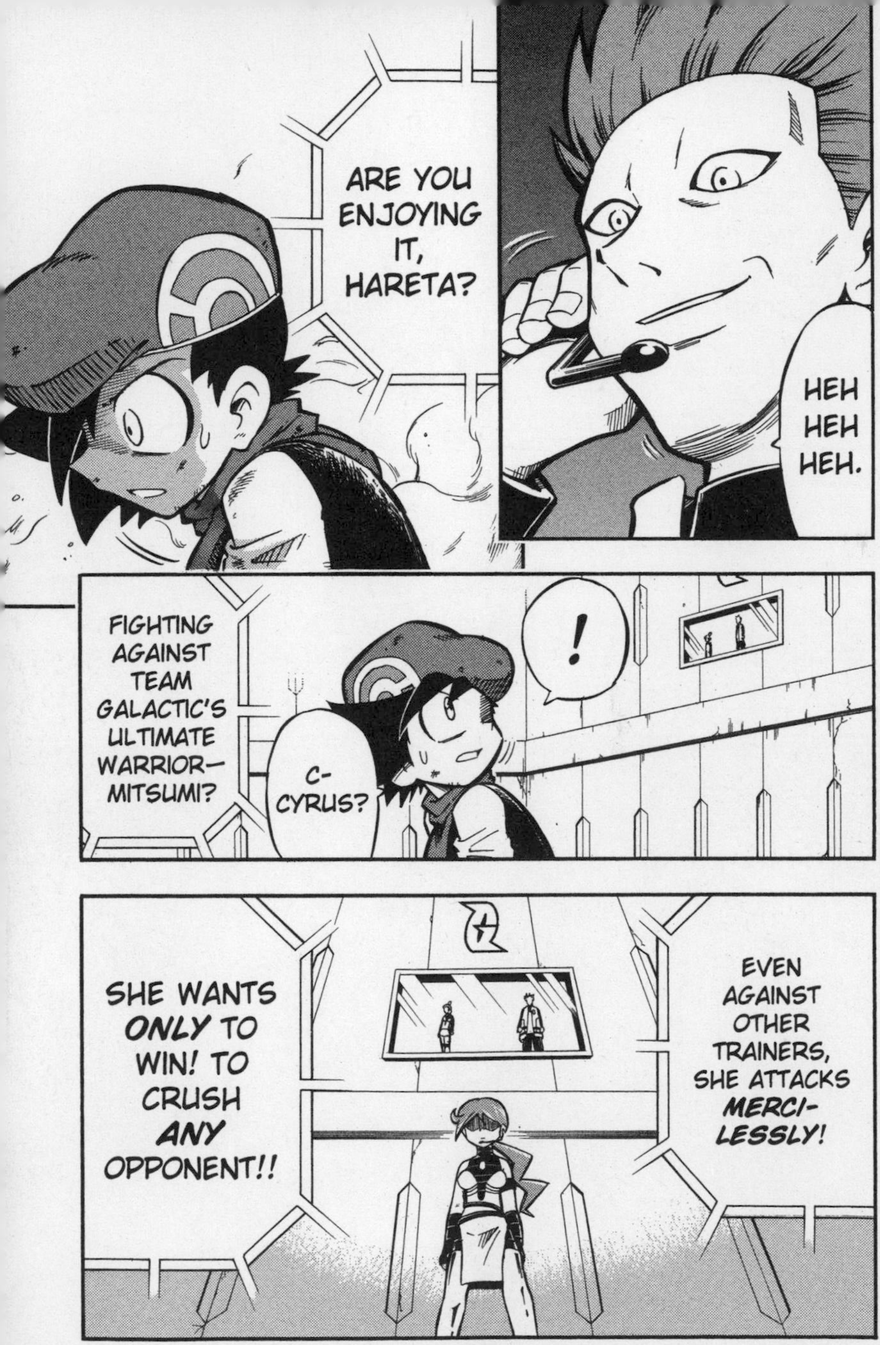
HEH HEH HEH.
ARE YOU ENJOYING IT, HARETA?
!
C- CYRUS?
FIGHTING AGAINST TEAM GALACTIC'S ULTIMATE WARRIOR—MITSUMI?
EVEN AGAINST OTHER TRAINERS, SHE ATTACKS MERCI-LESSLY!
SHE WANTS ONLY TO WIN! TO CRUSH ANY OPPONENT!!

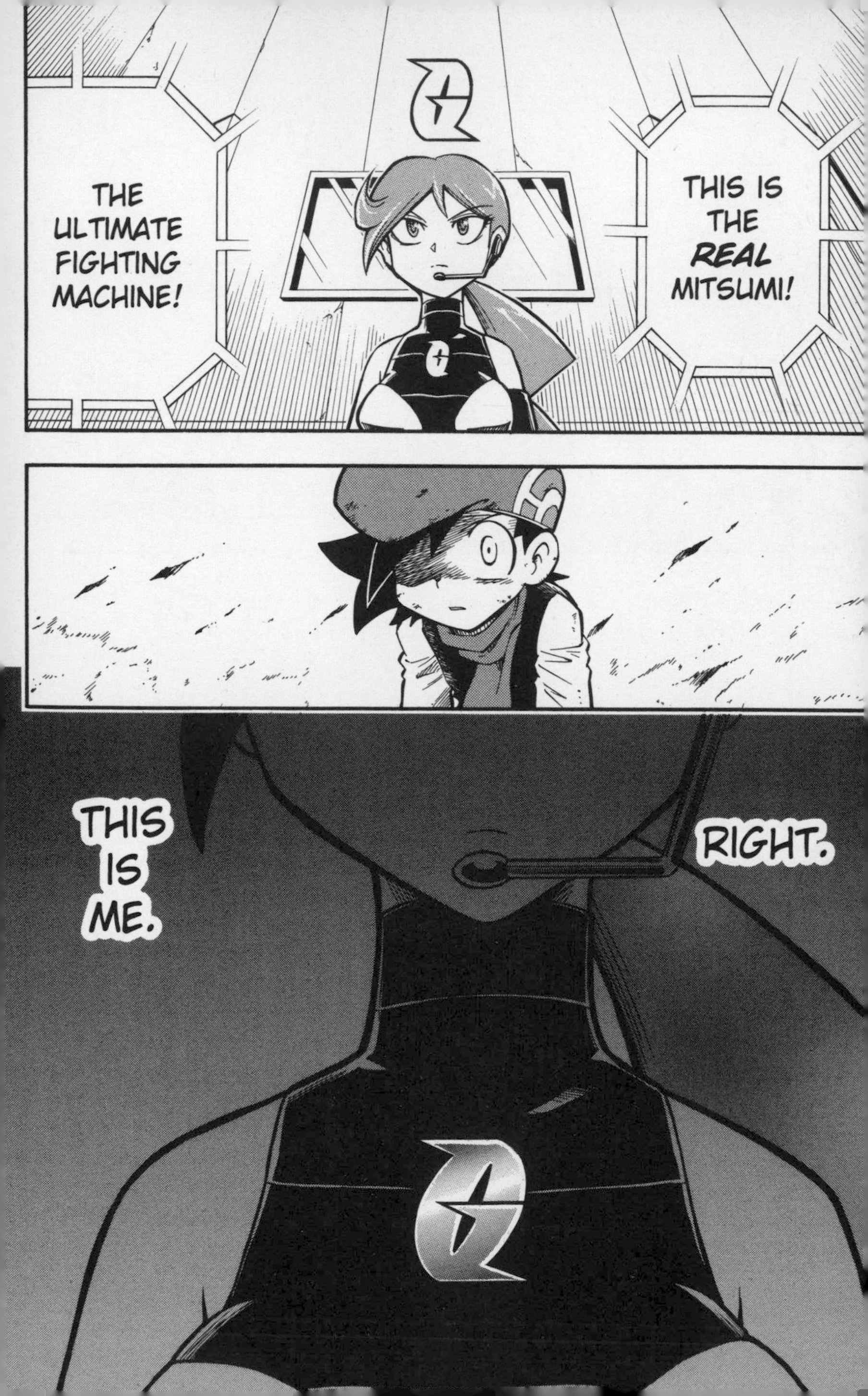
THIS IS THE REAL MITSUMI!
THE ULTIMATE FIGHTING MACHINE!
RIGHT.
THIS IS ME.

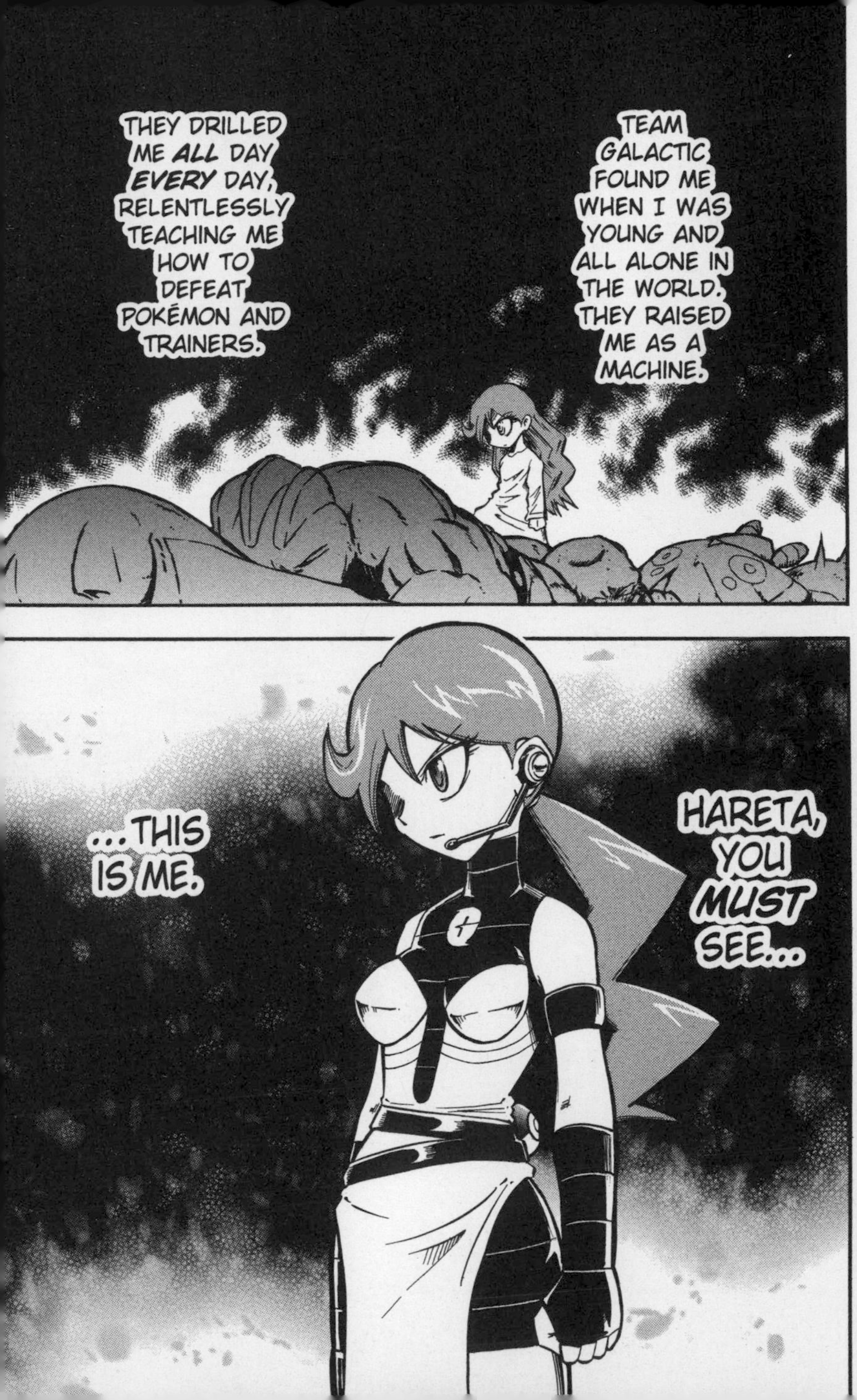
TEAM GALACTIC FOUND ME WHEN I WAS YOUNG AND ALL ALONE IN THE WORLD. THEY RAISED ME AS A MACHINE.
THEY DRILLED ME ALL DAY EVERY DAY, RELENTLESSLY TEACHING ME HOW TO DEFEAT POKÉMON AND TRAINERS.
HARETA, YOU MUST SEE...
...THIS IS ME.

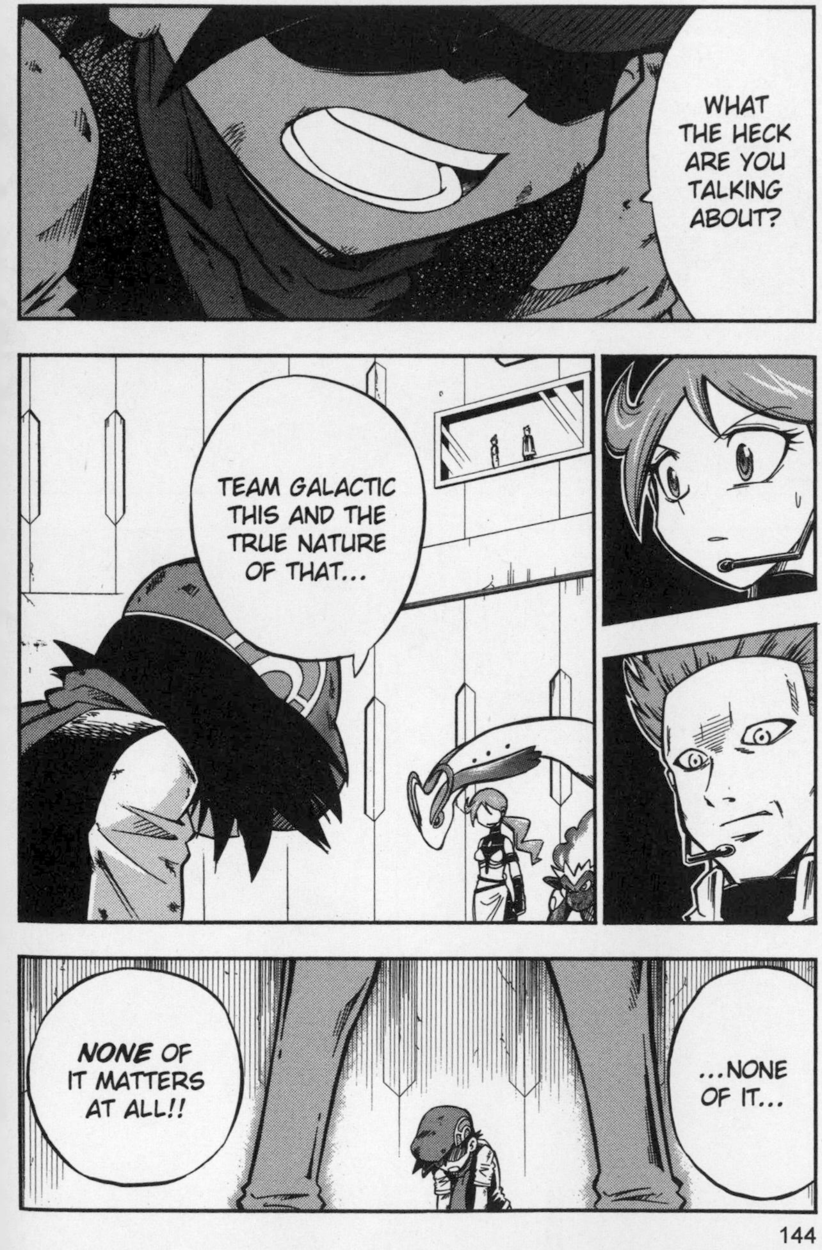
WHAT THE HECK ARE YOU TALKING ABOUT?
TEAM GALACTIC THIS AND THE TRUE NATURE OF THAT...
...NONE OF IT...
NONE OF IT MATTERS AT ALL!!

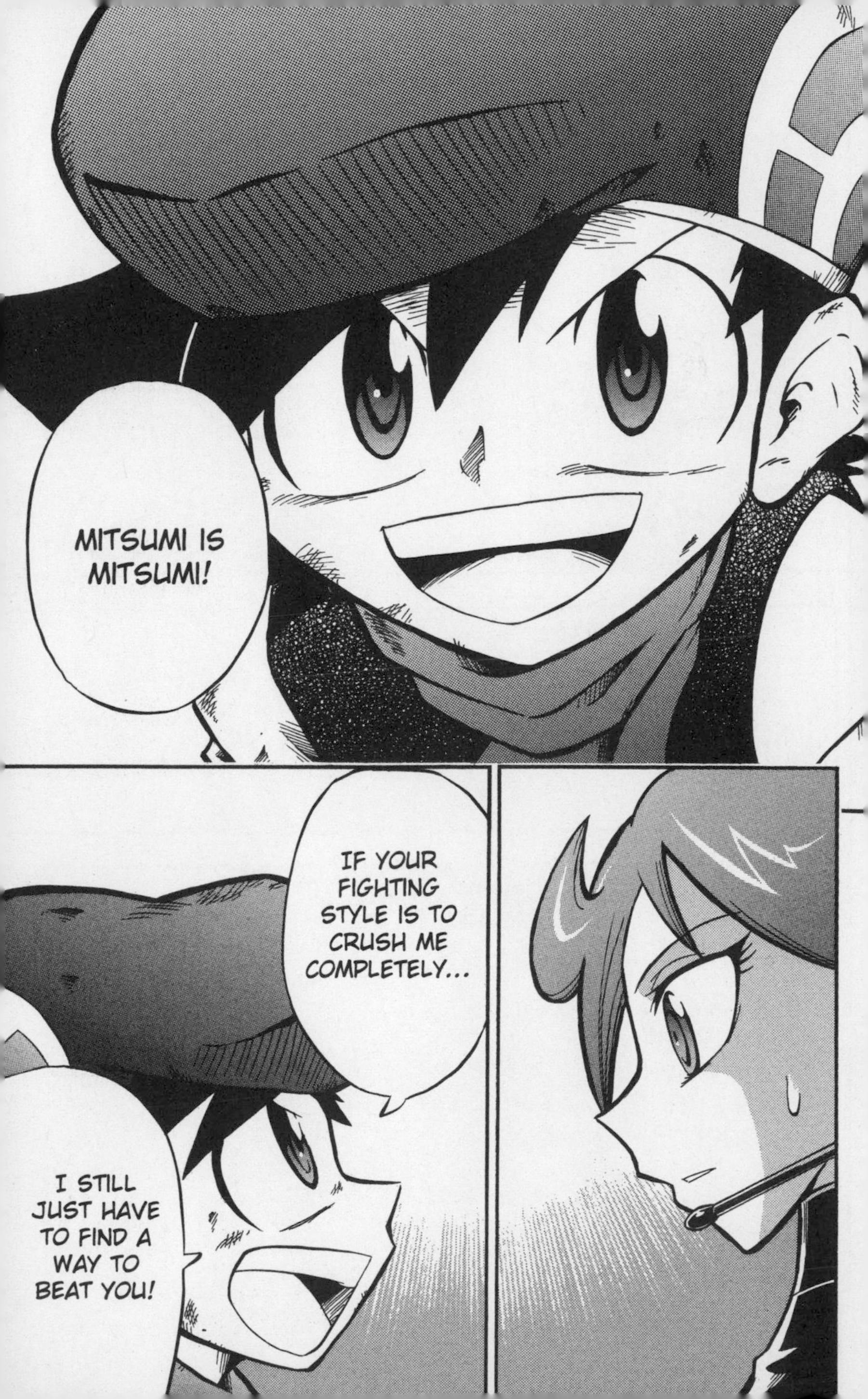
MITSUMI IS MITSUMI!
IF YOUR FIGHTING STYLE IS TO CRUSH ME COMPLETELY...
I STILL JUST HAVE TO FIND A WAY TO BEAT YOU!

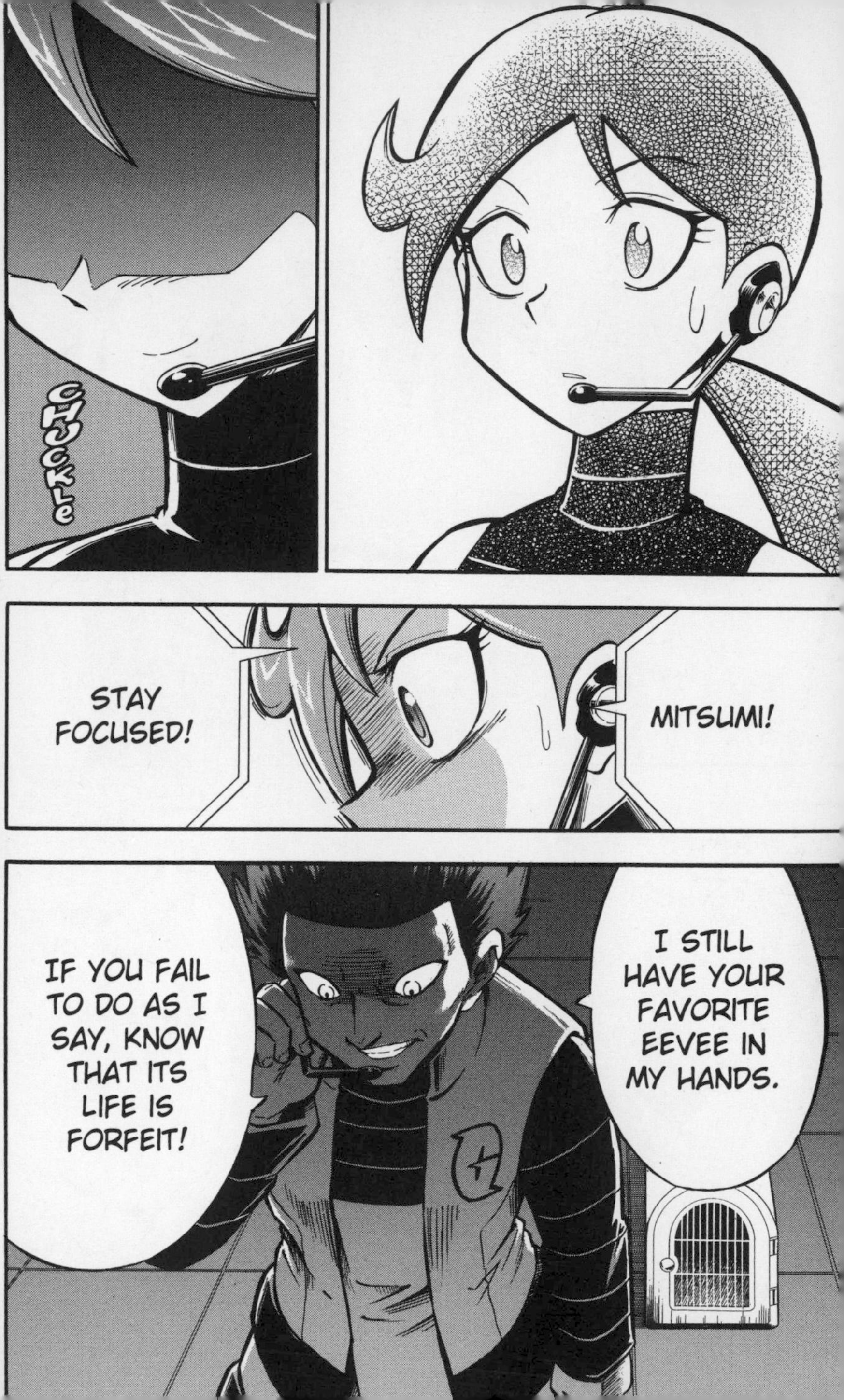
CHUCKLE
MITSUMI!
STAY FOCUSED!
I STILL HAVE YOUR FAVORITE EEVEE IN MY HANDS.
IF YOU FAIL TO DO AS I SAY, KNOW THAT ITS LIFE IS FORFEIT!

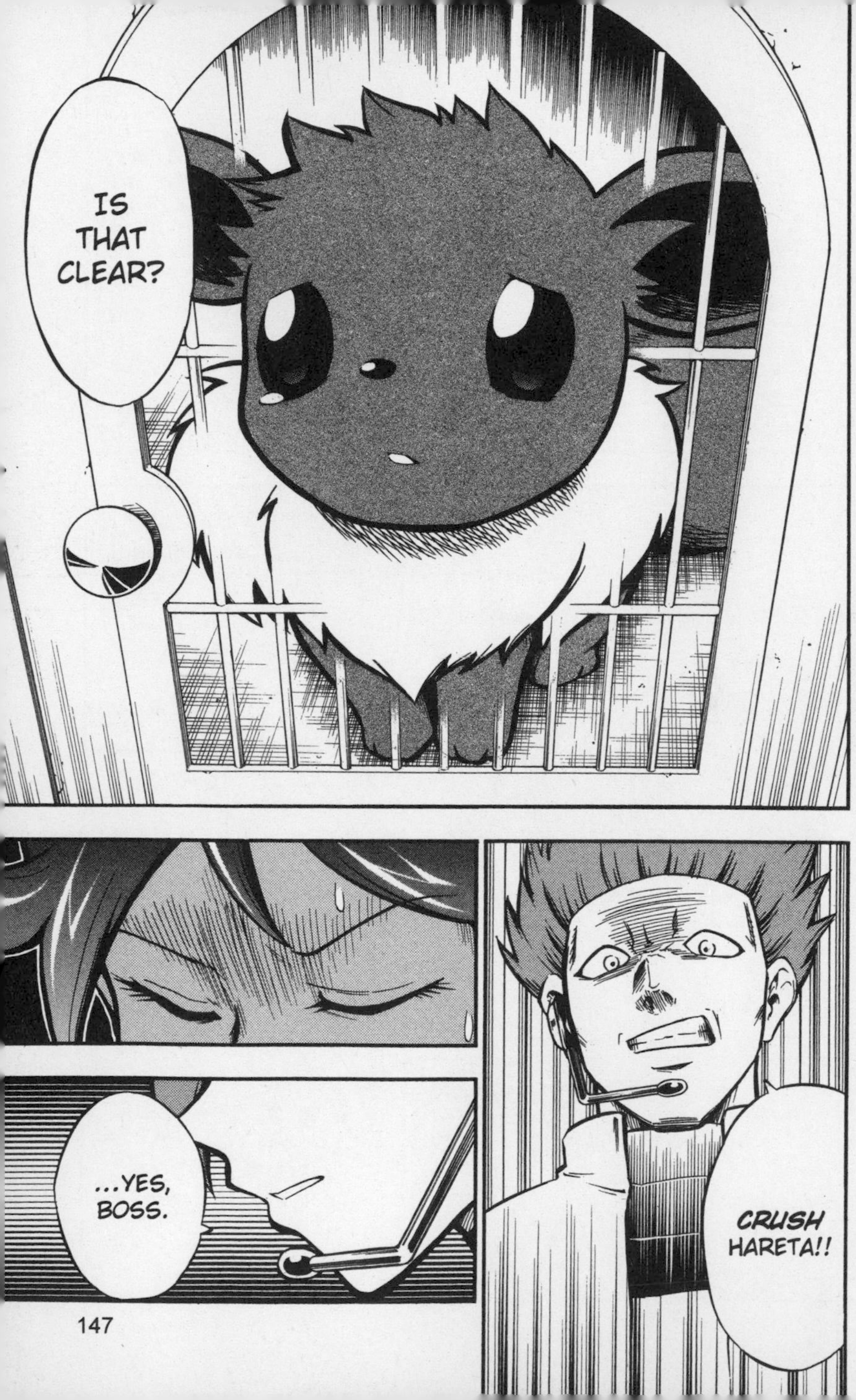
IS THAT CLEAR?
CRUSH HARETA!!
...YES, BOSS.

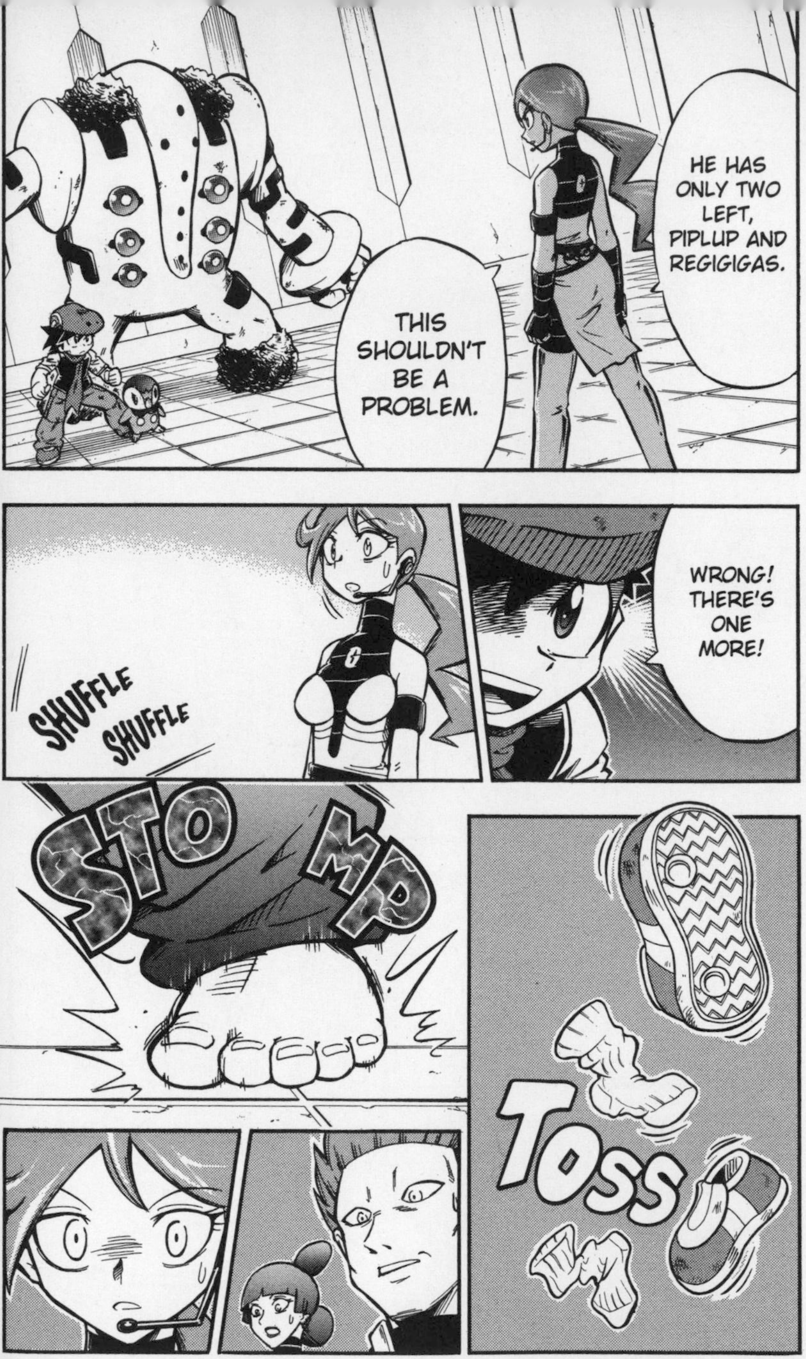
HE HAS ONLY TWO LEFT, PIPLUP AND REGIGIGAS.
THIS SHOULDN'T BE A PROBLEM.
WRONG! THERE'S ONE MORE!
SHUFFLE SHUFFLE
TOSS
STOMP

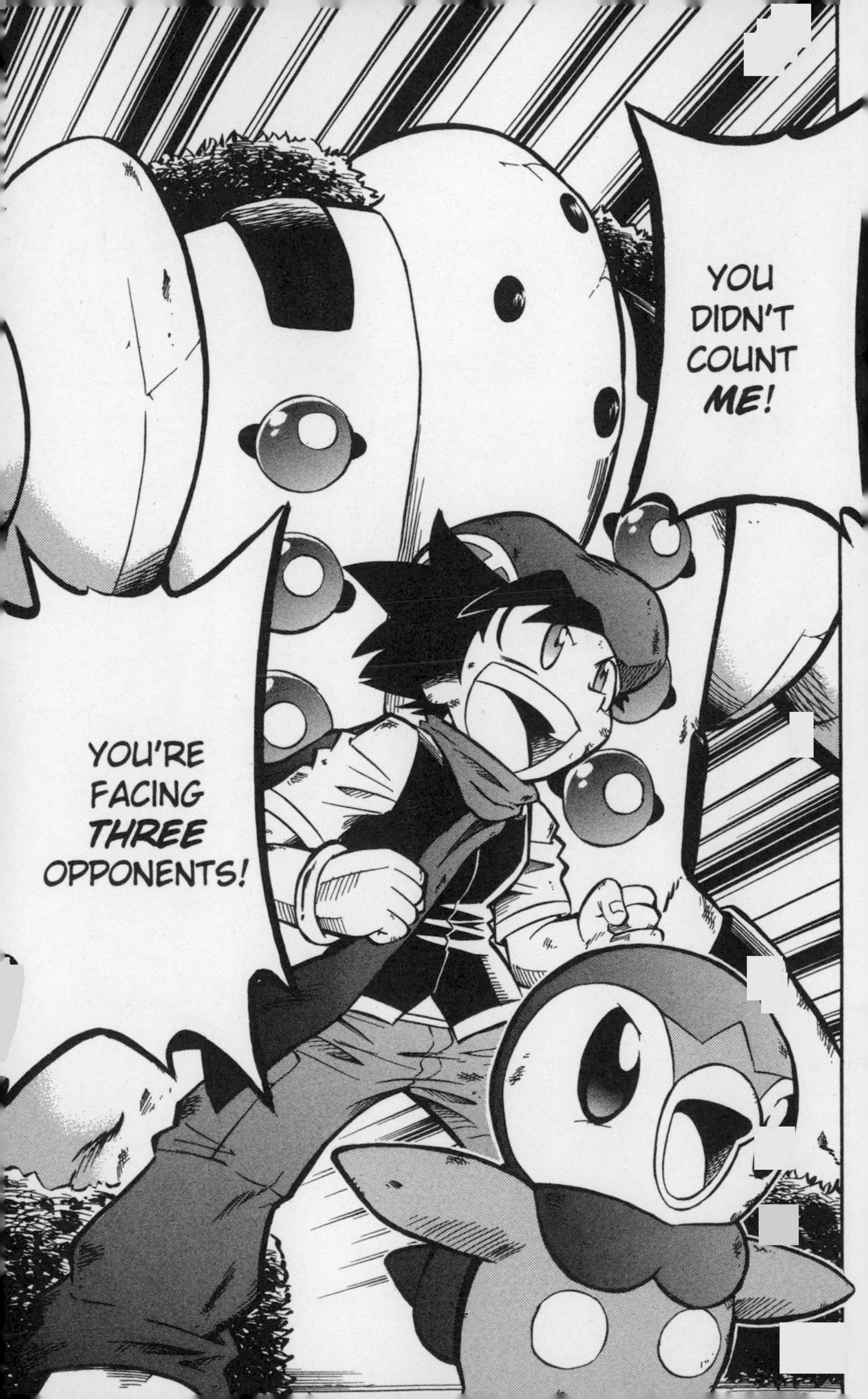
YOU DIDN'T COUNT ME!
YOU'RE FACING THREE OPPONENTS!

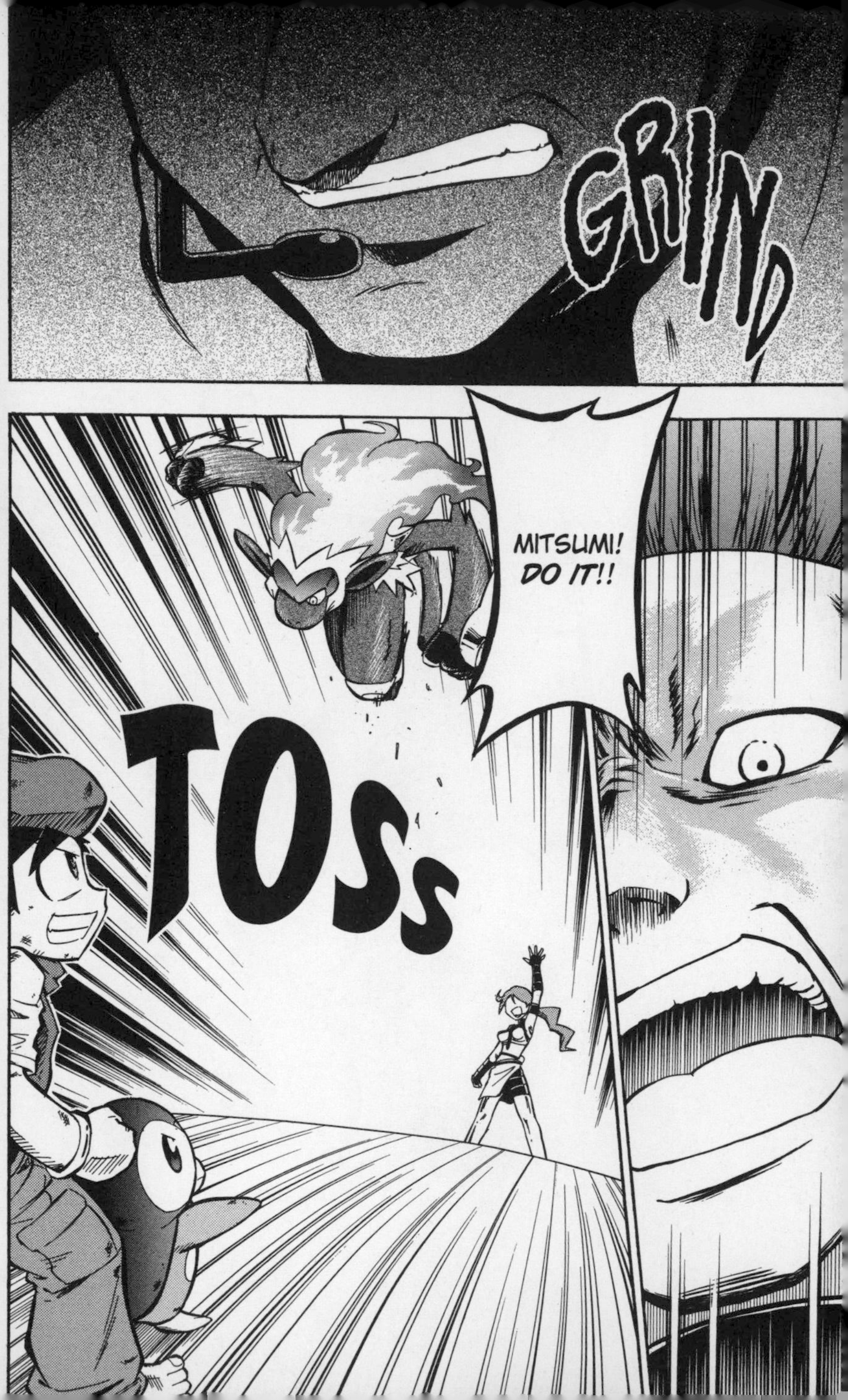
GRIND
MITSUMI! DO IT!!
TOSS

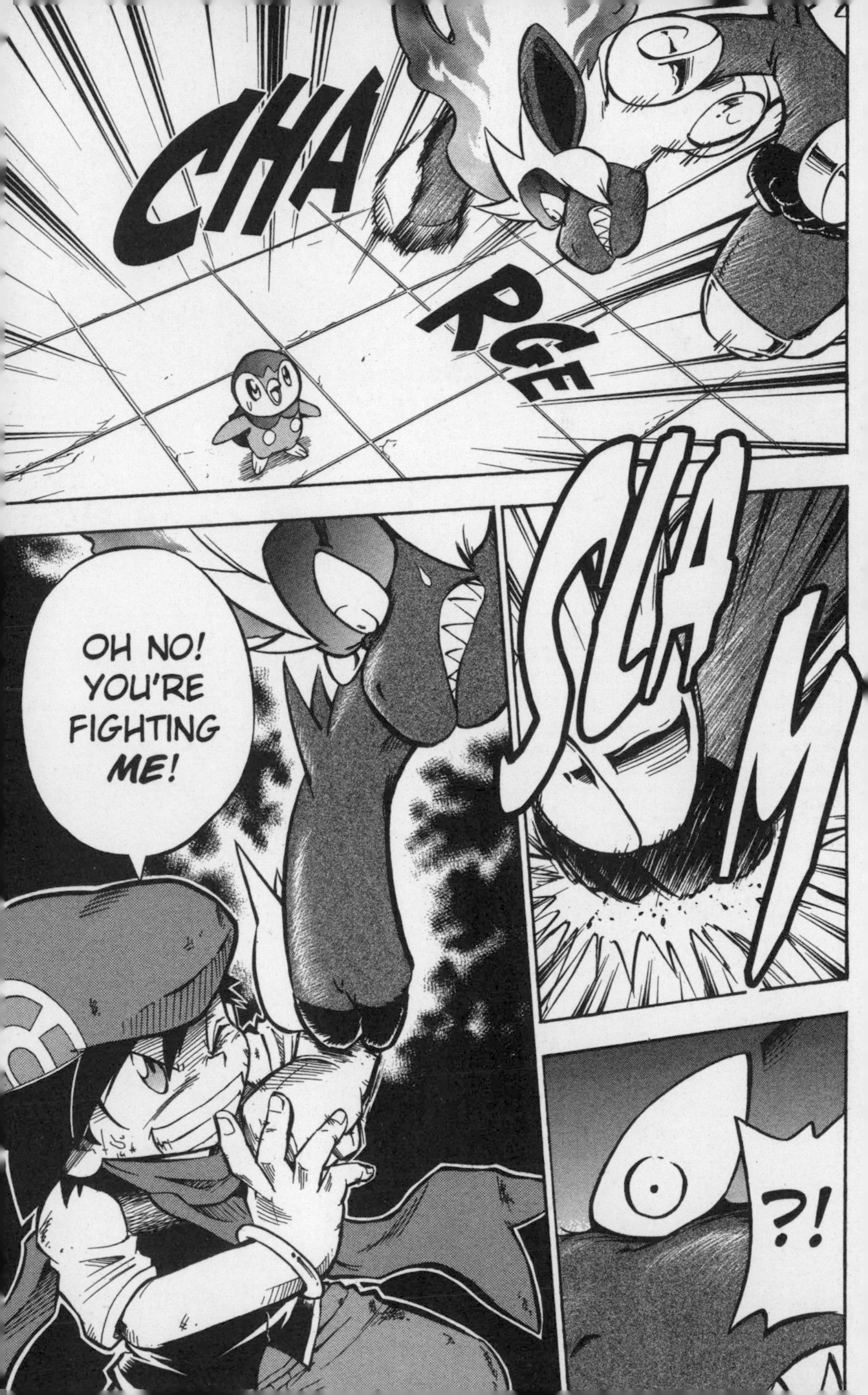
CHARGE
SLAM
?!
OH NO! YOU'RE FIGHTING ME!

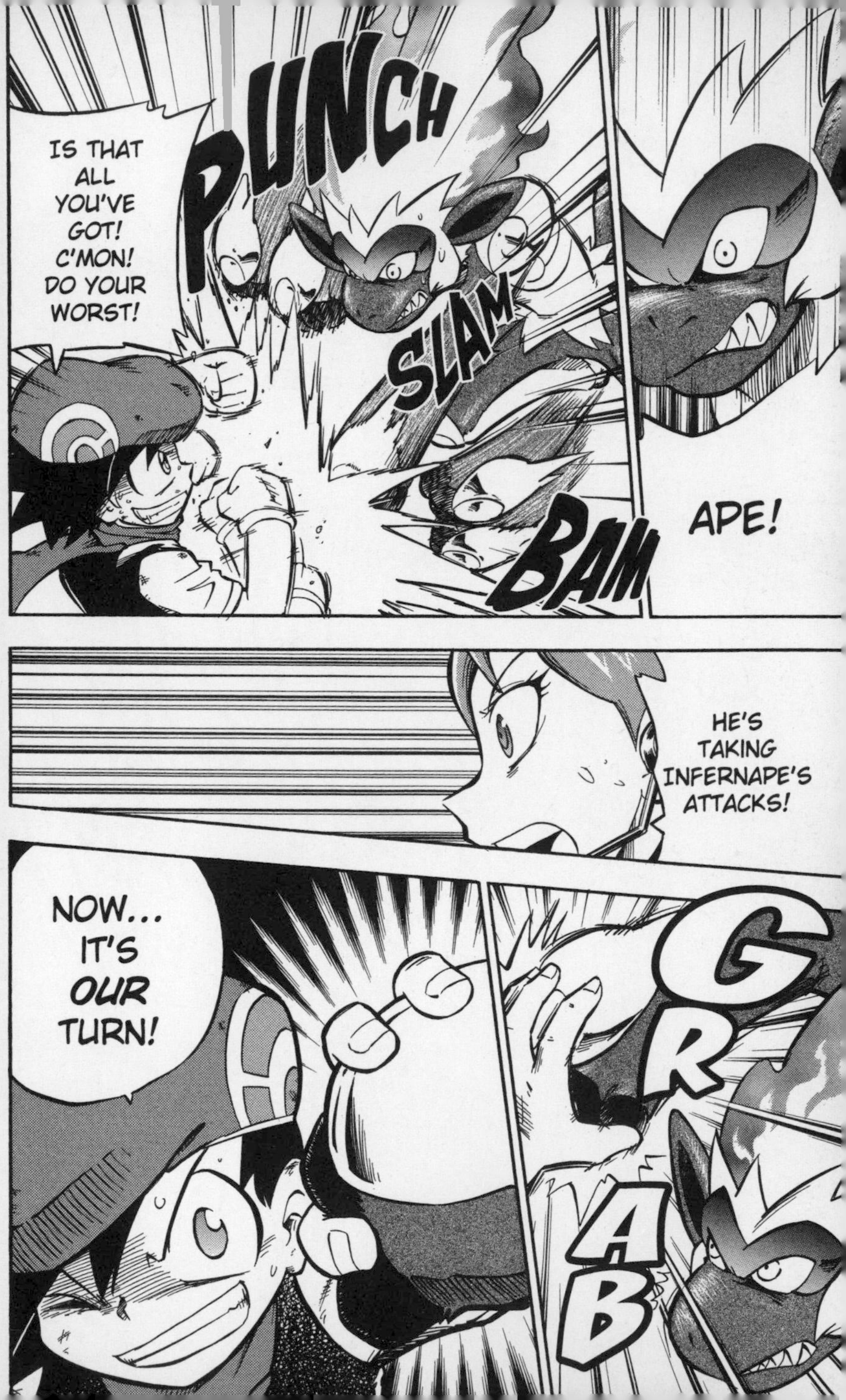
APE!
PUNCH
IS THAT ALL YOU'VE GOT! C'MON! DO YOUR WORST!
SLAM
BAM
HE'S TAKING INFERNAPE'S ATTACKS!
GRAB
NOW... IT'S OUR TURN!

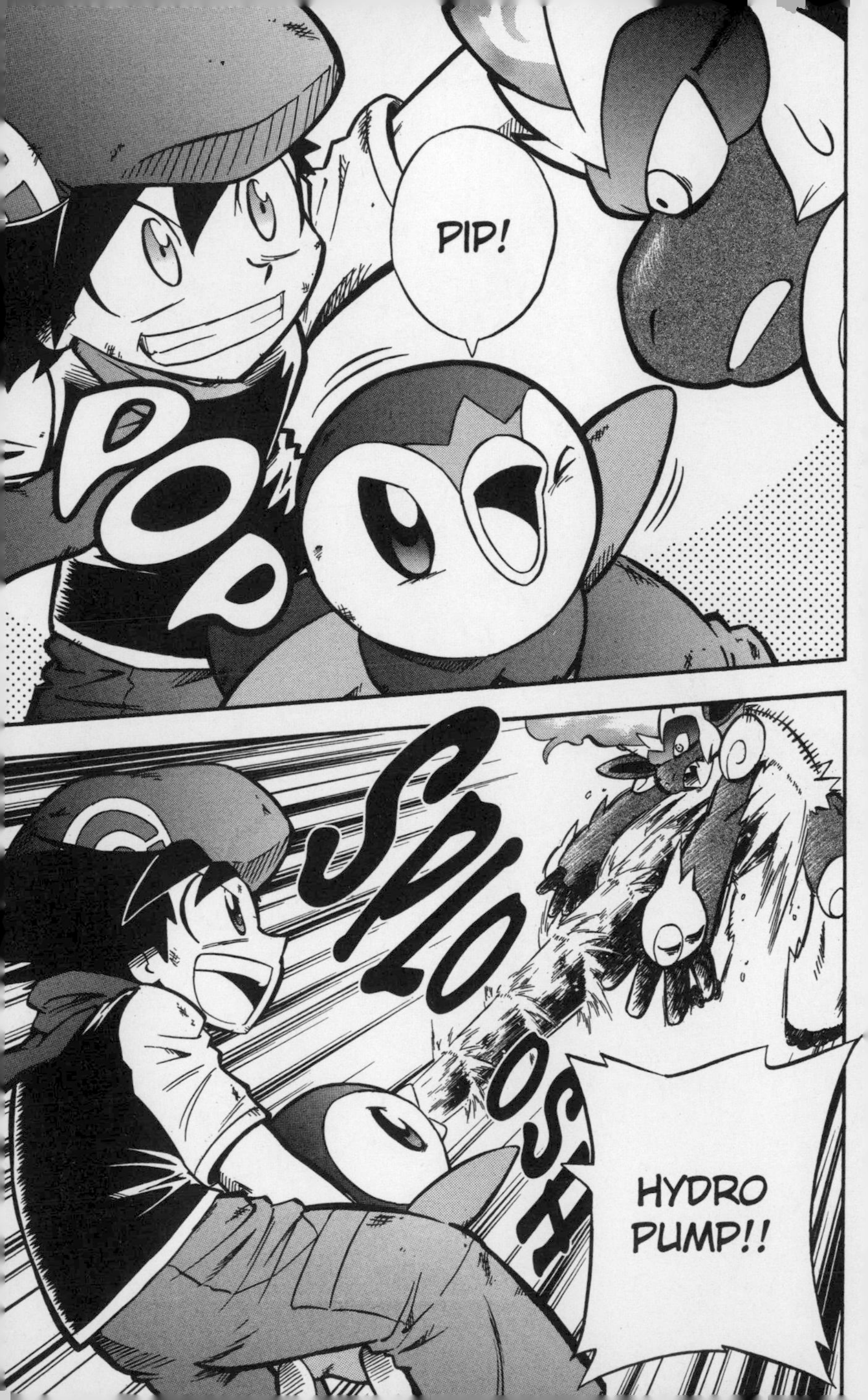
PIP!
POP
SPLOOSH
HYDRO PUMP!!

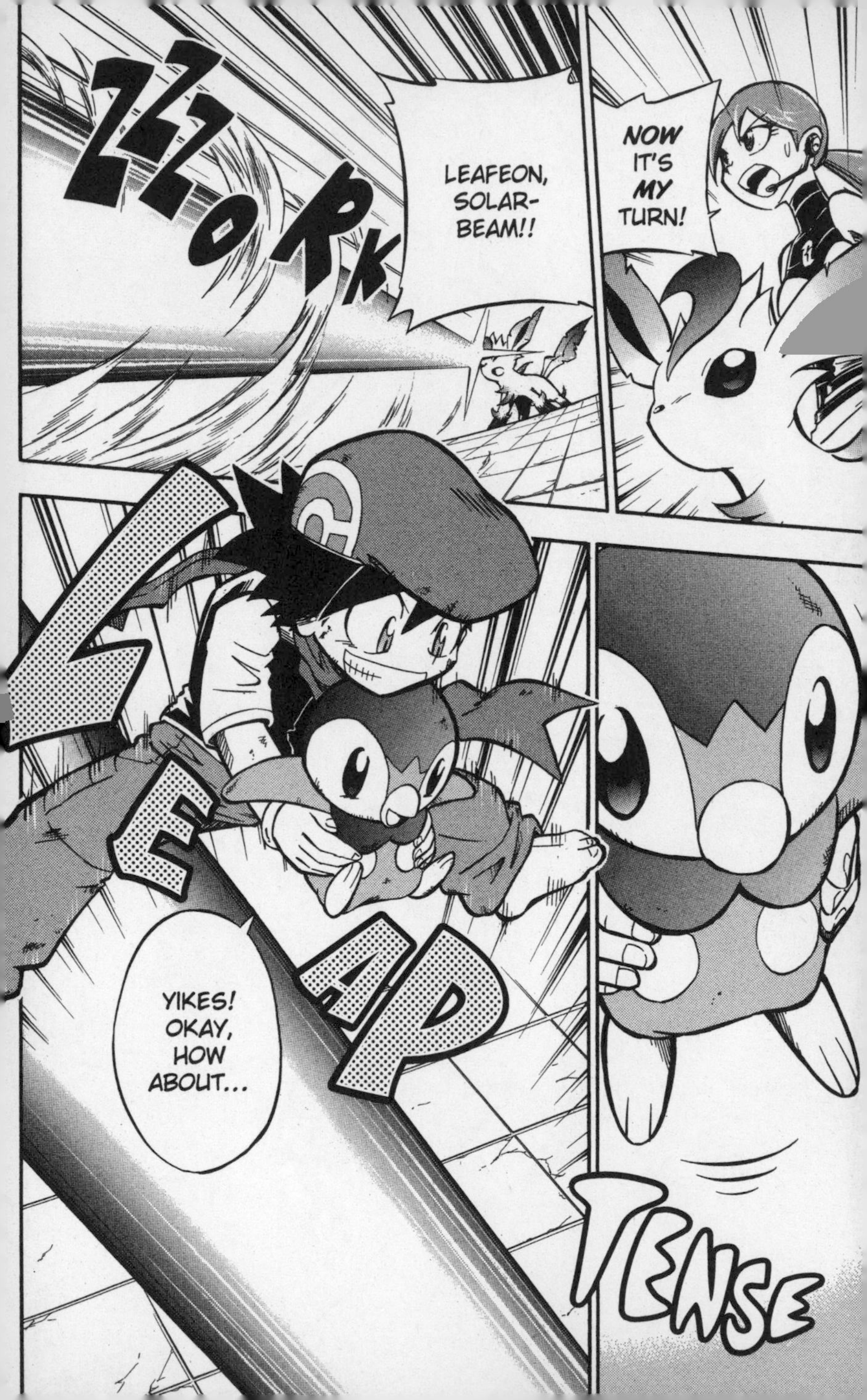
NOW IT'S MY TURN!
LEAFEON, SOLAR-BEAM!!
ZZZORK
TENSE
LEAP
YIKES! OKAY, HOW ABOUT...

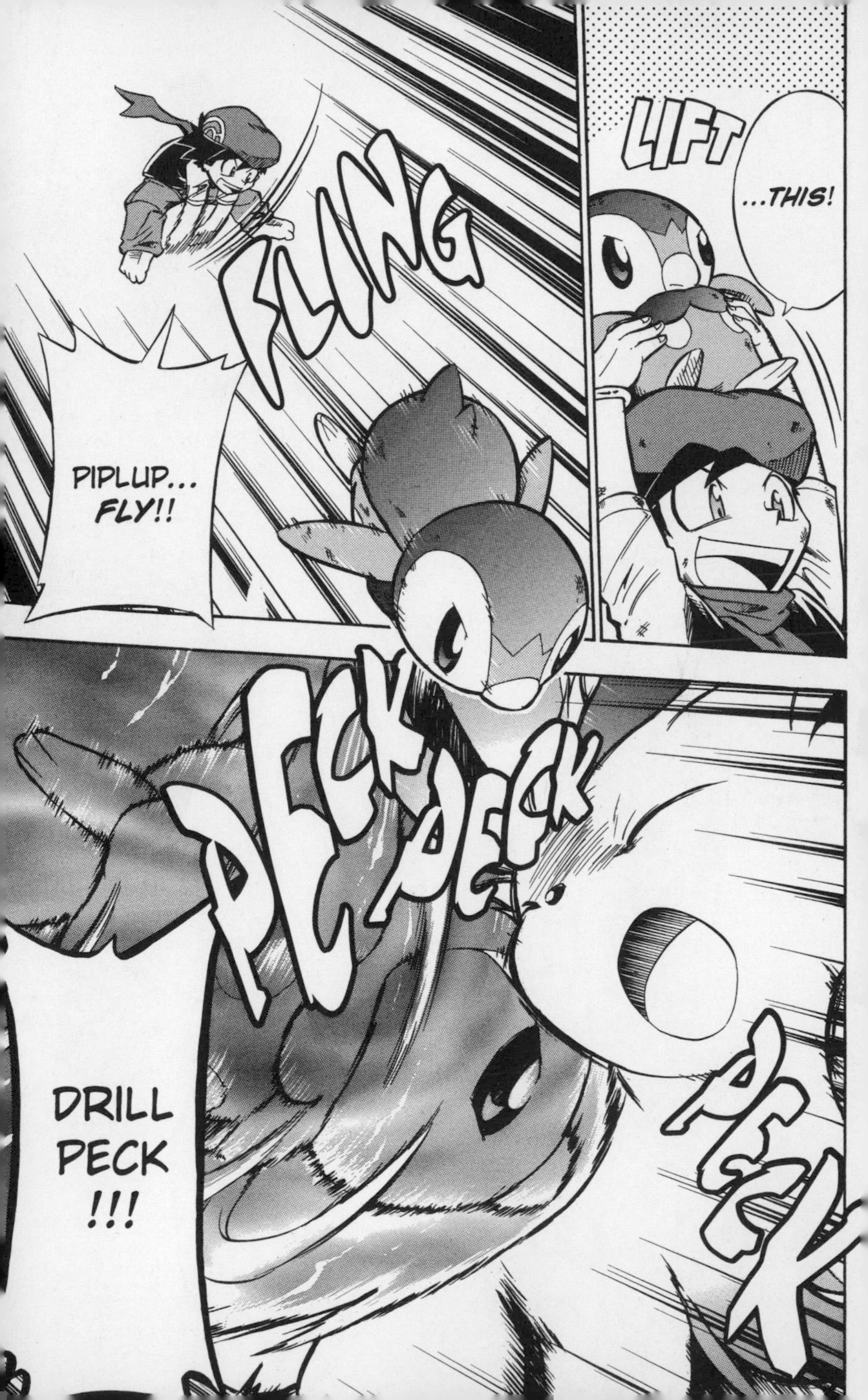
LIFT
...THIS!
FLING
PIPLUP... FLY!!
PECK PECK
PECK
DRILL PECK !!!

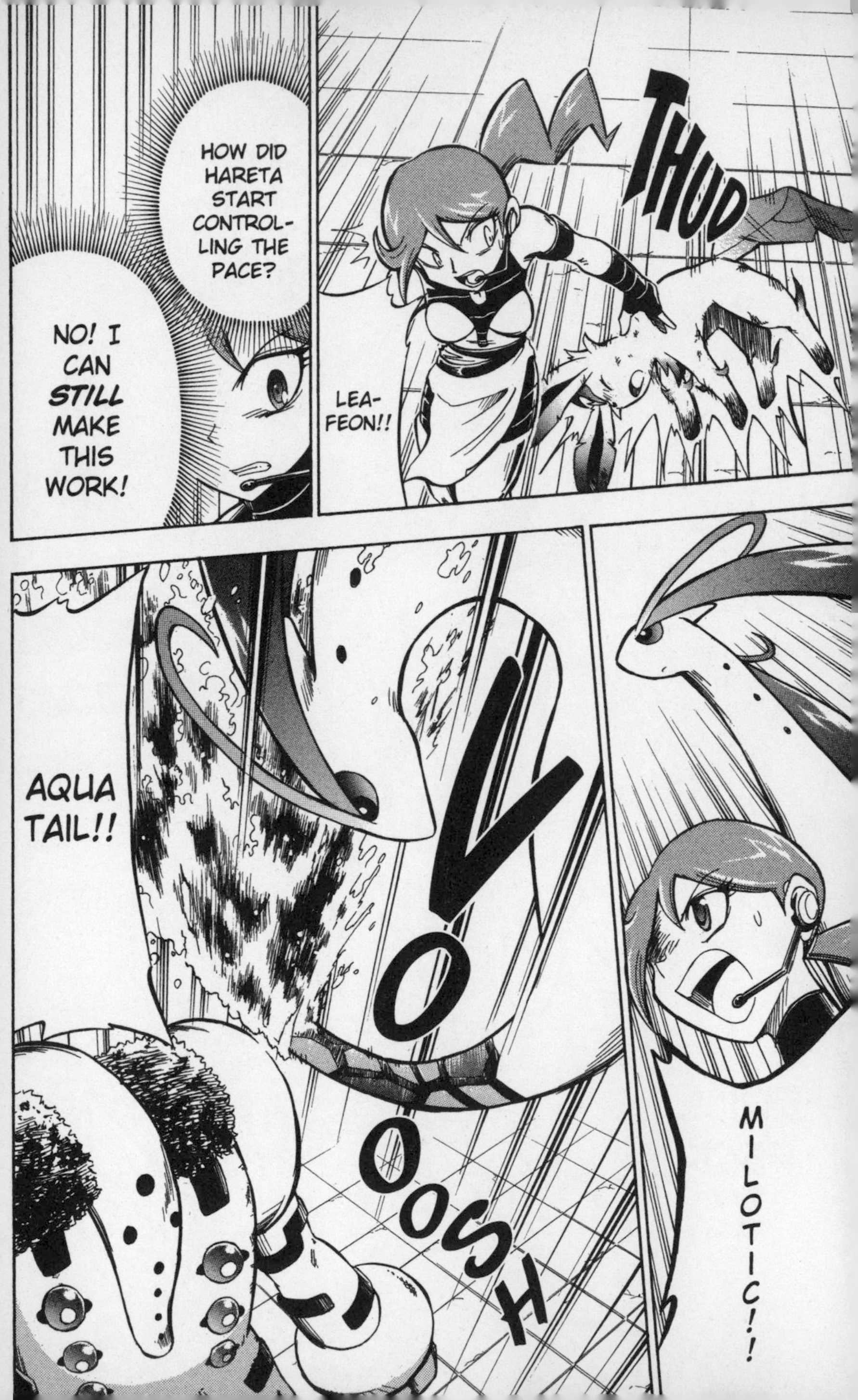
THUD
LEA-FEON!!
HOW DID HARETA START CONTROLLING THE PACE?
NO! I CAN STILL MAKE THIS WORK!
MILOTIC!!
AQUA TAIL!!
VOOOSH

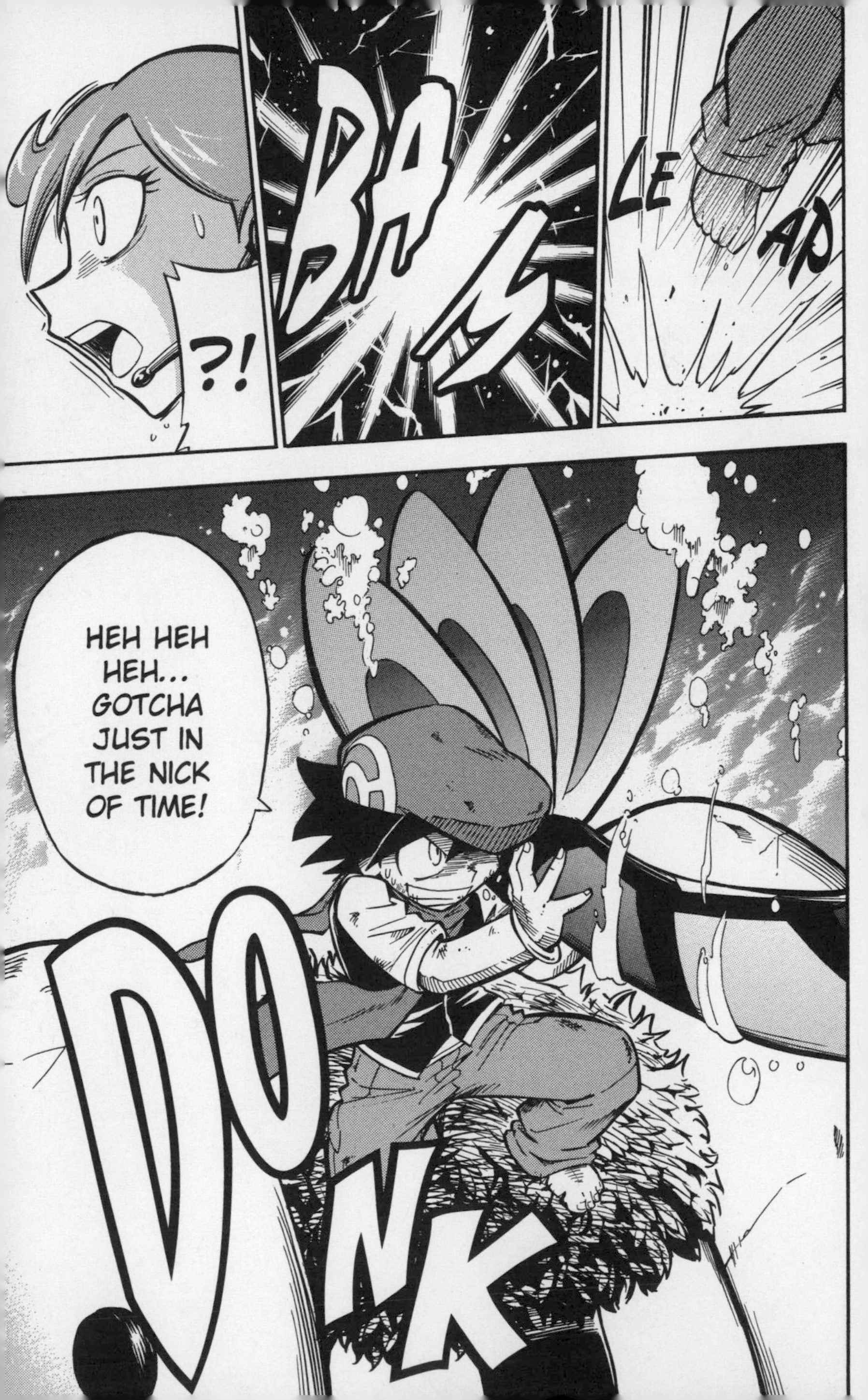
LEAP
BAS
?!
HEH HEH HEH... GOTCHA JUST IN THE NICK OF TIME!
DONK

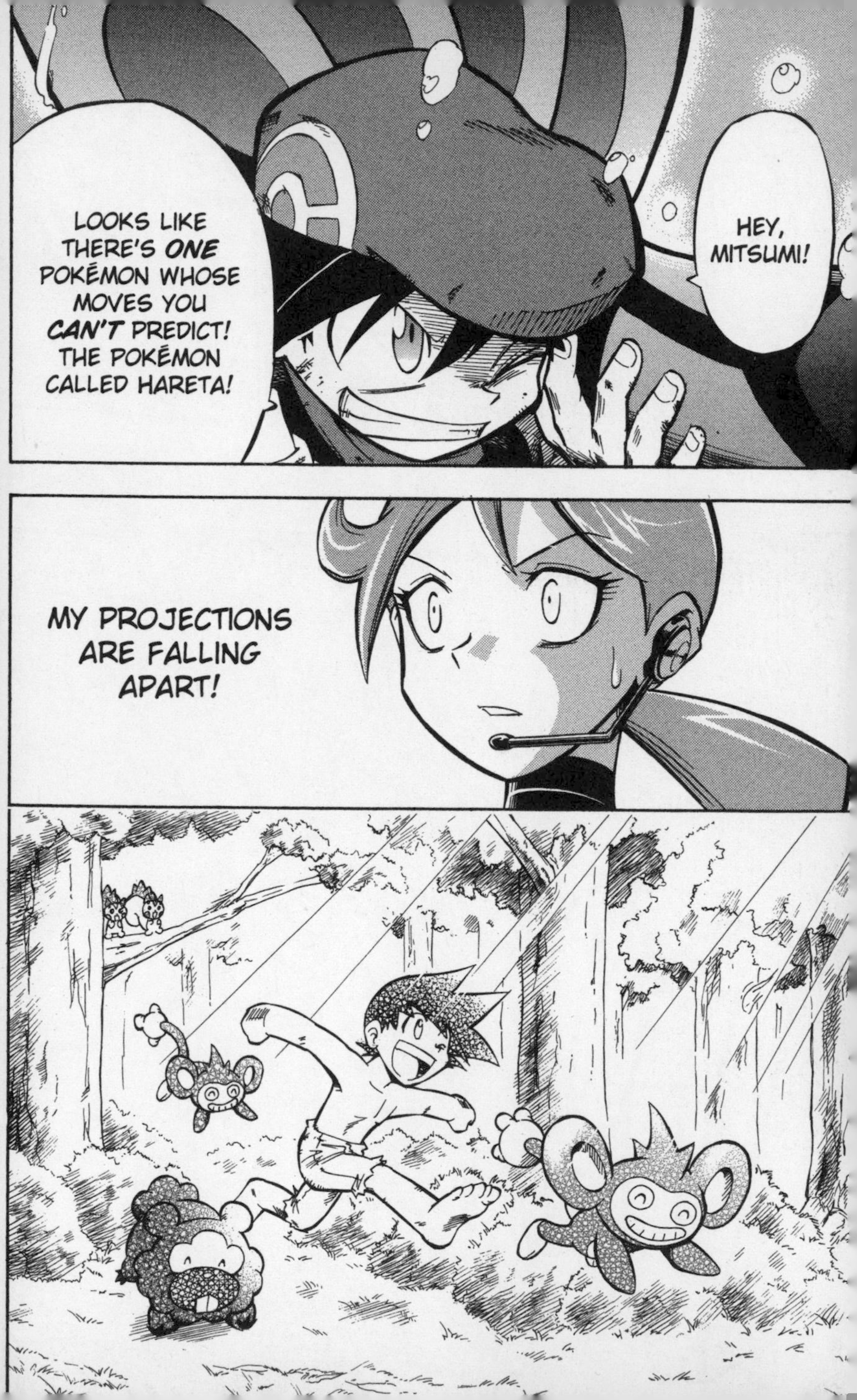
HEY, MITSUMI!
LOOKS LIKE THERE'S ONE POKÉMON WHOSE MOVES YOU CAN'T PREDICT! THE POKÉMON CALLED HARETA!
MY PROJECTIONS ARE FALLING APART!

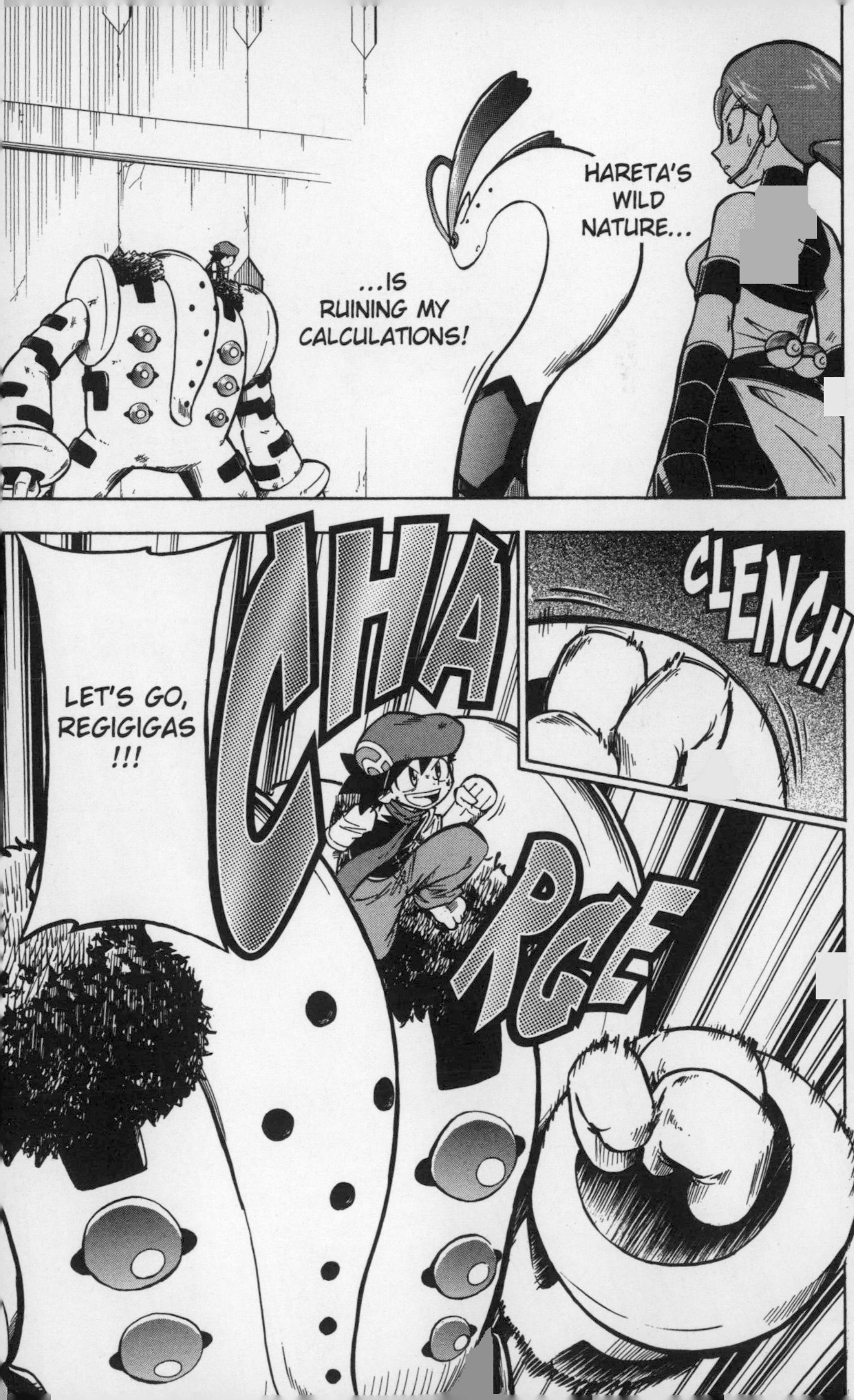
HARETA'S WILD NATURE...
...IS RUINING MY CALCULATIONS!
CLENCH
CHARGE
LET'S GO, REGIGIGAS!!!

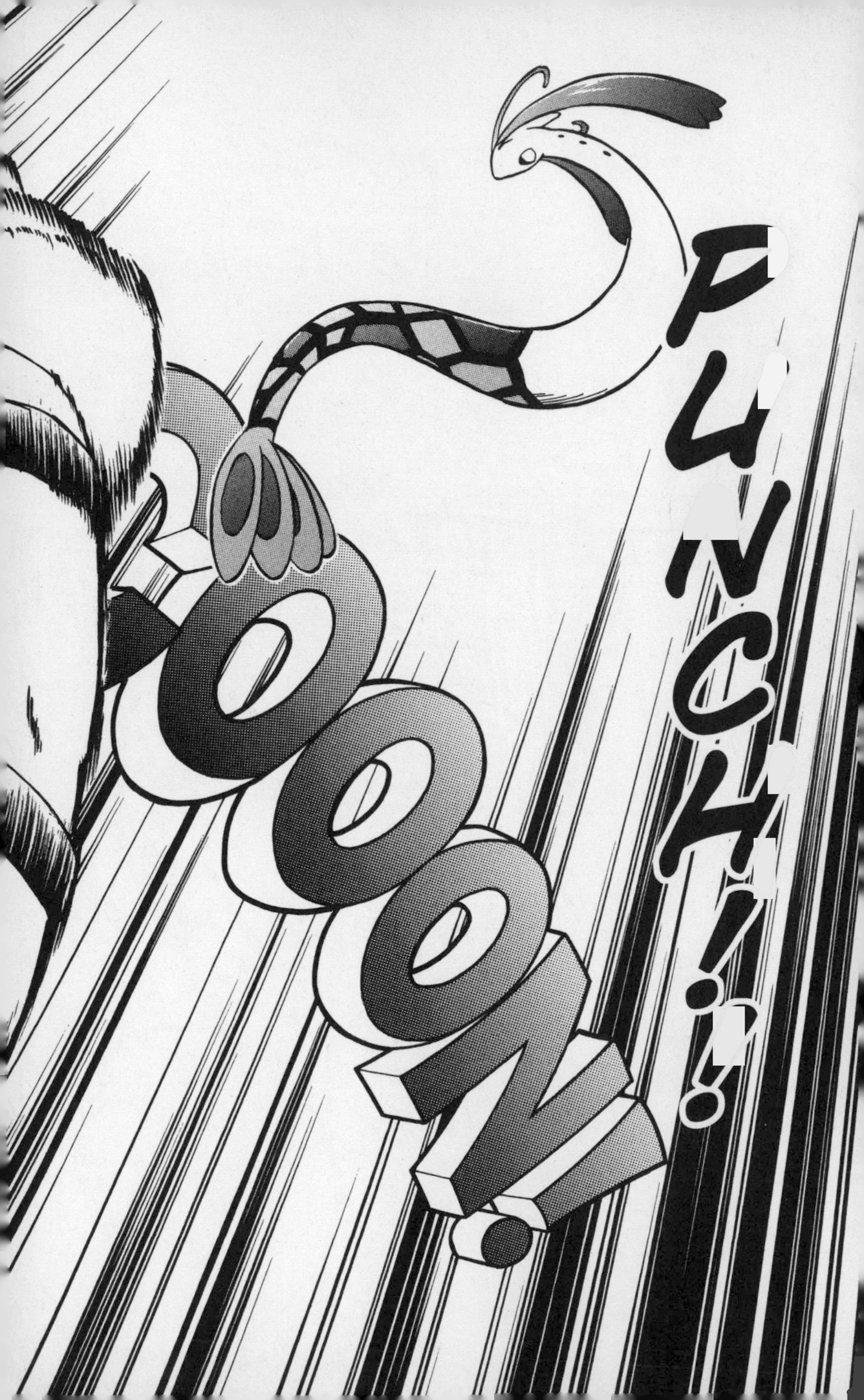
PUNCH!!
OOOM!

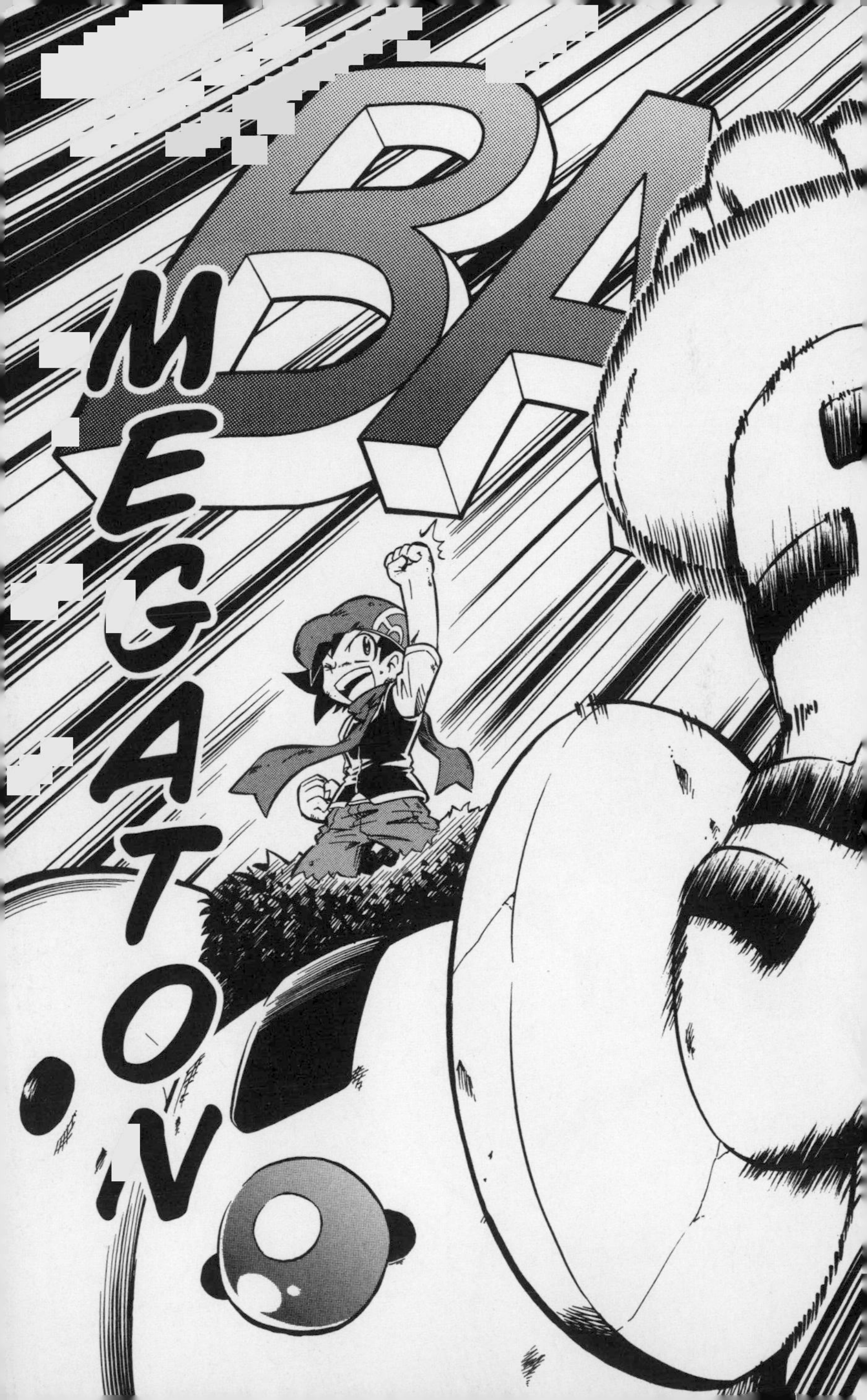
BA
MEGATON

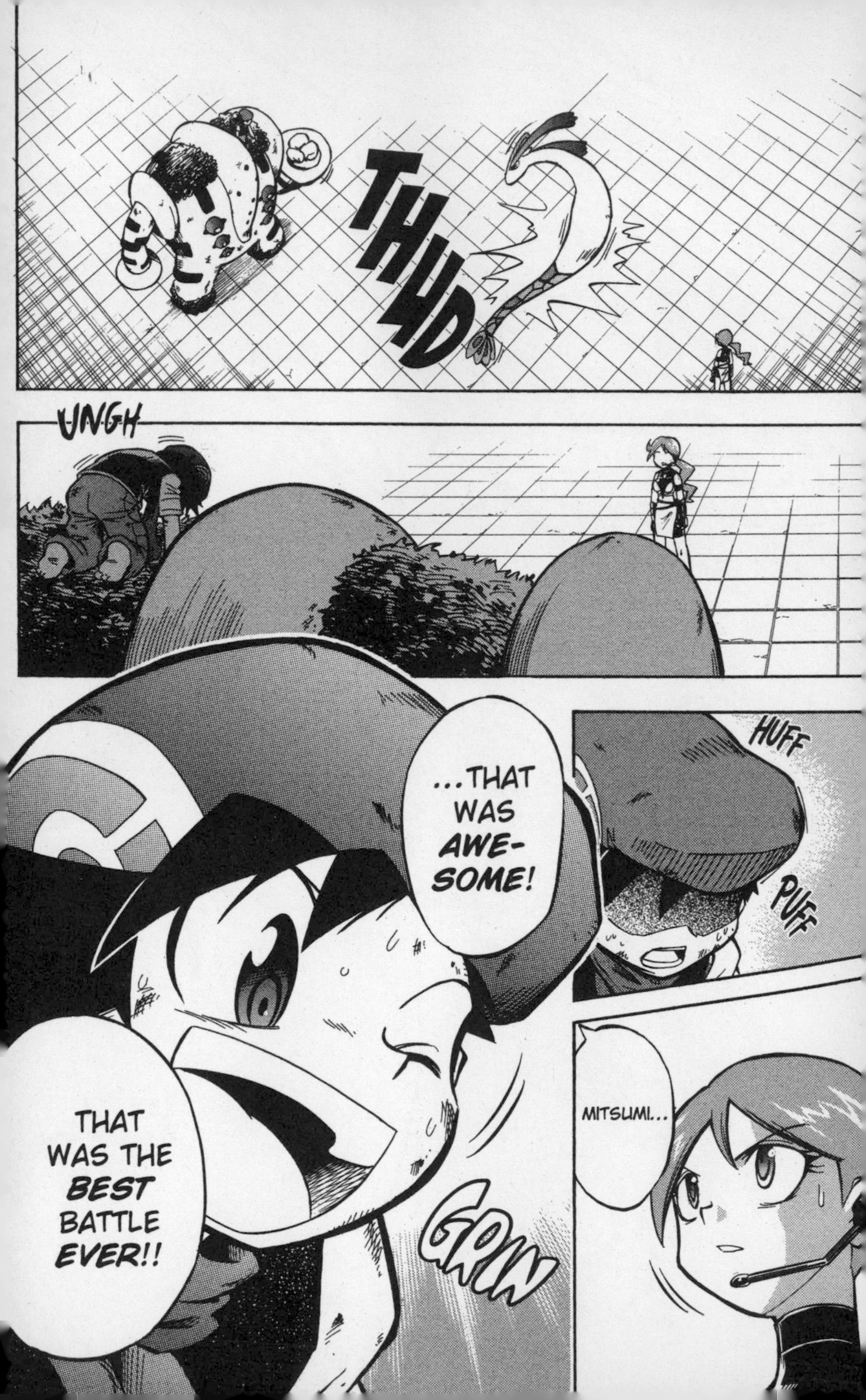
THUD
UNGH
HUFF
PUFF
...THAT WAS AWESOME!
MITSUMI...
THAT WAS THE BEST BATTLE EVER!!
GRIN

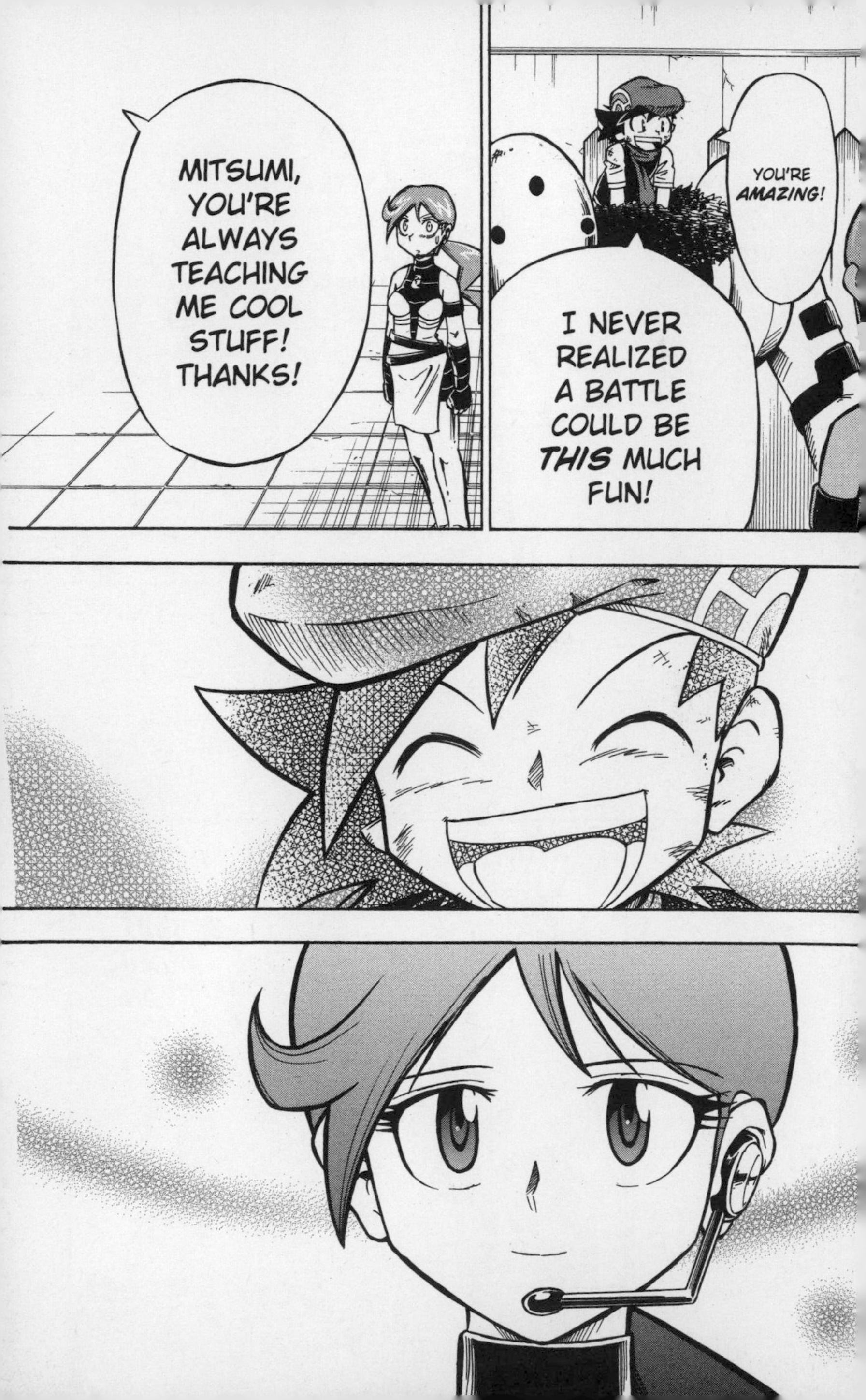
YOU'RE *AMAZING*!
I NEVER REALIZED A BATTLE COULD BE ***THIS*** MUCH FUN!
MITSUMI, YOU'RE ALWAYS TEACHING ME COOL STUFF! THANKS!

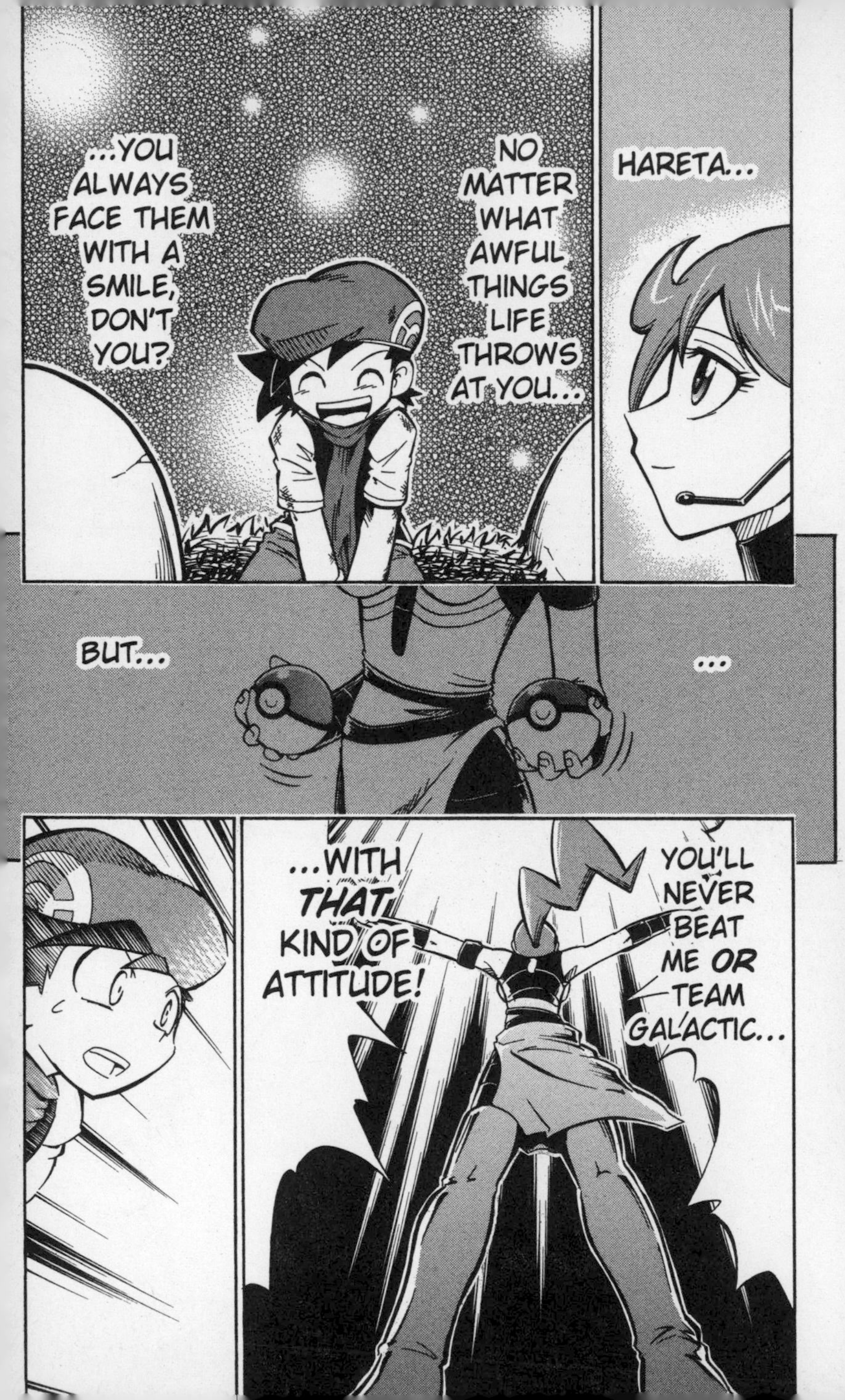
HARETA...
NO MATTER WHAT AWFUL THINGS LIFE THROWS AT YOU...
...YOU ALWAYS FACE THEM WITH A SMILE, DON'T YOU?
...
BUT...
YOU'LL NEVER BEAT ME OR TEAM GALACTIC...
...WITH THAT KIND OF ATTITUDE!

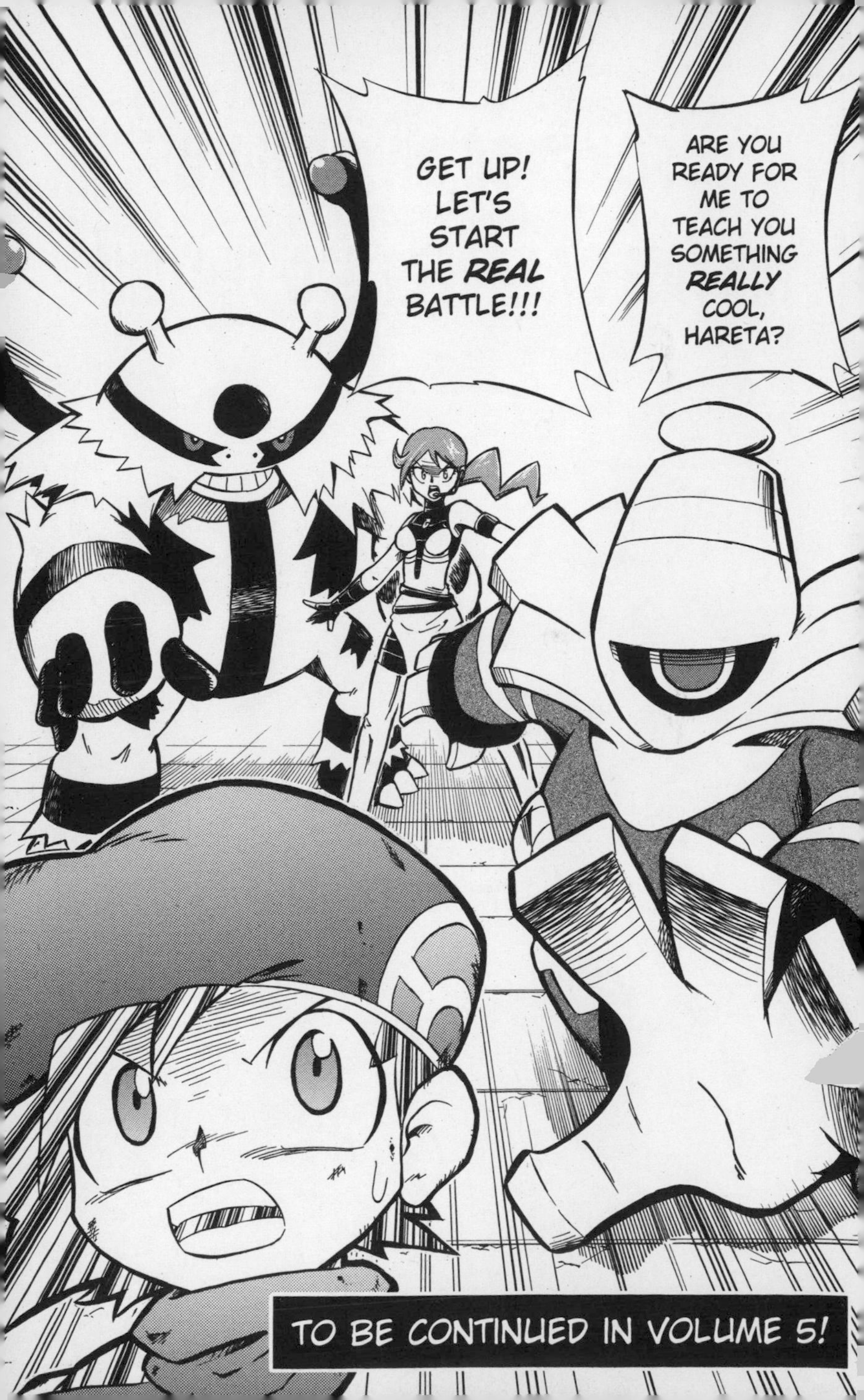
ARE YOU READY FOR ME TO TEACH YOU SOMETHING REALLY COOL, HARETA?
GET UP! LET'S START THE REAL BATTLE!!!
TO BE CONTINUED IN VOLUME 5!

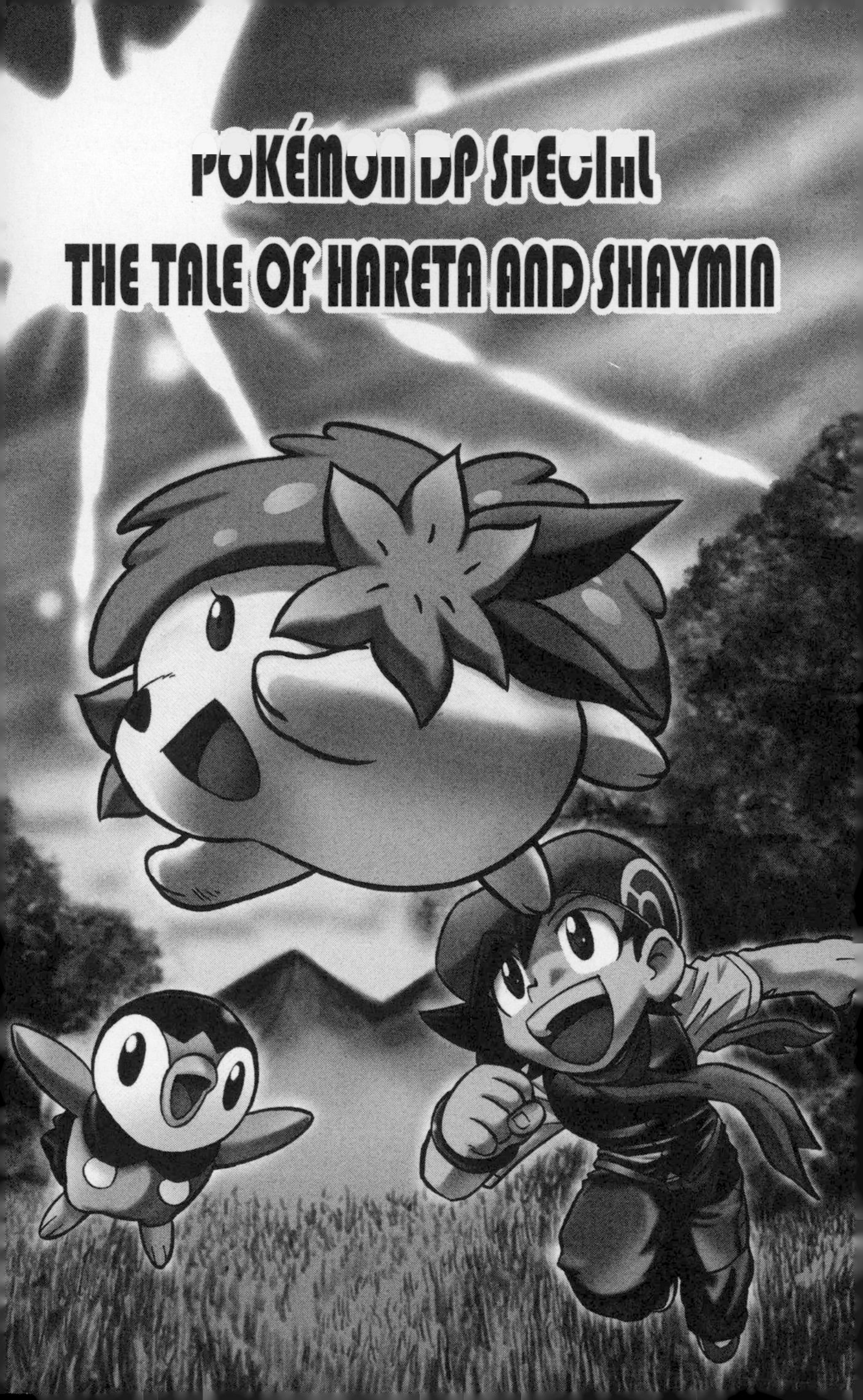
POKÉMON DP SPECIAL
THE TALE OF HARETA AND SHAYMIN

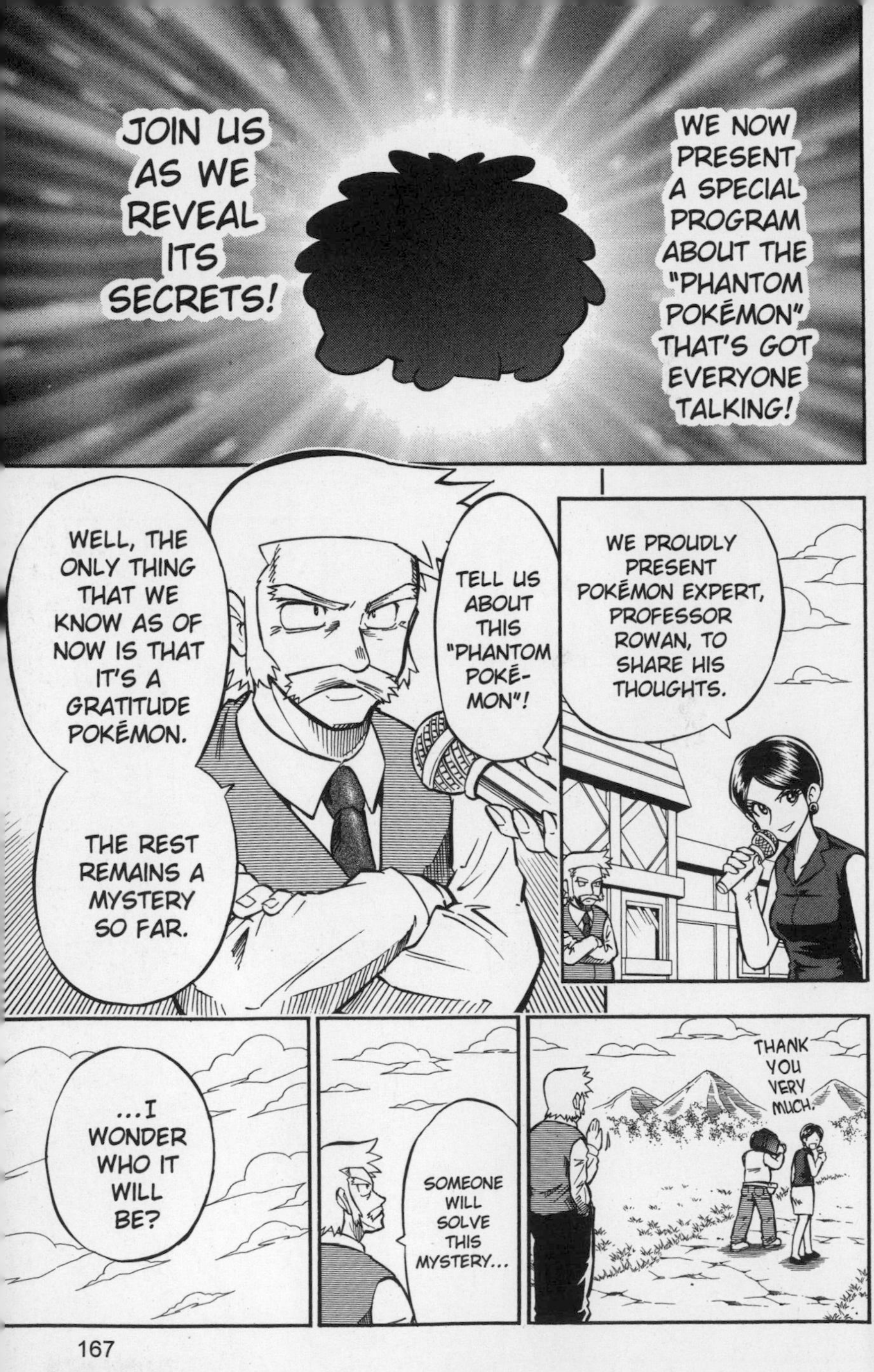
WE NOW PRESENT A SPECIAL PROGRAM ABOUT THE "PHANTOM POKÉMON" THAT'S GOT EVERYONE TALKING!
JOIN US AS WE REVEAL ITS SECRETS!
WE PROUDLY PRESENT POKÉMON EXPERT, PROFESSOR ROWAN, TO SHARE HIS THOUGHTS.
TELL US ABOUT THIS "PHANTOM POKÉMON"!
WELL, THE ONLY THING THAT WE KNOW AS OF NOW IS THAT IT'S A GRATITUDE POKÉMON.
THE REST REMAINS A MYSTERY SO FAR.
THANK YOU VERY MUCH.
SOMEONE WILL SOLVE THIS MYSTERY...
...I WONDER WHO IT WILL BE?

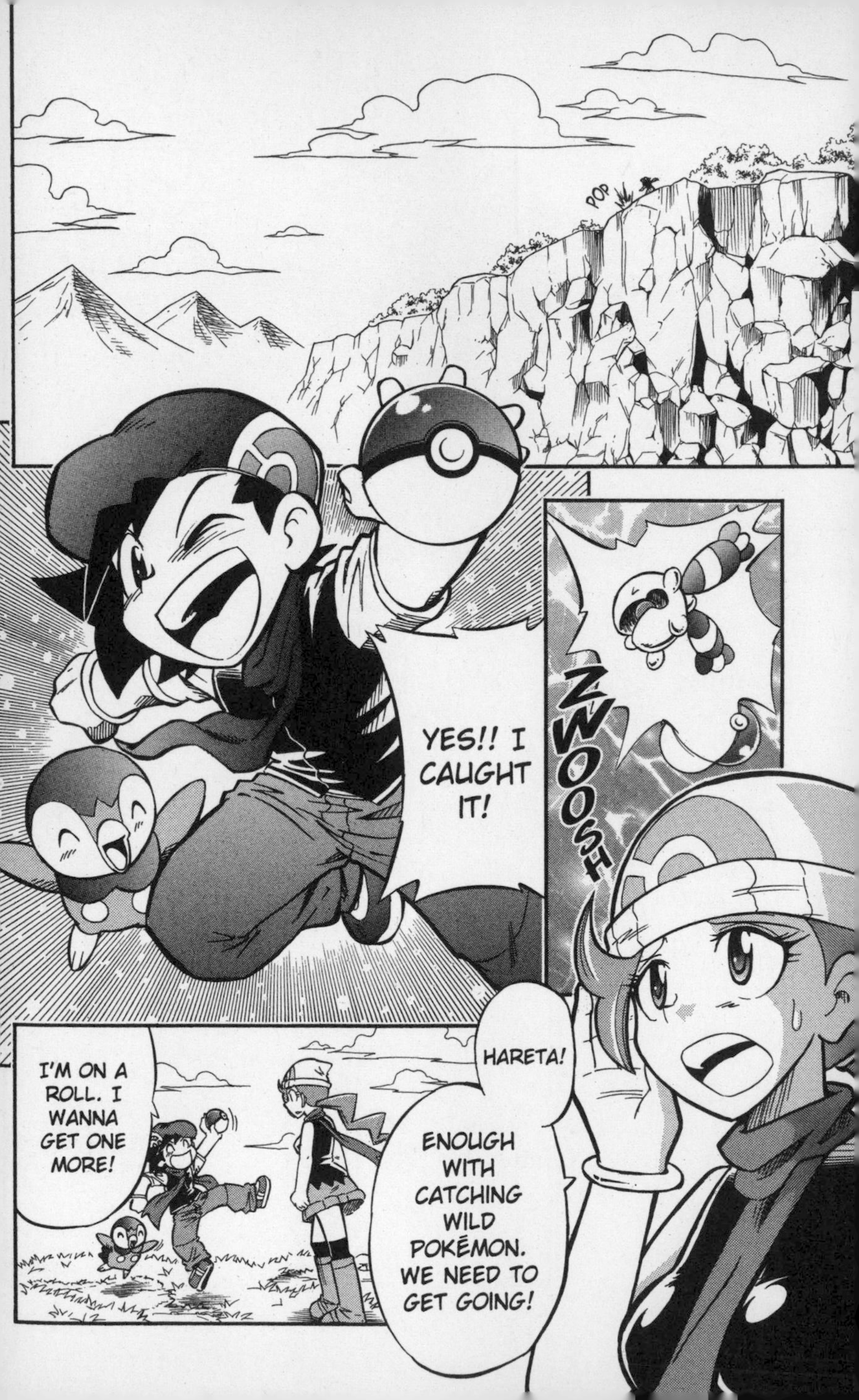
POP
ZWOOSH
YES!! I CAUGHT IT!
HARETA!
ENOUGH WITH CATCHING WILD POKÉMON. WE NEED TO GET GOING!
I'M ON A ROLL. I WANNA GET ONE MORE!

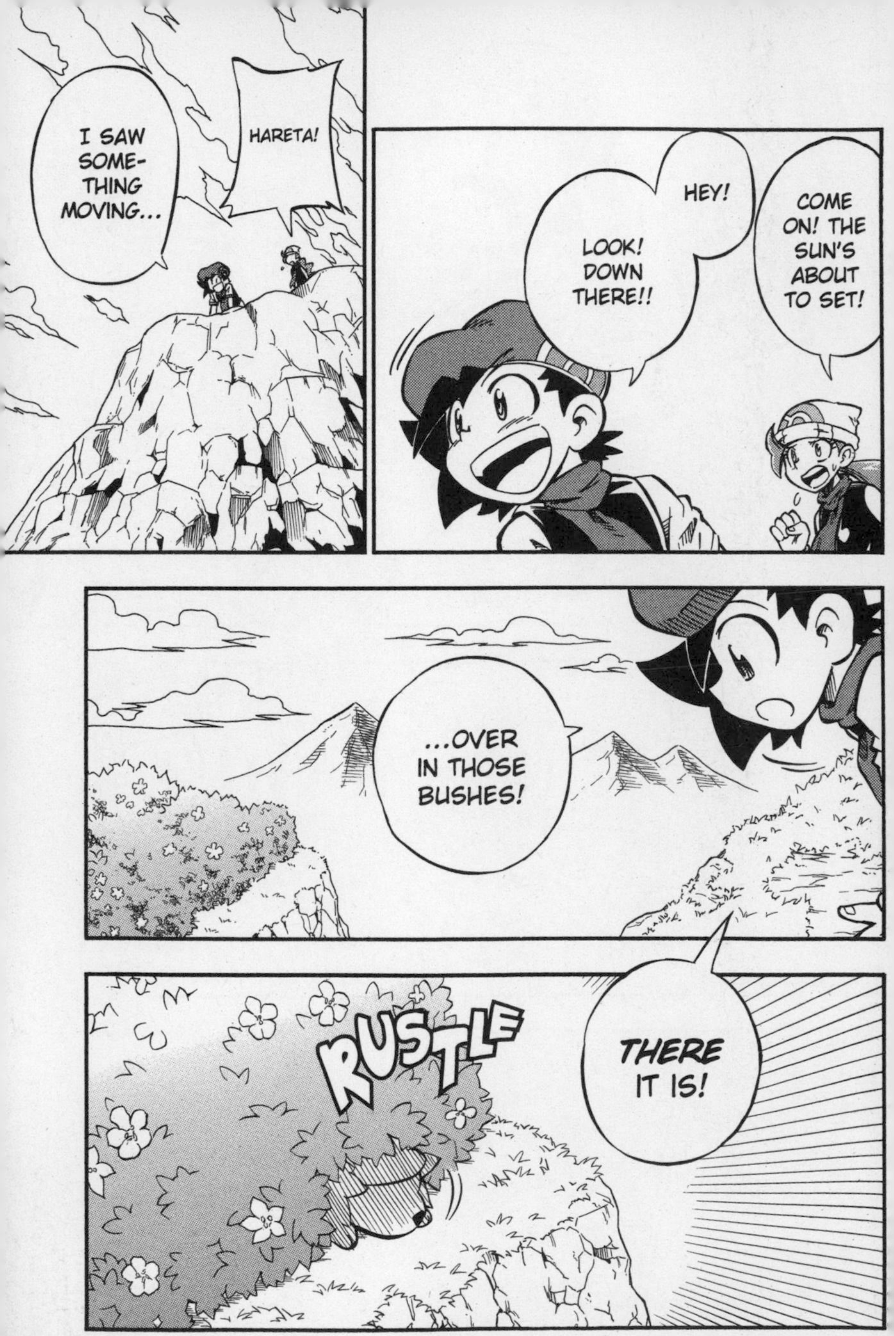
COME ON! THE SUN'S ABOUT TO SET!
HEY! LOOK! DOWN THERE!!
HARETA!
I SAW SOME-THING MOVING...
...OVER IN THOSE BUSHES!
THERE IT IS!
RUSTLE

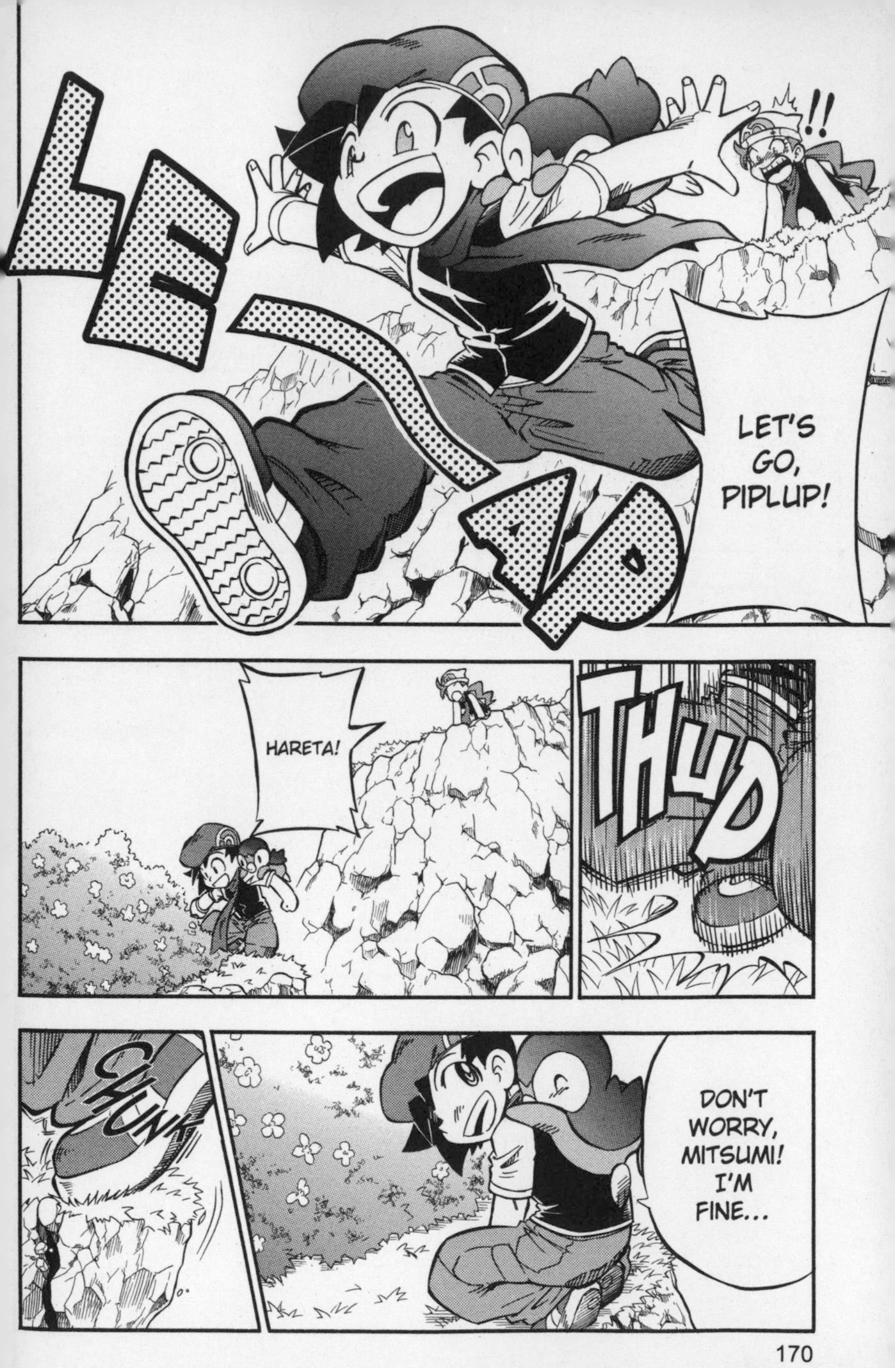
!!
LEAP
LET'S GO, PIPLUP!
THUD
HARETA!
DON'T WORRY, MITSUMI! I'M FINE...
CHUNK

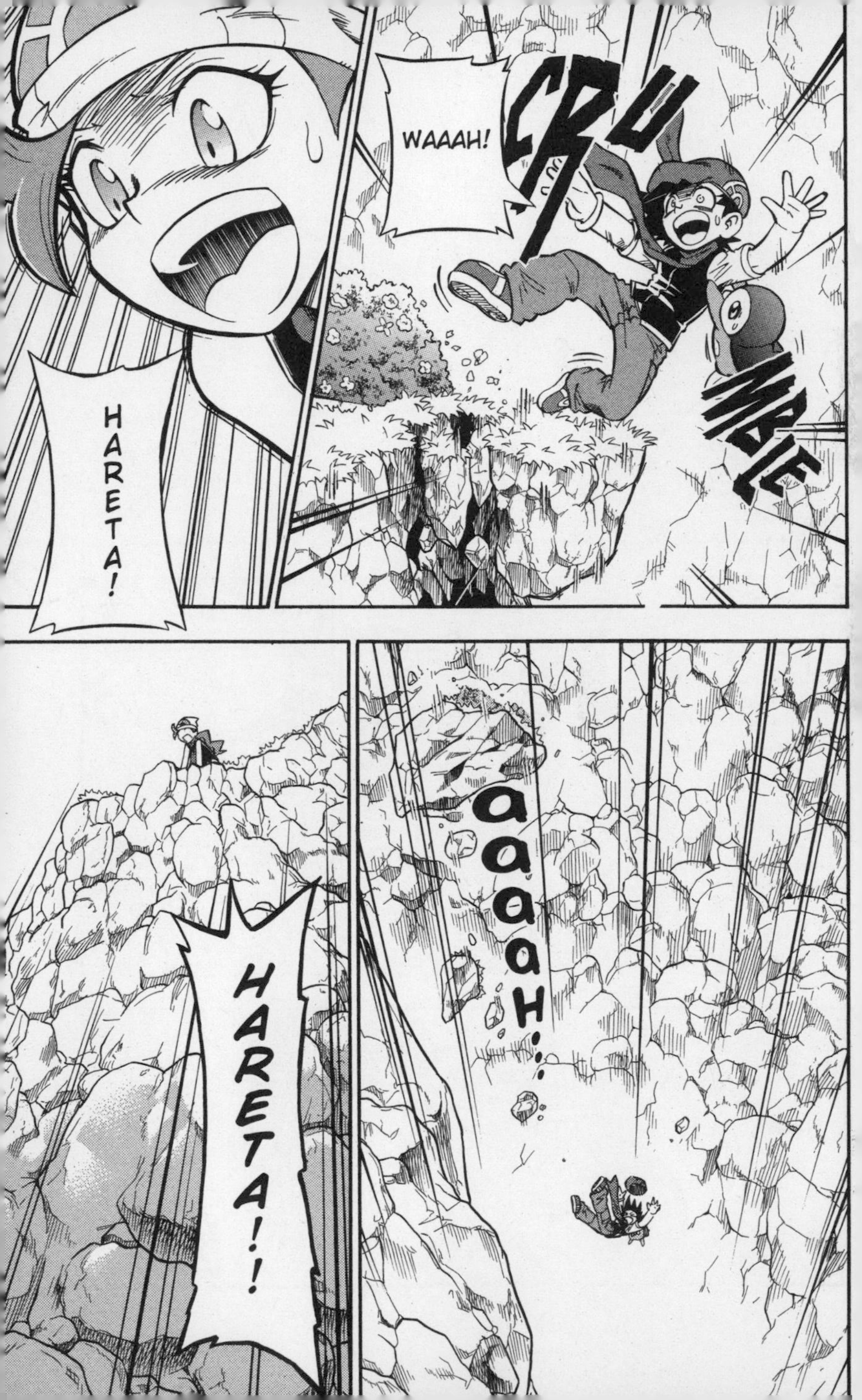

WAAAH!
CRUMBLE
HARETA!
AAAAAH...
HARETA!!!

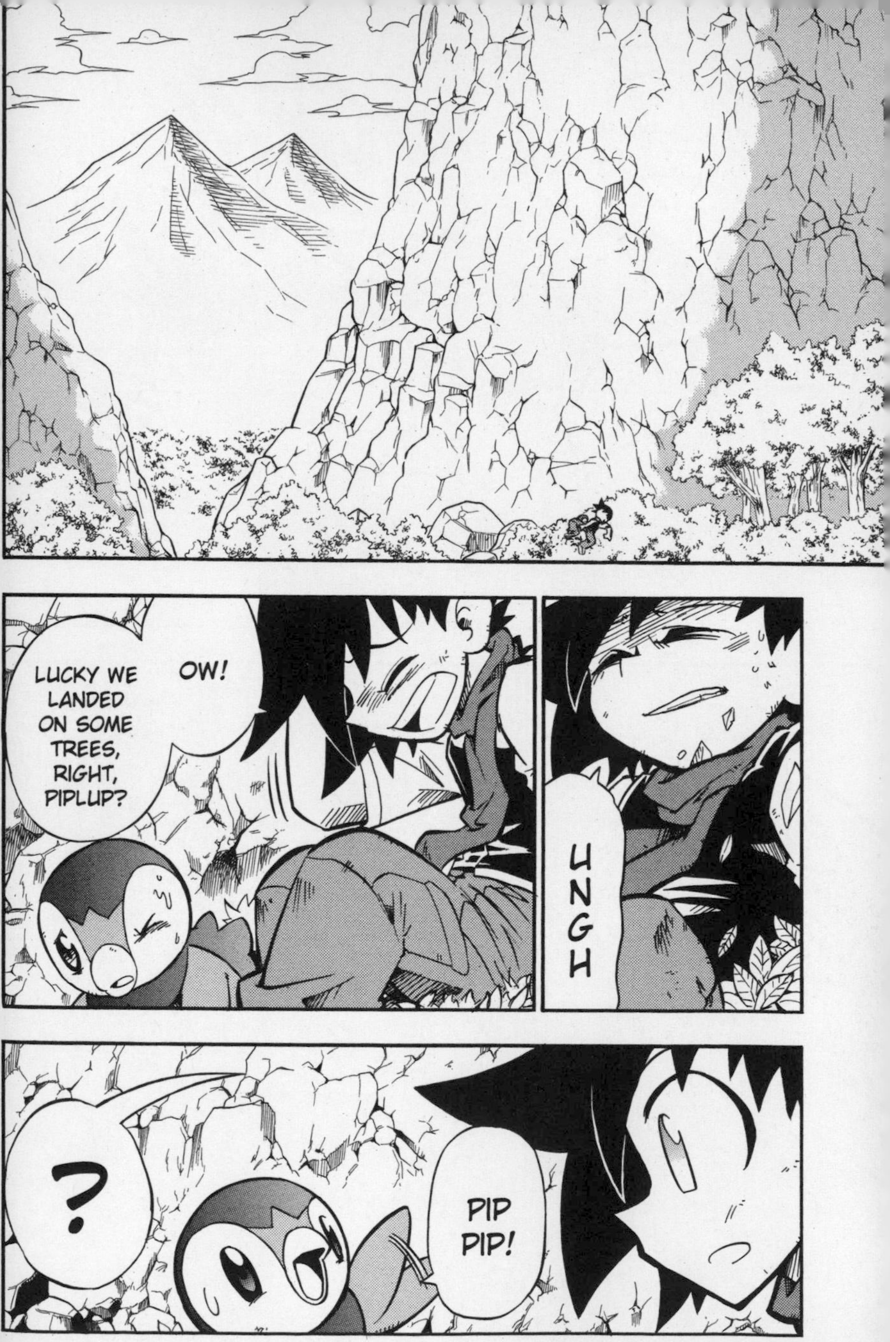
UNGH
OW!
LUCKY WE LANDED ON SOME TREES, RIGHT, PIPLUP?
PIP PIP!
?

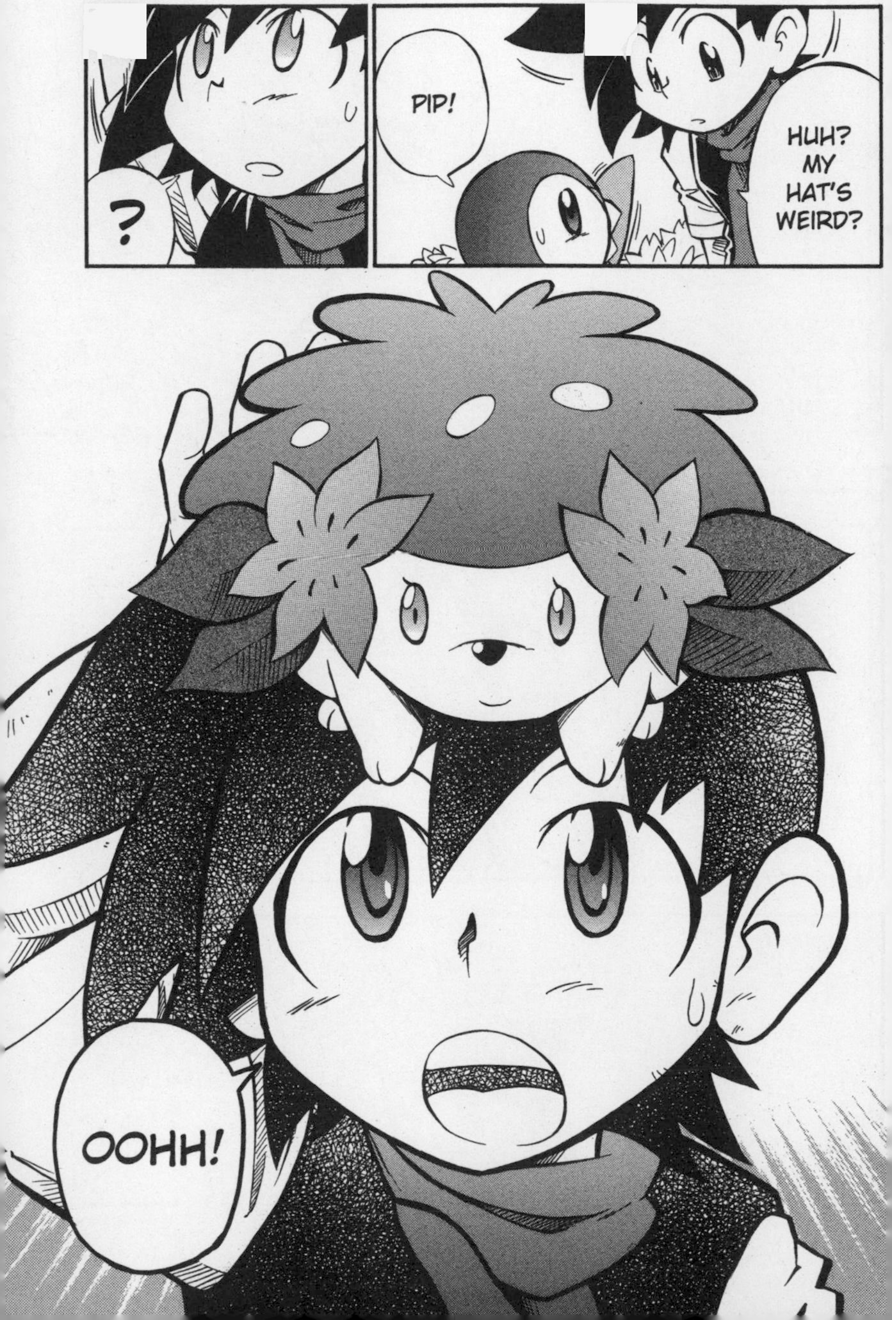
HUH? MY HAT'S WEIRD?
PIP!
?
OOHH!

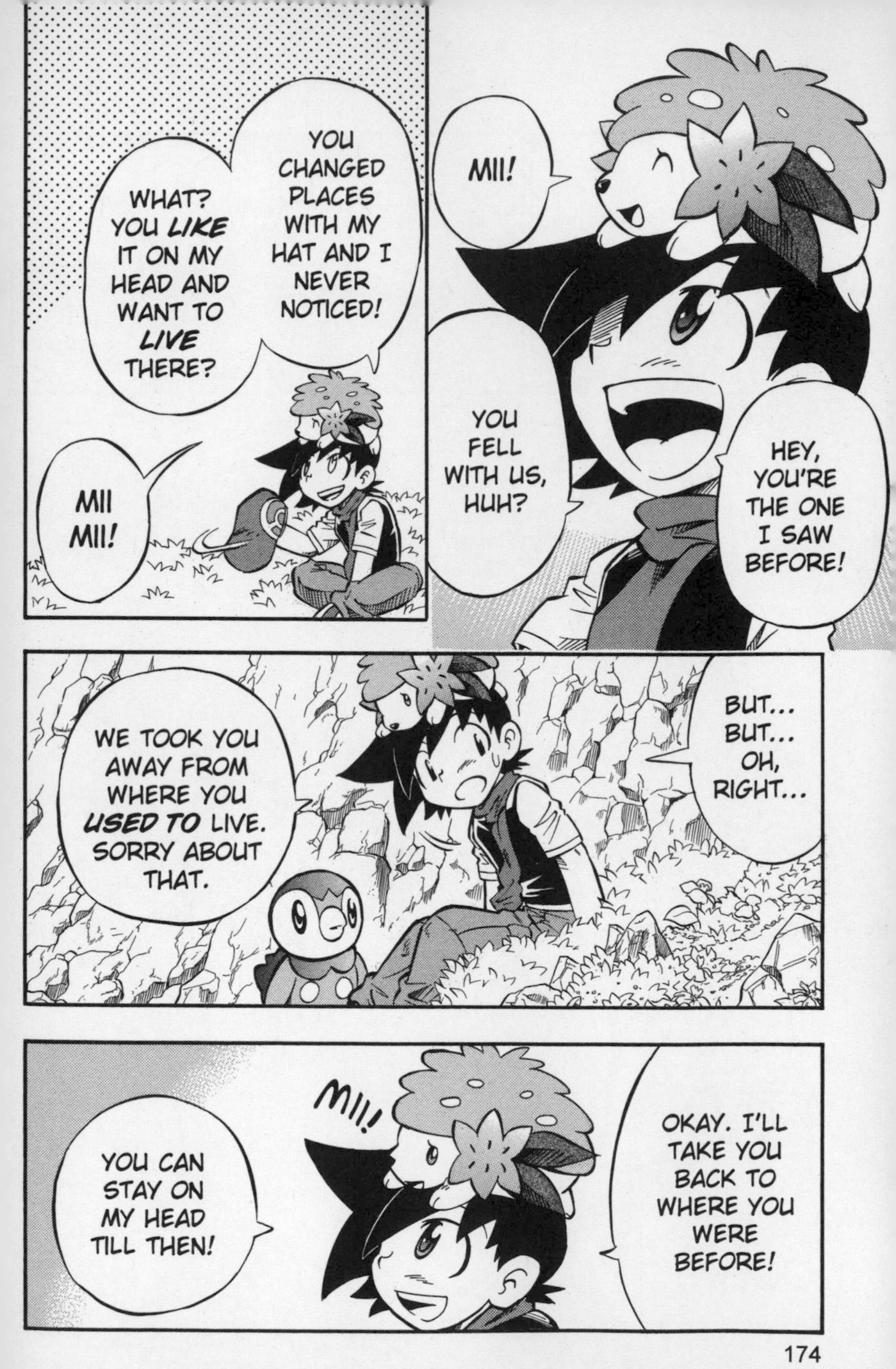
MII!
HEY, YOU'RE THE ONE I SAW BEFORE!
YOU FELL WITH US, HUH?
YOU CHANGED PLACES WITH MY HAT AND I NEVER NOTICED!
WHAT? YOU *LIKE* IT ON MY HEAD AND WANT TO *LIVE* THERE?
MII MII!
BUT... BUT... OH, RIGHT...
WE TOOK YOU AWAY FROM WHERE YOU ***USED TO*** LIVE. SORRY ABOUT THAT.
OKAY. I'LL TAKE YOU BACK TO WHERE YOU WERE BEFORE!
MII!
YOU CAN STAY ON MY HEAD TILL THEN!

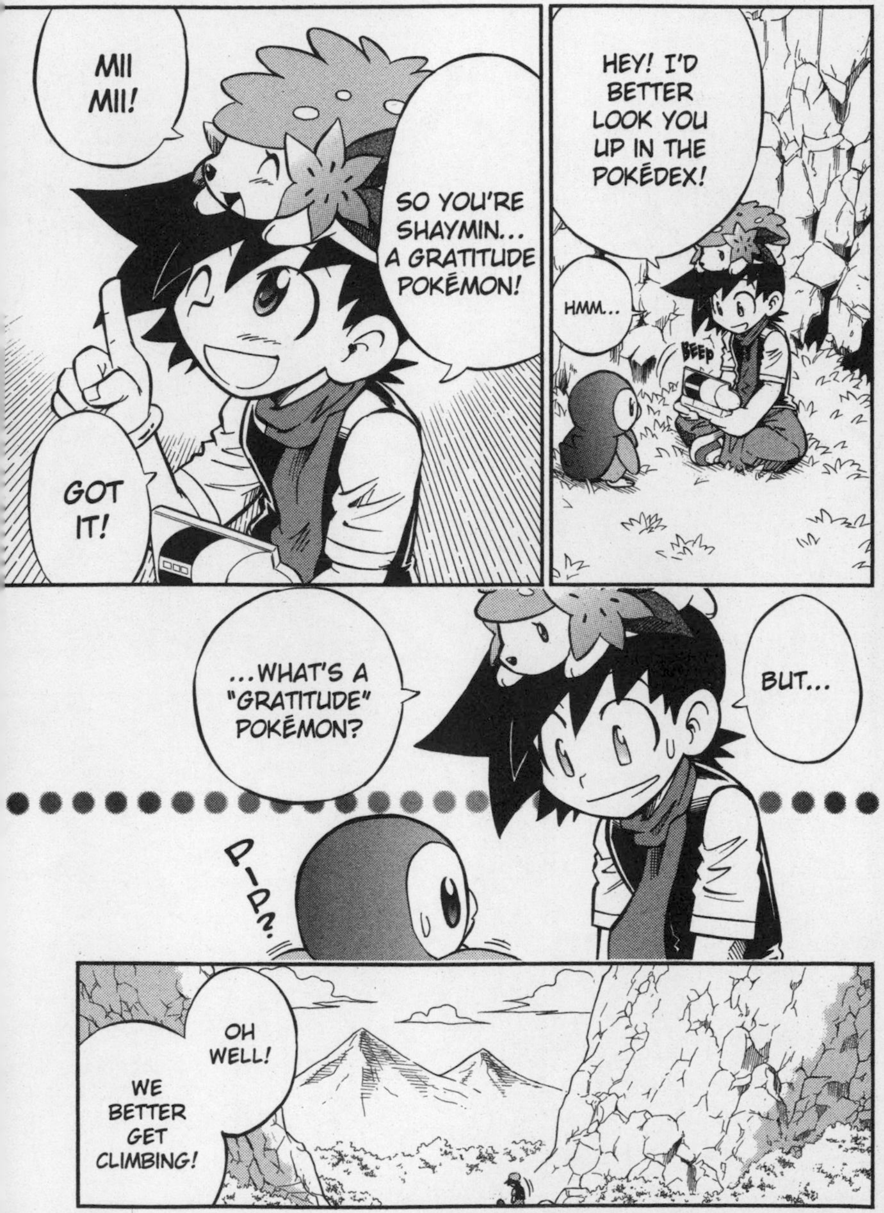
HEY! I'D BETTER LOOK YOU UP IN THE POKÉDEX!
HMM...
BEEP
GOT IT!
SO YOU'RE SHAYMIN... A GRATITUDE POKÉMON!
MII MII!
BUT...
...WHAT'S A "GRATITUDE" POKÉMON?
PIP?
OH WELL!
WE BETTER GET CLIMBING!

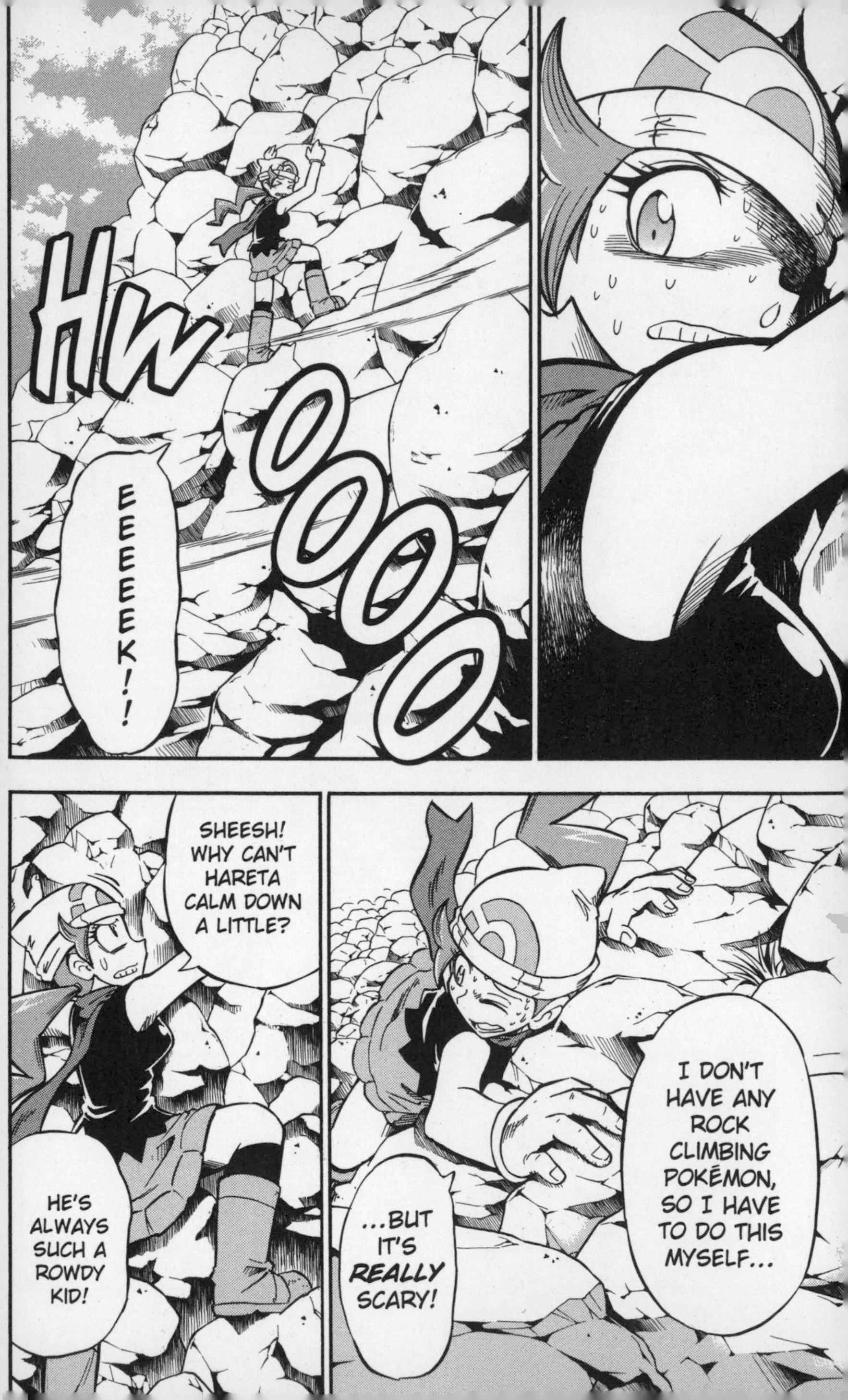
HWOOOOO
EEEEEK!!
I DON'T HAVE ANY ROCK CLIMBING POKÉMON, SO I HAVE TO DO THIS MYSELF...
...BUT IT'S *REALLY* SCARY!
SHEESH! WHY CAN'T HARETA CALM DOWN A LITTLE?
HE'S ALWAYS SUCH A ROWDY KID!

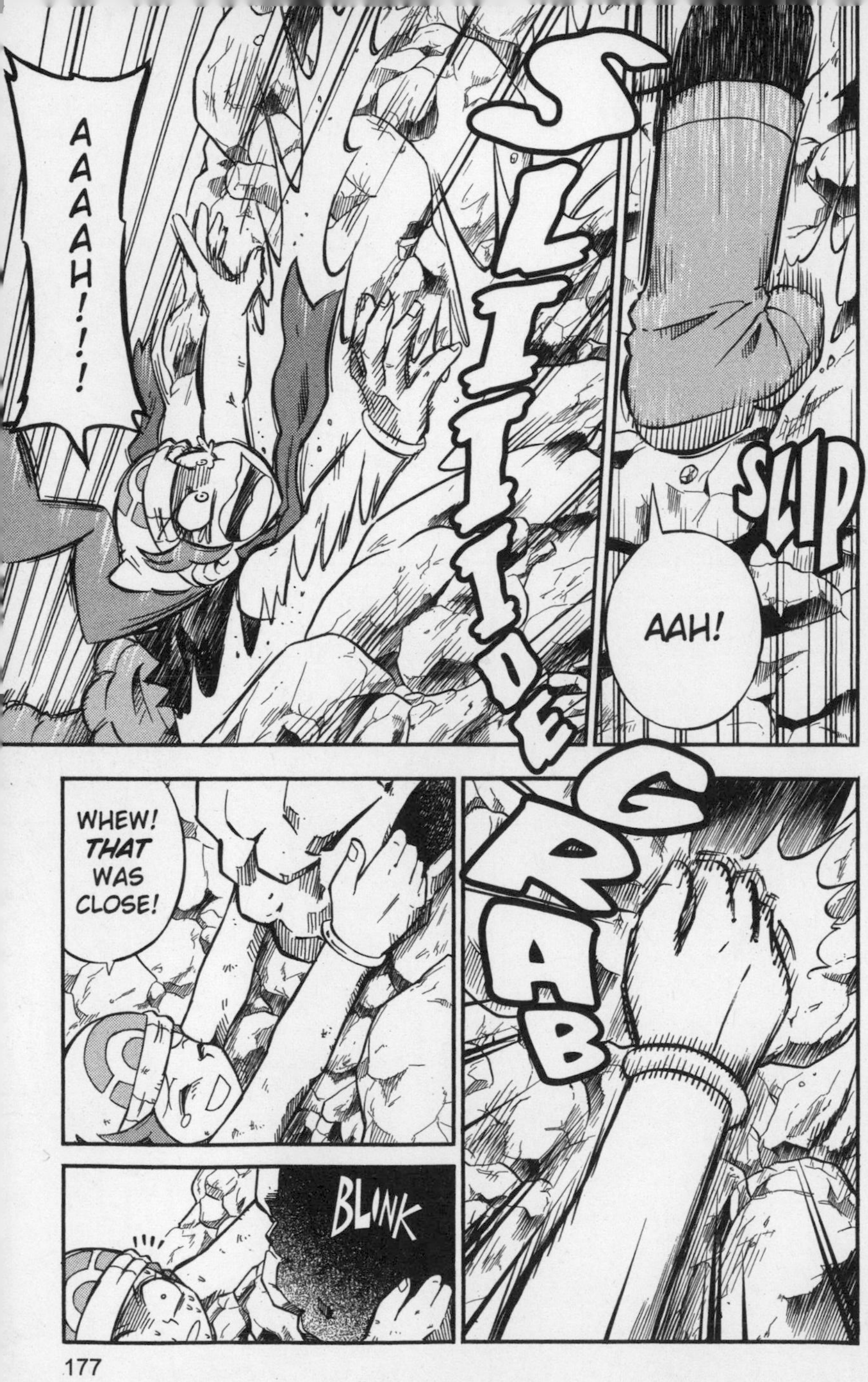
SLIP
AAH!
SLIIIDE
AAAAAH!!!!
GRAB
WHEW! *THAT* WAS CLOSE!
BLINK

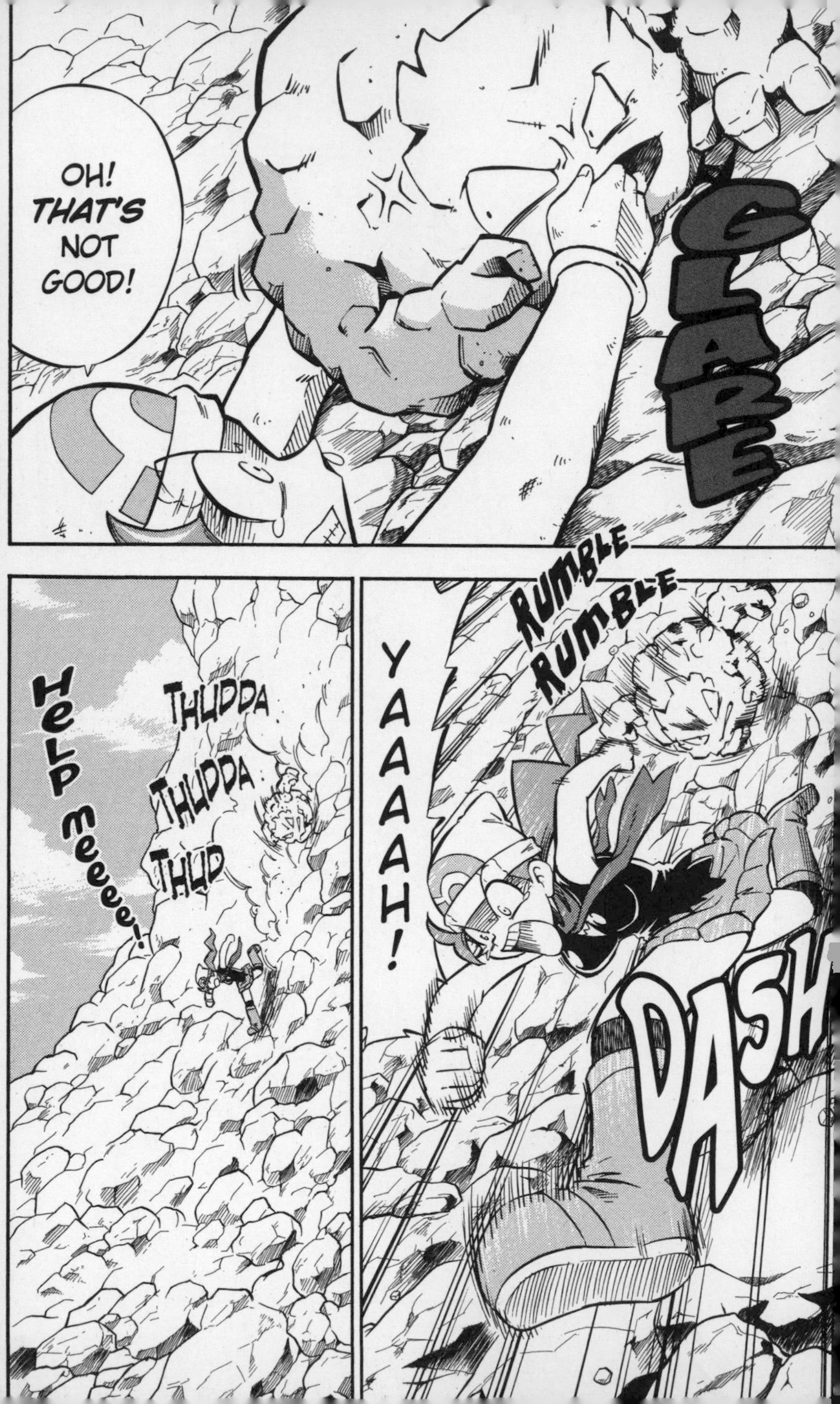
GLARE
OH! THAT'S NOT GOOD!
RUMBLE RUMBLE
YAAAAAH!
DASH
THUDDA THUDDA THUD
Help meeeee!

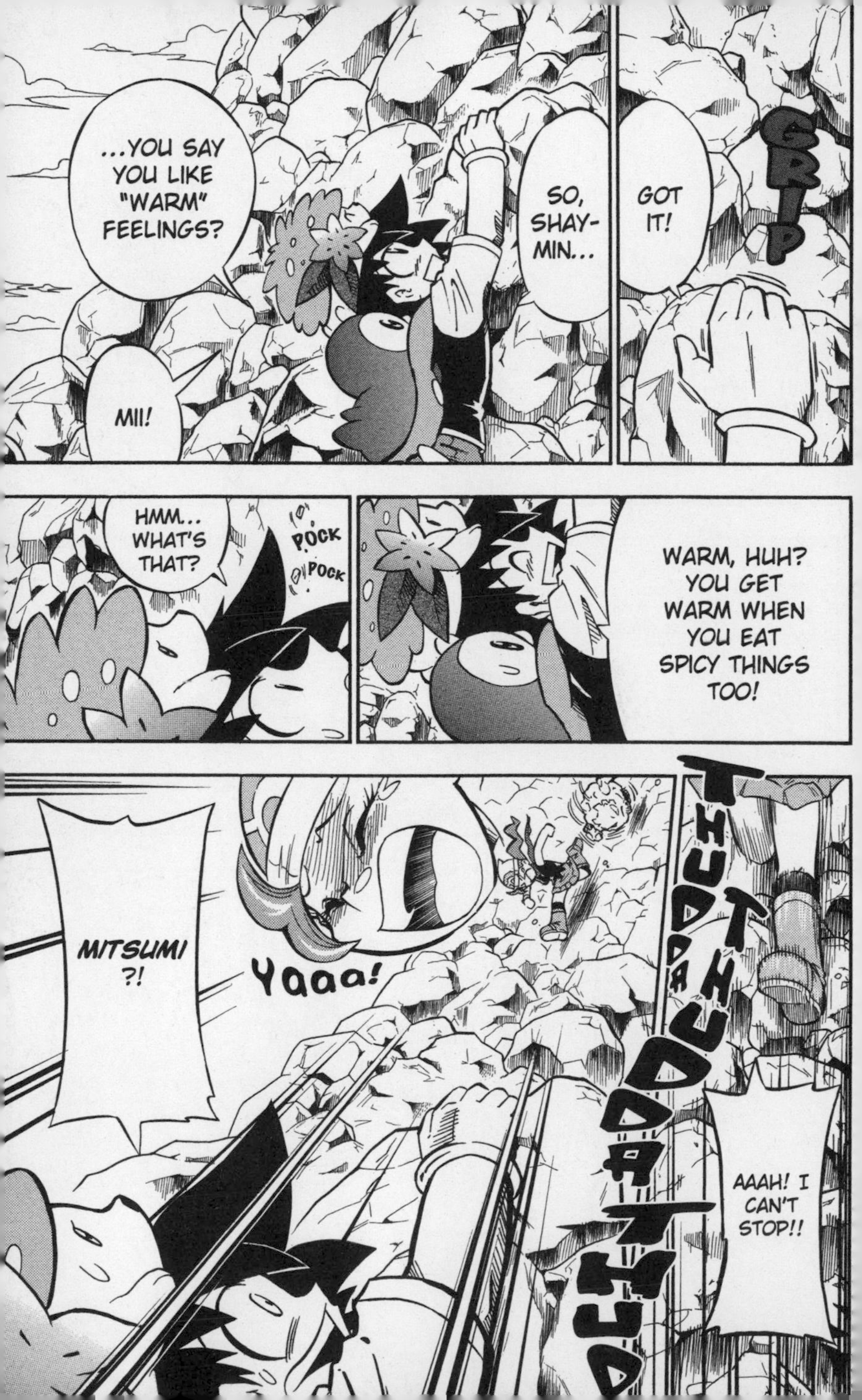
GRIP
GOT IT!
SO, SHAY-MIN...
...YOU SAY YOU LIKE "WARM" FEELINGS?
MII!
WARM, HUH? YOU GET WARM WHEN YOU EAT SPICY THINGS TOO!
POCK
POCK
HMM... WHAT'S THAT?
THUDDA
THUDDA THUD
AAAH! I CAN'T STOP!!
Yaaa!
MITSUMI?!

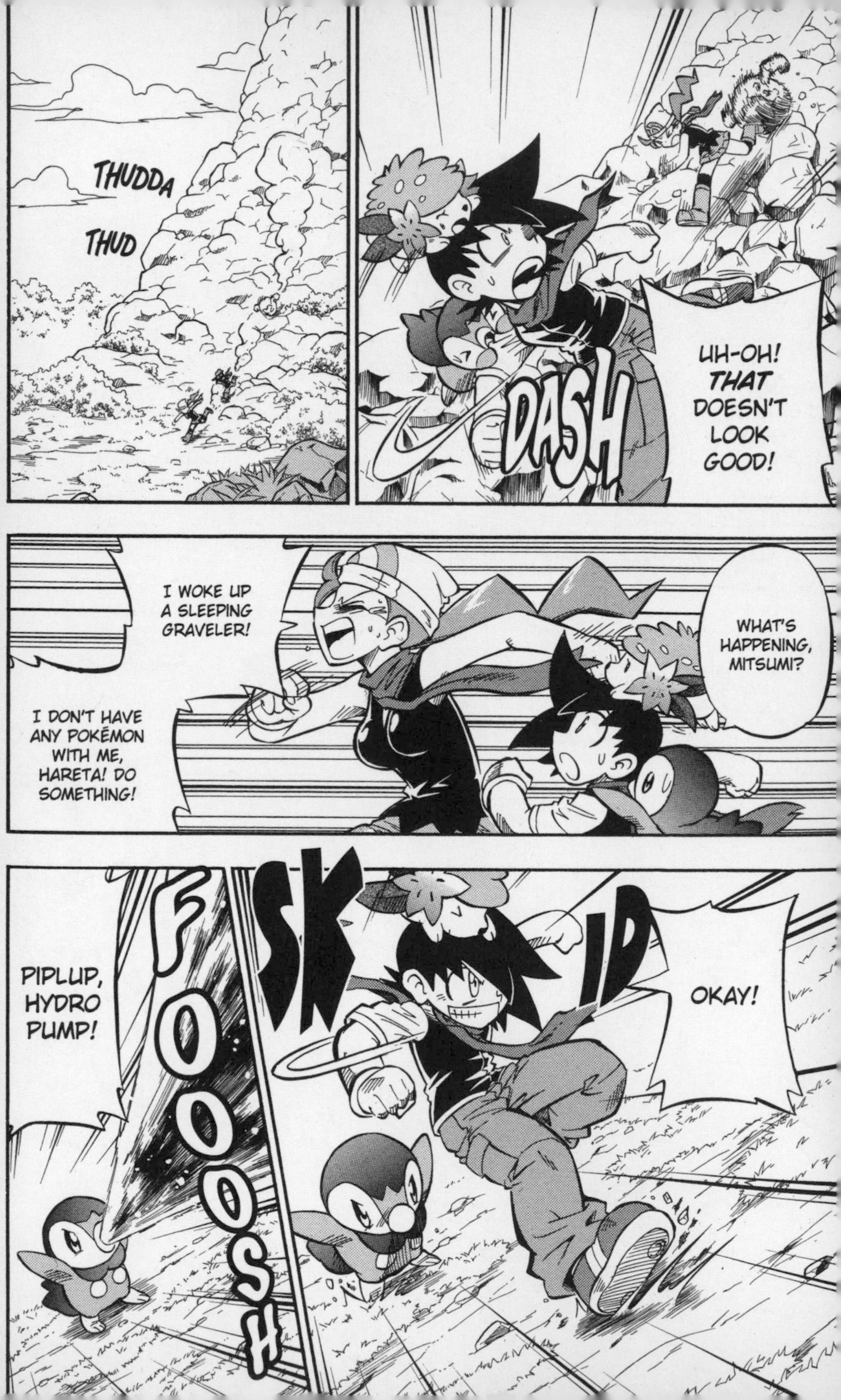
DASH
UH-OH! THAT DOESN'T LOOK GOOD!
THUDDA
THUD
WHAT'S HAPPENING, MITSUMI?
I WOKE UP A SLEEPING GRAVELER!
I DON'T HAVE ANY POKÉMON WITH ME, HARETA! DO SOMETHING!
OKAY!
SKID
PIPLUP, HYDRO PUMP!
FOOOOSH

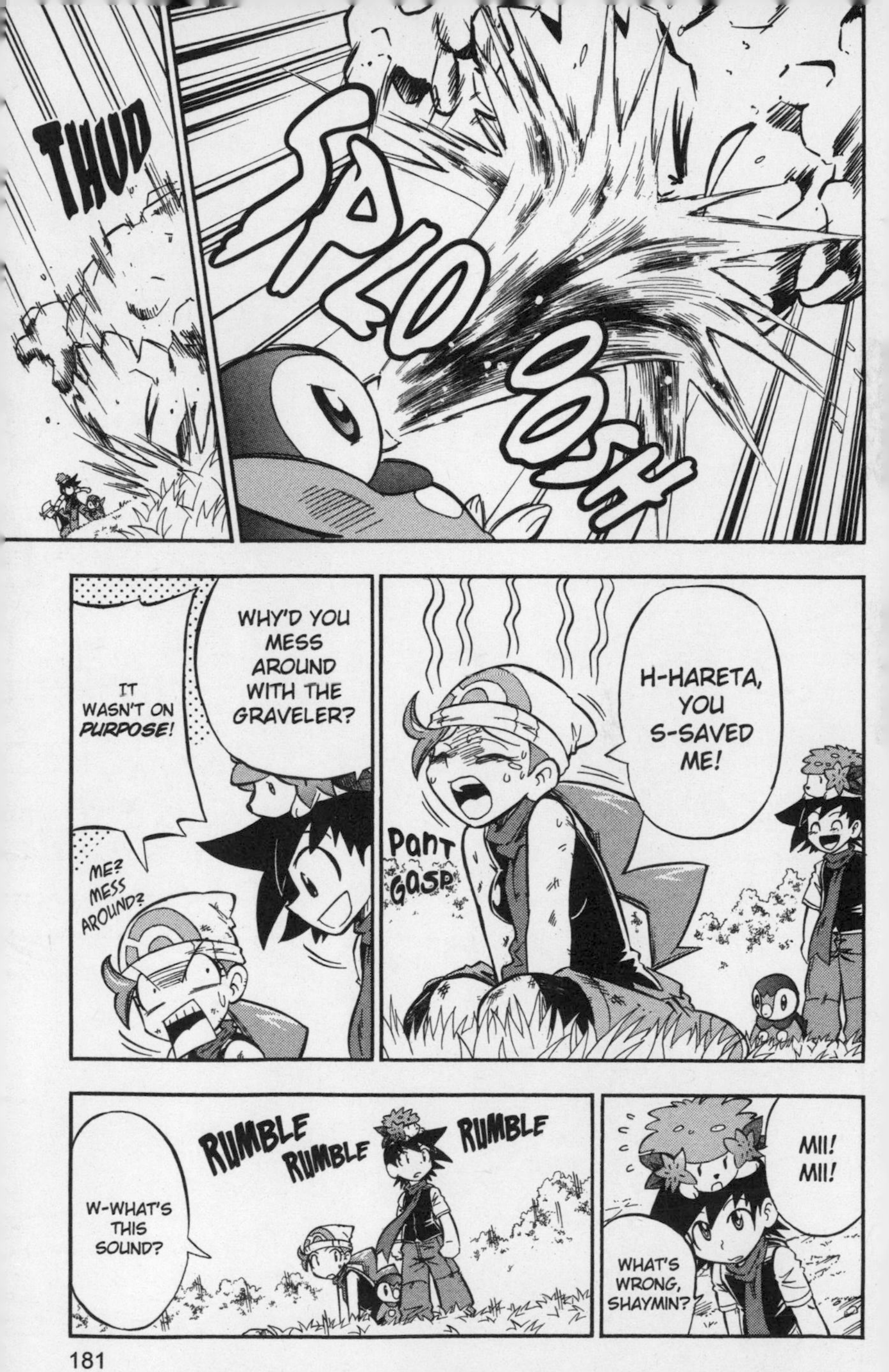
SPLOOOSH
THUD
H-HARETA, YOU S-SAVED ME!
Pant Gasp
WHY'D YOU MESS AROUND WITH THE GRAVELER?
IT WASN'T ON *PURPOSE*!
ME? MESS AROUND?
MII! MII!
WHAT'S WRONG, SHAYMIN?
RUMBLE RUMBLE RUMBLE
W-WHAT'S THIS SOUND?

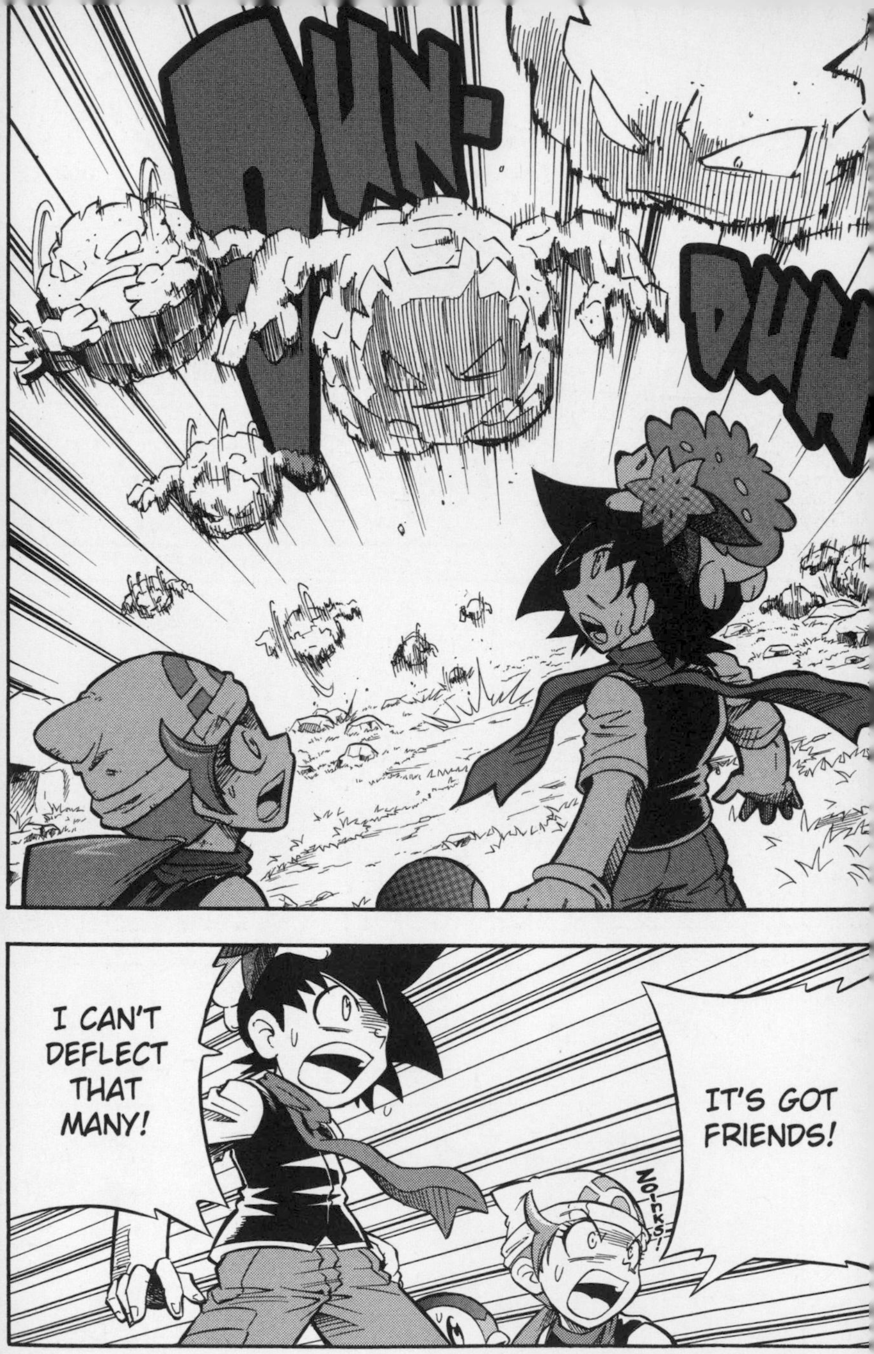
DUN-
IT'S GOT FRIENDS!
ZOINKS!
I CAN'T DEFLECT THAT MANY!

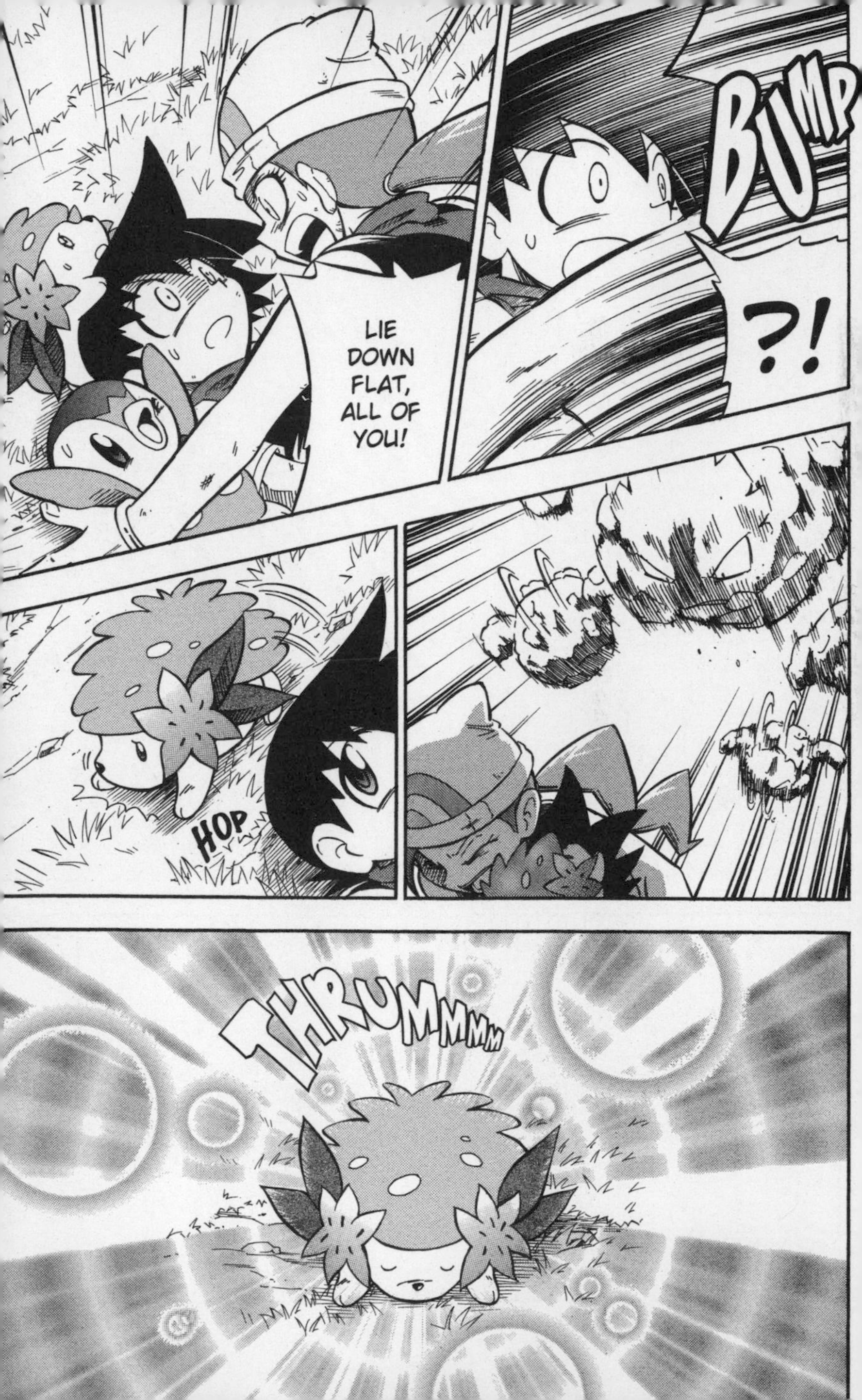
BUMP
?!
LIE DOWN FLAT, ALL OF YOU!
HOP
THRUMMMM

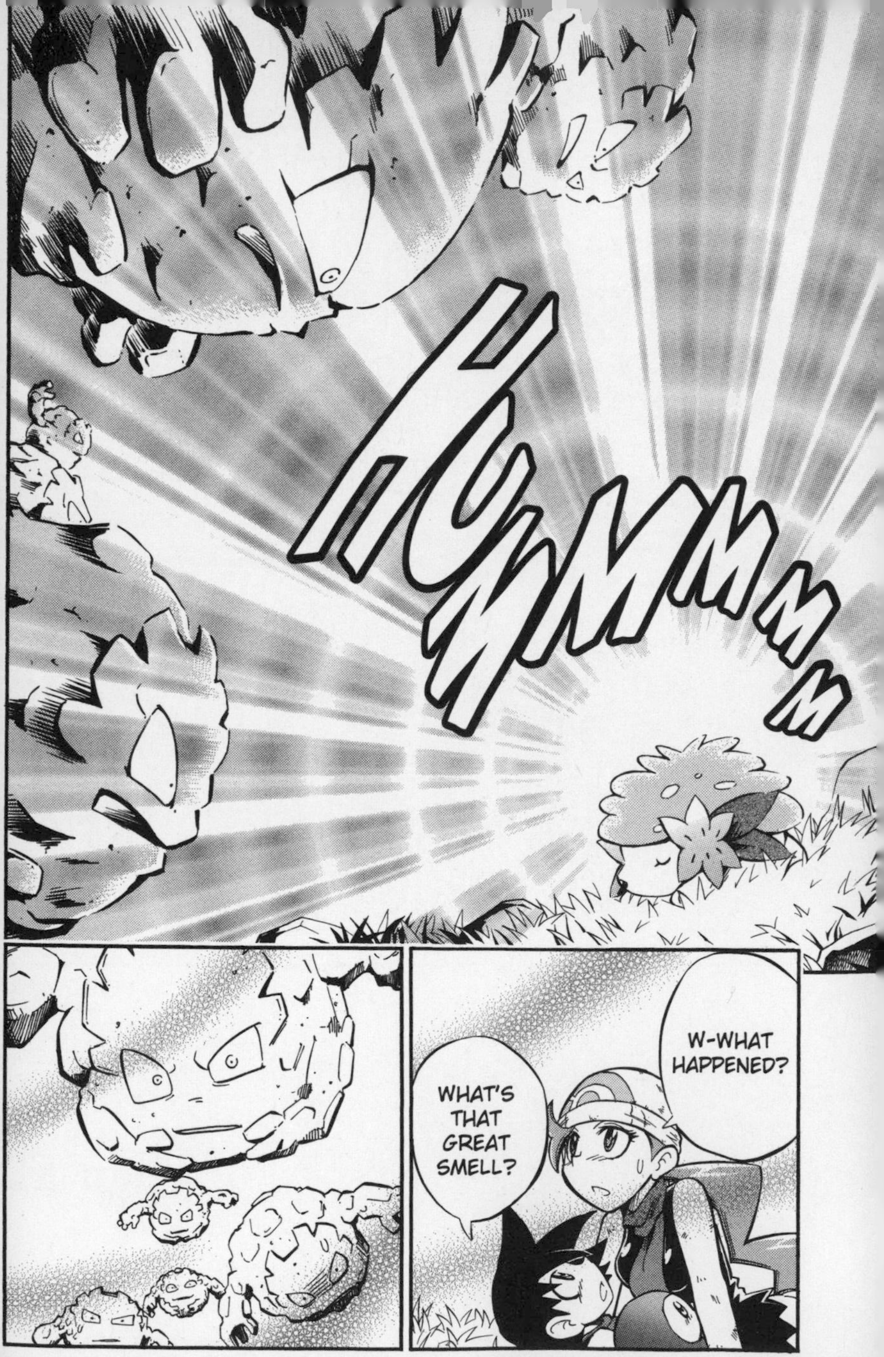
HUMMMMM
W-WHAT HAPPENED?
WHAT'S THAT GREAT SMELL?

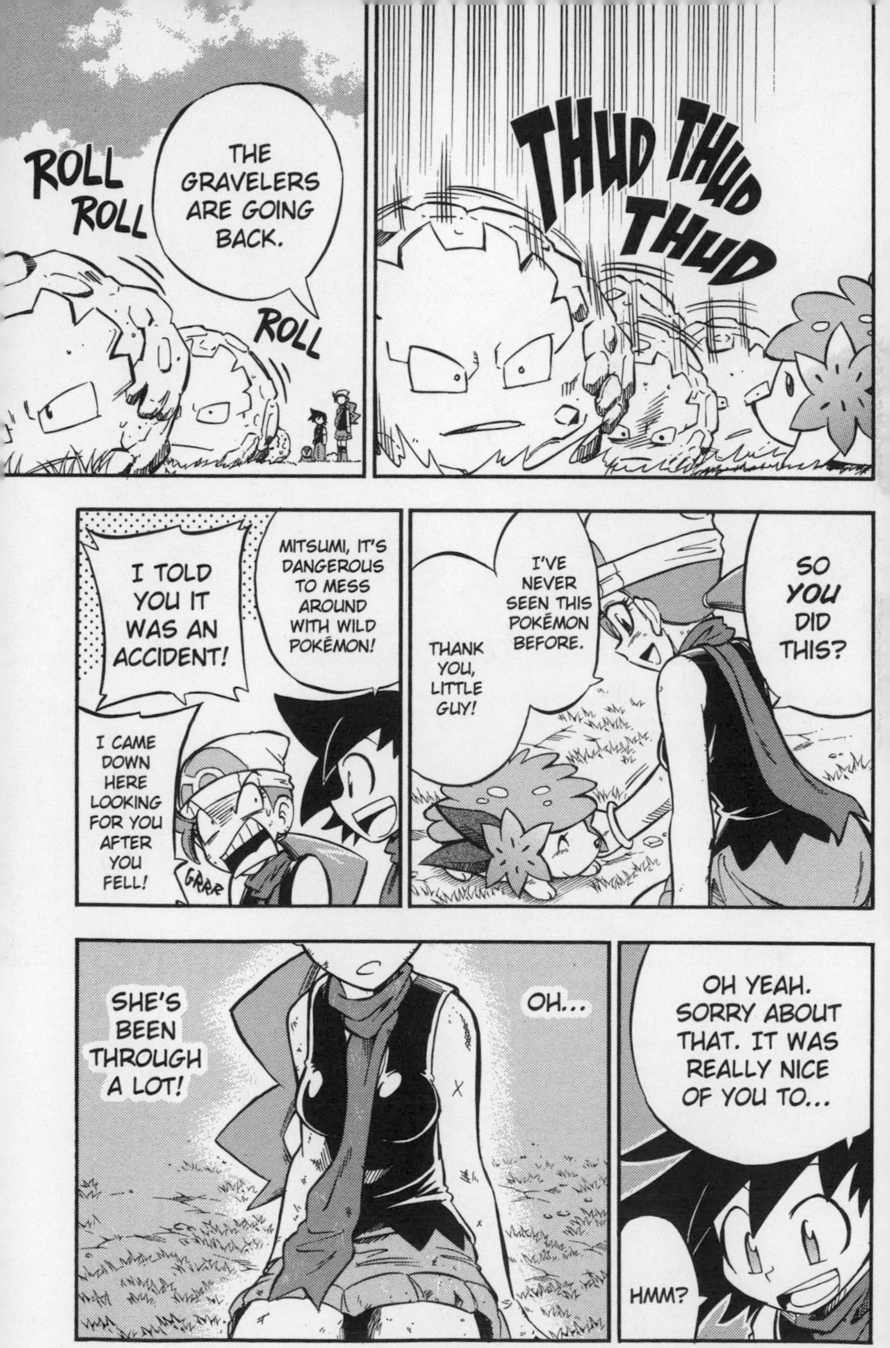
THUD THUD THUD
ROLL ROLL
THE GRAVELERS ARE GOING BACK.
ROLL
SO YOU DID THIS?
I'VE NEVER SEEN THIS POKÉMON BEFORE.
THANK YOU, LITTLE GUY!
MITSUMI, IT'S DANGEROUS TO MESS AROUND WITH WILD POKÉMON!
I TOLD YOU IT WAS AN ACCIDENT!
I CAME DOWN HERE LOOKING FOR YOU AFTER YOU FELL!
GRRR
OH YEAH. SORRY ABOUT THAT. IT WAS REALLY NICE OF YOU TO...
HMM?
OH...
SHE'S BEEN THROUGH A LOT!

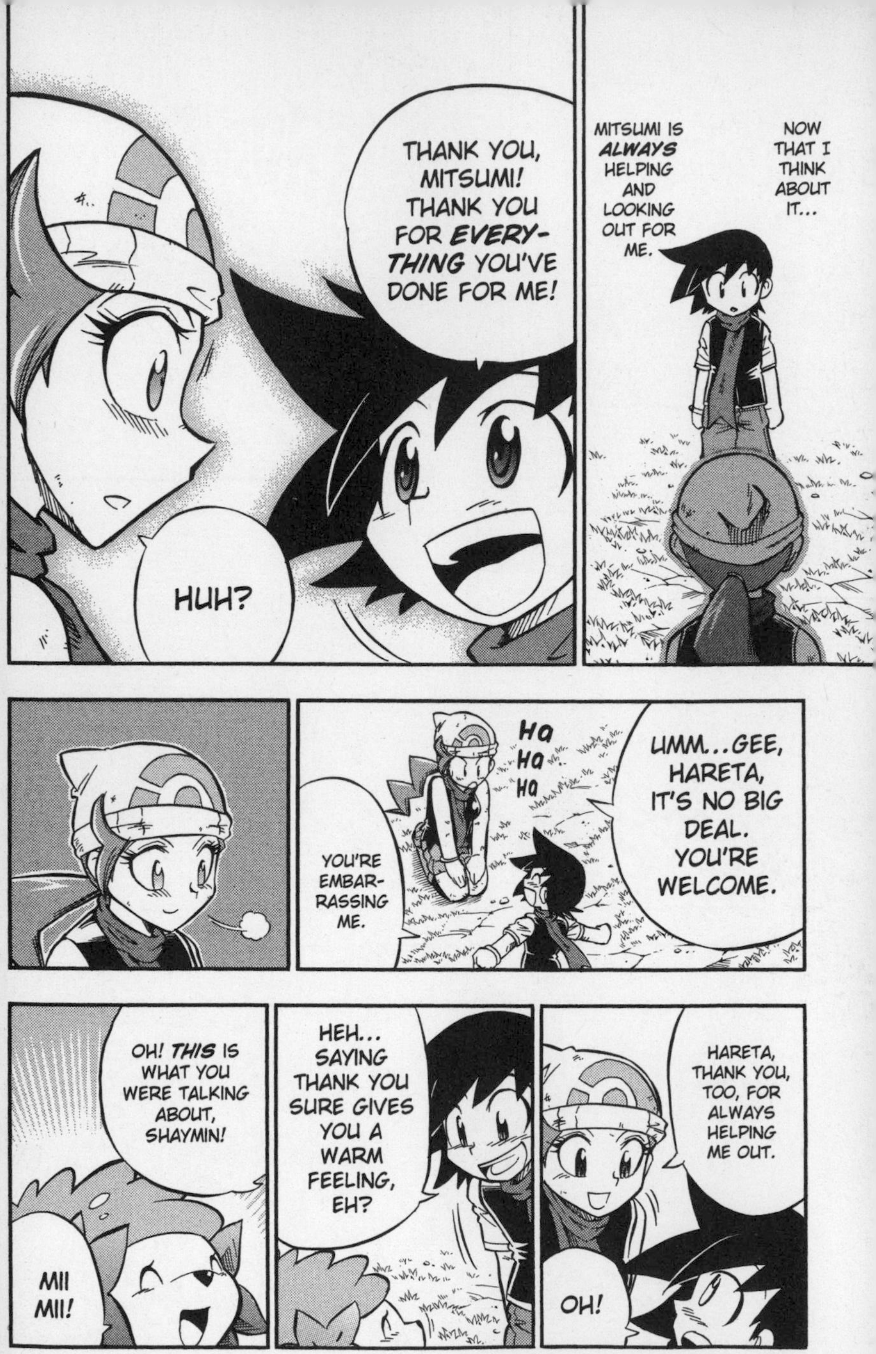
NOW THAT I THINK ABOUT IT...
MITSUMI IS ALWAYS HELPING AND LOOKING OUT FOR ME.
THANK YOU, MITSUMI! THANK YOU FOR EVERYTHING YOU'VE DONE FOR ME!
HUH?
UMM...GEE, HARETA, IT'S NO BIG DEAL. YOU'RE WELCOME.
Ha Ha Ha
YOU'RE EMBARRASSING ME.
HARETA, THANK YOU, TOO, FOR ALWAYS HELPING ME OUT.
OH!
HEH... SAYING THANK YOU SURE GIVES YOU A WARM FEELING, EH?
OH! THIS IS WHAT YOU WERE TALKING ABOUT, SHAYMIN!
MII MII!

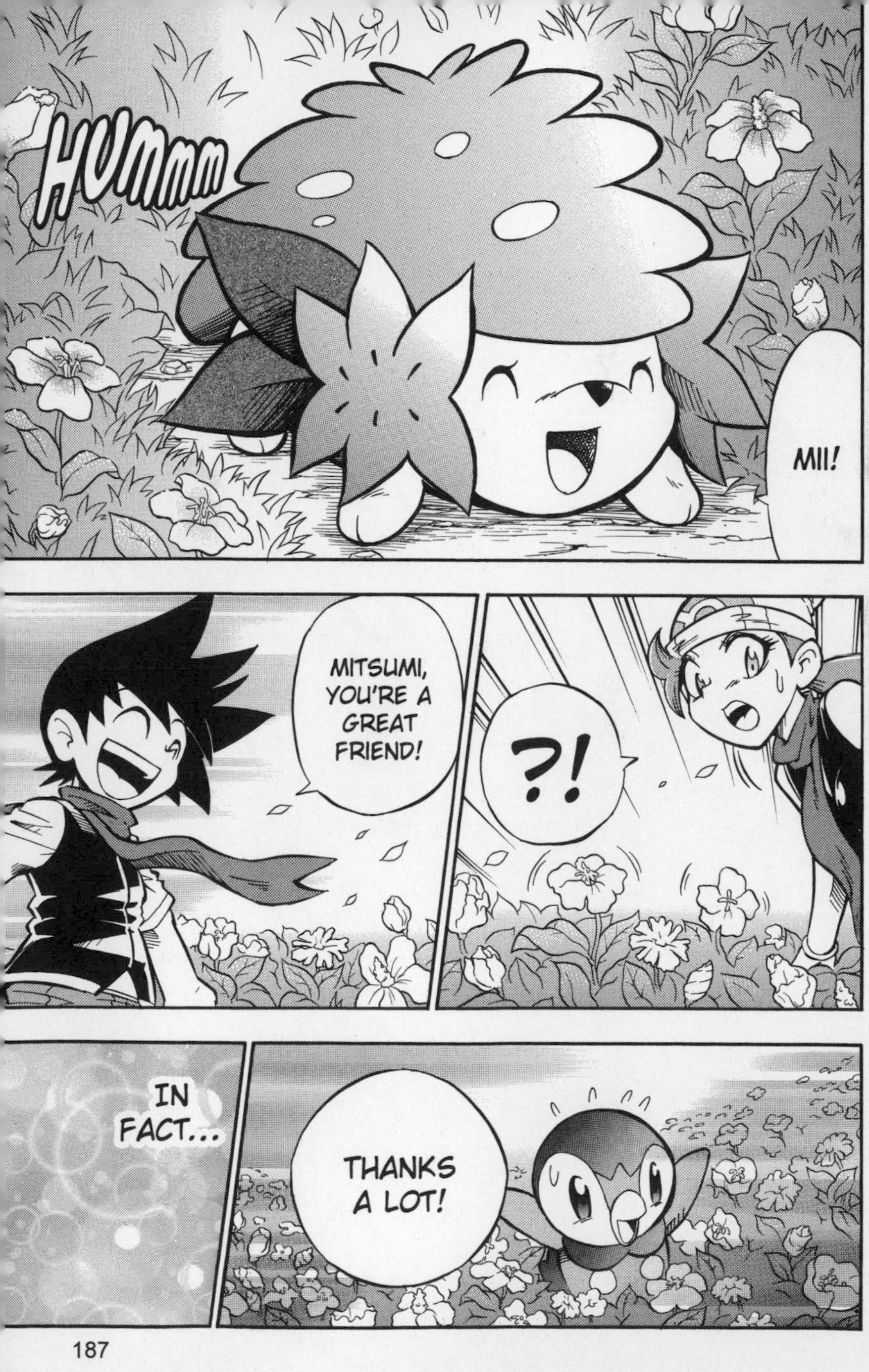
HUMMM
MII!
?!
MITSUMI, YOU'RE A GREAT FRIEND!
THANKS A LOT!
IN FACT...

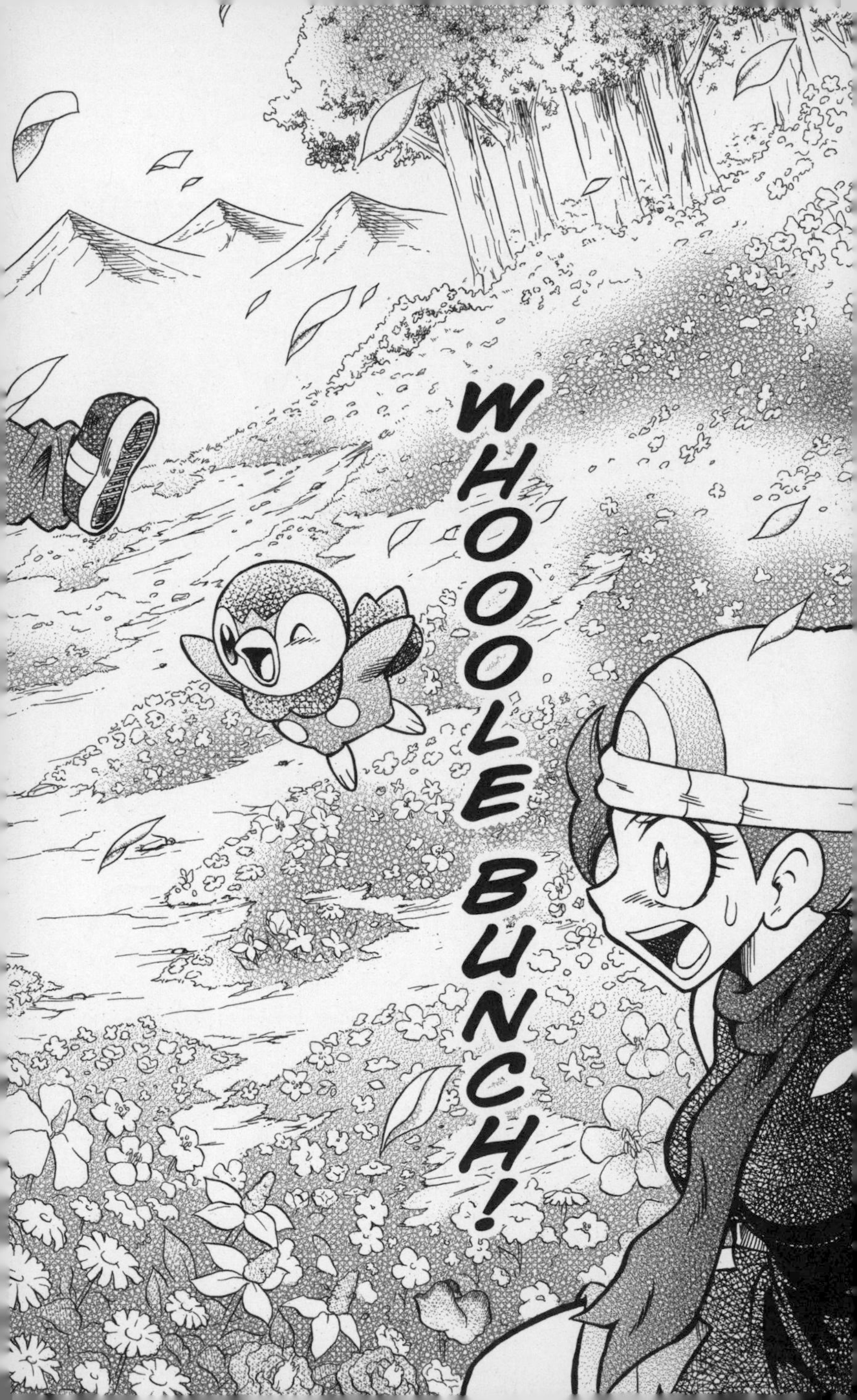
WHOOOOLE BUNCH!

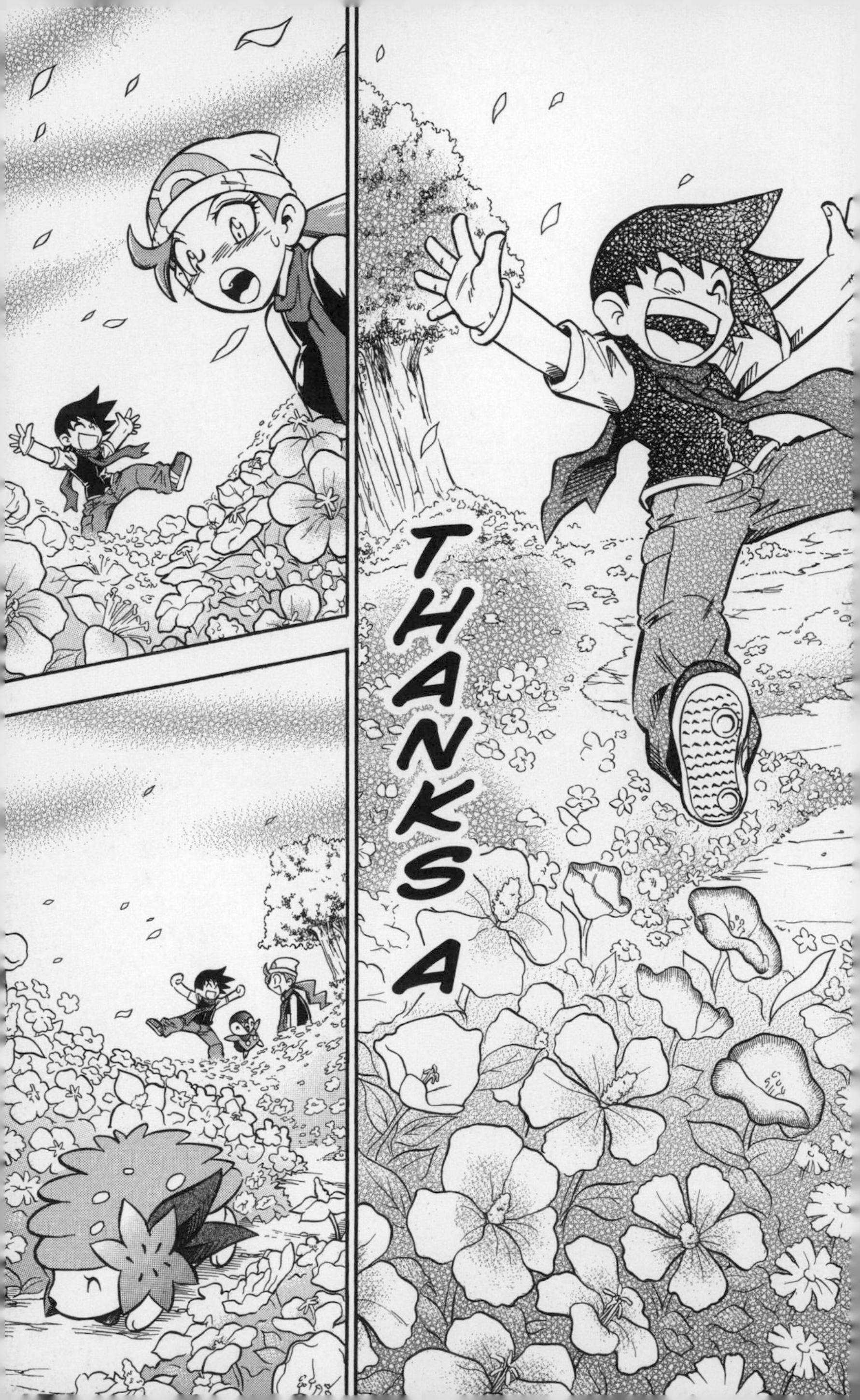
THANKS A

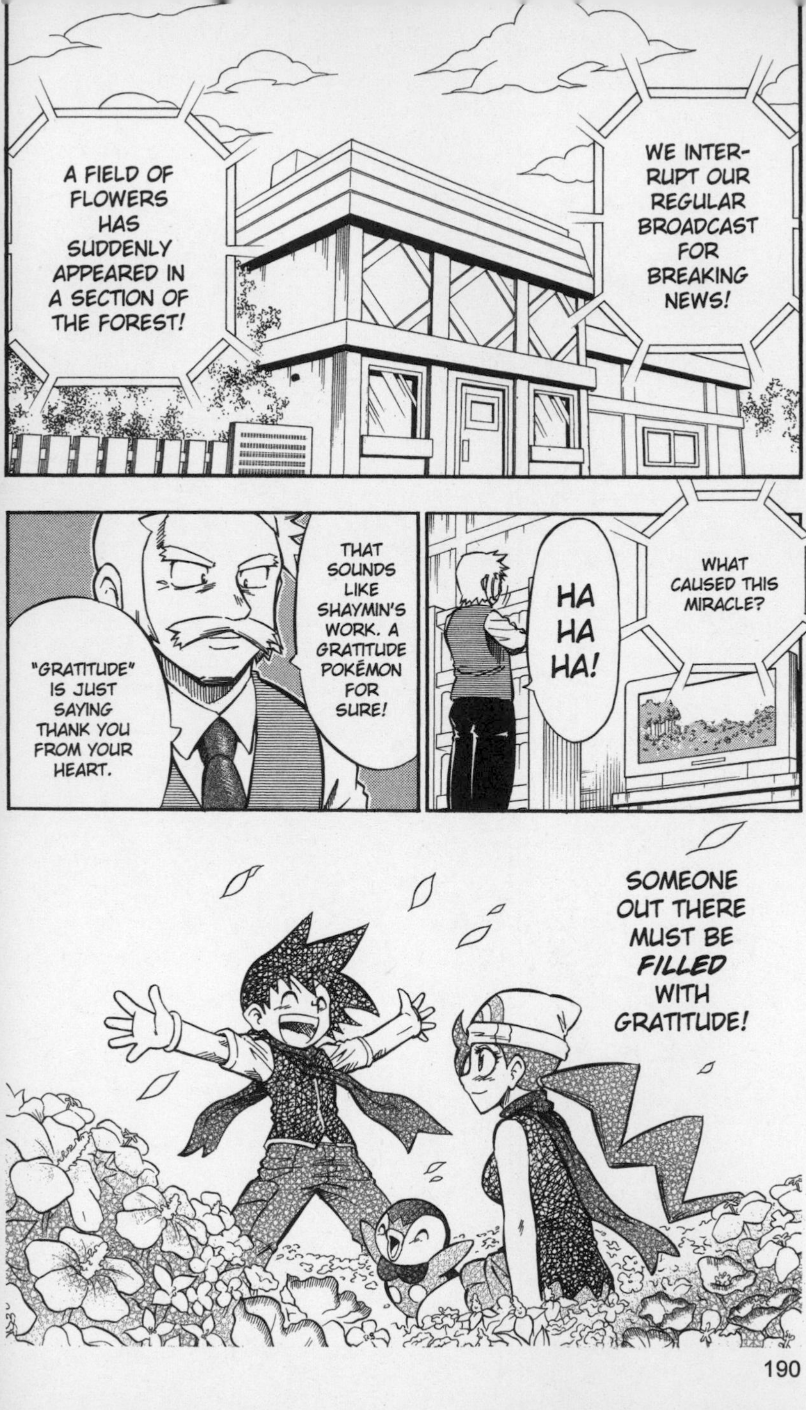
WE INTERRUPT OUR REGULAR BROADCAST FOR BREAKING NEWS!
A FIELD OF FLOWERS HAS SUDDENLY APPEARED IN A SECTION OF THE FOREST!
WHAT CAUSED THIS MIRACLE?
HA HA HA!
THAT SOUNDS LIKE SHAYMIN'S WORK. A GRATITUDE POKÉMON FOR SURE!
"GRATITUDE" IS JUST SAYING THANK YOU FROM YOUR HEART.
SOMEONE OUT THERE MUST BE *FILLED* WITH GRATITUDE!

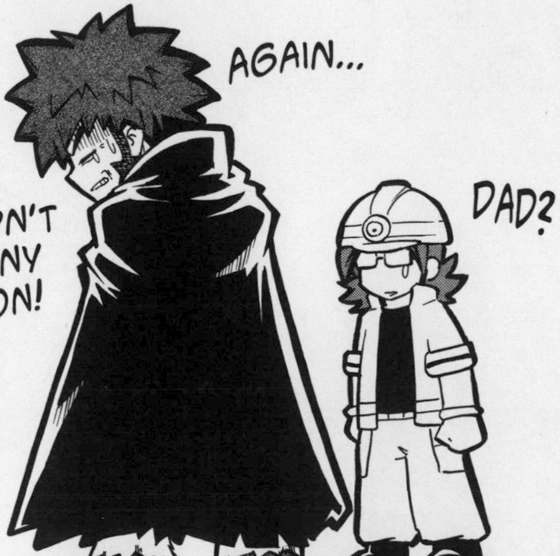
AGAIN...
DAD?
...I DIDN'T SEE ANY ACTION!

POKÉMON DIAMOND AND PEARL. POKÉMON D-P VOLUME 4 THE END.
TO BE CONTINUED IN VOLUME 5.

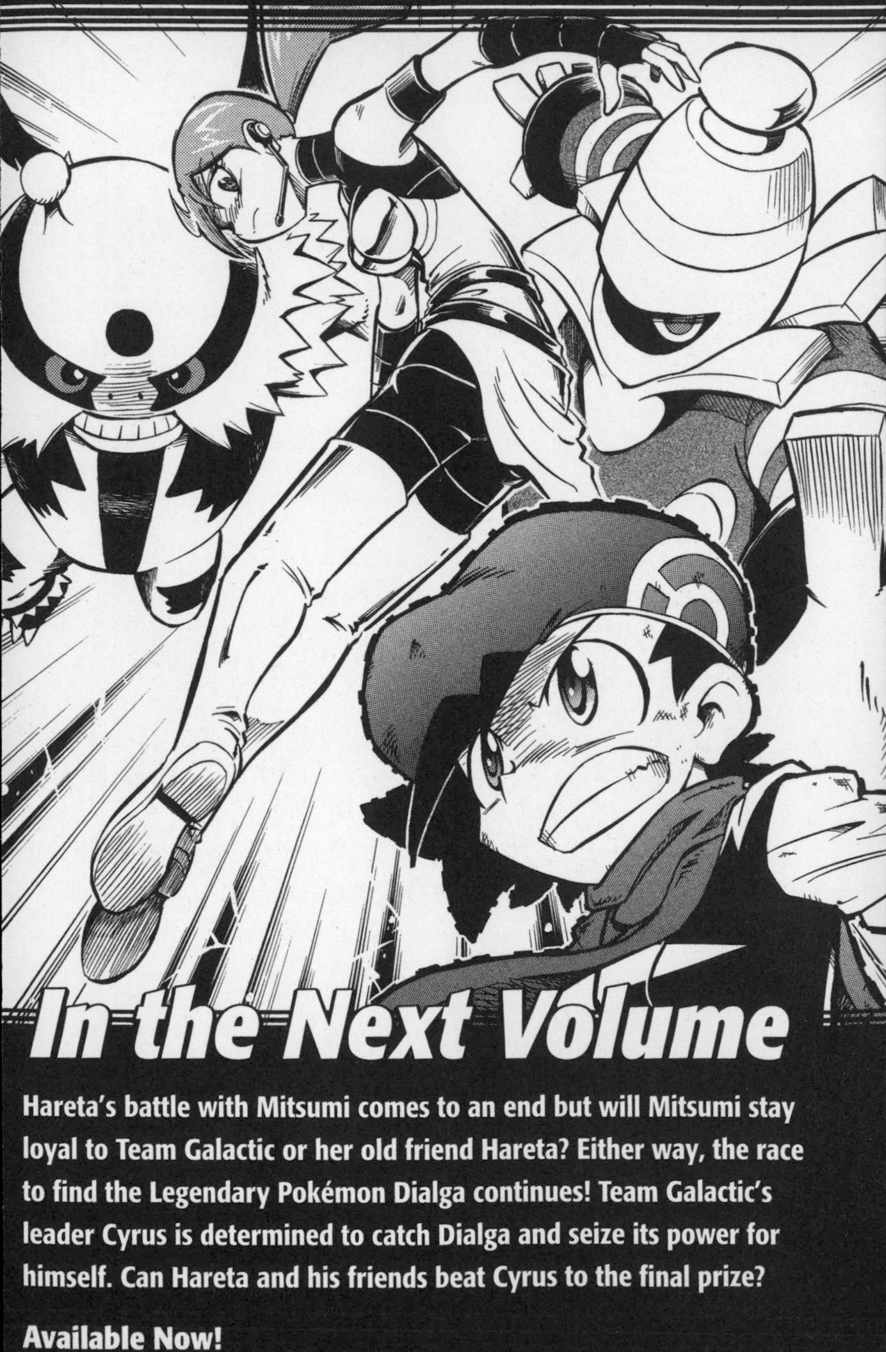

In the Next Volume

Hareta's battle with Mitsumi comes to an end but will Mitsumi stay loyal to Team Galactic or her old friend Hareta? Either way, the race to find the Legendary Pokémon Dialga continues! Team Galactic's leader Cyrus is determined to catch Dialga and seize its power for himself. Can Hareta and his friends beat Cyrus to the final prize?

Available Now!

PI**!**NG

Hareta's fierce fight against Team
Galactic continues. In the midst of all
this, a mysterious girl challenges Hareta
to battle. And if that wasn't enough,
Team Galactic reveals their ultimate
warrior! This volume also contains
a special story about Hareta and the
Gratitude Pokémon, Shaymin! Now
Hareta's all pumped up and raring to go,
and so am I! How about you?

– *Shigekatsu Ihara*

Shigekatsu Ihara's other manga titles include
*Pokémon: Lucario and the Mystery of Mew,
Pokémon Emerald Challenge!!* and
Battle Frontier, Dual Jack!!

Pokémon DIAMOND AND PEARL ADVENTURE!

Pokémon DIAMOND AND PEARL ADVENTURE!
Vol. 4
VIZ Kids Edition

Story & Art by SHIGEKATSU IHARA

Original Japanese edition
"Pokémon D•P POCKET MONSTER DIAMOND PEARL MONOGATARI"
published by SHOGAKUKAN Inc.

English Adaptation/Stan! Brown
Translation/Kaori Inoue
Touch-up Art & Lettering/Eric Erbes
Graphics & Cover Design/Hitomi Yokoyama Ross
Editor/Mike Montesa

Printed in the U.S.A.

Published by VIZ Media, LLC
P.O. Box 77010
San Francisco, CA 94107

10 9 8 7 6 5 4 3
First printing, June 2009
Third printing, July 2010

vizkids
www.vizkids.com

viz media
www.viz.com

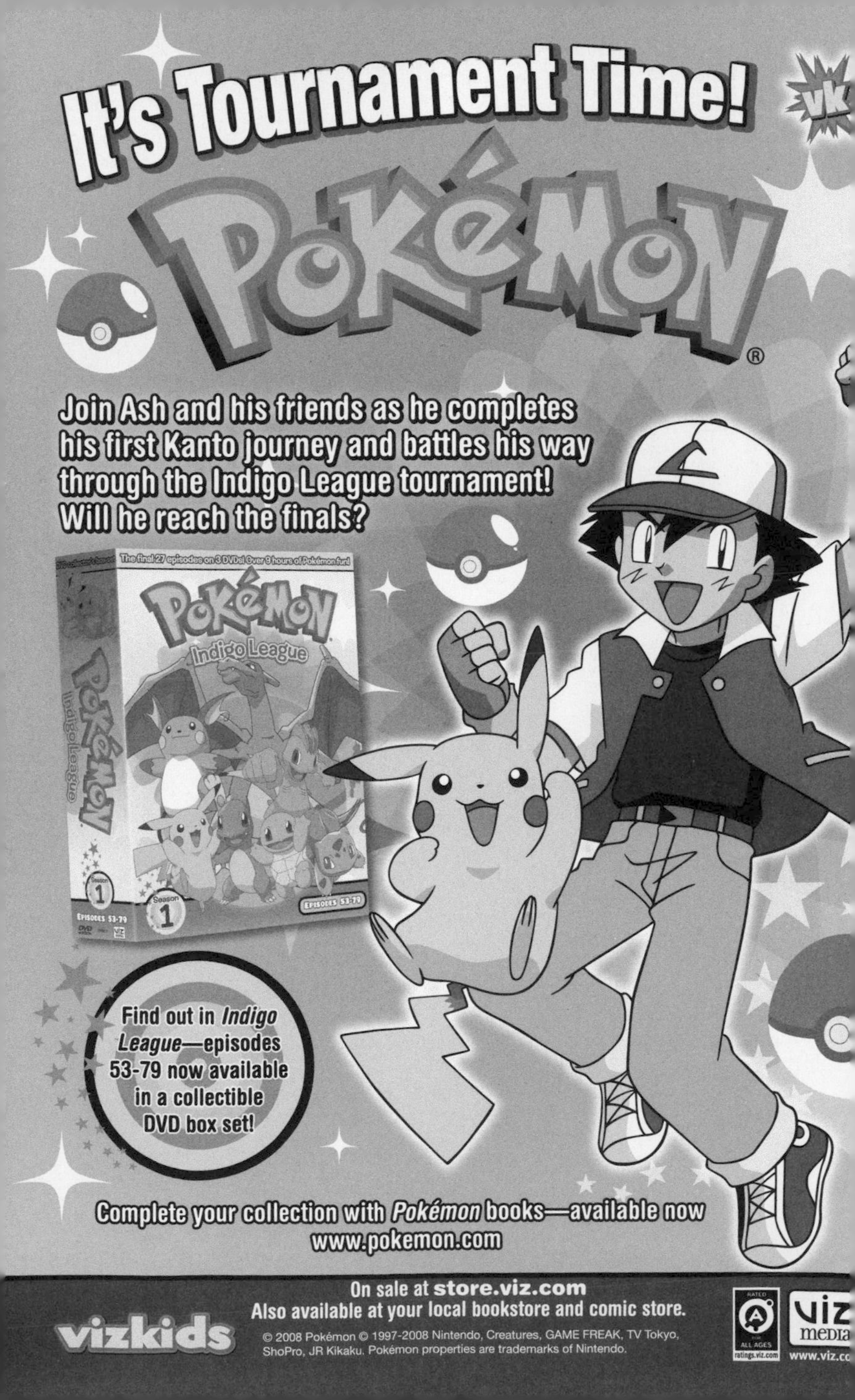
It's Tournament Time!
Pokémon®
Join Ash and his friends as he completes his first Kanto journey and battles his way through the Indigo League tournament! Will he reach the finals?
The final 27 episodes on 3 DVDs! Over 9 hours of Pokémon fun!
Pokémon Indigo League
Season 1
Episodes 53-79
Find out in *Indigo League*—episodes 53-79 now available in a collectible DVD box set!
Complete your collection with *Pokémon* books—available now
www.pokemon.com
On sale at store.viz.com
Also available at your local bookstore and comic store.
vizkids
© 2008 Pokémon © 1997-2008 Nintendo, Creatures, GAME FREAK, TV Tokyo, ShoPro, JR Kikaku. Pokémon properties are trademarks of Nintendo.
RATED A ALL AGES ratings.viz.com
viz media
www.viz.co

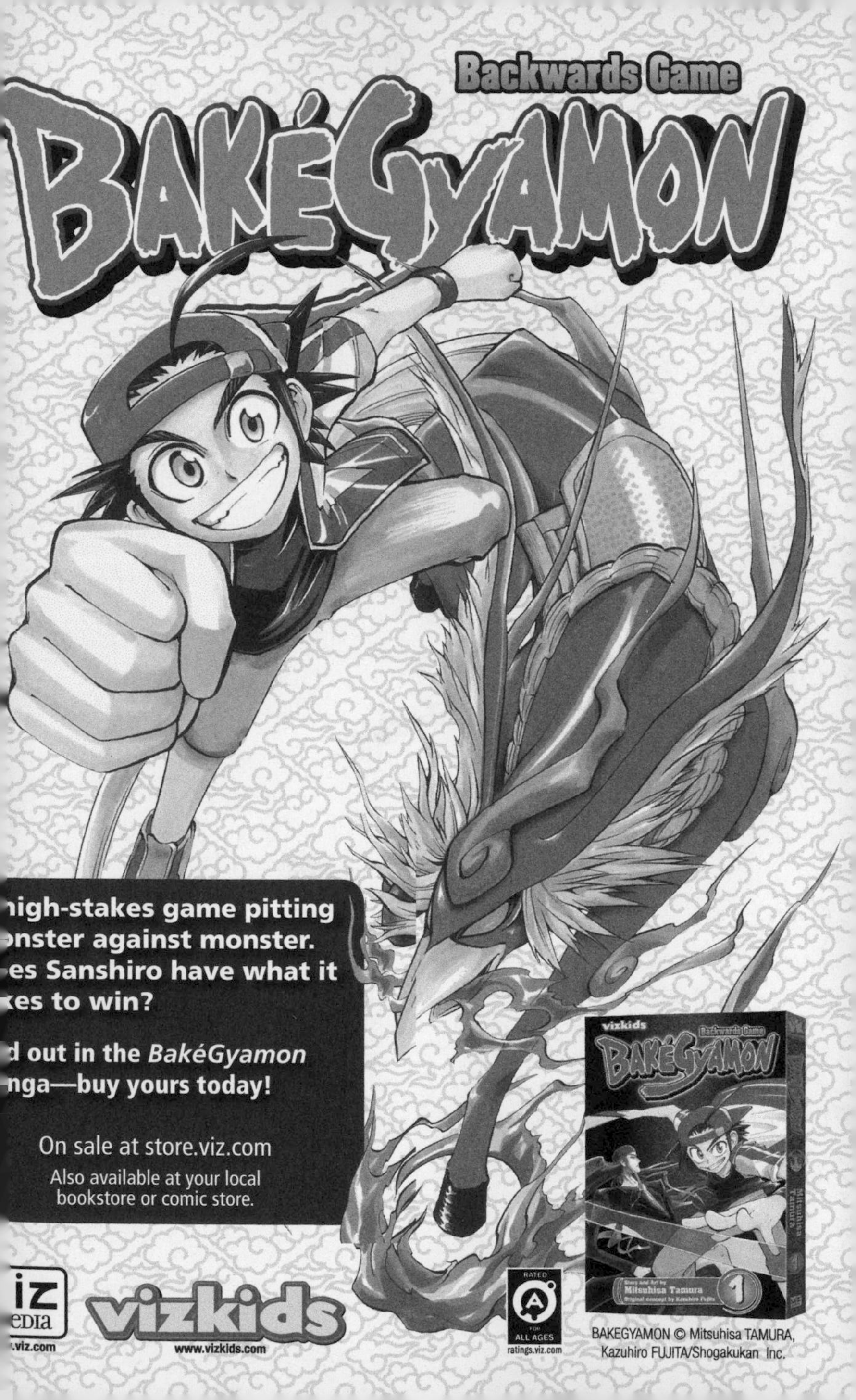
Backwards Game
BAKÉGYAMON
high-stakes game pitting
onster against monster.
es Sanshiro have what it
kes to win?
d out in the BakéGyamon
nga—buy yours today!
On sale at store.viz.com
Also available at your local
bookstore or comic store.
vizkids
Backwards Game
BAKÉGYAMON
Mitsuhisa Tamura
1
iz
EDIA
.viz.com
vizkids
www.vizkids.com
RATED
A
ALL AGES
ratings.viz.com
BAKEGYAMON © Mitsuhisa TAMURA,
Kazuhiro FUJITA/Shogakukan Inc.